PRAISE FOR
BERNARD CORNWELL'S
ACCLAIMED SHARPE SERIES

"Consistently exciting. . . . The history is brilliantly realized, and the stories are real by-god stories."

—Stephen King

"Marvelous! Bravery and audacity amidst the drama and turmoil of war."

—*Los Angeles Herald Examiner*

"A hero in the mold of James Bond, although his weapons are a baker carbine and a giant cavalry sword."

—*Philadelphia Inquirer*

"Apart from the rousing battle scenes, the author is at his best in evoking a long-gone era through clever detail."

—*New York Times Book Review*

"[A] first-rate series. . . . Cornwell [is] one of the great naval writers of this era."

—*Kirkus Reviews*

"[These] strengths . . . have come to characterize Bernard Cornwell's fiction—immaculate historical reconstruction and the ability to tell a ripping yarn."

—*Washington Post*

By Bernard Cornwell

SHARPE'S TIGER

RICHARD SHARPE AND THE
SIEGE OF SERINGAPATAM, 1799

BERNARD CORNWELL

Perennial

An Imprint of HarperCollinsPublishers

A hardcover edition of this book was published in Great Britain in 1997 by Harper-Collins Publishers.

HarperCollins books may be purchased for educational, business, or sales promotional use. For information please write: Special Markets Department, Harper-Collins Publishers, Inc., 10 East 53rd Street, New York, NY 10022.

First HarperPaperbacks edition published 1997.
First HarperPerennial edition published 1999.

Library of Congress Cataloging-in-Publication Data
Cornwell, Bernard.
   Sharpe's tiger : the Siege of Seringapatam, 1799 / Bernard
Cornwell.—1st ed.
     p. cm.
   ISBN 0-06-093230-9
   1. Sharpe, Richard (Fictitious character) Fiction. 2. Great
Britain—History, Military—18th century Fiction.
3. Śrīraṅgapaṭṭaṇa (India)—History—Siege, 1799 Fiction. 4. India—
History—Mysore War, 1799 Fiction. I. Title.
PR6053.075S56   1999
823'.914—dc21   99-30288
                                        CIP

Sharpe's Tiger is for
Muir Sutherland and Malcolm Craddock,
with many thanks.

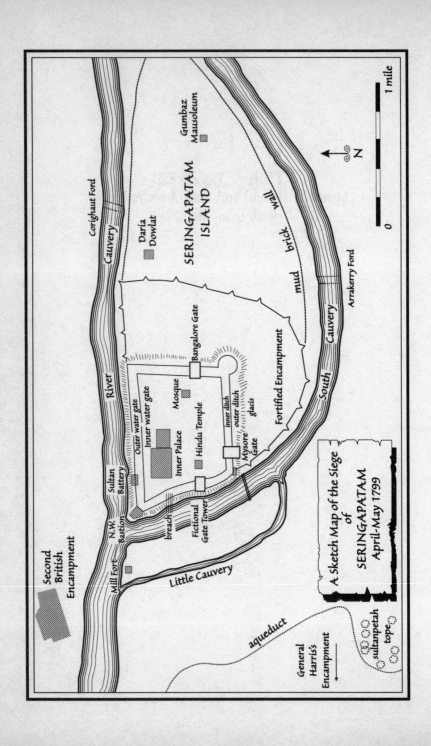

Second British Encampment

Mill Fort

N.W. Bastion

Sultan Battery

River

Corighaut Ford

Cauvery

Daria Dowlat

SERINGAPATAM ISLAND

Gumbaz Mausoleum

N

1 mile

0

wall

brick

mud

South Cauvery

Arrakerry Ford

Fortified Encampment

Bangalore Gate

Outer water gate

Inner water gate

Mosque

Hindu Temple

Inner Palace

inner ditch

outer ditch

glacis

Mysore Gate

Fictional Gate Tower

breach

Little Cauvery

aqueduct

General Harris's Encampment

sultanpetah tope

A Sketch Map of the Siege of SERINGAPATAM April–May 1799

SHARPE'S
TIGER

It was funny, Richard Sharpe thought, that there were no vultures in England. None that he had seen, anyway. Ugly things they were. Rats with wings.

He thought about vultures a lot, and he had a lot of time to think because he was a soldier, a private, and so the army insisted on doing a lot of his thinking for him. The army decided when he woke up, when he slept, when he ate, when he marched, and when he was to sit about doing nothing and that was what he did most of the time—nothing. Hurry up and do nothing, that was the army's way of doing things, and he was fed up with it. He was bored and thinking of running.

Him and Mary. Run away. Desert. He was thinking about it now, and it was an odd thing to worry about right now because the army was about to give Richard Sharpe his first proper battle. He had been in one fight, but that was five years ago and it had been a messy, confused business in fog, and no one had known why the 33rd Regiment was in Flanders or what they were supposed to be doing there, and in the end they had done nothing except fire some shots at the mist-shrouded French and the whole thing had been over almost before young Richard Sharpe had known it had begun. He had seen a couple of men killed. He remembered Sergeant Hawthorne's death best because the Sergeant had been hit by a musket ball that drove a rib clean out of his red coat. There was hardly a drop of blood to be seen, just the white rib sticking out of the faded red cloth. "You could hang your hat on that," Hawthorne had said in a tone of wonder, then he had sobbed, and after that he had choked up blood and collapsed. Sharpe had gone on loading and firing, and then, just as he was beginning to enjoy himself, the battalion had marched away and sailed back to England. Some battle.

Now he was in India. He did not know why he was invading Mysore and nor did he particularly care. King George III wanted Richard Sharpe to be in India, so in India Richard Sharpe was, but Richard Sharpe had now become bored with the King's service. He was young and he reckoned life had more to offer than hurrying up and doing nothing. There was money to be made. He was not sure how to make money, except by thieving, but he did know that he was bored and that he could do better than stay on the bottom of the dungheap. That was where he was, he kept telling himself, the bottom of a dungheap and everyone knew what was piled on top of a dungheap. Better to run, he told himself. All that was needed to get ahead in the world was a bit of sense and the ability to kick a bastard faster than the bastard could kick you, and Richard Sharpe reckoned he had those talents right enough.

Though where to run in India? Half the natives seemed to be in British pay and those would turn you in for a handful of tin pice, and the pice was only worth a farthing, and the other Indians were all fighting against the British, or readying to fight them, and if he ran to them he would just be forced to serve in their armies. He would fetch more pay in a native army, probably far more than the tuppence a day Sharpe got now after stoppages, but why change one uniform for another? No, he would have to run to some place where the army would never find him, or else it would be the firing squad on some hot morning. A blast of musket shots, a scrape in the red earth for a grave, and next day the rats with wings would be yanking the guts out of your belly like a bunch of blackbirds tugging worms out of a lawn.

That was why he was thinking about vultures. He was thinking that he wanted to run, but that he did not want to feed the vultures. Do not get caught. Rule number one in the army, and the only rule that mattered. Because if you got caught the bastards would flog you to death or else reorganize your ribs with musket balls, and either way the vultures got fat.

The vultures were always there, sometimes circling on long wings that tilted to the sudden winds of the warm upper air and sometimes standing hunched on branches. They fed on death and a marching army gave them a glutton's diet, and now, in this last year of the eighteenth century, two allied armies were crossing this hot fertile plain in southern India. One was a British army and the other belonged to a British ally, the Nizam of Hyderabad, and both armies provided a feast of vulture fodder. Horses died, oxen died, camels died, even two of the elephants that had seemed so indestructible had died, and then the people died. The twin armies had a tail ten times longer than themselves: a great sprawl of camp followers, merchants, herders, whores, wives, and children, and among all of those people, as it did among the armies themselves, the plagues ran riot. Men died with bloody dysentery, or shaking with a fever or choking on their own vomit. They died struggling for breath or drenched in sweat or raving like mad things or with skins blistered raw. Men, women, and children all died, and whether they were buried or burned it did not matter because, in the end, the vultures fed on them anyway, for there was never enough time nor sufficient timber to make a proper funeral pyre and so the vultures would rip the half-cooked flesh off the scorched bones, and if the bodies were buried then no amount of stones heaped on the soil would stop the scavenging beasts from digging up the swollen, rotting flesh and the vultures' hooked beaks took what the ravenous teeth left behind.

And this hot March day promised food in abundance and the vultures seemed to sense it for, as the early afternoon passed, more and more birds joined the spiring column of wings that circled above the marching men. The birds did not flap their wings, but simply soared in the warm air as they glided, tilted, slid, and waited, always waited, as if they knew that death's succulence would fill their gullets soon enough. "Ugly bastard birds," Sharpe said, "just rats with wings," but no one in the 33rd's Light Company answered him. No one had the breath to answer him. The air was choking from the dust kicked up by the men ahead so that the rearward ranks stumbled through a warm, gritty mix that parched their throats and stung their eyes. Most of the men were not even aware of the vultures, while others were so weary that they had not even noticed the troop of cavalry that had suddenly appeared a half-mile to the north. The horsemen trotted beside a grove of trees that were bright with red blossom, then accelerated away. Their drawn sabres flashed reflected sunlight as they wheeled away from the infantrymen, but then, as inexplicably as they had hurried and swerved away, they suddenly stopped. Sharpe noticed them. British cavalry, they were. The fancy boys come to see how proper soldiers fought.

Ahead, from the low rise of land where a second group of horsemen was silhouetted against the furnace whiteness of the sky, a gun fired. The crack of the cannon was immense, a billow of sound that punched hollow and malignant across the plain. The gun's smoke billowed white as the heavy ball thrashed into some bushes, tore leaves and blossoms to tatters, struck dust from the baked ground, then ran on in ever decreasing bounces to lodge against a gnarled fallen tree from which a pale shower of decaying wood spurted. The shot had missed the red-coated infantry by a good two hundred paces, but the sound of the cannon woke up the weary. "Jesus!" a voice in the rear file said. "What was that?"

"A bleeding camel farted, what the hell do you think it was?" a corporal answered.

"It was a bloody awful shot," Sharpe said. "My mother could lay a gun better than that."

"I didn't think you had a mother," Private Garrard said.

"Everyone's got a mother, Tom."

"Not Sergeant Hakeswill," Garrard said, then spat a mix of dust and spittle. The column of men had momentarily halted, not because of any orders, but rather because the cannon shot had unnerved the officer leading the front company who was no longer sure exactly where he was supposed to lead the battalion. "Hakeswill wasn't born of a mother," Garrard said vehemently. He took off his shako and used his sleeve to wipe the dust and sweat from his face. The woollen sleeve left a faint trace of red dye on his forehead. "Hakeswill was spawned of the devil," Garrard said, jamming the shako back on his white-powdered hair.

Sharpe wondered whether Tom Garrard would run with him. Two men might survive better than one. And what about Mary? Would she come? He thought about Mary a lot, when he was not thinking about everything else, except that Mary was inextricably twisted into everything else. It was confusing. She was Sergeant Bickerstaff's widow and she was half Indian and half English and she was twenty-two, which was the same age as Sharpe, or at least he thought it was the same age. It could be that he was twenty-one, or twenty-three; he was not really sure on account of not ever having had a mother to tell him. Of course he did have a mother, everyone had a mother, but not everyone had a Cat Lane whore for a mother who disappeared just after her son was born. The child had been named for the wealthy patron of the foundling home that had raised him, but the naming had not brought Richard Sharpe any patronage, only brought him to the reeking bottom of the army's dungheap. Still, Sharpe reckoned, he could have a future, and Mary spoke one or two Indian languages which could be useful if he and Tom did run.

The cavalry off to Sharpe's right spurred into a trot again and disappeared beyond the red-blossomed trees, leaving only a drifting cloud of dust behind. Two galloper guns, light six-pounder cannons, followed them, bouncing dangerously on the uneven ground behind their teams of horses. Every other cannon in the army was drawn by oxen, but the galloper guns had horse teams that were three times as fast as the plodding draught cattle. The lone enemy cannon fired again, its brutal sound punching the warm air with an almost palpable impact. Sharpe could see more enemy guns on the ridge, but they were smaller than the gun that had just fired and Sharpe presumed they did not have the long range of the bigger cannon. Then he saw a trace of gray in the air, a flicker like a vertical pencil stroke drawn against the pale blue sky and he knew that the big gun's shot must be coming straight toward him, and he knew too that there was no wind to carry the heavy ball gently aside, and all that he realized in the second or so that the ball was in the air, too short a time to react, only to recognize death's approach, but then the ball slammed into the ground a dozen paces short of him and bounced on up over his head to run harmlessly into a field of sugar cane. "I reckon the bastards have got your mother laying the gun now, Dick," Garrard said.

"No talking now!" Sergeant Hakeswill's voice screeched suddenly. "Save your godless breath. Was that you talking, Garrard?"

"Not me, Sarge. Ain't got the breath."

"You ain't got the breath?" Sergeant Hakeswill came hurrying down the company's ranks and thrust his face up toward Garrard. "You ain't got the breath? That means you're dead, Private Garrard! Dead! No use to King or country if you's dead, but you never was any bleeding use anyway." The Sergeant's malevolent eyes flicked to Sharpe. "Was it you talking, Sharpie?"

"Not me, Sarge."

"You ain't got orders to talk. If the King wanted you to have a conversation I'd have told you so. Says so in the scriptures. Give me your firelock, Sharpie. Quick now!"

Sharpe handed his musket to the Sergeant. It was Hakeswill's arrival in the company that had persuaded Sharpe that it was time to run from the army. He had been bored anyway, but Hakeswill had added injustice to boredom. Not that Sharpe cared about injustice, for only the rich had justice in this world, but Hakeswill's injustice was touched with such malevolence that there was hardly a man in the Light Company not ready to rebel, and all that kept them from mutiny was the knowledge that Hakeswill understood their desire, wanted it, and wanted to punish them for it. He was a great man for provoking insolence and then punishing it. He was always two steps ahead of you, waiting around a corner with a bludgeon. He was a devil, was Hakeswill, a devil in a smart red coat decorated with a sergeant's badges.

Yet to look at Hakeswill was to see the perfect soldier. It was true that his oddly lumpy face twitched every few seconds as though an evil spirit was twisting and jerking just beneath his sun-reddened skin, but his eyes were blue, his hair was powdered as white as the snow that never fell on this land, and his uniform was as smart as though he stood guard at Windsor Castle. He performed drill like a Prussian, each movement so crisp and clean that it was a pleasure to watch, but then the face would twitch and his oddly childlike eyes would flicker a sideways glance and you could see the

devil peering out. Back when he had been a recruiting sergeant Hakeswill had taken care not to let the devil show, and
that was when Sharpe had first met him, but now, when the
Sergeant no longer needed to gull and trick young fools into
the ranks, Hakeswill did not care who saw his malignancy.

Sharpe stood motionless as the Sergeant untied the scrap
of rag that Sharpe used to protect his musket's lock from the
insidious red dust. Hakeswill peered at the lock, found nothing wrong, then turned away from Sharpe so that the sun
could fall full on the weapon. He peered again, cocked the
gun, dry-fired it, then seemed to lose interest in the musket
as a group of officers spurred their horses towards the head
of the stalled column. "Company!" Hakeswill shouted.
"Company! 'Shun!"

The men shuffled their feet together and straightened as
the three officers galloped past. Hakeswill had stiffened into
a grotesque pose; his right boot tucked behind his left, his
legs straight, his head and shoulders thrown back, his belly
thrust forward and his bent elbows straining to meet in the
concavity at the small of his back. None of the other companies of the King's 33rd Regiment had been stood to attention
in honor of the passing officers, but Hakeswill's gesture of
respect was nevertheless ignored. The neglect had no effect
on the Sergeant who, when the trio of officers had gone past,
shouted at the company to stand easy and then peered again
at Sharpe's musket.

"You'll not find 'owt wrong with it, Sarge," Sharpe said.

Hakeswill, still standing at attention, did an elaborate
about turn, his right boot thumping down to the ground.
"Did you hear me give you permission to speak, Sharpie?"

"No, Sarge."

"No, Sarge. No, you did not. Flogging offence that,
Sharpie." Hakeswill's right cheek twitched with the involuntary spasm that disfigured his face every few seconds and the

vehement evil of the face was suddenly so intense that the whole Light Company momentarily held its breath in expectation of Sharpe's arrest, but then the thumping discharge of the enemy cannon rolled across the countryside and the heavy ball splashed and bounced and tore its way through a bright-green patch of growing rice, and the violence of the harmless missile served to distract Hakeswill who turned to watch as the ball rolled to a stop. "Poor bloody shooting," Hakeswill said scathingly. "Heathens can't lay guns, I dare say. Or maybe they're toying with us. Toying!" The thought made him laugh. It was not, Sharpe suspected, the anticipation of excitement that had brought Sergeant Obadiah Hakeswill to this state of near joviality, but rather the thought that a battle would cause casualties and misery, and misery was the Sergeant's delight. He liked to see men cowed and frightened, for that made them biddable, and Sergeant Hakeswill was always at his happiest when he was in control of unhappy men.

The three officers had stopped their horses at the head of the column and now used telescopes to inspect the distant ridge which was clouded by a ragged fringe of smoke left from the last discharge of the enemy cannon. "That's our Colonel, boys," Hakeswill announced to the 33rd's Light Company, "Colonel Arthur Wellesley himself, God bless him for a gentleman, which he is and you ain't. He's come to see you fight, so make sure you do. Fight like the Englishmen you are."

"I'm a Scot," a sour voice spoke from the rear rank.

"I heard that! Who said that?" Hakeswill glared at the company, his face twitching uncontrollably. In a less blithe mood the Sergeant would have ferreted out the speaker and punished him, but the excitement of pending battle persuaded him to let the offence pass. "A Scot!" he said derisively instead. "What is the finest thing a Scotsman ever saw?

Answer me that!" No one did. "The high road to England, that's what. Says so in the scriptures, so it must be true." He hefted Sharpe's musket as he looked down the waiting ranks. "I shall be watching you," he snarled. "You ain't none of you been in a proper fight before, not a proper fight, but on the other side of that bleeding hill there's a horde of black-faced heathens what can't wait to lay their filthy hands on your womenfolk, so if so much as one of you turns his back I'll have the skin off the lot of you! Bare bones and blood, that's what you'll be. But you does your duty and obeys your orders and you can't go wrong. And who gives the orders?"

The Sergeant waited for an answer and eventually Private Mallinson offered one. "The officers, Sergeant."

"The officers! The officers!" Hakeswill spat his disgust at the answer. "Officers are here to show us what we are fighting for. Gentlemen, they are. Proper gentlemen! Men of property and breeding, not broken potboys and scarlet-coated pickpockets like what you are. Sergeants give the orders. Sergeants is what the army is. Remember that, lads! You're about to go into battle against heathens and if you ignore me then you'll be dead men!" The face twitched grotesquely, its jaw wrenched suddenly sideways, and Sharpe, watching the Sergeant's face, wondered if it was nervousness that had made Hakeswill so voluble. "But keeps your eyes on me, lads," Hakeswill went on, "and you'll be right as trivets. And you know why?" He cried the last word out in a high dramatic tone as he stalked down the Light Company's front rank. "You know why?" he asked again, now sounding like some dissenting preacher ranting in a hedgerow. "Because I cannot die, boys, I cannot die!" He was suddenly intense, his voice hoarse and full of fervor as he spoke. It was a speech that all the Light Company had heard many times before, but it was remarkable for all that, though Sergeant Green, who was outranked by Hakeswill, turned away in disgust.

Hakeswill jeered at Green, then tugged at the tight constriction of the leather stock that circled his neck, pulling it down so that an old dark scar was visible at his throat. "The hangman's noose, boys!" he cried. "That's what marked me there, the hangman's noose! See it? See it? But I am alive, boys, alive and on two feet instead of being buried under the sod, proof as never was that you needs not die!" His face twitched again as he released the stock. "Marked by God," he finished, his voice gruff with emotion, "that's what I am, marked by God!"

"Mad as a hare," Tom Garrard muttered.

"Did you speak, Sharpie?" Hakeswill whipped around to stare at Sharpe, but Sharpe was so palpably still and staring mutely ahead that his innocence was indisputable. Hakeswill paced back down the Light Company. "I have watched men die, better men than any of you pieces of scum, proper men, but God has spared me! So you do what I says, boys, or else you'll be carrion." He abruptly thrust the musket back into Sharpe's hands. "Clean weapon, Sharpie. Well done, lad." He paced smartly away and Sharpe, to his surprise, saw that the scrap of rag had been neatly retied about the lock.

The compliment to Sharpe had astonished all the Light Company. "He's in a rare good mood," Garrard said.

"I heard that, Private Garrard!" Hakeswill shouted over his shoulder. "Got ears in the back of me head, I have. Silence now. Don't want no heathen horde thinking you're frit! You're white men, remember, bleached in the cleansing blood of the bleeding lamb, so no bleeding talking in the ranks! Nice and quiet, like them bleeding nuns what never utters a sound on account of having had their papist tongues cut out." He suddenly crashed to attention once again and saluted by bringing his spear-tipped halberd across his body. "Company all present, sir!" he shouted in a voice that must have been audible on the enemy-held ridge. "All present and quiet, sir! Have their backs whipped bloody else, sir."

Lieutenant William Lawford curbed his horse and nodded at Sergeant Hakeswill. Lawford was the Light Company's second officer, junior to Captain Morris and senior to the brace of young ensigns, but he was newly arrived in the battalion and was as frightened of Hakeswill as were the men in the ranks. "The men can talk, Sergeant," Lawford observed mildly. "The other companies aren't silent."

"No, sir. Must save their breath, sir. Too bleeding hot to talk, sir, and besides, they got heathens to kill, sir, mustn't waste breath on chit-chat, not when there are black-faced heathens to kill, sir. Says so in the scriptures, sir."

"If you say so, Sergeant," Lawford said, unwilling to provoke a confrontation, then he found he had nothing else to say and so, awkwardly aware of the scrutiny of the Light Company's seventy-six men, he stared at the enemy-held ridge. But he was also conscious of having ignominiously surrendered to the will of Sergeant Hakeswill and so he slowly colored as he gazed toward the west. Lawford was popular, but thought to be weak, though Sharpe was not so sure of that judgement. He thought the Lieutenant was still finding his way among the strange and sometimes frightening human currents that made up the 33rd, and that in time Lawford would prove a tough and resilient officer. For now, though, William Lawford was twenty-four years old and had only recently purchased his lieutenancy, and that made him unsure of his authority.

Ensign Fitzgerald, who was only eighteen, strolled back from the column's head. He was whistling as he walked and slashing with a drawn sabre at tall weeds. "Off in a moment, sir," he called up cheerfully to Lawford, then seemed to become aware of the Light Company's ominous silence. "Not frightened, are you?" he asked.

"Saving their breath, Mister Fitzgerald, sir," Hakeswill snapped.

"They've got breath enough to sing a dozen songs and still beat the enemy," Fitzgerald said scornfully. "Ain't that so, lads?"

"We'll beat the bastards, sir," Tom Garrard said.

"Then let me hear you sing," Fitzgerald demanded. "Can't bear silence. We'll have a quiet time in our tombs, lads, so we might as well make a noise now." Fitzgerald had a fine tenor voice that he used to start the song about the milkmaid and the rector, and by the time the Light Company had reached the verse that told how the naked rector, blindfolded by the milkmaid and thinking he was about to have his heart's desire, was being steered toward Bessie the cow, the whole company was bawling the song enthusiastically.

They never did reach the end. Captain Morris, the Light Company's commanding officer, rode back from the head of the battalion and interrupted the singing. "Half-companies!" he shouted at Hakeswill.

"Half-companies it is, sir! At once, sir. Light Company! Stop your bleeding noise! You heard the officer!" Hakeswill bellowed. "Sergeant Green! Take charge of the after ranks. Mister Fitzgerald! I'll trouble you to take your proper place on the left, sir. Forward ranks! Shoulder firelocks! Twenty paces, forward, march! Smartly now! Smartly!"

Hakeswill's face shuddered as the front ten ranks of the company marched twenty paces and halted, leaving the other nine ranks behind. All along the battalion column the companies were similarly dividing, their drill as crisp as though they were back on their Yorkshire parade ground. A quarter-mile off to the 33rd's left another six battalions were going through the same maneuver, and performing it with just as much precision. Those six battalions were all native soldiers in the service of the East India Company, though they wore red coats just like the King's men. The six sepoy battalions shook out their colors and Sharpe, seeing the bright flags, looked ahead to where the 33rd's two great regimental banners were being loosed from their leather tubes to the fierce Indian sun. The first, the King's Color, was a British flag on which the regiment's battle honors were embroidered, while the second was the Regimental Color and had the 33rd's badge displayed on a scarlet field, the same scarlet as the men's jacket facings. The tasseled silk banners blazed, and the sight of them prompted a sudden cannonade from the ridge. Till now there had only been the one heavy gun firing, but abruptly six other cannon joined the fight. The new guns were smaller and their round shot fell well short of the seven battalions.

Major Shee, the Irishman who commanded the 33rd while its Colonel, Arthur Wellesley, had control of the whole brigade, cantered his horse back, spoke briefly to Morris, then wheeled away toward the head of the column. "We're going to push the bastards off the ridge!" Morris shouted at the Light Company, then bent his head to light a cigar with a tinderbox. "Any bastard that turns tail, Sergeant," Morris went on when his cigar was properly alight, "will be shot. You hear me?"

"Loud and clear, sir!" Hakeswill shouted. "Shot, sir! Shot like the coward he is." He turned and scowled at the two half-companies. "Shot! And your names posted in your church porch at home as the cowards you are. So fight like Englishmen!"

"Scotsmen," a voice growled behind Sharpe, but too softly for Hakeswill to hear.

"Irish," another man said.

"We ain't none of us cowards," Garrard said more loudly.

Sergeant Green, a decent man, hushed him. "Quiet, lads. I know you'll do your duty."

The front of the column was marching now, but the rearmost companies were kept waiting so that the battalion could advance with wide intervals between its twenty half-companies. Sharpe guessed that the scattered formation was intended to reduce any casualties caused by the enemy's bombardment which, because it was still being fired at extreme range, was doing no damage. Behind him, a long way behind, the rest of the allied armies were waiting for the ridge to be cleared. That mass looked like a formidable horde, but Sharpe knew that most of what he saw was the two armies' civilian tail: the chaos of merchants, wives, sutlers, and herdsmen who kept the fighting soldiers alive and whose supplies would make the siege of the enemy's capital possible. It needed more than six thousand oxen just to carry the cannonballs for the big siege guns, and all those oxen had to be herded and fed and the herdsmen all traveled with their families who, in turn, needed more oxen to carry their own supplies. Lieutenant Lawford had once remarked that the expedition did not look like an army on the march, but like a great migrating tribe. The vast horde of civilians and animals was encircled by a thin crust of red-coated infantry, most of them Indian sepoys, whose job was to protect the merchants, ammunition, and draught animals from the quick-riding, hard-hitting light cavalry of the Tippoo Sultan.

The Tippoo Sultan. The enemy. The tyrant of Mysore and the man who was presumably directing the gunfire on the ridge. The Tippoo ruled Mysore and he was the enemy, but what he was, or why he was an enemy, or whether he was a tyrant, beast, or demigod, Sharpe had no idea. Sharpe was here because he was a soldier and it was sufficient that he had been told that the Tippoo Sultan was his enemy and so he waited patiently under the Indian sun that was soaking his lean tall body in sweat.

Captain Morris leaned on his saddle's pommel. He took

off his cocked hat and wiped sweat from his forehead with a handkerchief that had been soaked in cologne water. He had been drunk the previous night and his stomach was still churning with pain and wind. If the battalion had not been going into battle he would have galloped away, found a private spot, and voided his bowels, but he could hardly do that now in case his men thought it a sign of weakness and so he raised his canteen instead and swallowed some arrack in the hope that the harsh spirit would calm the turmoil in his belly. "Now, Sergeant!" he called when the company in front had moved sufficiently far ahead.

"Forward half-company!" Hakeswill shouted. "Forward march! Smartly now!"

Lieutenant Lawford, given supervision of the last half-company of the battalion, waited until Hakeswill's men had marched twenty paces, then nodded at Sergeant Green. "Forward, Sergeant."

The redcoats marched with unloaded muskets for the enemy was still a long way off and there was no sign of the Tippoo Sultan's infantry, nor of his feared cavalry. There were only the enemy's guns and, high in the fierce sky, the circling vultures. Sharpe was in the leading rank of the final half-company and Lieutenant Lawford, glancing at him, thought once again what a fine-looking man Sharpe was. There was a confidence in Sharpe's thin, sun-darkened face and hard blue eyes that spoke of an easy competence, and that appearance was a comfort to a young nervous lieutenant advancing toward his first battle. With men like Sharpe, Lawford thought, how could they lose?

Sharpe was ignorant of the Lieutenant's glance and would have laughed had he been told that his very appearance inspired confidence. Sharpe had no conception of how he looked, for he rarely saw a mirror and when he did the reflected image meant nothing, though he did know that the

ladies liked him and that he liked them. He knew, too, that
he was the tallest man in the Light Company, so tall, indeed,
that he should have been in the Grenadier Company that
led the battalion's advance, but when he had first joined the
regiment, six years before, the commanding officer of the
Light Company had insisted on having Sharpe in his ranks.
Captain Hughes was dead now, killed by a bowel-loosening
flux in Calcutta, but in his time Hughes had prided himself
on having the quickest, smartest men in his company, men
he could trust to fight alone in the skirmish line, and it had
been Hughes's tragedy that he had only ever seen his picked
men face an enemy once, and that once had been the misbe-
gotten, fever-ridden expedition to the foggy island off the
coast of Flanders where no amount of quick-wittedness by
the men could salvage success from the commanding general's stupidity. Now, five years later, on an Indian field, the
33rd again marched toward an enemy, though instead of the
enthusiastic and generous Captain Hughes, the Light Company was now commanded by Captain Morris who did not
care how clever or quick his men were, only that they gave
him no trouble. Which was why he had brought Sergeant
Hakeswill into the company. And that was why the tall, good-
looking, hard-eyed private called Richard Sharpe was thinking of running.

Except he would not run today. Today there would be a
fight and Sharpe was happy at that prospect. A fight meant
plunder, what the Indian soldiers called loot, and any man
who was thinking of running and striking up life on his own
could do with a bit of loot to prime the pump.

The seven battalions marched toward the ridge. They
were all in columns of half-companies so that, from a vulture's view, they would have appeared as one hundred and
forty small scarlet rectangles spread across a square mile of
green country as they advanced steadily toward the waiting

line of guns on the enemy-held ridge. The sergeants paced beside the half-companies while the officers either rode or walked ahead. From a distance the red squares looked smart, for the men's red coats were bright scarlet and slashed with white crossbelts, but in truth the troops were filthy and sweating. Their coats were wool, designed for battlefields in Flanders, not India, and the scarlet dye had run in the heavy rains so that the coats were now a pale pink or a dull purple, and all were stained white with dried sweat. Every man in the 33rd wore a leather stock, a cruel high collar that dug into the flesh of his neck, and each man's long hair had been pulled harshly back, greased with candle wax, then twisted about a small sand-filled leather bag that was secured with a strip of black leather so that the hair hung like a club at the nape of the neck. The hair was then powdered white with flour, and though the clubbed and whitened hair looked smart and neat, it was a haven for lice and fleas. The native sepoys of the East India Company were luckier. They did not cake their hair with powder, nor did they wear the heavy trousers of the British troops but instead marched bare-legged. They did not wear the leather stocks either and, even more amazing, there was no flogging in the Indian battalions.

An enemy cannonball at last found a target and Sharpe saw a half-company of the 33rd broken apart as the round shot whipped through the ranks. He thought he glimpsed an instant red mist appear in the air above the formation as the ball slashed through, but maybe that was an illusion. Two men stayed on the ground as a sergeant closed the ranks up. Two more men were limping and one of them staggered, reeled, and finally collapsed. The drummer boys, advancing just behind the unfurled colors, marked the rhythm of the march with steady beats interspersed with quicker flourishes, but when the boys marched past the twin heaps of offal that had been soldiers of the Grenadier Company a few seconds before they began to hurry their sticks and thus quickened the regiment's pace until Major Shee turned in his saddle and damned their eagerness.

"When are we going to load?" Private Mallinson asked Sergeant Green.

"When you're told to, lad, when you're told to. Not before. Oh, sweet Jesus!" This last imprecation from Sergeant Green had been caused by a deafening ripple of gunfire from the ridge. A dozen more of the Tippoo's smaller guns had opened fire and the crest of the ridge was now fogged by a grey-white cloud of smoke. The two British galloper guns off to the right had unlimbered and started to return the fire, but the enemy cannon were hidden by their own smoke and that thick screen obscured any damage the small galloper guns might be inflicting. More cavalry trotted forward to the 33rd's right. These newcomers were Indian troops dressed in scarlet turbans and holding long, wicked-pointed lances.

"So what are we bleeding supposed to do?" Mallinson complained. "Just march straight up the bloody ridge with empty muskets?"

"If you're told to," Sergeant Green said, "that's what you'll do. Now hold your bloody tongue."

"Quiet back there!" Hakeswill called from the half-company in front. "This ain't a bleeding parish outing! This is a fight, you bastards!"

Sharpe wanted to be ready and so he untied the rag from his musket's lock and stuffed it into the pocket where he kept the ring Mary had given him. The ring, a plain band of worn silver, had belonged to Sergeant Bickerstaff, Mary's husband, but the Sergeant was dead now and Green had taken Bickerstaff's sergeant's stripes and Sharpe his bed. Mary came from Calcutta. That was no place to run, Sharpe thought. Place was full of redcoats.

Then he forgot any prospect of deserting, for suddenly the

landscape ahead was filling with enemy soldiers. A mass of infantry was crossing the northern end of the low ridge and marching down onto the plain. Their uniforms were pale purple, they had wide red hats and, like the British Indian troops, were bare-legged. The flags above the marching men were red and yellow, but the wind was so feeble that the flags hung straight down to obscure whatever device they might have shown. More and more men appeared until Sharpe could not even begin to estimate their numbers.

"Thirty-third!" a voice shouted from somewhere ahead. "Line to the left!"

"Line to the left!" Captain Morris echoed the shout.

"You heard the officer!" Sergeant Hakeswill bawled. "Line to the left! Smartly now!"

"On the double!" Sergeant Green called.

The leading half-company of the 33rd had halted and every other half-company angled to their left and sped their pace, with the final half-company, in which Sharpe marched, having the farthest and fastest to go. The men began to jog, their packs and pouches and bayonet scabbards bumping up and down as they stumbled over the small fields of crops. Like a swinging door, the column, that had been marching directly toward the ridge, was now turning itself into a line that would lie parallel to the ridge and so bar the advance of the enemy infantry.

"Two files!" a voice shouted.

"Two files!" Captain Morris echoed.

"You heard the officer!" Hakeswill shouted. "Two files! On the right! Smartly now!"

All the running half-companies now split themselves into two smaller units, each of two ranks and each aligning itself on the unit to its right so that the whole battalion formed a fighting line two ranks deep. As Sharpe ran into position he glanced to his right and saw the drummer boys taking their place behind the regiment's colors which were guarded by a squad of sergeants armed with long, axe-headed poles.

The Light Company was the last into position. There were a few seconds of shuffling as the men glanced right to check their alignment, then there was stillness and silence except for the corporals fussily closing up the files. In less than a minute, in a marvellous display of drill, the King's 33rd had deployed from column of march into line of battle so that seven hundred men, arrayed in two long ranks, now faced the enemy.

"You may load, Major Shee!" That was Colonel Wellesley's voice. He had galloped his horse close to where Major Shee brooded under the regiment's twin flags. The six Indian battalions were still hurrying forward on the left, but the enemy infantry had appeared at the northern end of the ridge and that meant the 33rd was the nearest unit and the one most likely to receive the Tippoo's assault.

"Load!" Captain Morris shouted at Hakeswill.

Sharpe felt suddenly nervous as he dropped the musket from his shoulder to hold it across his body. He fumbled with the musket's hammer as he pulled it back to the half cock. Sweat stung his eyes. He could hear the enemy drummers.

"Handle cartridge!" Sergeant Hakeswill shouted, and each man of the Light Company pulled a cartridge from his belt pouch and bit through the tough waxed paper. They held the bullets in their mouths, tasting the sour salty gunpowder.

"Prime!" Seventy-six men trickled a small pinch of powder from the opened cartridges into their muskets' pans, then closed the locks so that the priming was trapped.

"Cast about!" Hakeswill called and seventy-six right hands released their musket stocks so that the weapons' butts dropped toward the ground. "And I'm watching you!" Hakeswill added. "If any of you lilywhite bastards don't use all his powder, I'll skin your hides off you and rub salt on your miserable flesh. Do it proper now!" Some old soldiers advised only using half the powder of a cartridge, letting the rest trickle to the ground so that the musket's brutal kick would be diminished, but faced by an advancing enemy, no man thought of employing that trick this day. They poured the remainder of their cartridges' powder down their musket barrels, stuffed the cartridge paper after the powder, then took the balls from their mouths and pushed them into the muzzles. The enemy infantry was two hundred yards away and advancing steadily to the beat of drums and the blare of trumpets. The Tippoo's guns were still firing, but they had turned their barrels away from the 33rd for fear of hitting their own infantry and were instead aiming at the six Indian regiments that were hurrying to close the gap between themselves and the 33rd.

"Draw ramrod!" Hakeswill shouted and Sharpe tugged the ramrod free of the three brass pipes that held it under the musket's thirty-nine-inch barrel. His mouth was salty with the taste of gunpowder. He was still nervous, not because the enemy was tramping ever closer, but because he had a sudden idiotic idea that he might have forgotten how to load a musket. He twisted the ramrod in the air, then placed the ramrod's flared tip into the barrel.

"Ram cartridge!" Hakeswill snapped. Seventy-six men thrust down, forcing the ball, wadding and powder charge to the bottom of the barrels.

"Return ramrod!" Sharpe tugged the ramrod up, listening to it scrape against the barrel, then twirled it about so that its narrow end would slide down into the brass pipes. He let it drop into place.

"Order arms!" Captain Morris called and the Light Company, now with loaded muskets, stood to attention with their guns held against their right sides. The enemy was still too far off for a musket to be either accurate or lethal and the long, two-deep line of seven hundred redcoats would wait until their opening volley could do real damage.

"'Talion!" Sergeant Major Bywaters's voice called from the center of the line. "Fix bayonets!"

Sharpe dragged the seventeen-inch blade from its sheath which hung behind his right hip. He slotted the blade over the musket's muzzle, then locked it in place by twisting its slot onto the lug. Now no enemy could pull the bayonet off the musket. Having the blade mounted made reloading the musket far more difficult, but Sharpe guessed that Colonel Wellesley had decided to shoot one volley and then charge. "Going to be a right mucky brawl," he said to Tom Garrard.

"More of them than us," Garrard muttered, staring at the enemy. "The buggers look steady enough."

The enemy indeed looked steady. The leading troops had momentarily paused to allow the men behind to catch up, but now, re-formed into a solid column, they were readying to advance again. Their ranks and files were ramrod straight. Their officers wore waist sashes and carried highly curved sabres. One of the flags was being waved to and fro and Sharpe could just make out that it showed a golden sun blazoned against a scarlet sky. Vultures swooped lower. The galloper guns, unable to resist the target of the great column of infantry, poured solid shot into its flank, but the Tippoo's men stoically endured the punishment as their officers made certain that the column was tight packed and ready to deliver its crushing blow on the waiting redcoat line.

Sharpe licked his dry lips. So these, he thought, were the Tippoo's men. Fine-looking bastards they were, too, and close enough now so that he could see that their tunics were not plain pale purple, but were instead cut from a creamy-white cloth decorated with mauve tiger stripes. Their crossbelts were black and their turbans and waist sashes crimson. Heathens, they might be, but not to be despised for that, for only fifteen years before these same tiger-striped men had torn apart a British army and forced its survivors to surrender. These were the famed tiger troops of Mysore, the warriors of the Tippoo Sultan who had dominated all of southern India until the British thought to climb the ghats from the coastal plain and plunge into Mysore itself. The French were these men's allies, and some Frenchmen served in the Tippoo's forces, but Sharpe could see no white faces in the massive column that at last was ready and, to the deep beat of a single drum, lurched ponderously forward. The tiger-striped troops were marching directly toward the King's 33rd and Sharpe, glancing to his left, saw that the sepoys of the East India Company regiments were still too far away to offer help. The 33rd would have to deal with the Tippoo's column alone.

"Private Sharpe!" Hakeswill's sudden scream was loud enough to drown the cheer that the Tippoo's troops gave as they advanced. "Private Sharpe!" Hakeswill screamed again. He was hurrying along the back of the Light Company and Captain Morris, momentarily dismounted, was following him. "Give me your musket, Private Sharpe!" Hakeswill bellowed.

"Nothing wrong with it," Sharpe protested. He was in the front rank and had to turn and push his way between Garrard and Mallinson to hand the gun over.

Hakeswill snatched the musket and gleefully presented it to Captain Morris. "See, sir!" the Sergeant crowed. "Just as I thought, sir! Bastard sold his flint, sir! Sold it to an 'eathen darkie." Hakeswill's face twitched as he gave Sharpe a triumphant glance. The Sergeant had unscrewed the musket's doghead, extracted the flint in its folded leather pad, and now offered the scrap of stone to Captain Morris. "Piece of common rock, sir, no good to man or beast. Must have flogged his flint, sir. Flogged it in exchange for a pagan whore, sir, I dare say. Filthy beast that he is."

Morris peered at the flint. "Sell the flint, did you, Private?" he asked in a voice that mingled derision, pleasure, and bitterness.

"No, sir."

"Silence!" Hakeswill screamed into Sharpe's face, spattering him with spittle. "Lying to an officer! Flogging offence, sir, flogging offence. Selling his flint, sir? Another flogging offence, sir. Says so in the scriptures, sir."

"It is a flogging offence," Morris said with a tone of satisfaction. He was as tall and lean as Sharpe, with fair hair and a fine-boned face that was just beginning to show the ravages of the liquor with which the Captain assuaged his boredom. His eyes betrayed his cynicism and something much worse: that he despised his men. Hakeswill and Morris, Sharpe thought as he watched them, a right bloody pair.

"Nothing wrong with that flint, sir," Sharpe insisted.

Morris held the flint in the palm of his right hand. "Looks like a chip of stone to me."

"Common grit, sir," Hakeswill said. "Common bloody grit, sir, no good to man or beast."

"Might I?" A new voice spoke. Lieutenant William Lawford had dismounted to join Morris and now, without waiting for his Captain's permission, he reached over and took the flint from Morris's hand. Lawford was blushing again, astonished by his own temerity in thus intervening. "There's an easy way to check, sir," Lawford said nervously, then he drew out his pistol, cocked it, and struck the loose flint against the pistol's steel. Even in the day's bright sunlight there was an obvious spark. "Seems like a good flint to me, sir," Lawford said mildly. Ensign Fitzgerald, standing behind Lawford, gave Sharpe a conspiratorial grin. "A perfectly good flint," Lawford insisted less diffidently.

Morris gave Hakeswill a furious look then turned on his heel and strode back toward his horse. Lawford tossed the flint to Sharpe. "Make your gun ready, Sharpe," he said.

"Yes, sir. Thank you, sir."

Lawford and Fitzgerald walked away as Hakeswill, humiliated, thrust the musket back at Sharpe. "Clever bastard, Sharpie, aren't you?"

"I'll have the leather as well, Sergeant," Sharpe said and, once he had the flint's seating back, he called after Hakeswill who had begun to walk away. "Sergeant!"

Hakeswill turned back.

"You want this, Sergeant?" Sharpe called. He took a chip of stone out of his pocket. He had found it when he had untied the rag from the musket's lock and realized that Hakeswill had substituted the stone for the flint when he had pretended to inspect Sharpe's musket. "No use to me, Sergeant," Sharpe said. "Here." He tossed the stone at Hakeswill who ignored it. Instead the Sergeant spat and turned away. "Thanks, Tom," Sharpe said, for it had been Garrard who had supplied him with a spare flint.

"Worth being in the army to see that," Garrard said, and all around him men laughed to have seen Hakeswill and Morris defeated.

"Eyes to your front, lads!" Ensign Fitzgerald called. The Irish Ensign was the youngest officer in the company, but he had the confidence of a much older man. "Got some shooting to do."

Sharpe pushed back into his file. He brought up the musket, folded the leather over the flint, and seated it in the doghead, then looked up to see that the mass of the enemy was now just a hundred paces away. They were shouting rhythmically and pausing occasionally to let a trumpet sound or a drum flourish a ripple, but the loudest sound was the beat of their feet on the dry earth. Sharpe tried to count the column's front rank, but kept losing count as enemy officers marched slantwise across the column's face. There had to be thousands of the tiger troops, all marching like a great sledgehammer to shatter the two-deep line of redcoats.

"Cutting it fine, aren't we?" a man complained.

"Wait lads, wait," Sergeant Green said calmly.

The enemy now filled the landscape ahead. They came in a column formed of sixty ranks of fifty men, three thousand in all, though to Sharpe's inexperienced eye it seemed as if there must be ten times that number. None of the Tippoo's men fired as they advanced, but held their fire just as the 33rd were holding theirs. The enemy's muskets were tipped with bayonets while their officers were holding deeply curved sabres. On they came and to Sharpe, who was watching the column from the left of the line so that he could see its flank as well as its leading file, the enemy formation seemed as unstoppable as a heavily loaded farm wagon that was rolling slowly and inexorably toward a flimsy fence.

He could see the enemy's faces now. They were dark, with black mustaches and oddly white teeth. The tiger men were close, so close, and their chanting began to dissolve into individual war shouts. Any second now, Sharpe thought, and the heavy column would break into a run and charge with leveled bayonets.

"Thirty-third!" Colonel Wellesley's voice called out sharply from beneath the regiment's colors. "Make ready!"

Sharpe put his right foot behind his left so that his body half turned to the right, then he brought his musket to hip height and pulled the hammer back to full cock. It clicked solidly into place, and somehow the pent-up pressure of the gun's mainspring was reassuring. To the approaching enemy it seemed as though the whole British line had half turned and the sudden movement, coming from men who had been waiting so silently, momentarily checked their eagerness.

Above the tiger troops of Mysore, beneath a bunch of flags on the ridge where the guns fired, a group of horsemen watched the column. Was the Tippoo himself there? Sharpe wondered. And was the Tippoo dreaming of that far-off day when he had broken three and a half thousand British and Indian troops and marched them off to captivity in his capital at Seringapatam? The cheers of the attackers were filling the sky now, but still Colonel Wellesley's voice was audible over the tumult. "Present!"

Seven hundred muskets came up to seven hundred shoulders. The muskets were tipped with steel, seven hundred muskets aimed at the head of the column and about to blast seven hundred ounces of lead at the leading ranks of that fast-moving, confident mass that was plunging straight toward the pair of British colors under which Colonel Arthur Wellesley waited. The tiger men were hurrying now, their front rank breaking apart as they began running. The wagon was about to hit the fence.

Arthur Wellesley had waited six years for this moment. He was twenty-nine years old and had begun to fear that he would never see battle, but now, at last, he would discover whether he and his regiment could fight, and so he filled his lungs to give the order that would start the slaughter.

Colonel Jean Gudin sighed, then, for the thousandth time in the last hour, he fanned his face to drive away the flies. He liked India, but he hated flies, which made India quite hard to like, but on balance, despite the flies, he did like India. Not nearly as much as he liked his native Provence, but where on earth was as lovely as Provence? "Your Majesty?" he ventured diffidently, then waited as his interpreter struggled to gain the Tippoo's attention. The interpreter was exchanging Gudin's French for the Tippoo's Persian tongue. The Tippoo did understand some French and he spoke the local Kanarese language well enough, but he preferred Persian for it reminded him that his lineage went back to the great Persian dynasties. The Tippoo was ever mindful that he was superior to the darker-skinned natives of Mysore. He was a Muslim, he was a Persian, and he was a ruler, while they were mostly Hindus, and all of them, whether rich, poor, great, or lowly, were his obedient subjects. "Your Majesty?" Colonel Gudin tried again.

"Colonel?" The Tippoo was a short man inclined to plumpness, with a mustached face, wide eyes, and a prominent nose. He was not an impressive-looking man, but Gudin knew the Tippoo's unprepossessing appearance disguised a decisive mind and a brave heart. Although the Tippoo acknowledged Gudin, he did not turn to look at the Colonel. Instead he leaned forward in his saddle with one hand clasped over the tiger hilt of his curved sabre as he watched his infantry march on the infidel British. The sword was slung on a silken sash that crossed the pale yellow silk jacket that the Tippoo wore above chintz trousers. His turban was of red silk and pinned with a gold badge showing a tiger's mask. The Tippoo's every possible accoutrement was decorated with the tiger, for the tiger was his mascot and inspiration, but the badge on his turban also incorporated his reverence for Allah, for the tiger's snarling face was formed by a cunning cipher that spelled out a verse of the Koran: "The Lion of God is the Conqueror." Above it, pinned to the turban's brief white plume and brilliant in the day's sunlight, there glittered a ruby the size of a pigeon's egg. "Colonel?" the Tippoo said again.

"It might be wise, Your Majesty," Gudin suggested hesitantly, "if we advanced cannon and cavalry onto the British flank." Gudin gestured to where the 33rd waited in its thin red line to receive the charge of the Tippoo's column. If the Tippoo threatened a flank of that fragile line with cavalry then the British regiment would be forced to shrink into square and thus deny three quarters of their muskets a chance to fire at the column.

The Tippoo shook his head. "We shall sweep that scum away with our infantry, Gudin, then send the cavalry against the baggage." He let go of his sword's hilt to touch his fingers fleetingly together. "Please Allah."

"And if it does not please Allah?" Gudin asked, and suspected that his interpreter would change the insolence of the question into something more acceptable to the Tippoo.

"Then we shall fight them from the walls of Seringapatam," the Tippoo answered, and turned briefly from watching the imminent battle to offer Colonel Gudin a quick smile. It was not a friendly smile, but a feral grimace of anticipation. "We shall destroy them with cannon, Colonel," the Tippoo continued with relish, "and shatter them with rockets, and in a few weeks the monsoon will drown their survivors, and after that, if Allah pleases, we shall hunt fugitive Englishmen from here to the sea."

"If Allah pleases," Gudin said resignedly. Officially he was an adviser to the Tippoo, sent by the Directorate in Paris to help Mysore defeat the British, and the patient Gudin had just done his best to give advice and it was none of his fault if the advice was spurned. He brushed flies from his face, then watched as the 33rd brought their muskets to their shoulders. When those muskets flamed, the Frenchman thought, the front of the Tippoo's column would crumple like a honeycomb hit by a hammer, but at least the slaughter would teach the Tippoo that battles could not be won against disciplined troops unless every weapon was used against them: cavalry to force them to bunch up in protection, then artillery and infantry to pour fire into the massed ranks. The Tippoo surely knew that, yet he had insisted on throwing his three thousand infantry forward without cavalry support, and

Gudin could only suppose that either the Tippoo believed Allah would be fighting on his side this afternoon, or else he was so consumed by his famous victory over the British fifteen years before that he believed he could always beat them in open conflict.

Gudin slapped at flies again. It was time, he thought, to go home. Much as he liked India he felt frustrated. He suspected that the government in Paris had forgotten about his existence, and he was keenly aware that the Tippoo was not receptive to his advice. He did not blame the Tippoo; Paris had made so many promises, but no French army had come to fight for Mysore and Gudin sensed the Tippoo's disappointment and even sympathized with it, while Gudin himself felt useless and abandoned. Some of his contemporaries were already generals; even little Bonaparte, a Corsican whom Gudin had known slightly in Toulon, now had an army of his own, while Jean Gudin was stranded in distant Mysore. Which made victory all the more important, and if the British were not broken here then they would have to be beaten by the massed artillery and rockets that waited on Seringapatam's walls. That was also where Gudin's small battalion of European soldiers was waiting, and Seringapatam, he suspected, was where this campaign would be decided. And if there was victory, and if the British were thrown out of southern India, then Gudin's reward would surely be back in France. Back home where the flies did not swarm like mice.

The enemy regiment waited with leveled muskets. The Tippoo's men cheered and charged impetuously onward. The Tippoo leaned forward, unconsciously biting his lower lip as he waited for the impact.

Gudin wondered whether his woman in Seringapatam would like Provence, or whether Provence would like her. Or maybe it was time for a new woman. He sighed, slapped at flies, then involuntarily shuddered.

For, beneath him, the killing had begun.

✶ ✶ ✶

''Fire!'' Colonel Wellesley shouted.

Seven hundred men pulled their triggers and seven hundred flints snapped forward onto frizzens. The sparks ignited the powder in the pans, there was a pause as the fire fizzed through the seven hundred touchholes, then an almighty crackling roar as the heavy muskets flamed.

The brass butt of the gun slammed into Sharpe's shoulder. He had aimed the weapon at a sashed officer leading the enemy column, though even at sixty yards' range it was hardly worth aiming a musket for it was a frighteningly inaccurate weapon, but unless the ball flew high it ought to hit someone. He could not tell what damage the volley had caused for the instant the musket banged into his shoulder his vision was obscured by the filthy bank of rolling smoke coughed out of the seven hundred musket muzzles. He could hardly hear anything either, for the sound of the rear rank muskets, going off close beside his head, had left his ears ringing. His right hand automatically went to find a new cartridge from his pouch, but then, above the ringing in his ears, he heard the Colonel's brusque voice. "Forward! Thirty-third, forward!"

"Go on, boys!" Sergeant Green called. "Steady now! Don't run! Walk!"

"Damn your eagerness!" Ensign Fitzgerald shouted at the company. "Hold your ranks! This ain't a race!"

The regiment marched into the musket smoke which stank like rotting eggs. Lieutenant Lawford suddenly remembered to draw his sword. He could see nothing beyond the smoke, but imagined a terrible enemy waiting with raised muskets. He touched the pocket of his coat in which he kept the Bible given to him by his mother.

The front rank advanced clear of the stinking smoke fog

and suddenly there was nothing ahead but chaos and carnage.

The seven hundred lead balls had converged on the front
of the column to strike home with a brutal efficiency. Where
there had been orderly ranks there were now only dead men
and dying men who writhed on the ground. The rearward
ranks of the enemy could not advance over the barrier of the
dead and injured, so they stood uncertainly as, out of the
smoke, the seven hundred bayonets appeared.

"On the double! On the double! Don't let them stand!"
Colonel Wellesley called.

"Give them a cheer, boys!" Sergeant Green called. "Go
for them now! Kill the buggers!"

Sharpe had no thought of deserting now, for now he was
about to fight. If there was any one good reason to join the
army, it was to fight. Not to hurry up and do nothing, but to
fight the King's enemies, and this enemy had been shocked
by the awful violence of the close-range volley and now they
stared in horror as the redcoats screamed and ran toward
them. The 33rd, released from the tight discipline of the
ranks, charged eagerly. There was loot ahead. Loot and food
and stunned men to slaughter and there were few men in
the 33rd who did not like a good fight. Not many had joined
the ranks out of patriotism; instead, like Sharpe, they had
taken the King's shilling because hunger or desperation had
forced them into uniform, but they were still good soldiers.
They came from the gutters of Britain where a man survived
by savagery rather than by cleverness. They were brawlers
and bastards, alley-fighters with nothing to lose but tuppence
a day.

Sharpe howled as he ran. The sepoy battalions were closing up on the left, but there was no need for their musketry
now, for the Tippoo's vaunted tiger infantry were not staying
to contest the afternoon. They were edging backward, look-

ing for escape, and then, out of the north where they had been half hidden by the red-blossomed trees, the British and Indian cavalry charged to the sound of a trumpet's call. Lances were lowered and sabres held like spears as the horsemen thundered onto the enemy's flank.

The Tippoo's infantry fled. A few, the lucky few, scrambled back up the ridge, but most were caught in the open ground between the 33rd and the ridge's slope and there the killing became a massacre. Sharpe reached the pile of dead and leapt over them. Just beyond the bloody pile a wounded man tried to bring up his musket, but Sharpe slammed the butt of his gun onto the man's head, kicked the musket out of his enfeebled hands, and ran on. He was aiming for an officer, a brave man who had tried to rally his troops and who now hesitated fatally. The man was carrying a drawn sabre, then he remembered the pistol in his belt and fumbled to draw it, but saw he was too late and turned to run after his men. Sharpe was faster. He rammed his bayonet forward and struck the Indian officer on the side of the neck. The man turned, his sabre whistling as he sliced the curved blade at Sharpe's head. Sharpe parried the blow with the barrel of his musket. A sliver of wood was slashed off the stock as Sharpe kicked the officer between the legs. Sharpe was screaming a challenge, a scream of hate that had nothing to do with Mysore or the enemy officer, and everything to do with the frustrations of his life. The Indian staggered, hunched over, and Sharpe slammed the musket's heavy butt into the dark face. The enemy officer went down, his sabre falling from his hand. He shouted something, maybe offering his surrender, but Sharpe did not care. He just put his left foot on the man's sword arm, then drove the bayonet hard down into his throat. The fight might have lasted three seconds.

Sharpe advanced no farther. Other men ran past, screaming as they pursued the fleeing enemy, but Sharpe had found his victim. He had thrust the bayonet so hard that the blade had gone clean through the officer's neck into the soil beneath and it was hard work to pull the steel free, and in the end he had to put a boot on the dying man's forehead before he could tug the bayonet out. Blood gushed from the wound, then subsided to a throbbing pulse of spilling red as Sharpe knelt and began rifling the man's gaudy uniform, oblivious of the choking, bubbling sound that the officer was making as he died. Sharpe ripped off the yellow silk sash and tossed it aside together with the silver-hilted sabre and the pistol. The sabre scabbard was made of boiled leather, nothing of any value to Sharpe, but behind it was a small embroidered pouch and Sharpe drew out his knife, unfolded the blade, and slashed through the pouch's straps. He fumbled the pouch open to find that it was filled with nothing but dry rice and one small scrap of what looked like cake. He smelled it gingerly and guessed it was made of some kind of bean. He tossed the food aside and spat a curse at the dying man. "Where's your bleeding money?"

The man gasped, made a choking sound, then his whole body jerked as his heart finally gave up the struggle. Sharpe tore at the tunic that was decorated with mauve tiger stripes. He felt the seams, looking for coins, found none so pulled off the wide red turban that was sticky with fresh blood. The dead man's face was already crawling with flies. Sharpe pulled the turban apart and there, in the very center of the greasy cloth, he found three silver and a dozen small copper coins. "Knew you'd have something," he told the dead man, then pushed the coins into his own pouch.

The cavalry was finishing off the remnants of the Tippoo's infantry. The Tippoo himself, with his entourage and standard-bearers, had gone from the top of the ridge, and there were no cannon firing there either. The enemy had slipped away, abandoning their trapped infantry to the sabres and lances of the British and Indian cavalry. The Indian cavalry had been recruited from the city of Madras and the East Coast states which had all suffered from the Tippoo's raids and now they took a bloody revenge, whooping and laughing as their blades cut down the terrified fugitives. Some cavalry-men, running out of targets, were already dismounted and searching the dead for plunder. The sepoy infantry, too late to join the killing, arrived to join the plunder.

Sharpe twisted the bayonet off his musket, wiped it clean on the dead man's sash, scooped up the sabre and pistol, then went to find more loot. He was grinning, and thinking that there was nothing to this fighting business, nothing at all. A few shots in Flanders, one volley here; and neither fight was worthy of the name battle. Flanders had been a muddle and this fight had been as easy as slaughtering sheep. No wonder Sergeant Hakeswill would live for ever. And so would he, Sharpe reckoned, because there was nothing to this business. Just a couple of bangs and it was all over. He laughed, slid the bayonet into its sheath, and knelt beside another dead man. There was work to do and a future to finance.

If only he could decide where it would be safe to run.

CHAPTER 2

Sergeant Obadiah Hakeswill glanced about to see what his men were doing. Just about all of them were plundering, and quite right too. That was a soldier's privilege. Fight the battle then strip the enemy of anything worth a penny. The officers were not looting, but officers never did, at least not so that anyone noticed them, but Hakeswill did see that Ensign Fitzgerald had somehow managed to get himself a jeweled sabre that he was now flashing around like a shilling whore given a guinea fan. Mister bloody Ensign Fitzgerald was getting above himself in Sergeant Hakeswill's considered opinion. Ensigns were the lowest of the low, apprentice officers, lads in silver lace, and Mister bloody Fitzgerald had no business countermanding Hakeswill's orders so Mister bloody Fitzgerald must be taught his place, but the trouble was that Mister Fitzgerald was Irish and Hakeswill was of the opinion that the Irish were only half civilized and never did understand their place. Most of them, anyway. Major Shee was Irish, and he was civilized, at least when he was sober, and Colonel Wellesley, who was from Dublin, was wholly civilized, but the Colonel had possessed the sense to make himself more English than the English, while Mister bloody Fitzgerald made no pretence about his birth.

"See this, Hakeswill?" Fitzgerald, sublimely unaware of

Hakeswill's glowering thoughts, stepped across a body to show off his new sabre.

"See what, sir?"

"Damned blade is made in Birmingham! Will you credit that? Birmingham! Says so on the blade, see? 'Made in Birmingham.'"

Hakeswill dutifully examined the legend on the blade, then fingered the sabre's pommel which was elegantly set with a ring of seven small rubies. "Looks like glass to me, sir," he said dismissively, hoping he could somehow persuade Fitzgerald to relinquish the blade.

"Nonsense!" Fitzgerald said cheerfully. "Best rubies! Bit small, maybe, but I doubt the ladies will mind that. Seven pieces of glitter? That adds up to a week of sin, Sergeant. It was worth killing the rascal for that."

If you did kill him, Hakeswill thought sourly as he stumped away from the exuberant Ensign. More likely picked it up off the ground. And Fitzgerald was right; seven rubies, even small ones, would buy a lot of Naig's ladies. "Nasty" Naig was a merchant from Madras, one of the many traveling with the army, and he had brought his brothel with him. It was an expensive brothel, officers only, or at least only those who could pay an officer's price, and that made Hakeswill think of Mary Bickerstaff. Mrs. Mary Bickerstaff. She was a half and half, half Indian and half British, and that made her valuable. Very valuable. Most of the women who followed the army were dark as Hades, and while Obadiah Hakeswill had no distaste for dark skin he did miss the touch of white flesh. So did many of the officers, and there was a guinea or two to be made out of that lust. Naig would pay well for a skin as pale as Mary Bickerstaff's.

She was a rare beauty, Mary Bickerstaff. A beauty amongst a pack of ugly, rancid women. Hakeswill watched as a group of the battalion's wives ran to take part in the plundering and almost shuddered as he contemplated their ugliness. About two thirds of the wives were *bibbis*, Indians, and most of those, Hakeswill knew, were not properly married with the Colonel's permission, while the rest were those lucky British women who had won the brutal lottery that had taken place on the night before the battalion had sailed from England. The wives had been gathered in a barrack room, their names had been put into ten shakos, one for each company, and the first ten names drawn from each hat were allowed to accompany their husbands. The rest had to stay in Britain, and what happened to them there was anybody's guess. Most went on the parish, but parishes resented feeding soldiers' wives, so as like as not they were forced to become whores. Barrack-gate whores, for the most part, because they lacked the looks for anything better. But a few, a precious few, were pretty, and none was prettier than Sergeant Bickerstaff's half and half widow.

The women spread out among the dead and dying Mysoreans. If anything they were even more efficient than their men at plundering the dead, for the men tended to hurry and so missed the hiding places where a soldier secreted his money. Hakeswill watched Flora Placket strip the body of a tall tiger-striped corpse whose throat had been slashed to the backbone by the slice of a cavalryman's sabre. She did not rush her work, but searched carefully, garment by garment, then handed each piece of clothing to one of her two children to fold and stack. Hakeswill approved of Flora Placket for she was a large and steady woman who kept her man in good order and made no fuss about a campaign's discomforts. She was a good mother too, and that was why Obadiah did not care that Flora Placket was as ugly as a haversack. Mothers were sacred. Mothers were not expected to be pretty. Mothers were Obadiah Hakeswill's guardian angels, and Flora Placket reminded Obadiah of his own mother who was the only person in all his life who had shown him kindness. Biddy Hakeswill was long dead now, she had died a year before the twelve-year-old Obadiah had dangled on a scaffold for the trumped-up charge of sheep stealing and, to amuse the crowd, the executioner had not let any of that day's victims drop from the gallows, but had instead hoisted them gently into the air so that they choked slowly as their piss-soaked legs jerked in the death dance of the gibbet. No one had taken much notice of the small boy at the scaffold's end and, when the heavens had opened and the rain come down in bucketfuls to scatter the crowd, no one had bothered when Biddy Hakeswill's brother had cut the boy down and set him loose. "Did it for your mother," his uncle had snarled. "God rest her soul. Now be off with you and don't ever show your face in the dale again." Hakeswill had run south, joined the army as a drummer boy, had risen to sergeant and had never forgotten his dying mother's words. "No one will ever get rid of Obadiah," she had said, "not my Obadiah. Death's too good for him." The gallows had proved that. Touched by God, he was, indestructible!

A groan sounded near Hakeswill and the Sergeant snapped out of his reverie to see a tiger-striped Indian struggling to turn onto his belly. Hakeswill scurried over, forced the man onto his back again and placed his halberd's spear point at the man's throat. "Money?" Hakeswill snarled, then held out his left hand and motioned the counting of coins. "Money?"

The man blinked slowly, then said something in his own language.

"I'll let you live, you bugger," Hakeswill promised, leering at the wounded man. "Not that you'll live long. Got a goolie in your belly, see?" He pointed at the wound in the man's belly where the bullet had driven home. "Now where's your money? Money! Pice? Dan? Pagodas? Annas? Rupees?"

The man must have understood for his hand fluttered weakly toward his chest.

"Good boy, now," Hakeswill said, smiling again, then his face jerked in its involuntary spasms as he pushed the spear point home, but not too quickly for he liked to see the realization of death on a man's face. "You're a stupid bugger, too," Hakeswill said when the man's death throes had ended, then he cut open the tunic and found that the man had strapped some coins to his chest with a cotton sash. He undid the sash and pocketed the handful of copper change. Not a big haul, but Hakeswill was not dependent on his own plundering to fill his purse. He would take a cut from whatever the soldiers of the Light Company found. They knew they would have to pay up or else face punishment.

He saw Sharpe kneeling beside a body and hurried across. "Got a sword there, Sharpie?" Hakeswill asked. "Stole it, did you?"

"I killed the man, Sergeant." Sharpe looked up.

"Doesn't bleeding matter, does it, lad? You ain't permitted to carry a sword. Officer's weapon, a sword is. Mustn't get above your station, Sharpie. Get above yourself, boy, and you'll be cut down. So I'll take the blade, I will." Hakeswill half expected Sharpe to resist, but the Private did nothing as the Sergeant picked up the silver-hilted blade. "Worth a few bob, I dare say," Hakeswill said appreciatively, then he laid the sword's tip against the stock at Sharpe's neck. "Which is more than you're worth, Sharpie. Too clever for your own good, you are."

Sharpe edged away from the sword and stood up. "I ain't got a quarrel with you, Sergeant," he said.

"But you do, boy, you do." Hakeswill grimaced as his face went into spasm. "And you know what the quarrel's about, don't you?"

Sharpe backed away from the sword. "I ain't got a quarrel with you," he repeated stubbornly.

"I think our quarrel is called Mrs. Bickerstaff," Hakeswill said, and grinned when Sharpe said nothing. "I almost got you with that flint, didn't I? Would have had you flogged raw, boy, and you'd have died of a fever within a week. A flogging does that in this climate. Wears a man down, a flogging does. But you got a friendly officer, don't you? Mister Lawford. He likes you, does he?" He prodded Sharpe's chest with the sword's tip. "Is that what it is? Officer's pet, are you?"

"Mister Lawford ain't nothing to me," Sharpe said.

"That's what you say, but my eyes tell different." Hakeswill giggled. "Sweet on each other, are you? You and Mister Lawford? Ain't that nice, Sharpie, but it don't make you much use to Mrs. Bickerstaff, does it? Reckon she'd be better off with a real man."

"She ain't your business," Sharpe said.

"Ain't my business! Oh, listen to it!" Hakeswill sneered, then prodded the sword forward again. He wanted to provoke Sharpe into resisting, for then he could charge him with attacking a superior, but the tall young man just backed away from the blade. "You listen, Sharpie," Hakeswill said, "and you listen well. She's a sergeant's wife, not the whore of some common ranker like you."

"Sergeant Bickerstaff's dead," Sharpe protested.

"So she needs a man!" Hakeswill said. "And a sergeant's widow doesn't get rogered by a stinking bit of dirt like you. It ain't right. Ain't natural. It's beneath her station, Sharpie, and it can't be allowed. Says so in the scriptures."

"She can choose who she wants," Sharpe insisted.

"Choose, Sharpie? Choose?" Hakeswill laughed. "Women don't choose, you soft bugger. Women get taken by the strongest. Says so in the scriptures, and if you stand in my way, Sharpie"—he pushed the sword hard forward—"then I'll have your spine laid open to the daylight. A lost flint? That would have been two hundred lashes, lad, but next time? A thousand. And laid on hard! Real hard! Be blood and bones, boy, bones and blood, and who'll look after your Mrs. Bickerstaff then? Eh? Tell me that. So you takes your filthy hands off her. Leave her to me, Sharpie." He leered at Sharpe, but still the younger man refused to be provoked and Hakeswill at last abandoned the attempt. "Worth a few guineas, this sword," the Sergeant said again as he backed away. "Obliged to you, Sharpie."

Sharpe swore uselessly at Hakeswill's back, then turned as a woman hailed him from among the heaped bodies that had been the leading ranks of the Tippoo's column. Those bodies were now being dragged apart to be searched and Mary Bickerstaff was helping the work along.

He walked toward her and, as ever, was struck by the beauty of the girl. She had black hair, a thin face, and dark big eyes that could spark with mischief. Now, though, she looked worried. "What did Hakeswill want?" she asked.

"You."

She spat, then crouched again to the body she was searching. "He can't touch you, Richard," she said, "not if you do your duty."

"The army's not like that. And you know it."

"You've just got to be clever," Mary insisted. She was a soldier's daughter who had grown up in the Calcutta barrack lines. She had inherited her dark Indian beauty from her mother and learned the ways of soldiers from her father who had been an engineer sergeant in the Old Fort's garrison before an outbreak of cholera had killed him and his native wife. Mary's father had always claimed she was pretty enough to marry an officer and so rise in the world, but no officer would marry a half-caste, at least no officer who cared about advancement, and so after her parents' death Mary had married Sergeant Jem Bickerstaff of the 33rd, a good man, but Bickerstaff had died of the fever shortly after the army had left Madras to climb to the Mysore plateau and Mary, at twenty-two, was now an orphan and a widow. She was also wise to the army's ways. "If you're made up to sergeant, Richard," she told Sharpe now, "then Hakeswill can't touch you."

Sharpe laughed. "Me? A sergeant? That'll be the day, lass. I made corporal once, but that didn't last."

"You can be a sergeant," she insisted, "and you should be a sergeant. And Hakeswill couldn't touch you if you were."

Sharpe shrugged. "It ain't me he wants to touch, lass, but you."

Mary had been cutting a tiger-striped tunic from a dead man, but now she paused and looked quizzically up at Sharpe. She had not been in love with Jem Bickerstaff, but she had recognized that the Sergeant was a good, kind man, and she saw the same decency in Sharpe. It was not exactly the same decency, for Sharpe, she reckoned, had ten times Jem Bickerstaff's fire and he could be as cunning as a snake when it suited him, but Mary still trusted Sharpe. She was also attracted to him. There was something very striking about Sharpe's lean good looks, something dangerous, she acknowledged, but very exciting. She looked at him for a few seconds, then shrugged. "Maybe he won't dare touch me if we're married," she said. "I mean proper married, with the Colonel's permission."

"Married!" Sharpe said, flustered by the word.

Mary stood. "It ain't easy being a widow in the army, Richard. Every man reckons you're loot."

"Aye, I know it's hard," Sharpe said, frowning. He stared at her as he thought about the idea of getting married. Till now he had only been thinking of desertion, but maybe marriage was not such a bad idea. At least it would make it much harder for Hakeswill to get his hands on Mary's skin. And a married man, Sharpe reckoned, was more likely to be promoted. But what was the point of rising an inch or two in the dunghill? Even a sergeant was still at the bottom of the heap. It was better to be out of the army altogether and Mary, Sharpe decided, would be more likely to desert with him if she was properly married to him. That thought made him nod slowly. "I reckon I might like to be married," he said shyly.

"Me too." She smiled and, awkwardly, Sharpe smiled back. For a moment neither had anything to say, then Mary excitedly fished in the pocket of her apron to produce a jewel she had taken from a dead man. "Look what I found!" She handed Sharpe a red stone, half the size of a hen's egg. "You reckon it's a ruby?" Mary asked eagerly.

Sharpe tossed the stone up and down. "I reckon it's glass, lass," he said gently, "just glass. But I'll get you a ruby for a wedding gift, just you watch me."

"I'll more than watch you, Dick Sharpe," she said happily and put her arm into his. Sergeant Hakeswill, a hundred paces away, watched them and his face twitched.

While on the edges of the killing place, where the looted and naked bodies lay scattered, the vultures came down, sidled forward, and began to tear at the dead.

The allied armies camped a quarter of a mile short of the place where the dead lay. The camp sprawled across the plain: an instant town where fifty thousand soldiers and thousands of camp followers would spend the night. Tents went up for officers well away from the places where the vast herds of cattle were guarded for the night. Some of the cattle were beeves, being herded and slaughtered for food, some were oxen that carried panniers filled with the eighteen- and twenty-four-pounder cannonballs that would be needed to blast a hole through the walls of Seringapatam, while yet others were bullocks that hauled the wagons and guns, and the heaviest guns, the big siege pieces, needed sixty bullocks apiece. There were more than two hundred thousand cattle with the army, but all were now scrawny for the Tippoo's cavalry was stripping the land of fodder as the British and Hyderabad armies advanced.

The common soldiers had no tents. They would sleep on the ground close to their fires, but first they ate and this night the feeding was good, at least for the men of the King's 33rd who had coins taken from the enemy dead to spend with the *bhinjarries*, the merchant clans that traveled with the army and had their own private guards to protect their goods. The *bhinjarries* all sold chickens, rice, flour, beans, and, best of all, the throat-burning skins of arrack which could make a man drunk even faster than rum. Some of the *bhinjarries* also hired out whores and the 33rd gave those men good business that night.

Captain Morris expected to visit the famous green tents of Naig, the *bhinjarrie* whose stock in trade was the most expensive whores of Madras, but for now he was stuck in his own tent where, under the feeble light of a candle that flickered on his table, he disposed of the company's business. Or rather Sergeant Hakeswill disposed of it while Morris, his coat unbuttoned and silk stock loosened, sprawled in a camp chair. Sweat dripped down his face. There was a small wind, but the muslin screen hanging at the entrance to the tent took away its cooling effects, and if the screen was discarded the tent would fill with savagely huge moths. Morris hated moths, hated the heat, hated India. "Guard rosters, sir," Hakeswill said, offering the papers.

"Anything I should know?"

"Not a thing, sir. Just like last week's, sir. Ensign Hicks

made up the roster, sir. A good man, sir, Ensign Hicks. Knows his place."

"You mean he does what you tell him to do?" Morris asked drily.

"Learning his trade, sir, learning his trade, just like a good little ensign should. Unlike some as I could mention."

Morris ignored the sly reference to Fitzgerald and instead dipped his quill in ink and scrawled his name at the foot of the rosters. "I assume Ensign Fitzgerald and Sergeant Green have been assigned all the night duty?" he asked.

"They needs the practice, sir."

"And you need your sleep, Sergeant?"

"Punishment book, sir," Hakeswill said, offering the leather-bound ledger and taking back the guard roster without acknowledging Morris's last comment.

Morris leafed through the book. "No floggings this week?"

"Will be soon, sir, will be soon."

"Private Sharpe escaped you today, eh?" Morris laughed. "Losing your touch, Obadiah." There was no friendliness in his use of the Christian name, just scorn, but Sergeant Hakeswill took no offence. Officers were officers, at least those above ensigns were proper officers in Hakeswill's opinion, and such gentlemen had every right to be scornful of lesser ranks.

"I ain't losing nothing, sir," Hakeswill answered equably. "If the rat don't die first shake, sir, then you puts the dog in again. That's how it's done, sir. Says so in the scriptures. Sick report, sir. Nothing new, except that Sears has the fever, so he won't be with us long, but he won't be no loss, sir. No good to man or beast, Private Sears. Better off dead, he is."

"Are we done?" Morris asked when he had signed the sick report, but then a tactful cough sounded at the tent's opening and Lieutenant Lawford ducked under the flap and pushed through the muslin screen.

"Busy, Charles?" Lawford asked Morris.

"Always pleased to see you, William," Morris said sarcastically, "but I was about to go for a stroll."

"There's a soldier to see you," Lawford explained. "Man's got a request, sir."

Morris sighed as though he was too busy to be bothered with such trifles, but then he shrugged and waved a hand as if to suggest he was making a great and generous gesture by giving the man a moment of his precious time. "Who?" he asked.

"Private Sharpe, sir."

"Troublemaker, sir," Hakeswill put in.

"He's a good man," Lawford insisted hotly, but then decided his small experience of the army hardly qualified him to make such judgements and so, diffidently, he added that it was only his opinion. "But he seems like a good man, sir," he finished.

"Let him in," Morris said. He sipped from a tin mug of arrack while Sharpe negotiated the muslin screen and then stood to attention beneath the ridge pole. "Hat off, boy!" Hakeswill snapped. "Don't you know to take your hat off in the presence of an officer?"

Sharpe snatched off his shako.

"Well?" Morris asked.

For a second it seemed that Sharpe did not know what to say, but then he cleared his throat and, staring at the tent wall a few inches above Captain Morris's head, he at last found his voice. "Permission to marry, sir."

Morris grinned. "Marry! Found yourself a *bibbi*, have you?" He sipped more arrack, then looked at Hakeswill. "How many wives are on the company strength now, Sergeant?"

"Full complement, sir! No room for more, sir! Full up, sir! Not a vacancy to be had. Shall I dismiss Private Sharpe, sir?"

"This girl's on the complement," Lieutenant Lawford intervened. "She's Sergeant Bickerstaff's widow."

Morris stared up at Sharpe. "Bickerstaff," he said vaguely as though the name was strange to him. "Bickerstaff. Fellow who died of a fever on the march, is that right?"

"Yes, sir," Hakeswill answered.

"Didn't know the man was even married," Morris said. "Official wife, was she?"

"Very official, sir," Hakeswill answered. "On the company strength, sir. Colonel's signature on the certificate, sir. Proper married before God and the army, sir."

Morris sniffed and looked up at Sharpe again. "Why on earth do you want to marry, Sharpe?"

Sharpe looked embarrassed. "Just do, sir," he said lamely.

"Can't say I disapprove of marriage," Morris said. "Steadies a man does marriage, but a fellow like you, Sharpe, can do better than a soldier's widow, can't you? Dreadful creatures, soldiers' widows! Used goods, Private. Fat and greasy, like lumps of lard wrapped up in linen. Get yourself a sweet little *bibbi*, man, something that ain't yet run to seed."

"Very good advice, sir," Hakeswill said, his face twitching. "Words of wisdom, sir. Shall I dismiss him, sir?"

"Mary Bickerstaff is a good woman, sir," Lieutenant Lawford said. The Lieutenant, whom Sharpe had first approached with his request, was eager to do his best. "Sharpe could do a lot worse than marry Mary Bickerstaff, sir."

Morris cut a cigar and lit it from the guttering candle that burned on his camp table. "White, is she?" he asked negligently.

"Half *bibbi* and half Christian, sir," Hakeswill said, "but she had a good man for her husband." He sniffed, pretending that he was suddenly overcome with emotion. "And Jem Bickerstaff ain't this month in his grave, sir. Too soon for the trollop to marry again. It ain't right, sir. Says so in the scriptures."

Morris offered Hakeswill a cynical glance. "Don't be absurd, Sergeant. Most army widows marry the next day! The ranks are hardly high society, you know."

"But Jem Bickerstaff was a friend of mine, sir," Hakeswill said, sniffing again and even cuffing at an invisible tear. "Friend of mine, sir," he repeated more hoarsely, "and on his dying bed, sir, he begged me to look after his little wife, sir. I know she ain't through and through white, he told me, but she deserves to be looked after. His very dying words, sir."

"He bloody hated you!" Sharpe could not resist the words.

"Quiet in front of an officer!" Hakeswill shouted. "Speak when you're spoken to, boy, and otherwise keep your filthy mouth buttoned like God wanted it."

Morris frowned as though Hakeswill's loud voice was giving him a headache. Then he looked up at Sharpe. "I'll talk to Major Shee about it, Sharpe. If the woman is on the strength and wants to marry you, then I don't suppose we can stop her. I'll talk to the Major. You're dismissed."

Sharpe hesitated, wondering whether he should thank the Captain for the laconic words, but before he could say anything, Hakeswill was bawling in his ear. "About turn! Smartly now! Hat on! Quick march! One two one two, smartly now. Mind the bleeding curtain, boy! This ain't a pig sty like what you grew up in, but an officer's quarters!"

Morris waited till Sharpe was gone, then looked up at Lawford. "Nothing more, Lieutenant?"

Lawford guessed that he too was dismissed. "You will talk to Major Shee, Charles?" he pressed Morris.

"I just said so, didn't I?" Morris glared up at the Lieutenant.

Lawford hesitated, then nodded. "Good night, sir," he said and ducked under the muslin screen.

Morris waited until he was certain that both men were out of earshot. "Now what do we do?" he asked Hakeswill.

"Tell the silly bugger that Major Shee refused permission, sir."

"And Willie Lawford will talk to the Major and find that he didn't. Or else he'll go straight to Wellesley. Lawford's uncle is on the staff, or had you forgotten that? Use your wits, man!" Morris slapped at a moth that had managed to slip through the screen. "What do we do?" he asked again.

Hakeswill sat on a stool opposite the camp table. He scratched his head, glanced into the night, then looked back to Morris. "He's a sharp one, Sharpie, he is. Slippery. But I'll do him." He paused. "Of course, sir, if you helped, it'd be quicker. Much quicker."

Morris looked dubious. "The girl will only find herself another protector," he said. "I think you're wasting my time, Sergeant."

"What me, sir? No, sir. Not at all, sir. I'll have the girl, sir, just you watch, and Nasty Naig says you can have all you want of her. Free and gratis, sir, like you ought to."

Morris stood, pulled on his jacket and picked up his hat and sword. "You think I'd share your woman, Hakeswill?" The Captain shuddered. "And get your pox?"

"Pox, sir? Me, sir?" Hakeswill stood. "Not me, sir. Clean as a whistle, I am, sir. Cured, sir. Mercury." His face twitched. "Ask the surgeon, sir, he'll tell you."

Morris hesitated, thinking of Mary Bickerstaff. He thought a great deal about Mary Bickerstaff. Her beauty ensured that, and men on campaign were deprived of beauty and so Mary's allure only increased with every mile the army marched westward. Morris was not alone. On the night when Mary's husband had died, the 33rd's officers, at least those who had a mind for such games, had wagered which of them would first take the widow to their bed and so far none of them had succeeded. Morris wanted to win, not only for the fourteen guineas that would accrue to the successful seducer, but because he had become besotted by the woman. Soon after she had become a widow he had asked Mary to do his laundry, thinking that thereby he could begin the intimacy he craved, but she had refused him with a lacerating scorn. Morris wanted to punish her for that scorn, and Hakeswill, with his intuition for other men's weaknesses, had sensed what Morris wanted and promised he would arrange everything. Naig, Hakeswill assured his bitter officer, had a way of breaking reluctant girls. "There ain't a *bibbi* born that Nasty can't break, sir," Hakeswill had promised Morris, "and he'd give a small fortune for a proper white one. Not that Mrs. Bickerstaff's proper white, sir, not like a Christian, but in the dark she'd pass well enough." The Sergeant needed Morris's help in ridding Mrs. Bickerstaff of Richard Sharpe and as an inducement he had offered Morris the free run of Naig's tent. In return, Morris knew, Hakeswill would expect a lifetime's patronage. As Morris climbed the army's ranks, so Hakeswill would be drawn ineluctably after him and with each step the Sergeant would garner more power and influence.

"So when will you free Mrs. Bickerstaff of Sharpe?" Morris asked, buckling his sword belt.

"Tonight, sir. With your help. You'll be back here by midnight, I dare say?"

"I might."

"If you are, sir, we'll do him. Tonight, sir."

Morris clapped the cocked hat on his head, made sure his purse was in his coattail pocket, and ducked under the muslin. "Carry on, Sergeant," he called back.

"Sir!" Hakeswill stood to attention for a full ten seconds

after the Captain was gone, and then, with a sly grin twitching on his lumpy face, followed Morris into the night.

Nineteen miles to the south lay a temple. It was an ancient place, deep in the country, one of the many Hindu shrines where the country folk came on high days and holidays to do honor to their gods and to pray for a timely monsoon, for good crops and for the absence of warlords. For the rest of the year the temple lay abandoned, its gods and altars and richly carved spires home to scorpions, snakes, and monkeys.

The temple was surrounded by a wall through which one gate led, though the wall was not high and the gate was never shut. Villagers left small offerings of leaves, flowers, and food in niches of the gateposts, and sometimes they would go into the temple itself, cross the courtyard, and climb to the inner shrine where they would place their small gifts beneath the image of a god, but at night, when the Indian sky lay black over a heat-exhausted land, no one would ever dream of disturbing the gods.

But this night, the night after battle, a man entered the temple. He was tall and thin, with white hair and a harsh, suntanned face. He was over sixty years old, but his back was still straight and he moved with the ease of a much younger man. Like many Europeans who had lived a long time in India he was prone to bouts of debilitating fever, but otherwise he was in sterling health, and Colonel Hector McCandless ascribed that good health to his religion and to a regimen that abjured alcohol, tobacco, and meat. His religion was Calvinism for Hector McCandless had grown up in Scotland and the godly lessons that had been whipped into his young, earnest soul had never been forgotten. He was an honest man, a tough man, and a wise one.

His soul was old in experience, but even so it was offended by the idols that reflected the small light of the lantern he had lit once he was through the temple's ever-open gate. He had lived in India for over sixteen years now and he was more accustomed to these heathen shrines than to the kirks of his childhood, but still, whenever he saw these strange gods with their multiplicity of arms, their elephant heads, their grotesquely colored faces, and their cobra-hooded masks, he felt a stab of disapproval. He never let that disapproval show, for that would have imperiled his duty, and McCandless was a man who believed that duty was a master second only to God.

He wore the red coat and the tartan kilt of the King's Scotch Brigade, a Highland regiment that had not seen McCandless's stern features for sixteen years. He had served with the brigade for over thirty years, but lack of funds had obstructed his promotion and so, with his Colonel's blessing, he had accepted a job with the army of the East India Company which governed those parts of India that were under British rule. In his time he had commanded battalions of sepoys, but McCandless's first love was surveying. He had mapped the Carnatic coast, he had charted the Sundarbans of the Hoogli, and he had once ridden the length and breadth of Mysore, and while he had been so engaged he had learned a half-dozen Indian languages and met a score of princes, rajahs, and nawabs. Few men understood India as McCandless did, which was why the Company had promoted him to Colonel and attached him to the British army as its chief of intelligence. It was McCandless's task to advise General Harris of the enemy's strength and dispositions, and, in particular, to discover just what defenses waited for the allied armies when they reached Seringapatam.

It was his search for that particular answer that had brought Colonel McCandless to this ancient temple. He had surveyed the temple seven years before, when Lord Cornwallis's army had marched against Mysore, and back then

McCandless had admired the extraordinary carvings that covered every inch of the temple's walls. The Scotsman's religion had been offended by so much decoration, but he was too honest a man to deny that the old stoneworkers had been marvellous craftsmen, for the sculpture here was as fine, if not finer, than anything produced in medieval Europe. The wan yellow light of his lantern washed across caparisoned elephants, fierce gods, and marching armies, all made of stone.

He climbed the steps to the central shrine, passed between its vast, squat pillars, and so went into the sanctuary. The roof here, beneath the temple's high carved tower, was fashioned into lotus blossoms. The idols stared blankly from their niches with flowers and leaves drying at their feet. The Colonel placed the lantern on the flagstone floor, then sat cross-legged and waited. He closed his eyes, letting his ears identify the noises of the night beyond the temple's walls. McCandless had come to this remote temple with an escort of six Indian lancers, but he had left that escort two miles away in case their presence should have inhibited the man he was hoping to meet. So now he just waited with eyes closed and arms folded, and after a while he heard the thump of a hoof on dry earth, the chink of a snaffle chain, and then, once again, silence. And still he waited with eyes closed.

"If you were not in that uniform," a voice said a few moments later, "I would think you were at your prayers."

"The uniform does not disqualify me from prayer, any more than does your uniform," the Colonel answered, opening his eyes. He stood. "Welcome, General."

The man who faced McCandless was younger than the Scot, but every inch as tall and lean. Appah Rao was now a general in the forces of the Tippoo Sultan, but once, many years before, he had been an officer in one of McCandless's sepoy battalions and it was that old acquaintanceship, which had verged upon friendship, that had persuaded McCandless it was worth risking his own life to talk to Appah Rao. Appah Rao had served under McCandless's orders until his father had died, and then, trained as a soldier, he had returned to his native Mysore. Today he had watched from the ridge as the Tippoo's infantry had been massacred by a single British volley. The experience had made him sour, but he forced a grudging courtesy into his voice. "So you're still alive, Major?" Appah Rao spoke in Kanarese, the language of the native Mysoreans.

"Still alive, and a full colonel now," McCandless answered in the same tongue. "Shall we sit?"

Appah Rao grunted, then sat opposite McCandless. Behind him, beyond the sunken courtyard where they were framed by the temple's gateway, were two soldiers. They were Appah Rao's escort and McCandless knew they must be trusted men, for if the Tippoo Sultan were ever to discover that this meeting had taken place then Appah Rao and all his family would be killed. Unless, of course, the Tippoo already knew and was using Appah Rao to make some mischief of his own.

The Tippoo's General was dressed in his master's tiger-striped tunic, but over it he wore a sash of the finest silk and slung across his shoulder was a second silk sash from which hung a gold-hilted sword. His boots were red leather and his hat a coil of watered red silk on which a milky-blue jewel gleamed soft in the lantern's flickering light. "You were at Malavelly today?" he asked McCandless.

"I was," McCandless said. Malavelly was the nearest village to where the battle had been fought.

"So you know what happened?"

"I know the Tippoo sacrificed hundreds of your people," McCandless said. "Your people, General, not his."

Appah Rao dismissed the distinction. "The people follow him."

"Because they have no choice. They follow, but do they love him?"

"Some do," Appah Rao answered. "But what does it matter? Why should a ruler want his people's love? Their obedience, yes, but love? Love is for children, McCandless, and for gods and for women."

McCandless smiled, tacitly yielding the argument which was not important. He did not have to persuade Appah Rao to treachery, the very presence of the Mysorean General was proof that he was already halfway to betraying the Tippoo, but McCandless did not expect the General to yield gracefully. There was pride at stake here, and Appah Rao's pride was great and needed to be handled as gently as a cocked dueling pistol. Appah Rao had always been thus, even when he was a young man in the Company's army, and McCandless approved of that pride. He had always respected Appah Rao, and still did, and he believed Appah Rao returned the respect. It was in that belief that the Colonel had sent a message to Seringapatam. The message was carried by one of the Company's native agents who wandered as a naked fakir through southern India. The message had been concealed in the man's long greasy hair and it had invited Appah Rao to a reunion with his old commanding officer. The reply had specified this temple and this night as the rendezvous. Appah Rao was flirting with treachery, but that did not mean he was finding it either easy or pleasant.

"I have a gift," McCandless said, changing the subject, "for your Rajah."

"He is in need of gifts."

"Then this comes with our most humble duty and high respect." McCandless took a leather bag from his sporran and placed it beside the lantern. The bag chinked as it was laid down and, though Appah Rao glanced at it, he did not take it. "Tell your Rajah," McCandless said, "that it is our desire to place him back on his throne."

"And who will stand behind his throne?" Appah Rao demanded. "Men in red coats?"

"You will," McCandless said, "as your family always did."

"And you?" the General asked. "What do you want?"

"To trade. That is the Company's business: trade. Why should we become rulers?"

Appah Rao sneered. "Because you always do. You come as merchants, but you bring guns and use them to make yourselves into taxmen, judges, and executioners. Then you bring your churches." He shuddered.

"We come to trade," McCandless insisted equably. "And what would you prefer, General? To trade with the British or be ruled by Muslims?"

And that, McCandless knew, was the question that had brought Appah Rao to this temple in the dark night. Mysore was a Hindu country and its ancient rulers, the Wodeyars, were Hindus like their people, but the Tippoo's father, the fierce Hyder Ali, had come from the north and conquered their state and the Tippoo had inherited his father's stolen throne. To give himself a shred of legality the Tippoo, like his father before him, kept the old ruling family alive, but the Wodeyars were now reduced to poverty and to ceremonial appearances only. The new Rajah was scarce more than a child, but to many of Mysore's Hindus he was still their rightful monarch, though that was an opinion best kept secret from the Tippoo.

Appah Rao had not answered the Scotsman's question, so McCandless phrased it differently. "Are you the last Hindu senior officer in the Tippoo's army?"

"There are others," Appah Rao said evasively.

"And the rest?"

Appah Rao paused. "Fed to his tigers," he eventually admitted.

"And soon, General," McCandless said softly, "there will be no more Hindu officers in Mysore and some very fat tigers. And if you defeat us you will still not be safe. The French will come."

Appah Rao shrugged. "There are already Frenchmen in Seringapatam. They demand nothing of us."

"Yet," McCandless said ominously. "But let me tell you what stirs in the wide world, General. There is a new French general named Bonaparte. His army sits on the Nile now, but there is nothing in Egypt that interests Bonaparte or the French. They have their eyes farther east. They have their eyes on India. Bonaparte wrote to the Tippoo earlier this year. Did the Tippoo show you his letter?" Appah Rao said nothing and McCandless took the silence to mean that Rao knew nothing of the French General's letter and so he took from his sporran a piece of paper. "Do you speak French, General?"

"No."

"Then let me translate for you. One of our agents copied the letter before it was sent and it reads, *'le sept pluviose, l'an six de la République Française.'* That's the twenty-seventh of January this year to the rest of us, and it says, 'I have reached the borders of the Red Sea with an innumerable and invincible army, full of the desire to deliver you from the yoke of England.' Here." McCandless offered Appah Rao the letter. "There's plenty more in the letter like that. Take it back with you and find someone who will translate it."

"I believe you," Appah Rao said, ignoring the proffered letter. "But why should I fear this French General?"

"Because Bonaparte's ally is the Tippoo and Bonaparte's ambition is to take away the Company's trade. His victory will strengthen the Muslims and weaken the Hindus. But if he sees Mysore defeated, and if he sees your Rajah back on his ancestor's throne, and if he sees a Hindu army led by General Appah Rao then he will think twice before he takes ship. Bonaparte needs allies in this land, and without Mysore he will have none."

Appah Rao frowned. "This Bonaparte, he is a Muslim?"

"He's friendly to Muslims, but he has no religion that we know of."

"If he's friendly to Muslims," Appah Rao observed, "why should he not be friendly to Hindus also?"

"Because it is to the Muslims that he looks for allies. He will reward them."

Appah Rao shifted on the hard floor. "Why should we not let this Bonaparte come and defeat you?"

"Because then he will have made the Tippoo all-powerful, and after that, General, how long will there be any Hindus in his service? And how long will the surviving Wodeyars live? The Tippoo keeps the Wodeyar family alive for he needs Hindu infantry and cavalry, but if he no longer has enemies, why will he need reluctant friends?"

"And you will restore the Wodeyars?"

"I promise it."

Appah Rao looked past McCandless, gazing up at the small light reflecting off the serene image of a Hindu goddess. The temple was still here, as were all Mysore's temples, for though the Tippoo was a Muslim he had not torn down the Hindu sanctuaries. Indeed, like his father, the Tippoo had restored some of the temples. Life was not hard under the Tippoo, but all the same the Tippoo was not the ancestral ruler of Appah Rao's country. That ruler was a boy kept in poverty in a small house in a back alley of Seringapatam, and Appah Rao's hidden loyalty was to the Wodeyar dynasty, not to the Muslim interlopers. The General's dark eyes shifted to McCandless. "You British captured the city seven years ago. Why didn't you replace the Tippoo then?"

"A mistake," McCandless admitted candidly. "We thought he could be trusted to keep his promises, but we were wrong. This time, if God wills it, we shall replace him. A man bitten by a snake once does not let the snake live a second time."

Appah Rao brooded for a while. Bats flickered in the courtyard. The two men in the gateway watched as McCandless let the silence stretch. The Colonel knew it would not serve to pressure this General too hard, but McCandless also knew he did not need to press. Appah Rao might not be certain that a British victory would be in Mysore's best interest, but what would serve that interest in these hard, confusing times? Appah Rao's choice lay between the Muslim usurpers and foreign domination, and McCandless knew only too well of the simmering distrust that lay between Hindus and Muslims. It was that breach that the Scotsman was assaulting in the hope that he could widen the rift into full betrayal.

Appah Rao finally shook his head, then raised an arm and beckoned. One of the two men in the gateway came running forward and knelt beside the General. He was a young man of startling good looks, black-haired and with a fine long face of strong bones and defiant eyes. Like Appah Rao he wore the tiger tunic and had a gold-hilted sword slung at his hip. "This is Kunwar Singh," Appah Rao introduced the young man. "He is the son of a cousin of mine"—he announced the relationship vaguely, intimating that it was not close—"and the commander of my bodyguard."

McCandless looked into Kunwar Singh's eyes. "Do your job well, my friend. Your master is valuable."

Kunwar Singh smiled and then, at a signal from Appah Rao, he took a roll of paper from inside his tunic. He unrolled the sheet and weighted its corners with a pistol, a knife, a handful of bullets, and the lantern.

McCandless leaned forward. The scroll was a map and it showed the big island in the River Cauvery on which the Tippoo's capital of Seringapatam was built. The fortress town occupied the island's western tip, while beyond its walls, to the east, were pleasure gardens, suburbs, the Tippoo's summer palace, and the mausoleum where the fearsome Hyder Ali was entombed.

Appah Rao drew a knife from his belt. He tapped the island's northern bank where it fronted the Cauvery's main channel. "That is where General Cornwallis crossed. But since then the walls have been strengthened. The French advised us how to do it. There are new guns on the walls, hundreds of them." He looked up into McCandless's eyes. "I mean hundreds, McCandless. That is not an exaggeration. The Tippoo is fond of cannon and rockets. He has thousands of rocketmen and deep arsenals crammed with weapons. All this"—he swept the knife's tip around the walls that faced the river—"has been rebuilt, refortified, and given cannon and rockets."

"We have cannon too," McCandless said.

Appah Rao ignored the comment. Instead he tapped the knife against the western ramparts that overlooked the Cauvery's smaller channel. "At this time of year, McCandless, the river here is shallow. The crocodiles have gone to the deeper pools and a man can walk across the river with dry knees. And when your army reaches Seringapatam they will see that these walls"—he tapped the western fortifications again—"have not been rebuilt. They are made of mud bricks and the rains have crumbled the rampart. It looks like a weak place and you will be tempted to attack there. Do not, for that is where the Tippoo wants you to attack." A beetle flew onto the map and crawled along the line marking the western

walls. Appah Rao gently swept the insect aside. "There is
another wall there, a new wall, hidden behind that rampart,
McCandless, and when your men get through the first wall
they will be in a trap. Here"—he pointed to a bastion that
connected the outer and inner walls—"that used to be a
water gate, but it's been blocked up and there are hundreds
of pounds of gunpowder inside. Once your men are trapped
between the two walls the Tippoo plans to blow the mine."
Appah Rao shrugged. "Hundreds of pounds of powder,
McCandless, just waiting for you. And when that attack has
failed you will have no time to make another before the monsoon comes, and when the rains do come the river will rise
and the roads will turn to mud and you will be forced to
retreat, and every foot of your way back to Madras will be
dogged by the Tippoo's cavalry. That is how he plans to beat
you."

"So we must attack anywhere but in the west?"

"Anywhere but from the west," Appah Rao said. "The new
inner wall"—he demonstrated on the map with the tip of his
knife—"extends all the way around the north. These other
walls"—he tapped the southern and eastern ramparts—"look
stronger, but don't be deceived. The west wall is a trap, and
if you fall into it, it will be your death." He moved the
weights off the corners of the map and let it roll itself up.
Then he unshielded McCandless's lantern and held one end
of the scroll in the candle flame. The paper blazed, lighting
the intricate carvings of the shrine. The three men watched
as the paper burned to ash. "Anywhere but from the west,"
Appah Rao said, then, after a moment's hesitation, he lifted
the bag of gold coins from beside the lantern. "All this will
go to my Rajah," he said. "I shall keep none."

"I never expected you to," McCandless said. "You have
my thanks, General."

"I don't want your thanks. I want my Rajah back. That is

why I came. And if you disappoint me, then you English will have a new enemy."

"I'm a Scot."

"But you would still be my enemy," Appah Rao said, then turned away, but paused and looked back from the inner shrine's threshold. "Tell your General that his men should be gentle with the people of the city."

"I will tell General Harris."

"Then I shall look to see you in Seringapatam," Appah Rao said heavily.

"Me and thousands of others," McCandless said.

"Thousands!" Appah Rao's tone mocked the claim. "You may have thousands, Colonel, but the Tippoo has tigers." He turned and walked to the temple's outer gateway, followed by Kunwar Singh.

McCandless burned the copy of Bonaparte's letter, waited another half-hour, and then, as silently as he had come to the temple, he left it. He would join his escort, sleep a few hours, then ride with his precious secret to the waiting army.

Few men of the 33rd slept that night for the excitement of fighting and beating the Tippoo's vaunted troops had filled them with a nervous energy. Some spent their loot on arrack, and those fell asleep soon enough, but the others stayed around their fires and relived the day's brief excitement. For most of the troops it had been their first battle, and on its slim evidence they built a picture of war and their own valor.

Mary Bickerstaff sat with Sharpe and listened patiently to the tales. She was accustomed to soldiers' stories and shrewd enough to know which men exaggerated their prowess and which pretended not to have been nauseated by the horrors of the dead and wounded. Sharpe, after he returned from Captain Morris's tent with the news that the Captain would ask Major Shee's permission for them to marry, was silent and Mary sensed he was not really listening to the tales, not even when he pretended to be amused or amazed. "What is it?" she asked him after a long while.

"Nothing, lass."

"Are you worried about Captain Morris?"

"If he says no, we just ask Major Shee," Sharpe said with a confidence he did not entirely feel. Morris was a bastard, but Shee was a drunk, and in truth there was little to choose between them. Sharpe had an idea that Lieutenant Colonel Arthur Wellesley, the 33rd's real commanding officer, was a man who might be reasonable, but Wellesley had been temporarily appointed as one of the army's two deputy commanders and had thus shrugged off all regimental business. "We'll get our permission," he told Mary.

"So what's worrying you?"

"I told you. Nothing."

"You're miles away, Richard."

He hesitated. "Wish I was."

Mary tightened the grip of her hand on his fingers, then lowered her voice to something scarce above a whisper. "Are you thinking of running, Richard Sharpe?"

He leaned away from the fire, trying to make a small private space where they could talk without being overheard. "Got to be a better life than this, love," he said.

"Don't do it!" Mary said fiercely, but laying a hand on his cheek as she spoke. Some of the men on the other side of the fire saw the tender gesture and greeted it with a chorus of jeers and whistles. Mary ignored them. "They'll catch you, Richard," she insisted, "catch you and shoot you."

"Not if we run far enough."

"We?" she asked cautiously.

"I'd want you, lass."

Mary took hold of one of his hands and squeezed it. "Listen," she hissed. "Work to become a sergeant! Once you're a sergeant, you're made. You could even become an officer! Don't laugh, Richard! Mister Lambert in Calcutta, he was a sergeant once, and he was a private before that. They made him up to ensign."

Sharpe smiled and traced a finger down her cheek. "You're mad, Mary. I love you, but you're mad. I couldn't be an officer! You have to know how to read!"

"I can teach you," Mary said.

Sharpe glanced at her with some surprise. He had never known she could read and the knowledge made him somewhat nervous of her. "I wouldn't want to be an officer anyway," he said scathingly. "Stuck-up bastards, all of them."

"But you can be a sergeant," Mary insisted, "and a good one. But don't run, love. Whatever you do, don't run."

"Is that the lovebirds?" Sergeant Hakeswill's mocking voice cut through their conversation. "Ah, it's sweet, isn't it? Good to see a couple in love. Restores a man's faith in human nature, it does."

Sharpe and Mary sat up and disentangled their fingers as the Sergeant stalked through the ring of men beside the fire. "I want you, Sharpie," Hakeswill said when he reached their side. "Got a message for you, I have." He touched his hat to Mary. "Not you, Ma'am," he said as she stood to accompany Sharpe. "This is men's business, Mrs. Bickerstaff. Soldiers' business. No business for *bibbis*. Come on, Sharpie! Ain't got all night! Look lively now!" He strode away, thumping the ground with the butt of his halberd as he threaded his way between the fires. "Got news for you, Sharpie," he called over his shoulder, "good news, lad, good news."

"I can marry?" Sharpe asked eagerly.

Hakeswill threw a sly glance over his shoulder as he led Sharpe toward the picketed lines of officers' horses. "Now why would a lad like you want to marry? Why throw all your spunk away on one *bibbi*, eh? And that one used goods, too?

Another man's leavings, that's all Mary Bickerstaff is. You should spread it about, boy. Enjoy yourself when you're still young." Hakeswill pushed his way between the horses to reach the dark space between the two picketed lines where he turned and faced Sharpe. "Good news, Sharpe. You can't marry. Permission is refused. You want to know why, boy?"

Sharpe felt his hopes crumbling. At that moment he hated Hakeswill more than ever, but his pride forced him not to show that hate, nor his disappointment. "Why?" he asked.

"I'll tell you why, Sharpie," Hakeswill said. "And stand still, boy! When a sergeant condescends to talk to you, you stand still! 'Tenshun! That's better, lad. Bit of respect, like what is proper to show to a sergeant." His face twitched as he grinned. "You want to know why, boy? Because I don't want you to marry her, Sharpie, that is why. I don't want little Mrs. Bickerstaff married to anyone. Not to you, not to me, not even to the King of England himself, God bless him." He was circling Sharpe as he talked. "And do you know why, boy?" He stopped in front of Sharpe and pushed his face up toward the younger man. "Because that Mrs. Bickerstaff is a *bibbi*, Sharpie, with possibilities. Possi*bibbi*bilities!" He giggled at his joke. "Got a future, she has." He grinned again, and the grin was suddenly twisted as his face shuddered with its distorting rictus. "You familiar with Naig? Nasty Naig? Answer me, boy!"

"I've heard of him," Sharpe said.

"Fat bugger, Sharpie, he is. Fat and rich. Rides a helephant, he does, and he's got a dozen green tents. One of the army's followers, Sharpie, and rich as a rich man can be. Richer than you'll ever be, Sharpie, and you know why? 'Cos Nasty Naig provides the officers with their women, that's why. And I'm not talking about those rancid slags the other heathens hires out to you nasty common soldiers, I'm talking about the desirable women, Sharpie. Desirable." He lingered on the word. "Nasty's got a whole herd of expensive whores, Sharpie, he does, all riding in those closed wagons with the colored curtains. Full of officers' meat, those wagons are, fat ones, skinny ones, dark ones, light ones, dirty ones, clean ones, tall ones, short ones, all sorts of ones, and all of 'em are prettier than you could ever dream of, but there ain't one of them as pretty as little Mrs. Bickerstaff, and there ain't one who looks as white as pretty little Mary does, and if there's one thing an English officer abroad wants once in a while, Sharpie, it's a spot of the white meat. That's the itch Morris has got, Sharpie, got it bad, but he ain't no different from the others. They get bored with the dark meat, Sharpie. And the Indian officers! Naig tells me they'll pay a month's wages for a white. You following me, Sharpie? You and me marching in step, are we?"

Sharpe said nothing. It had taken all his self-discipline not to hit the Sergeant, and Hakeswill knew it and mocked him for it. "Go on, Sharpie! Hit me!" Hakeswill taunted him, and when Sharpe did not move, the Sergeant laughed. "You ain't got the guts, have you?"

"I'll find a place and time," Sharpe said angrily.

"Place and time! Listen to him!" Hakeswill chuckled, then began pacing around Sharpe once again. "We've made a deal, Nasty and me. Like brothers, we are, me and him, just like brothers. We understand each other, see, and Nasty's right keen on your little Mary. Profit there, you see, boy. And I'll get a cut of it."

"Mary stays with me, Sarge," Sharpe said stubbornly, "married or not."

"Oh, Sharpie, dear me. You don't understand, do you? You didn't hear me, boy, did you? Nasty and me, we've made a bargain. Drunk to it, we did, and not in arrack, neither, but in proper gentlemen's brandy. I give him little Mrs. Bickerstaff and he gives me half the money she earns. He'll cheat me, of course he'll cheat me, but she'll make so much that it won't signify. She won't have a choice, Sharpie. She'll get snatched on the march and given to one of Nasty's men. One of the ugly buggers. She'll be raped wicked for a week, whipped every night, and at the end of it, Sharpie, she'll do whatever she's told. That's the way the business works, Sharpie, says so in the scriptures, and how are you going to stop it? Answer me that, boy. Are you going to pay me more than Nasty will?" Hakeswill stopped in front of Sharpe where he waited for an answer and, when none came, he shook his head derisively. "You're a boy playing in men's games, Sharpie, and you're going to lose unless you're a man. Are you man enough to fight me here? Put me down? Claim I was kicked by a horse in the night? You can try, Sharpie, but you're not man enough, are you?"

"Hit you, Sergeant," Sharpe said, "and be put on a flogging charge? I'm not daft."

Hakeswill made an elaborate charade of looking right and left. "Ain't no one here but you and me, Sharpie. Nice and private!"

Sharpe resisted the urge to lash out at his persecutor. "I'm not daft," he said again, stubbornly remaining at attention.

"But you are, boy. Daft as a bucket. Don't you understand? I'm offering you the soldier's way out! Forget the bloody officers, you daft boy. You and me, Sharpie, we're soldiers, and soldiers settle their arguments by fighting. Says so in the scriptures, don't it? So beat me now, lad, beat me here and now, beat me in a square fight and I warrant you can keep Mrs. Bickerstaff all to your little self." He paused, grinning up into Sharpe's face. "That's a promise, Sharpie. Fight me now, fair and honest, and our argument's over. But you're not man enough, are you? You're just a boy."

"I'm not falling for your tricks, Sergeant," Sharpe said.

"There ain't no trick, boy," Hakeswill said hoarsely. He

stepped two paces away from Sharpe, reversed his halberd, and thrust its steel point hard into the turf. "I can beat you, Sharpie, that's what I'm reckoning. I've been around a bit. Know how to fight. You might be taller than me, and you might be stronger, but you ain't as quick as me and you ain't half as dirty. I'm going to pound the bloody guts out of you, and when I've finished with you I'll take little Mary down to Nasty's tents and earn my money. But not if you beat me, boy. You beat me, and on a soldier's honor, I'll persuade Captain Morris to let you marry. You've got my word on it, boy. A soldier's honor." He waited for an answer. "You ain't a soldier," he said scornfully when Sharpe still kept quiet. "You ain't got the guts!" He stepped up to Sharpe and slapped him hard across the face. "Nothing but a lily, ain't you? Lieutenant Lawford's lily-boy. Maybe that's why you ain't got the guts to fight for your Mary!"

The last insult provoked Sharpe to hit Hakeswill. He did it hard and fast. He slammed a low blow into Hakeswill's belly that folded the Sergeant over, then cut his other hand hard up into the Sergeant's face to split open Hakeswill's nose and jerk his head back up. Sharpe brought up his knee, missed the Sergeant's crotch, but his left hand had hold of Hakeswill's clubbed hair now and he was just feeling with his right fingers for the squealing Sergeant's eyeballs when a voice was suddenly shouting close behind him.

"Guard!" the voice called. "Guard!"

"Jesus!" Sharpe let go of his enemy, turned, and saw Captain Morris standing just beyond the picketed horses. Ensign Hicks was with him.

Hakeswill had sunk onto the ground, but now hauled himself upright on the staff of his halberd. "Assaulted me, sir, he did!" The Sergeant could scarcely speak for the pain in his belly. "He went mad, sir! Just mad, sir!"

"Don't worry, Sergeant, Hicks and I both saw it," Morris said. "Came to check on the horses, ain't that right, Hicks?"

"Yes, sir," Hicks said. He was a small young man, very officious, who would never contradict a superior. If Morris claimed the clouds were made of cheese Hicks would just stand to attention, twitch his nose, and swear blind he could smell Cheddar. "Plain case of assault, sir," the Ensign said. "Unprovoked assault."

"Guard!" Morris shouted. "Here! Now!"

Blood was pouring down Hakeswill's face, but the Sergeant managed a grin. "Got you, Sharpie," he said softly, "got you. Flogging offence, that."

"You bastard," Sharpe said softly, and wondered if he should run. He wondered if he would stand any chance of making it safely away if he just sprinted into the dark, but Ensign Hicks had drawn his pistol and the sound of the hammer being cocked stilled Sharpe's tiny impulse to flee.

A panting Sergeant Green arrived with four men of the guard and Morris pushed the horses aside to let them through. "Arrest Private Sharpe, Sergeant," he told Green. "Close arrest. He struck Sergeant Hakeswill, and Hicks and I witnessed the assault. Ensign Hicks will do the paperwork."

"Gladly, sir," Hicks agreed. The Ensign was slurring his words, betraying that he had been drinking.

Morris looked at Sharpe. "It's a court martial offence, Sharpe," the Captain said, then he turned back to Green who had not moved to obey his orders. "Do it!"

"Sir!" Green said, stepping forward. "Come on, Sharpie."

"I didn't do nothing, Sergeant," Sharpe protested.

"Come on, lad. It'll sort itself out," Green said quietly, then he took Sharpe's elbow and led him away. Hicks went with them, happy to please Morris by writing up the charge.

Morris waited until the prisoner and his escort had gone,

then grinned at Hakeswill. "The boy was faster than you thought, Sergeant."

"He's a devil, that one, sir, a devil. Broke my nose, he did." Hakeswill gingerly tried to straighten the cartilage and the bleeding nose made a horrible crunching noise. "But his woman's ours."

"Tonight?" Morris could not keep the eagerness from his voice.

"Not tonight, sir," Hakeswill said in a tone that suggested the Captain had made a foolish suggestion. "There'll be enough trouble in the company with Sharpe arrested, sir, and if we go after his *bibbi* tonight there'll be a rare brawl. Half the bastards are full of arrack. No, sir. Wait till the bastard's flogged to death. Wait for that, sir, and then they'll all be meek as lambs. Meek as lambs. Flogging does that to men. Quietens them down something proper, a good whipping does. All be done in a couple of days, sir."

Morris flinched as Hakeswill tried to straighten his nose again. "You'd better see Mister Micklewhite, Hakeswill."

"No, sir. Don't believe in doctors, sir, except for the pox. I'll strap it up, sir, and soon be right as rain. Besides, watching Sharpie flogged will be treatment enough. I reckon we done him, sir. You won't have long to wait, sir, not long at all."

Morris found Hakeswill's intimate tone unseemly, and stepped stiffly back. "Then I'll wish you a good night, Sergeant."

"Thank you kindly, sir, and the same to you, sir. And sweet dreams too, sir." Hakeswill laughed. "Just as sweet as sweet can ever be, sir."

For Sharpie was done.

CHAPTER 3

Colonel McCandless woke as the dawn touched the world's rim with a streak of fire. The crimson light glowed bright on the lower edge of a long cloud that lay on the eastern horizon like the smoke rill left by a musket volley. It was the only cloud in the sky. He rolled his plaid and tied it onto his saddle's cantle, then rinsed his mouth with water. His horse, picketed close by, had been saddled all night in case some enemy discovered McCandless and his escort. That escort, six picked men of the 4th Native Cavalry, had needed no orders to be about the day. They grinned a greeting at McCandless, stowed their meager bedding, then made a breakfast out of warm canteen water and a dry cake of ground lentils and rice. McCandless shared the cavalrymen's meal. He liked a cup of tea in the mornings, but he dared not light a fire for the smoke might attract the pestilential patrols of the Tippoo's Light Cavalry. "It will be a hot day, sahib," the Havildar remarked to McCandless.

"They're all hot," McCandless answered. "Haven't had a cold day since I came here." He thought for a second, then worked out that it must be Thursday the twenty-eighth of March. It would be cold in Scotland today and, for an indulgent moment, he thought of Lochaber and imagined the snow lying deep in Glen Scaddle and the ice edging the loch's foreshore, and though he could see the image clearly enough, he could not really imagine what the cold would feel

like. He had been away from home too long and now he
wondered if he could ever live in Scotland again. He certainly would not live in England, not in Hampshire where his
sister lived with her petulant English husband. Harriet kept
pressing him to retire to Hampshire, saying that they had no
relatives left in Scotland and that her husband had a wee
cottage that would suit McCandless's declining years to per-
fection, but the Colonel had no taste for a soft, plump,
English landscape, nor, indeed, for his soft, plump sister's
company. Harriet's son, McCandless's nephew William Lawford, was a decent enough young fellow even if he had forgotten his Scottish ancestry, but young William was now in
the army, here in Mysore indeed, which meant that the only
relative McCandless liked was close at hand and that circum-
stance merely strengthened McCandless's distaste for retir-
ing to Hampshire. But to Scotland? He often dreamed of
going back, though whenever the opportunity arose for him
to take the Company's pension and sail to his native land, he
always found some unfinished business that kept him in
India. Next year, he promised himself, the year of our Lord
1800, would be a good year to go home, though in truth he
had promised himself the same thing every year for the last
decade.

The seven men unpicketed the horses and hauled themselves into their worn saddles. The Indian escort was armed
with lances, sabres, and pistols, while McCandless carried a
claymore, a horse pistol, and a carbine that was holstered on
his saddle. He glanced once toward the rising sun to check
his direction, then led his men northward. He said nothing,
but he needed to give these men no orders. They knew well
enough to keep a keen lookout in this dangerous land.

For this was the kingdom of Mysore, high on the southern
Indian plateau, and as far as the horsemen could see the land
was under the rule of the Tippoo Sultan. Indeed this was the

Tippoo's heartland, a fertile plain rich with villages, fields, and water cisterns; only now, as the British army advanced and the Tippoo's retreated, the country was being blighted. McCandless could see six pillars of smoke showing where the Tippoo's cavalry had burned granaries to make sure that the hated British could not find food. The cisterns would all have been poisoned, the livestock driven westward, and every storehouse emptied, thus forcing the armies of Britain and Hyderabad to carry all their own supplies on the cumbersome bullock carts. McCandless guessed that yesterday's brief and unequal battle had been an attempt by the Tippoo to draw the escorting troops away from the precious baggage onto his infantry, after which he would have released his fearsome horsemen onto the wagons of grain and rice and salt, but the British had not taken the bait which meant that General Harris's ponderous advance would continue. Say another week until they arrived at Seringapatam? Then they would face two months of short rations and searing weather before the monsoon broke, but McCandless reckoned that two months was plenty enough time to do the job, especially as the British would soon know how to avoid the Tippoo's trap at the western walls.

He threaded his horse through a grove of cork trees, glad of the shade cast by the deep-green leaves. He paused at the grove's edge to watch the land ahead, which dropped gently into a valley where a score of people were working in rice paddies. The valley, McCandless supposed, lay far enough from the line of the British advance to have been spared the destruction of its stores and water supply. A small village lay to the west of the rice paddies, and McCandless could see another dozen people working in the small gardens around the houses, and he knew that he and his men would be spotted as soon as they left the cover of the cork grove, but he doubted that any of the villagers would investigate seven

strange horsemen. The folk of Mysore, like villagers throughout all the Indian states, avoided mysterious soldiers in the
hope that the soldiers would avoid them. At the far side of
the rice paddies were plantations of mango and date palms,
and beyond them a bare hill crest. McCandless watched that
empty crest for a few minutes and then, satisfied that no
enemy was nearby, he spurred his mare forward.

The people working the rice immediately fled toward their
homes and McCandless swerved eastward to show them he
meant no harm, then kicked the mare into a trot. He rode
beside a grove of carefully tended mulberry trees, part of the
Tippoo's scheme to make silk-weaving into a major industry
of Mysore, then he spurred into a canter as he approached
the bed of the valley. His escort's curb and scabbard chains
jingled behind him as the horses pounded down the slope,
splashed through the shrunken stream that trickled from the
paddies, then began the gentle climb to the date palm grove.

It was then that McCandless saw the flash of light in the
mango trees.

He instinctively dragged his horse around to face the rising sun and pricked back his spurs. He looked behind as he
rode, hoping that the flash of light was nothing but some
errant reflection, but then he saw horsemen spurring from
the trees. They carried lances and all of them were dressed
in the tiger-striped tunic. There were a dozen men at least,
but the Scotsman had no time to count them properly for he
was plunging his spurs back to race his mare diagonally up
the slope toward the crest.

One of the pursuing horsemen fired a shot that echoed
through the valley. The bullet went wide. McCandless
doubted it had been supposed to hit anything, but was rather
intended as a signal to alert other horsemen who must be in
the area. For a second or two the Scotsman debated turning
and charging directly at his pursuers, but he rejected the

idea. The odds were marginally too great and his news far
too important to be gambled on a skirmish. Flight was his
only option. He pulled the carbine from its saddle holster,
cocked it, then clapped his heels hard onto the mare's flank.
Once over the crest he reckoned there was a good chance he
could outrun his pursuers.

Goats scattered from his path as he spurred the mare over
the ridge's skyline. One glance behind satisfied McCandless
that he had gained a long enough lead to let him turn north
without being headed off, and so he twitched the rein and
let the mare run. A long stretch of open, tree-dotted country
lay ahead and beyond were thick stands of timber in which
he and his escort could lose themselves. "Run, girl!" he
called to the mare, then looked behind to make certain his
escort was closed up and safe. Sweat dripped down his face,
his scabbarded claymore thumped up and down on his hip,
but the strong mare was running like the wind now, her
speed blowing the kilt back up around his hips. This was not
the first time McCandless had raced away from enemies. He
had once run for a whole day, dawn to twilight, to escape a
Mahratta band and the mare had never once lost her footing.
In all India, and that meant all the world, McCandless had
no friend better than this mare. "Run, girl!" he called to her
again, then looked behind once more and it was then that
the Havildar shouted a warning. McCandless turned to see
more horsemen coming from the trees to the north.

There must have been fifty or sixty horsemen racing
toward the Scotsman and, even as he swerved the mare eastward, he realized that his original dozen pursuers must have
been the scouts for this larger party of cavalry and that by
running north he had been galloping toward the enemy
rather than away from them. Now he rode toward the rising
sun again, but there was no cover to the east and these new
pursuers were already dangerously close. He angled back to

the south, hoping he might find some shelter in the valley beyond the crest, but then a wild volley of shots sounded from his pursuers.

One bullet struck the mare. It was a fortunate shot, fired at the gallop, and ninety-nine times out of a hundred such a shot would have flown yards wide, but this ball struck the mare's haunch and McCandless felt her falter. He slapped her rump with the stock of his carbine and she tried to respond, but the bullet had driven close to the mare's spine and the pain was growing and she stumbled, neighed, yet still she tried to run again. Then one of her back legs simply stopped working and the horse slewed around in a cloud of dust. McCandless kicked his feet out of the stirrups as his escort galloped past. The Havildar was already hauling on his reins, wheeling his horse to rescue McCandless, but the Scotsman knew it was too late. He sprawled on the ground, hurled free of the falling mare, and shouted at the Havildar. "Go, man!" he called. "Go!" But the escort had sworn to protect the Colonel and, instead of fleeing, the Havildar led his men toward the rapidly approaching enemy.

"You fools!" McCandless shouted after them. Brave fools, but fools. He was bruised, but otherwise unhurt, though his mare was dying. She was whinnying and somehow she had managed to raise the front part of her body on her forelegs and seemed puzzled that her back legs would not work. She whinnied again, and McCandless knew she would never again run like the wind and so he did the friend's duty. He went to her head, pulled it down by the reins, kissed her nose, and then put a bullet into her skull just above her eyes. She reared back, white-eyed and with blood spraying, then she slumped down. Her forelegs kicked a few times and after that she was still. The flies came to settle on her wounds.

The Havildar's small group rode full tilt into the enemy's pursuit. That enemy had been scattered by their gallop and the Havildar's men were closed up and so the first few seconds were an easy victory. Two lances found Mysore bellies, two sabres drew more blood, but then the main body of the enemy crashed into the fight. The Havildar himself had ridden clean through the leading ranks, leaving his lance behind, and he now looked back to see his men fighting desperately among a milling group of enemy horsemen. He drew his sabre and turned back to help when he heard McCandless shouting. "Go, man, go! Go!" McCandless yelled, pointing north. The Havildar could not take back the vital news McCandless had gained from Appah Rao, but it was still important to let the army know that the Colonel had been captured. McCandless was not a vain man, but he knew his own value, and he had left some careful instructions that might retrieve some of the damage of his capture. Those instructions offered a chance for the army to rescue McCandless, and that dangerous expedient was now the Scotsman's only hope of passing on Appah Rao's message. "Go!" McCandless roared as loudly as he could.

The Havildar was caught between his duty to his men and his duty to obey McCandless's orders. He hesitated, and two of the pursuers swerved aside to pounce on him. That made up his mind. He clapped his spurs back, charged the pursuers, touched the rein at the last moment and swung his sabre as he went past the two men. The blade sliced across the nape of the nearer man's neck and then the Havildar curved away northwards, galloping free while the rest of the enemy gathered about the survivors for the kill.

McCandless threw down his pistol and carbine, drew his heavy claymore, and walked toward the mêlée. He never reached it, for an enemy officer detached himself from the clash of sabres and turned his horse to meet the Scotsman. The Mysorean officer sheathed his sabre, then mutely held out his right hand for McCandless's blade. Behind him the sabres and lances worked briefly, then the small fight was over and McCandless knew that his escort, all but the Havildar, was dead. He looked at the horseman above him. "This sword," he said bitterly, "belonged to my father and to his father." He spoke in English. "This sword," McCandless said, "was carried for Charles Stuart at Culloden."

The officer said nothing, just held his hand out, his eyes steady on McCandless. The Scotsman slowly reversed his blade, then held the hilt upwards. The Mysorean officer took it and seemed surprised by the claymore's weight. "What were you doing here?" the officer asked in Kanarese.

"Do you speak English?" McCandless asked in that tongue, determined to hide his knowledge of India's languages.

The officer shrugged. He looked at the old claymore then slid it into his sash. His men, their horses white with sweat, gathered excitedly to stare at the captured heathen. They saw an old man and some wondered if they had captured the enemy's General, but the captive seemed to speak no language any of them knew and so his identity would have to wait. He was given one of his dead escort's horses and then, as the sun climbed toward its daily furnace heat, McCandless was taken west toward the Tippoo's stronghold.

While behind him the vultures circled and at last, sure that nothing lived where the dust and flies had settled on the newly-made corpses, flew down for their feast.

It took two days to convene the court martial. The army could not spare the time in its march for the business to be done immediately and so Captain Morris had to wait until the great ponderous horde was given a half-day's rest to allow the straggling herds to catch up with the main armies. Only then was there time to assemble the officers and have Private Sharpe brought into Major Shee's tent which had one of its sides brailed up to make more space. Captain Morris laid the charge and Sergeant Hakeswill and Ensign Hicks gave evidence.

Major John Shee was irritable. The Major was irritable at the best of times, but the need to stay at least apparently sober had only shortened his already short Irish temper. He did not, in truth, enjoy commanding the 33rd. Major Shee suspected, when he was sober enough to suspect anything, that he did the job badly and that suspicion had given rise to a haunting fear of mutiny, and mutiny, to Major Shee's befuddled mind, was signaled by any sign of disrespect for established authority. Private Sharpe was plainly a man who brimmed over with such disrespect and the offence with which he was charged was plain and the remedy just as obvious, but the court proceedings were delayed because Lieutenant Lawford, who should have spoken for Sharpe, was not present. "Then where the devil is he?" Shee demanded.

Captain Fillmore, commander of the fourth company, spoke for Lawford. "He was summoned to General Harris's tent, sir."

Shee frowned at Fillmore. "He knew he was supposed to be here?"

"Indeed, sir. But the General insisted."

"And we're just supposed to twiddle our thumbs while he takes tea with the General?" Shee demanded.

Captain Fillmore glanced through the tent's open side as if he hoped to see Lawford hurrying toward the court martial, but there were only sentries to be seen. "Lieutenant Lawford did ask me to assure the court, sir, that Private Sharpe is a most reliable man," Fillmore said, fearing that he was not doing a very good job of defending the unfortunate prisoner. "The Lieutenant would have spoken most forcibly for the prisoner's character, sir, and begged the court to grant him the benefit of any doubt."

"Doubt?" Shee snapped. "What doubt is there? He struck a sergeant, he was seen doing it by two officers, and you think there's doubt? It's an open-and-shut case! That's what it is, open and shut!"

Fillmore shrugged. "Ensign Fitzgerald would also like to say something."

Shee glared at Fitzgerald. "Not much to say, Ensign, I trust?"

"Whatever it might take, sir, to prevent a miscarriage of justice." Fitzgerald, young and confident, stood and smiled at his commanding officer and fellow Irishman. "I doubt we've a better soldier in the regiment, sir, and I suspect Private Sharpe was given provocation."

"Captain Morris says not," Shee insisted, "and so does Ensign Hicks."

"I cannot contradict the Captain, sir," Fitzgerald said blandly, "but I was drinking with Timothy Hicks earlier that evening, sir, and if his eyes weren't crossed by midnight then he must possess a belly like a Flanders cauldron."

Shee looked dangerously belligerent. "Are you accusing a fellow officer of being under the influence of liquor?"

Fitzgerald reckoned that most of the 33rd's mess was ever under the influence of arrack, rum, or brandy, but he also knew better than to say as much. "I'm just agreeing with Captain Fillmore, sir, that we should give Private Sharpe the benefit of the doubt."

"Doubt?" Shee spat. "There is no doubt! Open and shut!" He gestured at Sharpe who stood hatless in front of his escort. Flies crawled on Sharpe's face, but he was not allowed to brush them away. Shee seemed to shudder at the thought of Sharpe's villainy. "He struck a sergeant in full view of two officers, and you think there's doubt about what happened?"

"I do, sir," Fitzgerald declared forcibly. "Indeed I do."

Sergeant Hakeswill's face twitched. He watched Fitzgerald with loathing. Major Shee stared at Fitzgerald for a few seconds, then shook his head as though questioning the Ensign's sanity.

Captain Fillmore tried one last time. Fillmore doubted the evidence of Morris and Hicks, and he had never trusted Hakeswill, but he knew Shee could never be persuaded to take the word of a private against that of two officers and a sergeant. "Might I beg the court," Fillmore said respectfully, "to suspend judgment until Lieutenant Lawford can speak for the prisoner?"

"What can Lawford say, in the name of God?" Shee demanded. There was a flask of arrack waiting in his baggage and he wanted to get these proceedings over and done. He had a brief, muttered conversation with his two fellow judges, both of them field officers from other regiments, then glared at the prisoner. "You're a damned villain, Sharpe, and the army has no need of villains. If you can't respect authority, then don't expect authority to respect you. Two thousand lashes." He ignored the shudder of astonishment and horror that some of the onlookers gave and looked instead at the Sergeant Major. "How soon can it be done?"

"This afternoon's as good a time as any, sir," Bywaters answered stolidly. He had expected a flogging verdict, though not as severe as this, and he had already made the necessary arrangements.

Shee nodded. "Parade the battalion in two hours. These proceedings are over." He gave Sharpe one foul glance, then pushed his chair back. He would need some arrack, Shee thought, if he was to sit his horse in the sun through two thousand lashes. Maybe he should have only given one thousand, for a thousand lashes were as liable to kill as two, but it was too late now, the verdict was given, and Shee's only hope of respite from the dreadful heat was his hope that the prisoner would die long before the awful punishment was finished.

Sharpe was kept under guard. His sentinels were not men from his own battalion, but six men from the King's 12th who did not know him and who could therefore be trusted not to connive in his escape. They kept him in a makeshift pen behind Shee's tent and no one spoke to Sharpe there until Sergeant Green arrived. "I'm sorry about this, Sharpie," Green said, stepping over the ammunition boxes that formed the crude walls of the pen.

Sharpe was sitting with his back against the boxes. He shrugged. "I've been whipped before, Sergeant."

"Not in the army, lad, not in the army. Here." Green held out a canteen. "It's rum."

Sharpe uncorked the canteen and drank a good slug of the liquor. "I didn't do nothing anyway," he said sullenly.

"Maybe, maybe not," Green said, "but the more you drink the less you'll feel. Finish it, lad."

"Tomkins says you don't feel a damn thing after the first thirty," Sharpe said.

"I hope he's right, lad, I hope he's right, but you drink that rum anyway." Green took off his shako and wiped the sweat from his bald head with a scrap of rag.

Sharpe tipped the canteen again. "And where was Mister Lawford?" he asked bitterly.

"You heard, son. He was called off to see the General." Green hesitated. "But what could he have said anyway?" he added.

Sharpe leaned his head against the box-built wall. "He could have said that Morris is a lying bastard and that Hicks will say anything to please him."

"No, he couldn't say that, lad, and you know it." Green filled a clay pipe with tobacco and lit it with his tinderbox. He sat on the ground opposite Sharpe and saw the fear in the younger man's eyes. Sharpe was doing his best to hide it, but it was plainly there and so it should be, for only a fool did not fear two thousand lashes and only a lucky man came away alive. No man had ever actually walked away from such a punishment, but a handful had recovered after a month in the sick tent. "Your Mary's all right," Green told Sharpe.

Sharpe gave a sullen grimace. "You know what Hakeswill told me? That he was going to sell her as a whore."

Green frowned. "He won't, lad. He won't."

"And how will you stop him?" Sharpe asked bitterly.

"She's being looked after now," Green reassured him. "The lads are making sure of that, and the women are all protecting her."

"But for how long?" Sharpe asked. He drank more of the rum which seemed to be having no effect that he could sense. He momentarily closed his eyes. He knew he had been given an effective death sentence, but there was always hope. Some men had survived. Their ribs might have been bared to the sun and their skin and flesh be hanging from their backs in bloody ribbons, yet they had lived, but how was he to look after Mary when he was bandaged in a bed? If he was even lucky enough to reach a sick bed instead of a grave. He felt tears pricking at his eyes, not for the punishment he faced, but for Mary. "How long can they protect her?" he asked gruffly, cursing himself for being so near to weeping.

"I tell you she'll be all right," Green insisted.

"You don't know Hakeswill," Sharpe said.

"Oh, but I do, lad, I do," Green said feelingly, then paused. For a second or two he looked embarrassed, then glanced up at Sharpe. "The bastard can't touch her if she's married. Married proper, I mean, with the Colonel's blessing."

"That's what I thought."

Green drew on the pipe. "If the worst does happen, Sharpie . . ." he said, then stopped in embarrassment again.

"Aye?" Sharpe prompted him.

"Not that it will, of course," Green said hurriedly. "Billy Nixon survived a couple of thousand tickles, but you probably don't remember him, do you? Little fellow, with a wall eye. He survived all right. He was never quite the same afterward, of course, but you're a tough lad, Sharpie. Tougher than Billy."

"But if the worst does happen?" Sharpe reminded the Sergeant.

"Well," Green said, coloring, but then at last he summoned the courage to say what he had come to say. "I mean if it don't offend you, lad, and only if the worst does happen, which of course it won't, and I pray it won't, but if it does then I thought I might ask for Mrs. Bickerstaff's hand myself, if you follow my meaning."

Sharpe almost laughed, but then the thought of two thousand lashes choked off even the beginnings of a smile. Two thousand! He had seen men with backs looking like offal after just a hundred lashes and how the hell was he to survive with another nineteen hundred strokes on top of that? Such survival really depended on the battalion surgeon. If Mister Micklewhite thought Sharpe was dying after five or six hundred lashes he might stop the punishment to give his back time to heal before the rest of the lashes were given, but Micklewhite was not known for stopping whippings. The rumor in the battalion was that so long as the man did not scream like a baby and thus disturb the more squeamish of the officers, the surgeon would keep the blows coming, even if they were falling onto a dead man's spine. That was the rumor, and Sharpe could only hope it was not true.

"Did you hear me, Sharpie?" Sergeant Green interrupted Sharpe's gloomy thoughts.

"I heard you, Sergeant," Sharpe said.

"So would you mind? If I asked her?"

"Have you asked her already?" Sharpe said accusingly.

"No!" Green said hastily. "Wouldn't be right! Not while you're still, well, you know."

"Alive," Sharpe said bitterly.

"It's only if the worst happens." Green tried to sound optimistic. "Which it won't."

"You won't need my permission when I'm dead, Sergeant."

"No, but if I can tell Mary you wanted her to accept me, then it'll help. Don't you see that? I'll be a good man to her, Sharpie. I was married before, I was, only she died on me, but she never complained about me. No more than any woman ever complains, anyhow."

"Hakeswill might stop you marrying her."

Green nodded. "Aye, he might, but I can't see how. Not if we tie the knot quick. I'll ask Major Shee, and he's always fair with me. Ask him tonight, see? But only if the worst happens."

"But you need a chaplain," Sharpe warned the Sergeant. The 33rd's own chaplain had committed suicide on the voyage to Madras and no marriage in the army was considered official unless it had the regimental commander's permission and the blessing of a chaplain.

"The lads in the Old Dozen tell me they've got a Godwalloper," Green said, gesturing at the soldiers guarding Sharpe, "and he can do the splicing tomorrow. I'll probably have to slip the bugger a shilling, but Mary's worth a bob."

Sharpe shrugged. "Ask her, Sergeant," he said, "ask her." What else could he say? And if Mary was properly married to Sergeant Green then she would be protected by the army's regulations. "But see what happens to me first," Sharpe added.

"Of course I will, Sharpie. Hope for the best, eh? Never say die."

Sharpe drained the canteen. "There's a couple of things in my pack, Sergeant. A good pistol I took off an Indian officer the other day and a few coins. You'll give them to Mary?"

"Of course I will," Green said, carefully hiding the fact that Hakeswill had already plundered Sharpe's pack. "She'll be all right, Sharpie. Promise you, lad."

"And some dark night, Sergeant, give bloody Hakeswill a kicking for me."

Green nodded. "Be a pleasure, Sharpie. Be a pleasure." He knocked the ashes of his pipe against the ammunition boxes, then stood. "I'll bring you some more rum, lad. The more the better."

The preparations for Sharpe's flogging had all been made. Not that they were many, but it took a few moments to make sure everything was to the Sergeant Major's satisfaction. A tripod had been constructed out of three sergeant's halberds, their spearpoints uppermost and lashed together so that the whole thing stood two feet higher than a tall man. The three halberd butts were sunk into the dry soil, then a fourth halberd was firmly lashed crosswise on one face of the tripod at the height of a man's armpits.

Sergeant Hakeswill personally selected two of the 33rd's drummer boys. The drummer boys always administered the floggings, a small element of mercy in a bestial punishment, but Hakeswill made certain that the two biggest and strongest boys were given the task and then he collected the two whips from the Sergeant Major and made the boys practice on a tree trunk. "Put your body into it, lads," he told them, "and keep the arm moving fast after the whip's landed. Like this." He took one of the whips and slashed it across the bark, then showed them how to keep the lash sliding across the target by following the stroke through. "I did it often enough when I was a drummer," he told them, "and I always did a good job. Best flogger in the battalion, I was. Second to none." Once he was sure their technique was sufficient for the task he warned them not to tire too quickly, and then, with a pocketknife, he nicked the edges of the leather lashes so that their abrasions would tear at the exposed flesh as they were dragged across Sharpe's back. "Do it well, lads," he promised them, "and there's one of these for each of you." He showed them one of the Tippoo's gold coins which had been part of the battle's loot. "I don't want this bastard walking again," he told them. "Nor do you neither, for if Sharpie ever finds his feet he'll give you two a rare kicking, so make sure you finish the bastard off proper. Whip him bloody then put him underground, like it says in the scriptures."

Hakeswill coiled the two whips and hung them on the halberd that was mounted crosswise on the tripod, then went to find the surgeon. Mister Micklewhite was in his tent where he was trying to tie his white silk stock in preparation for the punishment parade. He grunted when he saw Hakeswill. "You don't need more mercury, do you?" he snarled.

"No, sir. Cured, sir. Thanks to your worship's skill, sir. Clean as a whistle I am, sir."

Micklewhite swore as the knot in the damned stock loosened. He did not like Hakeswill, but like everyone else in the regiment he feared him. There was a wildness in the back of Hakeswill's childlike eyes that spoke of terrible mischief, and, though the Sergeant was always punctilious in his dealings with officers, Micklewhite still felt obscurely threatened. "So what do you want, Sergeant?"

"Major Shee asked me to say a word, sir."

"Couldn't speak to me himself?"

"You know the Major, sir. No doubt he's thirsty. A hot day." Hakeswill's face quivered in a series of tremors. "It's about the prisoner, sir."

"What about him?"

"Troublemaker, sir. Known for it. A thief, a liar, and a cheat."

"So he's a redcoat. So?"

"So Major Shee ain't keen to see him back among the living, sir, if you follow my meaning. Is this what I owe you for the mercury, sir?" Hakeswill held up a gold coin, a *haideri*, which was worth around two shillings and sixpence. The coin was certainly not payment for the cure of his pox, for that cost had already been deducted from the Sergeant's pay, so Micklewhite knew it was a bribe. Not a great bribe, but half a crown could still go a long way. Micklewhite glanced at it, then nodded. "Put it on the table, Sergeant."

"Thank you, sir."

Micklewhite tugged the silk stock tight, then waved Hakeswill off. He pulled on his coat and pocketed the gold coin. The bribe had not been necessary, for Micklewhite's opposition to the coddling of flogging victims was well enough known in the battalion. Micklewhite hated caring for men who had been flogged, for in his experience they almost always died, and if he did stop a punishment then the recovering victim only cluttered up his sick cots. And if, by some miracle, the man was restored to health, it was only so he could be strapped to the triangle to be given the rest of his punishment and that second dose almost always proved fatal and so, all things considered, it was more prudent to let a man die at the first flogging. It saved money on medicine and, in Micklewhite's view, it was kinder too. Micklewhite buttoned his coat and wondered just why Sergeant Hakeswill wanted this particular man dead. Not that Micklewhite really cared, he just wanted the bloody business over and done.

The 33rd paraded under the afternoon's burning sun. Four companies faced the tripod, while three were arraigned at either side so that the battalion's ten companies formed a hollow oblong with the tripod standing in the one empty long side. The officers sat on their horses in front of their companies while Major Shee, his aides, and the adjutant stood their horses just behind the tripod. Mister Micklewhite, his head protected from the sun by a wide straw hat, stood to one side of the triangle. Major Shee, fortified by arrack and satisfied that everything was in proper order, nodded to Bywaters. "You will begin punishment, Sergeant Major."

"Sir!" Bywaters acknowledged, then turned and bellowed for the prisoner to be fetched. The two drummer boys stood nervously with their whips in hand. They alone of the parading soldiers were in shirtsleeves, while everyone else was in full wool uniform. Women and children peered between the company intervals. Mary Bickerstaff was not there. Hakeswill had looked for her, wanting to enjoy her horror, but Mary had stayed away. The women who had come for the spectacle, like their men, were silent and sullen. Sharpe was a popular man, and Hakeswill knew that everyone here was hating him for engineering this flogging, but Obadiah Hakeswill had never been concerned by such enmity. Power did not lie in being liked, but in being feared.

Sharpe was brought to the triangle. He was bareheaded and already stripped to the waist. The skin of his chest and back were as white as his powdered hair and contrasted oddly with his darkly tanned face. He walked steadily, for though he had the best part of a pint of rum in his belly, the liquor had not seemed to have the slightest effect. He did not look at either Hakeswill or Morris as he walked to the tripod.

"Arms up, lad," the Sergeant Major said quietly. "Stand against the triangle. Feet apart. There's a good lad."

Sharpe obediently stepped up to the triangular face of the tripod. Two corporals knelt at his feet and lashed his ankles to the halberds, then stood and pushed his arms over the crosswise halberd. They pulled his hands down and tied them to the uprights, thus forcing his naked back up and outward. That way he could not sag between the triangle and so hope to exhaust some of the blows on the halberd staffs. The corporals finished their knots, then stepped back.

The Sergeant Major went to the back of the triangle and brought from his pouch a folded piece of leather that was deeply marked by tooth prints. "Open your mouth, lad," he said softly. He smelled the rum on the prisoner's breath and hoped it would help him survive, then he pushed the leather between Sharpe's teeth. The gag served a double purpose. It would stifle any cries the victim might make and would stop him biting off his tongue. "Be brave, boy," Bywaters said quietly. "Don't let the regiment down."

Sharpe nodded.

Bywaters stepped smartly back and came to attention. "Prisoner ready for punishment, sir!" he called to Major Shee.

The Major looked to the surgeon. "Is the prisoner fit for punishment, Mister Micklewhite?"

Micklewhite did not even give Sharpe a glance. "Hale and fit, sir."

"Then carry on, Sergeant Major."

"Right, boys," the Sergeant Major said, "do your duty! Lay it on hard now, and keep the strokes high. Above his trousers. Drummer! Begin."

A third drummer boy was standing behind the floggers. He lifted his sticks, paused, then brought the first stick down.

The boy to the right brought his whip hard down on Sharpe's back.

"One!" Bywaters shouted.

The whip had left a red mark across Sharpe's shoulder blades. Sharpe had flinched, but the rope fetters restricted his movement and only those close to the triangle saw the tremor run through his muscles. He stared up at Major Shee who took good care to avoid the baleful gaze.

"Two!" Bywaters called and the drummer brought down his stick as the second boy planted a red mark crosswise on the first.

Hakeswill's face twitched uncontrollably, but he was smiling under the rictus. For the drumbeat of death had begun.

Colonel McCandless stood alone in the center of the courtyard of the Tippoo's Inner Palace inside Seringapatam. The Scotsman was still in his full uniform: red-coated, tartan-kilted, and with his feather-plumed hat cocked on his head. Six tigers were chained to the courtyard's walls and those tigers sometimes strained to reach him, but they were always checked by the heavy chains that quivered tautly whenever one of the muscled beasts sprang toward the Scotsman. McCandless did not move and the tigers, after one or two fruitless lunges, contented themselves with snarling at him. The tigers' keepers, big men armed with long staves, watched from the courtyard entrance. It was those men who might receive the orders to unleash the tigers and McCandless was determined to show them a calm face.

The courtyard was covered with sand, its lower walls were of dressed stone, but above the stone the palace's second story was a riot of stuccoed teak that had been painted red, white, green, and yellow. That decorated second story was composed of Moorish arches and McCandless knew just enough Arabic to guess that the writing incised above each arch was a *surah* from the Koran. There were two entrances to the courtyard. The one behind McCandless, through which he had entered and where the tiger's keepers now stood, was a plain double gateway that led to a tangle of stables and storehouses behind the palace, while in front of him, and evidently leading into the palace's staterooms, was a brief marble staircase rising to a wide door of black wood that had been decorated with patterns of inlaid ivory. Above that lavish door was a balcony that jutted out from three of the stuccoed arches. A screen of intricately carved wood hid the balcony, but McCandless could see that there were men behind the screen. He suspected the Tippoo was there and, the Scotsman trusted, so was the Frenchman who had first questioned him. Colonel Gudin had struck him as an honest fellow and right now, McCandless hoped, Gudin was pleading to let him live, though McCandless had taken good care not to offer the Frenchman his real name. He feared that the Tippoo would recognize it, and realize just what a prize his cavalry had taken, and so the Scotsman had given his name as Ross instead.

McCandless was right. Colonel Gudin and the Tippoo were both staring down through the screen. "This Colonel Ross," the Tippoo asked, "he says he was looking for forage?"

"Yes, sir," Gudin replied through the interpreter.

"You believe him?" It was plain from his tone that the Tippoo was skeptical.

Gudin shrugged. "Their horses are thin."

The Tippoo grunted. He had done his best to deny the advancing enemy any food, but the British had taken to making sudden marches north or south of their approach to enter territory where his horsemen had not yet destroyed the villagers' supplies. Not only that, but they had brought a vast amount of food with them. Yet even so the Tippoo's spies reported that the enemy was going hungry. Their horses and oxen were especially ill fed, so it was not unlikely that this British officer had been searching for forage. But why would a full colonel be sent on such an errand? The Tippoo could find no answer to that, and the question fed his suspicions. "Could he have been spying?"

"Scouting, maybe," Gudin said, "but not spying. Spies do not ride in uniform, Your Majesty."

The Tippoo grunted when the answer was translated into Persian. He was a naturally suspicious man, as any ruler should be, but he consoled himself with the observation that whatever this Britisher had been doing, he must have failed. The Tippoo turned to his entourage and saw the tall, dark-faced Appah Rao. "You think this Colonel Ross was looking for food, General?"

Appah Rao knew exactly who Colonel Ross truly was, and what McCandless had been looking for, and worse, Rao now knew that his own treachery was in dire danger of being discovered which meant that this was no time to look weak in front of the Tippoo. But nor was Appah Rao ready to betray McCandless. That was partly because of an old friendship, and partly because Appah Rao half suspected he might have a better future if he was allied to the British. "We know they're short of food," he said, "and that man looks thin enough."

"So you don't consider him a spy?"

"Spy or not," Appah Rao said coldly, "he is your enemy."

The Tippoo shrugged at the evasive answer. His good sense suggested that the prisoner was not a spy, for why would he wear his uniform? But even if he was, that did not worry the Tippoo overmuch. He expected Seringapatam was full of spies, just as he had two score of his own men marching with the British, but most spies, in the Tippoo's experience, were useless. They passed on rumors, they inflated guesses, and they muddled far more than they ever made plain.

"Kill him," one of the Tippoo's Muslim generals suggested.

"I shall think about it," the Tippoo said, and turned back through one of the balcony's inner archways into a gorgeous room of marble pillars and painted walls. The room was dominated by his throne, which was a canopied platform eight feet wide, five foot deep, and held four feet above the tiled floor by a model of a snarling tiger that supported the platform's center and was flanked on each side by four carved tiger legs. Two silver gilt ladders gave access to the throne's platform which was made of ebony wood on which a sheet of gold, thick as a prayer mat, had been fixed with silver nails. The edge of the platform was carved with quotations from the Koran, the Arabic letters picked out in gold, while above each of the throne's eight legs was a finial in the form of a tiger's head. The tiger heads were each the size of a pineapple, cast from solid gold and studded with rubies, emeralds, and diamonds. The central tiger, whose long, lean body supported the middle of the throne, was made of wood covered with gold, while its head was entirely of gold. The tiger's mouth was open, revealing teeth cut from rock crystal between which a gold tongue was hinged so that it could be moved up and down. The canopy above the golden platform was supported by a curved pole which, like the canopy itself, had been covered with sheet gold. The fringes of the canopy were made of strung pearls, and at its topmost point was a golden model of the fabulous *hummah*, the royal bird that rose from fire. The *hummah*, like the tiger finials, was studded with jewels; its back was one solid glorious emerald and its peacock-like tail a dazzle of precious stones arrayed so thickly that the underlying gold was scarcely visible.

The Tippoo did not spare the gorgeous throne a glance. He had ordered the throne made, but had then sworn an oath that he would never climb its silver steps nor sit on the cushions of its golden platform until he had at last driven the British from southern India. Only then would he take his royal place beneath the pearl-strung canopy and until that bright day the tiger throne would stay empty. The Tippoo had made his oath, and the oath meant that he would either sit on the tiger throne or else he would die, and the Tippoo's dreams had given him no presentiment of death. Instead he expected to expand Mysore's frontiers and to drive the infidel British into the sea where they belonged, for they had no business here. They had their own land, and if that far country was not good enough for them, then let them all drown.

So the British must go, and if their destruction meant an alliance with the French, then that was a small price to pay for the Tippoo's ambitions. He envisaged his empire spreading throughout southern India, then northward into the Mahratta territories which were all ruled by weak kings or child kings or by tired kings and in their place the Tippoo would offer what his dynasty had already given to Mysore: a firm and tolerant government. The Tippoo was a Muslim, and a devout one, but he knew the surest way to lose his throne was to upset his Hindu subjects and so he took good care to show their temples reverence. He did not entirely trust the Hindu aristocracy, and he had done what he could to weaken that elite over the years, but he wished only prosperity on his other Hindu subjects for if they were prosperous then they would not care what god was worshipped in the new mosque that the Tippoo had built in the city. In time, he prayed, every person in Mysore would kneel to Allah, but until that happy day he would take care not to stir the Hindus into rebellion. He needed them. He needed them to fight for him against the infidel British. He needed them to cut down the red-coated enemy before the walls of Seringapatam.

For it was here, on his island capital, that the Tippoo expected to defeat the British and their allies from Hyderabad. Here, in front of his tiger-muzzled guns, the redcoats would be beaten down like rice under a flail. He hoped they could be lured into the slaughteryard he was preparing on the western bastions, but even if they did not take the bait and came at the southern or eastern walls, he was still ready for them. He had thousands of cannon and thousands of rockets and thousands of men ready to fight. He would turn their infidel army into blood and he would destroy the army of Hyderabad and then he would hunt down the Nizam of Hyderabad, a fellow Muslim, and torture him to a slow and deserved death which the Tippoo would watch from his canopied golden throne.

He walked past the throne to stare at his favorite tiger. This one was a lifesize model, made by a French craftsman, that showed a full-grown beast crouching above the carved figure of a British redcoat. There was a handle in the tiger's flank and when it was turned the tiger's paw mauled at the redcoat's face and reeds hidden within the tiger's body made a growling sound and a pathetic noise that imitated the cries of a man dying. A flap opened in the tiger's flank to reveal a keyboard on which an organ, concealed in the tiger's belly, could be played, but the Tippoo rarely bothered with the instrument, preferring to operate the separate bellows that made the tiger growl and the victim cry out. He turned the handle now, delighting in the thin, reedy sound of the dying man. In a few days' time, he thought, he would stun the very heavens with the genuine cries of dying redcoats.

The Tippoo finally let the tiger organ fall silent. "I suspect the man is a spy," he said suddenly.

"Then kill him," Appah Rao said.

"A failed spy," the Tippoo said. "You say he is a Scot?" he asked Gudin.

"Indeed, Your Majesty."

"Not English, then?"

"No, sire."

The Tippoo shrugged at the distinction. "Whatever his

tribe, he is an old man, but is that reason to show him mercy?"

The question was directed at Colonel Gudin who, once it was translated, stiffened. "He was captured in uniform, Your Majesty, so he does not deserve death." Gudin would have liked to add that it would be uncivilized even to contemplate killing such a prisoner, but he knew the Tippoo hated being patronized and so he kept silent.

"He is here, is he not?" the Tippoo demanded. "Does that not deserve death? This is not his land, these are not his people, and the bread and water he consumes are not his."

"Kill him, Your Majesty," Gudin warned, "and the British will show no mercy on any prisoners they take."

"I am full of mercy," the Tippoo said, and mostly that was true. There was a time for being ruthless and a time for showing mercy, and maybe this Scotsman would be a useful pawn if there was a need to hold a hostage. Besides, the Tippoo's dream the night before had promised well, and this morning's auguries had been similarly hopeful, so today he could afford to show mercy. "Put him in the cells for now," the Tippoo said. Somewhere in the palace a French-made clock chimed the hour, reminding the Tippoo that it was time for his prayers. He dismissed his entourage, then went to the simple chamber where, facing west toward Mecca, he made his daily obeisances.

Outside, cheated of their prey, the tigers slunk back to the courtyard's shadows. One beast yawned, another slept. There would be other days and other men to eat. That was what the six tigers lived for, the days when their master was not merciful.

While up in the Inner Palace, with his back to the canopied throne of gold, Colonel Jean Gudin turned the tiger's handle. The tiger growled, the claws raked back and forth across the wooden, blood-painted flesh, and the redcoat cried aloud.

Sharpe had not meant to cry out. Before the punishment had begun he had been determined to show no weakness and he had even been angry with himself that he had flinched as the first blow fell, but that sudden pain had been so acute that he had involuntarily shuddered. Since then he had closed his eyes and bitten down on the leather, but in his head a silent scream shrilled as the lashes landed one after the other.

"One hundred and twenty-three!" Bywaters shouted hoarsely.

The drummer boys' arms were tiring, but they still knew better than to slacken their efforts for Sergeant Hakeswill was watching and savoring every blow.

"One hundred and twenty-four," Bywaters called, and it was then, through the silent scream that was filling his head, Sharpe heard a whimper. Then he heard another, and realized that it was he who was making the noise and so he snarled instead, opened his eyes, and stared his loathing at the bastard officers sitting on their horses a few paces away. He stared at them fixedly as if he could transfer the ghastly pain from his back onto their faces, but not one of them looked at him. They stared at the sky, they gazed at the ground, they all tried to ignore the sight of a man being beaten to death in front of their eyes.

"One hundred and thirty-six," Bywaters shouted and the drummer boy beat his instrument again.

Blood had run down Sharpe's back and stained the weave of his white trousers past his knees. More blood had spattered onto his greased and powdered hair, and still the lashes whistled down and each blow of the leather thongs splashed into the mess of broken flesh and ribboned skin, and more gleaming blood spurted away.

"One hundred and forty. Keep it high, boy, keep it high! Not on the kidneys," Bywaters snapped, and the Sergeant Major looked across at the surgeon and saw that Micklewhite was staring vaguely up over the tripod's peak, his jowly face looking as calm as though he was merely idling away a summer's day. "Want to look at him, Mister Micklewhite, sir?" the Sergeant Major suggested, but Micklewhite just shook his head. "Keep going, lads," the Sergeant Major told the drummer boys, not bothering to keep the disapproval from his voice.

The flogging went on. Hakeswill watched it with delight, but most of the men stared into the sky and prayed that Sharpe would not cry aloud. That would be his victory, even if he died in achieving it. Some Indian troops had gathered around the hollow square to watch the flogging. Such punishments were not permitted in the East India Company and most of the sepoys found it inexplicable that the British inflicted it upon themselves.

"One hundred and sixty-nine!" Bywaters shouted, then saw a gleam of white under a lash. The gleam was instantly obscured by a trickle of blood. "Can see a rib, sir!" the Sergeant Major called to the Surgeon.

Micklewhite waved a fly away from his face and stared up at a small cloud that was drifting northward. Must be some wind up there, he thought, and it was a pity that there was none down here to alleviate the heat. A tiny droplet of blood splashed onto his blue coat and he fastidiously backed farther away.

"One hundred and seventy-four," Bywaters shouted, trying to imbue the bare numbers with a tone of disapproval.

Sharpe was scarcely conscious now. The pain was beyond bearing. It was as if he was being burned alive and being stabbed at the same time. He was whimpering with each blow, but the sound was tiny, scarce loud enough to be audible to the two sweating boys whose aching arms brought the lashes down again and again. Sharpe kept his eyes closed. The breath hissed in and out of his mouth, past the gag, and the sweat and saliva dribbled down his chin and dripped onto the earth where his blood showed as dark splashes in the dust.

"Two hundred and one," Bywaters called, and wondered if he dared take a sip of water from his canteen. His voice was becoming hoarse.

"Stop!" a voice shouted.

"Two hundred and two."

"Stop!" the voice shouted again, and this time it was as if the whole battalion had been suddenly woken from a sleep. The drummer boy gave a last hesitant tap, then let his hands fall to his sides as Sergeant Major Bywaters held up his hand to stop the next stroke which was already faltering. Sharpe lifted up his head and opened his eyes, but saw nothing but a blur. The pain surged through him, he whimpered, then dropped his face again and a string of spittle fell slowly from his mouth.

Colonel Arthur Wellesley had ridden up to the tripod. For a moment Shee and his aides looked at their Colonel almost guiltily, as though they had been caught in some illicit pastime. No one spoke as the Colonel edged his horse closer to the prisoner. Wellesley looked down sourly, then put his riding crop under Sharpe's chin to lift up his head. The Colonel almost recoiled from the look of hatred he saw in the victim's eyes. He pulled the crop away, then wiped its tip on his saddle cloth to remove the spittle. "The prisoner is to be cut down, Major Shee," the Colonel said icily.

"Yes, sir." Shee was nervous, wondering if he had made

some terrible mistake. "At once, sir," he added, though he gave no orders.

"I dislike stopping a well-deserved punishment," Wellesley said loudly enough for all the nearby officers to hear, "but Private Sharpe is to be taken to General Harris's tent as soon as he's recovered."

"General Harris, sir?" Major Shee asked in astonishment. General Harris was the commander of this expedition against the Tippoo, and what possible business could the commanding General have with a half-flogged private? "Yes, sir, of course, sir," Shee added quickly when he saw that his query had annoyed Wellesley. "At once, sir."

"Then do it!" Wellesley snapped. The Colonel was a thin young man with a narrow face, hard eyes, and a prominently beaked nose. Many older men resented that the twenty-nine-year-old Wellesley was already a full colonel, but he came from a wealthy and titled family and his elder brother, the Earl of Mornington, was Governor-General of the East India Company's British possessions in India, so it was hardly surprising that the young Arthur Wellesley had risen so high so fast. Any officer given the money to buy promotion and lucky enough to possess relations who could put him in the way of advancement was bound to rise, but even the less fortunate men who resented Wellesley's privileges were forced to admit that the young Colonel had a natural and chilling authority, and maybe, some thought, even a talent for soldiering. He was certainly dedicated enough to his chosen trade if that was any sign of talent.

Wellesley nudged his horse forward and stared down as the prisoner's bonds were cut loose. "Private Sharpe?" He spoke with utter disdain, as though he dirtied himself by even addressing Sharpe.

Sharpe looked up, blinked, then made a guttural noise. Bywaters ran forward and worked the gag out of Sharpe's mouth. Freeing the pad took some manipulation, for Sharpe had sunk his teeth deep into the folded leather. "Good lad now," Bywaters said softly, "good lad. Didn't cry, did you? Proud of you, lad." The Sergeant Major at last managed to work the gag free and Sharpe tried to spit.

"Private Sharpe?" Wellesley's disdainful voice repeated.

Sharpe forced his head up. "Sir?" The word came out as a croak. "Sir," he tried again and this time it sounded like a moan.

Wellesley's face twitched with distaste for what he was doing. "You're to be fetched to General Harris's tent. Do you understand me, Sharpe?"

Sharpe blinked up at Wellesley. His head was spinning and the pain in his body was vying with disbelief at what he heard and with rage against the army.

"You heard the Colonel, boy," Bywaters prompted Sharpe.

"Yes, sir," Sharpe managed to answer Wellesley.

Wellesley turned to Micklewhite. "Bandage him, Mister Micklewhite. Put a salve on his back, whatever you think best. I want him *compos mentis* within the hour. You understand me?"

"Within an hour!" the surgeon said in disbelief, then saw the anger on his young Colonel's face. "Yes, sir," he said swiftly, "within an hour, sir."

"And give him clean clothes," Wellesley ordered the Sergeant Major before giving Sharpe one last withering look and spurring his horse away.

The last of the ropes holding Sharpe to the tripod were cut away. Shee and the officers watched, all of them wondering just what extraordinary business had caused a summons to General Harris's tent. No one spoke as the Sergeant Major plucked away the last strands of rope from Sharpe's right wrist, then offered his own hand. "Here, lad. Hold onto me. Gently now."

Sharpe shook his head. "I'm all right, Sergeant Major," he said. He was not, but he would be damned before he showed weakness in front of his comrades, and double damned before he showed it in front of Sergeant Hakeswill who had watched aghast as his victim was cut down from the triangle. "I'm all right," Sharpe insisted and he slowly pushed himself away from the tripod, then, tottering slightly, turned and took three steps.

A cheer sounded in the Light Company.

"Quiet!" Captain Morris snapped. "Take names, Sergeant Hakeswill!"

"Take names, sir! Yes, sir!"

Sharpe staggered twice and almost fell, but he forced himself to stand upright and then to take some steady steps toward the surgeon. "Reporting for bandaging, sir," he croaked. Blood had soaked his trousers, his back was carnage, but he had recovered most of his wits and the look he gave the surgeon almost made Micklewhite flinch because of its savagery.

"Come with me, Private," Micklewhite said.

"Help him! Help him!" Bywaters snapped at the drummer boys and the two sweating lads dropped their whips and hurried to support Sharpe's elbows. He had managed to remain upright, but Bywaters had seen him swaying and feared he was about to collapse.

Sharpe half walked and was half carried away. Major Shee took off his hat, scratched his graying hair, and then, unsure what he should do, looked down at Bywaters. "It seems we have no more business today, Sergeant Major."

"No, sir."

Shee paused. It was all so irregular.

"Dismiss the battalion, sir?" Bywaters suggested.

Shee nodded, glad to have been given some guidance. "Dismiss them, Sergeant Major."

"Yes, sir."

Sharpe had survived.

· CHAPTER 4 ·

It seemed airless inside General Harris's tent. It was a large tent, as big as a parish marquee, and though both its wide entrances had been brailed back there was no wind to stir the damp air trapped under the high ridge. The light inside the big tent was yellowed by the canvas to the color of urine and gave the grass underfoot a dank, unhealthy look.

Four men waited inside the tent. The youngest and most nervous was William Lawford who, because he was a mere lieutenant and by far the most junior officer present, was sitting far off to one side on a gilt chair of such spindly and fragile construction it seemed a miracle that it had survived its transport on the army's wagons. Lawford scarcely dared move lest he draw attention to himself, and so he sat awkward and uncomfortable as the sweat trickled down his face and dripped onto the crown of his cocked hat which rested on his thighs.

Opposite Lawford, and utterly ignoring the younger man, sat his Colonel, Arthur Wellesley. The Colonel made small talk, but gruffly, as though he resented being forced to wait. Once or twice he pulled a watch from his fob pocket, snapped open the lid, glared at the revealed face, then restored the watch to his pocket without making a comment.

General Harris, the army's commander, sat behind a long table that was spread with maps. The commander of the allied armies was a trim, middle-aged man who possessed an uncommon measure of common sense and a great deal of practical ability, and both were qualities he recognized in his younger deputy, Colonel Wellesley. George Harris was an affable man, but now, waiting in the tent's yellow gloom, he seemed distracted. He stared at the maps, he wiped the sweat from his face with a big blue handkerchief, but he rarely looked up to acknowledge the stilted conversation. Harris was uneasy for, like Wellesley, he did not really approve of what they were about to do. It was not so much the irregularity of the action that concerned the two men, for neither was hidebound, but rather because they suspected that the proposed operation would fail and that two good men, or rather one good man and one bad, would be lost.

The fourth man in the tent refused to sit, but instead strode up and down between the tables and the scatter of flimsy chairs. It was this man who kept alive what little conversation managed to survive the tent's stiff, damp, and airless atmosphere. He jollied his companions, he encouraged them, he tried to amuse them, though every now and then his efforts would fail and then he would stride to one of the tent doorways and stoop to peer out. "Can't be long now," he would say each time and then begin his pacing again. His name was Major General David Baird and he was the senior and older of General Harris's two deputy commanders. Unlike his colleagues he had discarded his uniform coat and waistcoat, stripping down to a dirty, much-darned shirt and letting the braces of his breeches hang down to his knees. His dark hair was damp and tousled, while his broad face was so tanned that, to Lawford's nervous gaze, Baird looked more like a laborer than a general. The resemblance was even more acute because there was nothing delicate or refined about David Baird's appearance. He was a huge Scotsman, tall as a giant, broad-shouldered and muscled like a coal-heaver. It had been Baird who had persuaded his two colleagues to act, or rather he had persuaded General Harris to act much against that officer's better judgement, and Baird frankly did not give a tinker's damn whether Colonel Arthur bloody Wellesley approved or not. Baird disliked Wellesley, and bitterly resented the fact that the younger man had been made into his fellow second-in-command. Baird, never a man to let his grudges simmer unspoken, had protested Arthur Wellesley's appointment to Harris. "If his brother wasn't Governor-General, Harris, you'd never have promoted him."

"Not true, Baird," Harris had answered mildly. "Wellesley has ability."

"Ability, my arse. He's got family!" Baird spat.

"We all have family."

"Not prinking English popinjay families with too much bloody money."

"He was born in Ireland."

"Poor bloody Ireland, then, but he ain't Irish, Harris, and you know it. The man doesn't even drink, for God's sake! A little wine, maybe, but nothing I'd call a proper drink. Have you ever met an Irishman so sober?"

"Some, quite a few, a good number, to tell the truth," Harris, a fair-minded man, had answered honestly, "but is inebriation such a desirable quality in a military commander?"

"Experience is," Baird had growled. "Hell, man, you and I have seen some service! We've lost blood! And what has Wellesley lost? Money! Nothing but money while he purchased his way up to colonel. Man's never been in a battle!"

"He will still make a very good second-in-command, and that's all that matters," Harris had insisted, and indeed Harris had been well pleased with Wellesley's performance. The Colonel's responsibilities lay mainly with the army of the Nizam of Hyderabad, and he had proved adept at persuading that potentate to submit to Harris's suggestions, a task Baird could never have performed even half so well for the Scotsman was notorious for his hatred of all Indians.

That hatred went back to the years Baird had spent in the dungeons of the Tippoo Sultan in Seringapatam. Nineteen years before, in battle against the Tippoo's fierce father, Hyder Ali, the young David Baird had been captured. He and the other prisoners had been marched to Seringapatam and there endured forty-four humiliating months of hot, damp hell in Hyder Ali's cells. For some of those months Baird had been manacled to the wall and now the Scotsman wanted revenge. He dreamed of carrying his Scottish claymore across the city's ramparts and cornering the Tippoo, and then, by Christ, the hell of Seringapatam's cells would be paid back a thousandfold.

It was the memory of that ordeal and the knowledge that his fellow Scotsman, McCandless, was now doomed to endure it, that had persuaded Baird that McCandless must be freed. Colonel McCandless had himself suggested how that release might be achieved for, before setting out on his mission, he had left a letter with David Baird. The letter, which had instructions penned on its cover saying that it should only be opened if McCandless failed to return, suggested that if the Colonel should be captured, and should General Harris feel it was important to make an attempt to release him, then a trusted man should be sent secretly into Seringapatam where he should contact a merchant named Ravi Shekhar. "If any man has the resources to free me, it is Shekhar," McCandless had written, "though I trust both you and the General will weigh well the risk of losing such a prized informant against whatever small advantages might be gained from my release."

Baird had no doubts about McCandless's worth. McCandless alone knew the identities of the British agents in the Tippoo's service and no one in the army knew as much of the Tippoo as did McCandless, and Baird was aware that should the Tippoo ever discover McCandless's true responsibilities then McCandless would be given to the tigers. It was Baird who had remembered that McCandless's English nephew, William Lawford, was serving in the army, and Baird who had persuaded Lawford to enter Seringapatam in an effort to free McCandless, and Baird who had then proposed the mission to General Harris. Harris had initially scorned the idea, though he had unbent sufficiently to suggest that maybe an Indian volunteer could be found who would stand a much greater chance of remaining undetected in the enemy capital, but Baird had vigorously defended his choice. "This is too important to be left to some blackamoor, Harris, and besides, only McCandless knows which of the bastards can be trusted. Me, I wouldn't trust any damned one of them."

Harris had sighed. He led two armies, fifty thousand men, and all but five thousand of those soldiers were Indians, and if "blackamoors" could not be trusted then Harris, Baird, and everyone else was doomed, but the General knew he would make no headway against Baird's stubborn dislike of all Indians. "I would like McCandless freed," Harris had allowed, "but, upon my soul, Baird, I can't see a white man living long in Seringapatam."

"We can't send a blackamoor," Baird had insisted. "They'll take money from us, then go straight to the Tippoo and get more money from him. Then you can kiss farewell to McCandless and to this Shekhar fellow."

"But why send this young man Lawford?" Harris had asked.

"Because McCandless is a secretive fellow, sir, more cautious than most, and if he sees Willie Lawford then he'll know that we sent him, but if it's some other British fellow he might think it's some deserter sent to trap him by the

Tippoo. Never underestimate the Tippoo, Harris, he's a clever little bastard. He reminds me of Wellesley. He's always thinking."

Harris had grunted. He had resisted the idea, but it had still tempted him, for the Havildar who had survived McCandless's ill-starred expedition had returned to the army, and his story suggested that McCandless had met with the man he hoped to meet, and, though Harris did not know who that man was, he did know that McCandless had been searching for the key to the Tippoo's city. Only a mission so important, a mission that could guarantee success, had persuaded Harris to allow McCandless to risk himself, and now McCandless was taken and Harris was being offered a chance to fetch him back, or at least to retrieve McCandless's news, even if the Colonel himself could not be fetched out of the Tippoo's dungeons. Harris was not so confident of British success in the campaign that he could disregard such a wind-fall. "But how in God's name is this fellow Lawford supposed to survive inside the city?" Harris had asked.

"Easy!" Baird had answered scornfully. "The Tippoo's only too damned eager for European volunteers, so we dress young Lawford in a private's uniform and he can pretend to be a deserter. He'll be welcomed with open arms! They'll be hanging bloody flowers round his neck and giving him first choice of the *bibbis*."

Harris had slowly allowed himself to be persuaded, though Wellesley, once introduced to the idea, had advised against it. Lawford, Wellesley insisted, could never pass himself off as an enlisted man, but Wellesley had been overruled by Baird's enthusiasm and so Lieutenant Lawford had been summoned to Harris's tent where he had complicated matters by agreeing with his Colonel. "I'd dearly like to help, sir," he had told Harris, "but I'm not sure I'm capable of the pretence."

"Good God, man," Baird intervened, "spit and swear! It ain't difficult!"

"It will be very difficult," Harris had insisted, staring at the diffident Lieutenant. He was doubtful whether Lawford had the resources to carry off the deception, for the Lieutenant, while plainly a decent man, seemed guileless.

Then Lawford had complicated matters still further. "I think it would be more plausible, sir," he suggested respectfully, "if I could take another man with me. Deserters usually run in pairs, don't they? And if the man is the genuine article, a ranker, it'll be altogether more convincing."

"Makes sense, makes sense," Baird had put in encouragingly.

"You have a man in mind?" Wellesley had asked coldly.

"His name is Sharpe, sir," Lawford said. "They're probably about to flog him."

"Then he'll be no damned use to you," Wellesley said in a tone which suggested the matter was now closed.

"I'll go with no one else, sir," Lawford retorted stubbornly, addressing himself to General Harris rather than to his Colonel, and Harris was pleased to see this evidence of backbone. The Lieutenant, it seemed, was not quite so diffident as he appeared.

"How many lashes is this fellow getting?" Harris asked.

"Don't know, sir. He's standing trial now, sir, and if I wasn't here I'd be giving evidence on his behalf. I doubt his guilt."

The argument over whether to employ Sharpe had continued over a midday meal of rice and stewed goat. Wellesley was refusing to intervene in the court martial or its subsequent punishment, declaring that such an act would be prejudicial to discipline, but William Lawford stubbornly and respectfully refused to take any other man. It had, he said, to be a man he could trust. "We could send another officer,"

Wellesley had suggested, but that idea had faltered when the difficulties of finding a reliable volunteer were explored. There were plenty of men who might go, but few were steady, and the steady ones would be too sensible to risk their precious commissions on what Wellesley scathingly called a fool's errand. "So why are you willing to go?" Harris had asked Lawford. "You don't look like a fool."

"I trust I'm not, sir. But my uncle gave me the money to purchase my commission."

"Did he, by God! That's damned generous."

"And I hope I'm damned grateful, sir."

"Grateful enough to die for him?" Wellesley put in sourly.

Lawford had colored, but stuck to his guns. "I suspect Private Sharpe is resourceful enough for both of us, sir."

The decision whether or not to employ Sharpe belonged, in the end, to General Harris who privately agreed with Wellesley that to spare a man his well-earned punishment was to display a dangerous laxity, but at last, persuaded that extraordinary measures were needed to save McCandless, the General surrendered to Baird's enthusiasm and so, with a heavy heart, Harris had ordered the unfortunate Sharpe fetched to the tent. Which was why, at long last, Private Richard Sharpe limped into the wan, yellow light cast through the tent's high canvas. He was dressed in a clean uniform, but everyone in the tent could see that he was still in dreadful pain. He moved stiffly, and the stiffness was not just caused by the yards of bandage that circled his torso, but by the agony of every movement of his body. He had tried to wash the blood out of his hair and had succeeded in taking out most of the powder as well so that when Colonel Wellesley told him to take off his shako he appeared with curiously mottled hair.

"I think you'd better sit, man," General Baird suggested, with a glance at Harris for his permission.

"Fetch that stool," Harris ordered Sharpe, then saw that the private could not bend down to pick it up.

Baird fetched the stool. "Is it hurting?" he asked sympathetically.

"Yes, sir."

"It's supposed to hurt," Wellesley said curtly. "Pain is the point of punishment." He kept his back to Sharpe, pointedly demonstrating his disapproval. "I do not like cancelling a flogging," Wellesley went on to no one in particular. "It erodes good order. Once men think their sentences can be curtailed, then God only knows what roguery they'll be up to." He suddenly twisted in his chair and gave Sharpe an icy glare. "If I had my way, Private Sharpe, I'd march you back to the triangle and finish the job."

"I doubt Private Sharpe even deserved the punishment," Lawford dared to intervene, blushing as he did.

"The time for that sentiment, Lieutenant, was during the court martial!" Wellesley snapped, his tone suggesting that it would have been a wasted sentiment anyway. "You've been lucky, Private Sharpe," Wellesley said with distaste. "I shall announce that you've been spared the rest of your punishment as a reward for fighting well the other day. Did you fight well?"

Sharpe nodded. "Killed my share of the enemy, sir."

"So I'm commuting your sentence. And tonight, damn your eyes, you'll reward me by deserting."

Sharpe wondered if he had heard right, decided it was best not to ask, and so he looked away from the Colonel, composed his face, and stared fixedly at the wall of the tent.

"Have you ever thought about deserting, Sharpe?" General Baird asked him.

"Me, sir?" Sharpe managed to look surprised. "Not me, sir, no, sir. Never crossed my mind, sir."

Baird smiled. "We need a good liar for this particular service. So maybe you're an excellent choice, Sharpe. Besides, anyone who looks at your back will know why you wanted to desert." Baird liked that idea and his face betrayed a sudden enthusiasm. "In fact if you hadn't already conveniently had yourself flogged, man, we might have had to give you a few lashes anyway!" He smiled.

Sharpe did not smile back. Instead he looked warily from one officer to the other. He could see that Mister Lawford was nervous, Baird was doing his best to be friendly, General Harris's face was unreadable, while Colonel Wellesley had turned away in disgust. But Wellesley had always been a cold fish, so there was no point in trying to gain his approval. Baird was the man who had saved him, Sharpe guessed, and that fitted with Baird's reputation in the army. The Scotsman was a soldier's general, a brave man and well liked by the troops.

Baird smiled again, trying to put Sharpe at his ease. "Let me explain why you're running, Sharpe. Three days ago we lost a good man, a Colonel McCandless. The Tippoo's forces captured him and, so far as we know, they took him back to Seringapatam. We want you to go to that city and be captured by the Tippoo's forces. Are you understanding me this far?"

"Yes, sir," Sharpe said obediently.

"Good man. Now, when you reach Seringapatam the Tippoo will want you to join his army. He likes to have white men in his ranks, so you won't have any trouble taking his shilling. And once you're trusted your job is to find Colonel McCandless and bring him out alive. Are you still following me, now?"

"Yes, sir," Sharpe said stoically, and wondered why they did not first ask him to hop over to London and steal the crown jewels. Bloody idiots! Put a bit of gold lace on a man's coat and his brain turned to mush! Still, they were doing what he wanted them to do, which was kicking him out of the army and so he sat very still, very quiet, and very straight, not so much out of respect, but because his back hurt like the very devil every time he moved.

"You won't be going alone," Baird told Sharpe. "Lieutenant Lawford volunteered your services and he's going as well. He'll pretend to be a private and a deserter, and your job is to look after him."

"Yes, sir," Sharpe said, and hid his dismay that perhaps things were not going to be quite so easy after all. He could not just run now, not with Lawford tied to his apron strings. He glanced at the Lieutenant, who gave him a reassuring smile.

"The thing is, Sharpe," Lawford said, still smiling, "I'm not too certain I can pass myself off as a private. But they'll believe you, and you can say I'm a new recruit."

A new recruit! Sharpe almost laughed. You could no more pass the Lieutenant off as a new recruit than you could pass Sharpe off as an officer! He had an idea then, and the idea surprised him, not because it was a good idea, but because it implied he was suddenly trying to make this idiotic scheme work. "Better if you said you was a company clerk, sir." He muttered the words too softly, made shy by the presence of so many senior officers.

"Speak up, man!" Wellesley snarled.

"It would be better, sir," Sharpe said so loudly that he was verging on insolence, "if the Lieutenant said he was a company clerk, sir."

"A clerk?" Baird asked. "Why?"

"He's got soft hands, sir. Clean hands, sir. Clerks don't muck about in the dirt like the rest of us. And recruits, sir, they're usually just as filthy-handed as the rest of us. But not clerks, sir." Harris, who had been writing, looked up with a faint expression of admiration. "Put some ink on his hands, sir," Sharpe still spoke to Baird, "and he won't look wrong."

"I like it, Sharpe, indeed I do!" Baird said. "Well done."

Wellesley sneered, then pointedly stared through one of the tent openings as though he found the proceedings tiresome. General Harris looked at Lawford. "You could manage to play the part of a disgruntled clerk, Lieutenant?" he asked.

"Oh, indeed, sir. I'm sure, sir." Lawford at last sounded confident.

"Good," Harris said, laying down his pen. The General wore a wig to hide the scar where an American bullet had torn away a scrap of his skull on Bunker Hill. Now, unconsciously, he lifted a corner of the wig and scratched at that old scar. "And I suppose, once you reach the city, you contact this merchant. Remind me of his name, Baird?"

"Ravi Shekhar, sir."

"And what if this fellow Shekhar ain't there?" Harris asked. "Or won't help?" There was silence after the question. The sentries outside the tent, moved far enough away so they could not overhear the conversation, stamped up and down. A dog barked. "You have to anticipate these things," Harris said mildly, scratching again under his wig. Wellesley offered a harsh laugh, but no suggestion.

"If Ravi Shekhar won't help us, sir," Baird suggested, "then Lawford and Sharpe must get themselves into McCandless's jail, then find a way of getting themselves out." The Scotsman turned to Sharpe. "Were you by any chance a thief before you joined up?"

A heartbeat's hesitation, then Sharpe nodded. "Yes, sir."

"What kind of a thief?" Wellesley asked in a disgusted voice as though he was astonished to discover the ranks of his battalion contained criminals, and, when Sharpe did not answer, the Colonel became even more irritable. "A diver? A scamp?"

Sharpe was surprised that his Colonel even knew such slang. He shook his head indignantly, denying he had ever been a mere pickpocket or a highwayman. "I was a house boner, sir," he said. "And proper trained, too," he added proudly. In fact he had done his share on the highway, not so much holding up coaches as slicing the leather straps that held the passengers' portmanteaus on the backs of coaches. The job was done while the coach was speeding along a road so that the noise of the hooves and wheels would hide the sound of the tumbling luggage. It was a job for agile youngsters and Sharpe had been good at it.

"A house boner means he was a burglar," Wellesley translated for his two senior officers, unable to hide his scorn.

Baird was pleased with Sharpe's answers. "Do you still have a picklock, Private?"

"Me, sir? No, sir. But I suppose I could find one, sir, if I had a guinea."

Baird laughed, suspecting the true cost was nearer a shilling, but he still went to his coat which was hanging from a hook on one of the tent poles and fished out a guinea which he tossed onto Sharpe's lap. "Find one before tonight, Private Sharpe," he said, "for who knows, it might be useful." He turned to Harris. "But I doubt it will come to that, sir. I pray it doesn't come to that for I'm not sure that any man, even Private Sharpe here, can escape from the Tippoo's dungeons." The tall General turned back to Sharpe. "I was near four years in those cells, Sharpe, and in all that time not one man escaped. Not one." Baird paced restlessly as he remembered the ordeal. "The Tippoo's cells have barred doors with padlocks, so your picklock could take care of that, but when I was there we always had four jailers in the daytime, and some days there were even *jettis* on guard."

"*Jettis*, sir?" Lawford asked.

"*Jettis*, Lieutenant. The Tippoo inherited a dozen of the

bastards from his father. They're professional strongmen and their favorite trick is executing prisoners. They have several ways of doing it, none of them pleasant. You want to know their methods?"

"No, sir," Lawford said hurriedly, blanching at the thought. Sharpe was disappointed, but dared not ask for the details.

Baird grimaced. "Very unpleasant executions, Lieutenant," he said grimly. "You still want to go?"

Lawford remained pale, but nodded. "I think it's worth a try, sir."

Wellesley snorted at the Lieutenant's foolishness, but Baird ignored the Colonel. "At night the guards are withdrawn," he went on, "but there's still a sentry."

"Just one?" Sharpe asked.

"Just one, Private," Baird confirmed.

"I can take care of one sentry, sir," Sharpe boasted.

"Not this one," Baird said grimly, "because when I was there he was eight feet long if he was an inch. He was a tiger, Sharpe. A man-eater, and the eight foot don't count his tail. He used to be put in the corridor every night, so pray you don't ever end up in the Tippoo's cells. Pray that Ravi Shekhar will know how to get McCandless out."

"Or at the very least," Harris intervened, "pray that Shekhar can discover what McCandless knows and that you can get that news out to us."

"So that's what we want of you!" Baird said to Sharpe with a brusque cheerfulness. "Are you willing to go, man?"

Sharpe reckoned it was all idiocy, and he did not much like the sound of the tiger, but he knew better than to show any reluctance. "I reckon three is better than two thousand, sir," he said.

"Three?" Baird asked, puzzled.

"Three stripes are better than two thousand lashes, sir. If

we find out what you want to know or else fetch this Colonel McCandless out of jail, sir, can I be a sergeant?" He asked the question of Wellesley.

Wellesley looked enraged at Sharpe's presumption, and for a second it was plain that he proposed to turn him down, but General Harris cleared his throat and mildly remarked that it sounded a reasonable suggestion to him.

Wellesley thought about opposing the General, then decided that it was most unlikely that Sharpe would even survive this nonsense and so, albeit reluctantly, he nodded. "A sergeant's stripes, Sharpe, if you succeed."

"Thank you, sir," Sharpe said.

Baird dismissed him. "Go with Lieutenant Lawford now, Sharpe, he'll tell you what to do. And one other thing . . ." The Scotsman's voice became urgent. "For God's sake, man, don't tell another soul what you're doing."

"Wouldn't dream of it, sir," Sharpe said, flinching as he stood up.

"Go then," Baird said. He waited till the two men were gone, then sighed. "A bright young fellow, that Sharpe." He spoke to Harris.

"A rogue," Wellesley interjected. "I could provide you with a hundred others just as disreputable. Scum, all of them, and the only thing that keeps them from riot is discipline."

Harris rapped the table to stop the squabbling of his two seconds-in-command. "But will the rogue succeed?" he asked.

"Not a chance," Wellesley said confidently.

"A woefully small chance," Baird admitted dourly, then added more vigorously, "but even a small chance is worth it if we can get McCandless back."

"At the risk of losing two good men?" Harris asked.

"One man who might become a decent officer," Wellesley

corrected the General, "and one man whose loss the world won't mourn for a second."

"But McCandless might hold the key to the city, General," Baird reminded Harris.

"True," Harris said heavily, then unrolled a map that had lain scrolled on the edge of his table. The map showed Seringapatam and whenever he gazed at it he wondered how he was to set about besieging the city. Lord Cornwallis, who had captured the city seven years before, had assaulted the north side of the island and then attacked the eastern walls, but Harris doubted that he would be given that route again. The Tippoo would have been forewarned by that earlier success, which meant this new assault must come from either the south or the west. A dozen deserters from the enemy's forces had all claimed that the west wall was in bad repair, and maybe that would give Harris his best chance. "South or west," he said aloud, reiterating the problem he had already discussed a score of times with his two deputies. "But either way, gentlemen, the place is crammed with guns, thick with rockets and filled with infantry. And we'll have only the one chance before the rains come. Just one. West or south, eh?" He stared at the map, hoping against hope that McCandless could be fetched from his dungeon to offer some guidance, but that, he admitted to himself, was a most unlikely outcome, which meant the decision would inevitably be all his to make. The final decision could wait till the army was close to the city and Harris had been given a chance to view the Tippoo's defenses, but once the army was ready to make camp the choice would have to be made swiftly and, all things being equal, Harris was fairly sure which route he would choose. For weeks now his instinct had been telling him where to attack, but he worried that the Tippoo might have foreseen the weakness in his city's defences. But there was no point in wondering whether the Tippoo was outfoxing him, that way lay indecision, and so Harris tapped his quill on the map. "My instincts tell me to attack here, gentlemen, right here." He was indicating the west wall. "Across the river shallows and right through the weakest stretch of the walls. It seems the obvious place." He tapped the map again. "Right here, right here."

Right where the Tippoo had set his trap.

Allah, in His infinite mercy, had been good to the Tippoo Sultan, for Allah, in His immeasurable wisdom, had revealed the existence of a merchant who was sending information to the British army. The man dealt in common metals, in copper, tin, and brass, and his wagons frequently passed through one of the city's two main gates loaded with their heavy cargoes. God alone knows how many such cargoes had passed out of Seringapatam in the last three months, but at least the gate guards had searched the right wagon, the one that carried a coded letter which, under interrogation, the wretched merchant had admitted contained a report of the strange work that was being done in the old closed gateway of the western wall. That work should have been a close secret, for the only men allowed near the gateway were Gudin's reliable European troops and a small band of the Tippoo's Muslim warriors whom he regarded as utterly trustworthy. The merchant, not surprisingly, was a Hindu, but when his wife was brought into the interrogation room and threatened with the red-hot pincers, the merchant had confessed the name of the Muslim soldier who had allowed himself to be suborned by the merchant's gold. And so much gold! A strongroom filled with the metal, far more than the Tippoo suspected could be earned from trading in tin, brass, and copper. It was British gold, the merchant confessed, given him so he could raise rebellion inside Seringapatam.

The Tippoo did not consider himself a cruel man, but nor,

indeed, did he think of himself as a gentle one. He was a ruler, and cruelty and mercy were both weapons of rulers. Any monarch who flinched from cruelty would not rule long, just as any ruler who forgot mercy would soon earn hatred, and so the Tippoo tried to balance mercy with cruelty. He did not want the reputation of being lenient any more than he wanted to be judged a tyrant, and so he tried to use both mercy and cruelty judiciously. The Hindu merchant, his confession made, had pleaded for mercy, but the Tippoo knew this was no time to show weakness. This was the time to let a shudder of horror ripple through the streets and alleys of Seringapatam. It was a time to let his enemies know that the price for treason was death, and so both the merchant and the Muslim soldier who had taken the merchant's gold were now standing on the hot sand of the Inner Palace's courtyard where they were being guarded by two of the Tippoo's favored *jettis*.

The *jettis* were Hindus, and their strength, which was remarkable, was devoted to their religion. That amused the Tippoo. Some Hindus sought the rewards of godliness by growing their hair and fingernails, others by denying themselves food, still others by abjuring all earthly pleasures, but the *jettis* did it by developing their muscles, and the results, the Tippoo admitted, were extraordinary. He might disagree with their religion, but he encouraged them all the same and like his father he had hired a dozen of the most impressive strongmen to amuse and serve him. Two of the finest now stood beneath the throne-room balcony, stripped to their waists and with their vast chests oiled so that their muscles shone dark in the early-afternoon sun. The six tigers, restless because they had been denied their midday meal of freshly slaughtered goat meat, glared with yellow eyes from the courtyard's edges.

The Tippoo came from his prayers to the balcony where

he threw open the filigree shutters so that he and his entourage could view the courtyard clearly. Colonel Gudin was in
attendance, as was Appah Rao. Both men had been summoned from the city ramparts where they had been making
the last preparations for the arrival of the British. Gun carriages were being repaired, ammunition being laid down in
magazines deep enough to be shielded from the fall of
enemy howitzer shells, while dozens of rockets were in the
ready magazines on the ramparts' firesteps. The Tippoo liked
to tour his defenses where he could imagine his rockets and
shells searing down into the enemy ranks, but now, in the
courtyard of his inner palace, he had an even more pleasur-
able duty to perform. He would kill traitors. "Both men
betrayed me," he told Colonel Gudin through the interpreter, "and one is also a spy. What would you do in France
with such men, Colonel?"

"Send them to Madame Guillotine, Your Majesty."

The Tippoo chuckled when the answer was translated. He
was curious about the guillotine and at one time he had
thought of having such a machine built in the city. He was
fascinated by all things French and indeed, when the revolution had swept France and destroyed the *ancien régime*, the
Tippoo had for a time embraced the new ideas of Liberty,
Equality, and Fraternity. He had erected a Tree of Liberty
in Seringapatam, ordered his guards to wear the red hats of
the revolution, and had even ordered revolutionary declarations to be posted in the city's main streets, but the fascination had not endured. The Tippoo had begun to fear that his
people might become too fond of liberty, or even infected
with equality, and so he had removed the Tree of Liberty
and had the declarations torn down, yet still the Tippoo
treasured a love of France. He had never built the guillotine,
not for lack of funds, but rather because Gudin had persuaded him that the machine was a device of mercy, con-

structed to end a criminal's life with such swiftness that the victim would never even realize he was being killed. It was an ingenious device, the Tippoo admitted, but much too merciful. How could such a machine deter traitors?

"That man"—the Tippoo now pointed to the Muslim soldier who had betrayed the secrets of the gatehouse—"will be killed first and then his body will be fed to pigs. I can think of no fate worse for a Muslim, and believe me, Colonel, he fears the pigs more than he fears his death. The other man will feed my tigers and his bones will be ground to powder and delivered to his widow. Their deaths will be short, not perhaps as quick as your machine, Colonel, but still mercifully short." He clapped his hands and the two chained prisoners were dragged forward until they stood in the center of the courtyard.

The Muslim soldier was forced to his knees. His tiger-striped uniform had been stripped from him and now he wore nothing but a short pair of loose cotton breeches. He stared up at the Tippoo who was gaudy in a yellow silk tunic and a jeweled turban, and the man raised his manacled hands in a mute appeal for clemency that the Tippoo ignored. Gudin tensed himself. He had seen the *jettis* at work before, but familiarity did not make the spectacle any more pleasant.

The first *jetti* placed a nail on the crown of the victim's bare head. The nail was of black iron and had a six-inch shank that was topped by a flat head that was a good three inches wide. The man held the nail in place with his left hand, then looked up at the balcony. The doomed soldier, feeling the touch of the iron point on his scalp, called for forgiveness. The Tippoo listened for a second to the soldier's desperate excuses, then pointed a finger at him. The Tippoo held the finger steady for a few seconds and the soldier held his breath as he dared to believe he might be forgiven, but then the Tippoo's hand abruptly dropped.

The *jetti* raised his right hand, its palm facing downward, then took a deep breath. He paused, summoning his huge strength, then he slapped the hand fast down so that his open palm struck the nail's flat top. He shouted aloud as he struck, and at the very instant that his right hand slapped the nail so he snatched his left hand away from the long shank which was driven hard and deep into the soldier's skull. It went so deep that the nail's flat head crushed the prisoner's black hair. Blood spurted from under the nail as its shank slammed home. The *jetti* stepped away, gesturing at the nail as if to show how much strength had been needed to so drive it through the thick bone of the skull. The traitor still lived. He was babbling and shrieking, and blood was spilling down his face in quick, lacing rivulets as he swayed on his knees. His body was shaking, but then, quite suddenly, his back arched, he stared wide-eyed up at the Tippoo, and then fell forward. His body shuddered twice, then was still. One of the six chained tigers stirred at the smell of blood and padded forward until its chain stretched to its full length and so held it back. The beast growled, then settled down to watch the second man die.

The Tippoo and his entourage applauded the first *jetti*'s skill, then the Tippoo pointed at the wretched Hindu merchant. This second prisoner was a big man, fat as butter, and his gross size would only make the second demonstration all the more impressive.

The first *jetti*, his execution successfully completed, fetched a stool from the gateway. He set it down and forced the fat, weeping merchant onto its seat. Then he knelt in front of the chair and pinned the man's manacled arms down tight against his sagging belly so that he could not move. The chair faced the Tippoo and the kneeling *jetti* made certain he stayed low so that he would not spoil his master's view. "It takes more strength than you would think," the Tippoo remarked to Gudin, "to drive a nail into a skull."

"So Your Majesty has been kind enough to inform me before," Gudin answered drily.

The Tippoo laughed. "You do not enjoy this, Colonel?"

"The death of traitors is ever necessary, sire," Gudin said evasively.

"But I should like to think you derive amusement from it. Surely you appreciate my men's strength?"

"I do admire it, sire."

"Then admire it now," the Tippoo said, "for the next death takes even more strength than the nail." The Tippoo smiled and turned back to look into the courtyard where the second *jetti* waited behind the prisoner. The Tippoo pointed at the merchant, held the gesture as before, then dropped his hand abruptly. The merchant screamed in anticipation, then began to shake like a leaf as the *jetti* placed his hands against the sides of the merchant's skull. His touch was gentle at first, almost a caress. His palms covered the merchant's ears as his fingers groped to find a purchase among the skull bones beneath the victim's fat cheeks. Then the *jetti* suddenly tightened his grip, distorting the plump face, and the merchant's scream became frantic until, at last, he had no breath left to scream and could only mew in terror. The *jetti* drew breath, paused to concentrate all his force, then gave a great shout that made the six tigers leap to their feet in alarm.

As he shouted the *jetti* twisted the merchant's head. He was wringing his victim's neck like a man would wring a chicken's gullet, only this neck was thick and fat, but the *jetti*'s first great effort twisted it so far around that the face was already looking back across its right shoulder when the executioner made his second effort, marked by a grunt, which pulled the head all the way around and Gudin, flinch-

ing from the sight on the balcony, heard the distinct crack as
the merchant's spine was broken. The *jetti* let go of the head
and sprang back, proud of his work as the dead merchant
collapsed off the stool. The Tippoo applauded, then tossed
down two small bags of gold. "Take that one to the pigs," he
said, pointing at the Muslim. "And leave the other here. Let
the tigers loose."

The balcony shutters were closed. Somewhere deep in the
palace, perhaps from the harem where the Tippoo's six hundred wives, concubines, and handmaidens all lived, a harp
tinkled prettily, while down in the courtyard the tigers' keepers used their long staves to herd the beasts as they released
them from their chains. The Tippoo smiled at his followers.
"Back to the walls, gentlemen," he said. "We have work to
do."

The keepers released the last tiger, then followed the *jettis*
out through the gateway. The dead soldier had been dragged
away. For a moment the tigers watched the remaining body,
then one of the beasts crossed to the merchant's corpse and
eviscerated the fat belly with one blow of its huge paw.

And so Ravi Shekhar had died. And now was eaten.

Sharpe was back with his company before sunset. He was
greeted ebulliently by men who saw in his release from the
flogging a small victory for the lower ranks against blind
authority. Private Mallinson even clapped Sharpe on the
back, and was rewarded with a stream of curses.

Sharpe ate with his usual six companions who, as ever,
were joined by three wives and by Mary. The supper was a
stew of beans, rice, and salt beef, and it was at the end of the
small meal, when they were sharing a canteen of arrack, that
Sergeant Hakeswill appeared. "Private Sharpe!" He was carrying a cane that he pointed toward Sharpe. "I wants you!"

"Sergeant." Sharpe acknowledged Hakeswill, but did not move.

"A word with you, Private. On your feet now!"

Sharpe still did not move. "I'm excused company duties, Sergeant. Colonel's orders."

Hakeswill's face wrenched itself in a grotesque twitch. "This ain't your duty," the Sergeant said, "this is your bleeding pleasure. So get on your bloody feet and come here."

Sharpe obediently stood, flinching as his coat tugged at his grievously wounded back. He followed the Sergeant to an open space behind the surgeon's tent where Hakeswill turned and rammed his cane into Sharpe's chest. "How the hell did you escape that flogging, Sharpie?"

Sharpe ignored the question. Hakeswill's broken nose was still swollen and bruised, and Sharpe could see the worry in the Sergeant's eyes.

"Didn't you hear me, boy?" Hakeswill shoved the cane's tip into Sharpe's belly. "How come you was cut down?"

"How come you were cut down from the scaffold, Sergeant?" Sharpe asked.

"No lip from you, boy. No lip, or by God I'll have you strapped to the tripod again. Now tell me what the General wanted."

Sharpe shook his head. "If you want to know that, Sergeant," he said, "you'd better ask General Harris yourself."

"Stand still! Stand straight!" Hakeswill snapped, then cut with his cane at a nearby guy rope. He sniffed, wondering how best to worm the information out of Sharpe and decided, for a change, to try gentleness. "I admire you, Sharpie," the Sergeant said hoarsely. "Not many men have the guts to walk after getting two hundred tickles of the whip. Takes a strong man to do that, Sharpie, and I'd hate to see you getting even more tickles. It's in your best interest to tell me, Sharpie. You know that. It'll go bad with you else. So why was you released, lad?"

Sharpe pretended to relent. "You know why I was released, Sergeant," he said. "The Colonel announced it."

"No, I don't know, lad," Hakeswill said. "Upon my soul, I don't. So you tell me now."

Sharpe shrugged. "Because we fought well the other day, Sergeant. It's a reward, like."

"No, it bleeding ain't!" Hakeswill shouted, then dodged to one side and slashed his cane onto Sharpe's wounded back. Sharpe almost screamed with the pain. "You don't get called away to a general's tent for that, Sharpie!" Hakeswill said. "Stands to reason! Never heard nothing like it in all my born days. So you tell me why, you bastard."

Sharpe turned to face his persecutor. "You lay that cane on me again, Obadiah," he said softly, "and I'll tell General Harris about you. I'll have you skinned of your stripes, I will, and turned back into a private. Would you like that, Obadiah? You and me in the same file? I'd like that, Obadiah."

"Stand still!" Hakeswill spat.

"Shut your face, Sergeant," Sharpe said. He had called Hakeswill's bluff, and there was pleasure in that. The Sergeant had doubtless thought he could bully the truth out of Sharpe, but Sharpe held all the trump cards here. "How's your nose?" he asked Hakeswill.

"Be careful, Sharpie. Be careful."

"Oh, I am, Sergeant, I am. I'm real careful. Have you done now?" Sharpe did not wait for an answer, but just walked away. The next time he faced Obadiah, he thought, he would have the stripes on his sleeve, and God help Hakeswill then.

He talked to Mary for half an hour, then it was time to make the excuses that Lieutenant Lawford had rehearsed with him. He picked up his pack, took his musket, and said he had to report to the paymaster's tent. "I'm on light duties till the stripes heal," he told his mates, "doing sentry-go on the money. I'll see you tomorrow."

Major General Baird had made all the arrangements. The camp's western perimeter was guarded by men he could trust, and those men had orders to disregard anything they saw, while next day, Baird promised Lawford, the army would take care not to send any cavalry patrols directly west in case those patrols discovered the two fugitives. "Your job is to go as far west as you can tonight," Baird told Sharpe and Lawford when he met them close to the western picquet line, "and then keep walking west in the morning. You understand now?"

"Yes, sir," Lawford answered. The Lieutenant, beneath a heavy cloak that disguised his uniform, was now dressed in the common soldier's red wool coat and white trousers. Sharpe had tugged Lawford's hair back, then wrapped it around the leather pad to form the queue, and after that he had smothered it with a mix of grease and powder so that Lawford looked no different from any other private except that his hands were still too soft, but at least they now had ink under the fingernails and ground into the pores. Lawford had grimaced as Sharpe had tugged at his hair, and protested when Sharpe had gouged two marks in his neck where a stock would have scraped twin calluses, but Baird had hushed him. Lawford winced again when he put on the leather stock and realized just what discomfort the ordinary soldier endured daily. Now, safe out of sight of the soldiers about their campfires, he dropped the cloak, pulled on a pack, and picked up his musket.

Baird hauled a huge watch from his pocket and tilted its face to the half moon. "Eleven o'clock," the General said. "Time you fellows were away." He put two fingers in his mouth and sounded a shrill quick whistle and the picquet, visible in the pale moonlight, magically parted north and south to leave an unguarded gap in the camp's perimeter. Baird had shaken Lawford's hand, then patted Sharpe's shoulder. "How's your back, Sharpe?"

"Hurts like hell, sir." It did too.

Baird looked worried. "You'll manage, though?"

"I ain't soft, sir."

"I never supposed you were, Private." Baird patted Sharpe's shoulder again, then gestured into the dark. "Off you go, lads, and God be with you." Baird watched the two men run across the open ground and disappear into the darkness on the farther side. He waited for a long time, hoping to catch a last glimpse of the two men's shadows, but he saw nothing, and his best judgement suggested that he would probably never see either soldier again and that reflection saddened him. He sounded the whistle again and watched as the sentries reformed the picquet line, then he turned and walked slowly back to his tent.

"This way, Sharpe," Lawford said when they were out of earshot of the sentries. "We're following a star."

"Just like the wise men, Bill," Sharpe said. It had taken Sharpe an extraordinary effort to use Mister Lawford's first name, but he knew he had to do it. His survival, and Lawford's, depended on everything being done right.

But the use of the name shocked Lawford, who stopped and stared at Sharpe. "What did you call me?"

"I called you Bill," Sharpe said, "because that's your bleeding name. You ain't an officer now, you're one of us. I'm Dick, you're Bill. And we ain't following any bloody star. We're going to those trees over there. See? The three big buggers?"

"Sharpe!" Lawford protested.

"No!" Sharpe turned savagely on Lawford. "My job is to keep you alive, Bill, so get one thing straight. You're a bleeding private now, not a bloody officer. You volunteered, remember? And we're deserters. There ain't no ranks here, no 'sirs,' no bloody salutes, no gentlemen. When we get back to the army I promise you I'll pretend this never happened and I'll salute you till my bloody arm drops off, but not now, and not till you and me get out of this bloody nonsense alive. So come on!"

Lawford, stunned by Sharpe's confidence, meekly followed. "But this is south of west!" he protested, glancing up at the stars to check the direction Sharpe was taking.

"We'll go west later," Sharpe said. "Now get your bleeding stock off." He ripped his own off and tossed it into some bushes. "First thing any runner does, sir"—the "sir" was accidental, a habit, and he silently cursed himself for using it —"is take off his stock. Then mess your hair. And get those trousers dirty. You look like you're standing guard on Windsor bleeding Castle." Sharpe watched as Lawford did his best to obey. "So where did you join up, Bill?" he asked.

Lawford was still resentful of this sudden reversal of roles, but he was sensible enough to realize Sharpe was right. "Join up?" he repeated. "I didn't."

"Of course you did! Where did they recruit you?"

"My home's near Portsmouth."

"That's no bloody good. Navy would press you in Portsmouth before a recruiting sergeant could get near to you. Ever been to Sheffield?"

"Good Lord, no!" Lawford sounded horrified.

"Good place, Sheffield," Sharpe said. "And there's a pub on Pond Street called The Hawle in the Pond. Can you remember that? The Hawle in the Pond in Sheffield. It's a favorite hunting hole for the 33rd's recruiters, especially on market days. You was tricked there by some bleeding sergeant. He got you drunk and before you knew it you'd taken the King's shilling. He was a sergeant of the 33rd, so what did he have on his bayonet?"

"His bayonet?" Lawford, fumbling to release the leather binding of his newly clubbed hair, frowned in perplexity. "Nothing, I should hope."

"We're the 33rd, Bill! The Havercakes! He carried an oatcake on his bayonet, remember? And he promised you'd be an officer inside two years because he was a lying bastard. What did you do before you met him?"

Lawford shrugged. "A farmer?"

"No one would ever believe you labored on a farm," Sharpe said scornfully. "You ain't got a farmer's arms. That General Baird now, he's got proper arms. Looks as if he could hoist hay all day long and not feel a damn thing, but not you. You were a lawyer's clerk."

Lawford nodded. "I think we should go now," he said, trying to reassert his rapidly vanishing authority.

"We're waiting," Sharpe said stubbornly. "So why the hell are you running?"

Lawford frowned. "Unhappiness, I suppose."

"Bleeding hell, you're a soldier! You ain't supposed to be happy! No, let's think now. You boned the Captain's watch, how about that? Got caught, and you faced a flogging. You saw me flogged and didn't fancy you could survive, so you and me, being mates like, ran."

"I really do think we must go!" Lawford insisted.

"In a minute, sir." Again Sharpe cursed himself for using the honorific. "Just let my back settle down."

"Oh, of course." Lawford was immediately contrite. "But we can't wait too long, Sharpe."

"Dick, sir. You call me Dick. We're friends, remember?"

"Of course." Lawford, as uncomfortable with this sudden intimacy as with the need to waste time, settled awkwardly by Sharpe at the base of a tree. "So why did you join up?" he asked Sharpe.

"The harmen were after me."

"The harmen? Oh yes, the constables." Lawford paused. Somewhere in the night a creature shrieked as it was caught by a predator, while off to the east the sergeants called to their sentries. The sky glowed with the light of the army's myriad fires. "What had you done?" Lawford asked.

"Killed a man. Put a knife in him."

Lawford gazed at Sharpe. "Murdered him, you mean?"

"Oh, aye, it was murder right enough, even though the bugger deserved it. But the judge at York Assizes wouldn't have seen it my way, would he? Which meant Dick Sharpe would have been morris-dancing at the end of a rope so I reckoned it was easier to put on the scarlet coat. The harmen don't bother a man once he's in uniform, not unless he killed one of the gentry."

Lawford hesitated, not sure whether he should inquire too deeply, then decided it was worth a try. "So who was the fellow you killed?"

"Bugger kept an inn. I worked for him, see? It was a coaching inn so he knew what coaches were carrying good baggage and my job was to snaffle the stuff once the coach was on the road. That and some prigging." Lawford did not like to ask what prigging was, so kept quiet. "He were a right bastard," Sharpe went on, "but that wasn't why I stuck him. It was over a girl, see? And he and I had a disagreement about who should keep her blanket warm. He lost and I'm here and God knows where the lass is now." He laughed.

"We're wasting time," Lawford said.

"Quiet!" Sharpe snapped, then picked up his musket and pointed it toward some bushes. "Is that you, lass?"

"It's me, Richard." Mary Bickerstaff emerged from the shadows carrying a bundle. "Evening, Mr. Lawford, sir," she said shyly.

"Call him Bill," Sharpe insisted, then stood and shouldered his musket. "Come on, Bill!" he said. "No point in wasting time here. There's three of us now and wise men always travel in threes, don't they? So find your bleeding star and let's be moving."

They walked all night, following Lawford's star toward the western skyline. Lawford took Sharpe aside at one point and, insisting on his ever-more precarious authority, ordered Sharpe to send the woman back. "That's an order, Sharpe," Lawford said.

"She won't go," Sharpe retorted.

"We can't take a woman!" Lawford snapped.

"Why not? Deserters always take their valuables, sir. Bill, I mean."

"Christ, Private, if you mess this up I'll make sure you get all the stripes you escaped yesterday."

Sharpe grinned. "It won't be me who messes it. It's the damn fool idea itself."

"Nonsense." Lawford strode ahead, forcing Sharpe to follow. Mary, guessing that they were arguing about her, kept a few paces behind. "There's nothing wrong with General Baird's notion," Lawford said. "We fall into the Tippoo's hands, we join his wretched army, find this man Ravi Shekhar, then leave everything to him. And just what part does Mrs. Bickerstaff play in that?" He asked the question angrily.

"Whatever part she wants," Sharpe said stubbornly.

Lawford knew he should argue, or rather that he should impose his authority on Sharpe, but he sensed he could never win. He was beginning to wonder whether it had been such a good idea to bring Sharpe after all, but from the first moment when Baird had suggested this desperate endeavor, Lawford had known he would need help and he had also known which of the Light Company's soldiers he wanted. Private Sharpe had always stood out, not just because of his height, but because he was by far the quickest-witted man in the company. But even so, Lawford had not been ready for the speed or force with which Sharpe had taken over this mission. Lawford had expected gratitude from Sharpe, and also deference; he even believed he deserved that deference purely by virtue of being an officer, but Sharpe had swiftly torn that assumption into tatters. It was rather as if Lawford had harnessed a solid-looking draught horse to his gig only to discover it was a runaway racer, but why had the racehorse insisted on bringing the filly? That offended Lawford, suggesting to him that Sharpe was taking advantage of the freedom offered by this mission. Lawford glanced at Sharpe, noting how pale and strained he looked, and he guessed that the flogging had taken far more from the Private than he realized. "I still think Mrs. Bickerstaff should go back to the army," he said gently.

"She can't," Sharpe said curtly. "Tell him, Mary."

Mary ran to catch up. "I'm not safe while Hakeswill's alive," she told Lawford.

"You could have been looked after," Lawford suggested vaguely.

"Who by?" Mary asked. "A man looks after a woman in the army and he wants his price. You know that, sir."

"Call him Bill!" Sharpe snarled. "Our lives might depend on it! If one of us calls him 'sir' then they'll feed us to their bloody tigers."

"And it isn't just Hakeswill," Mary went on. "Sergeant Green wants to marry me now, which is at least more than Hakeswill does, but I don't want either. I just want to be left in peace with Richard."

"God knows," Lawford said bitterly, "but you've probably jumped out of the frying pan into the fire."

"I'll take my chances," Mary said obstinately, though she had taken what care she could to reduce her chances of being raped. She had dressed herself in a torn dark frock and a filthy apron, both garments as drab and greasy as she could find. She had smeared ashes and dirt into her hair, but she had done nothing to disguise the lively beauty in her face. "Besides," she said to Lawford, "neither you nor Richard speak any of the languages. You need me. And I brought some more food." She hoisted the cloth bundle.

Lawford grunted. Behind them the horizon was now marked with a pale glow that silhouetted trees and bushes. He guessed they had traveled about a dozen miles and, as the pale glow turned brighter and the dawn's light seeped across the landscape, he suggested they stop and rest. Mary's bundle held a half-dozen loaves of flat unleavened bread and had two canteens of water which they shared as their breakfast. After he had eaten, Lawford went into the bushes for privacy and, as he came back, he saw Sharpe hit Mary hard in the face. "For God's sake, man," Lawford shouted, "what are you doing?"

"Blacking my eye," Mary answered. "I asked him to."

"Dear God!" Lawford said. Mary's left eye was already swelling, and tears were running down her cheeks. "Whatever for?"

"Keep the buggers off her, of course," Sharpe said. "Are you all right, love?"

"I'll live," Mary said. "You hit hard, Richard."

"No point in hitting softly. Didn't mean to hurt you, though."

Mary splashed water on her eye, then they all started walking again. They were now in an open stretch of country that was dotted with groves of bright-blossomed trees. There were no villages in sight, though they did come to an aqueduct an hour after dawn and wasted another hour trying to find a way across before simply plunging into the weed-filled water and wading through. Seringapatam lay well below the horizon, but Lawford knew the city was almost due west and he planned to angle southward until he reached the Cauvery and then follow that river to the city.

The Lieutenant's spirits were low. He had volunteered for this mission readily enough, but in the night it had begun to dawn on him just how risky the errand was. He felt lonely, too. He was only two years older than Sharpe and he envied Sharpe Mary's companionship, and he still resented the Private's lack of deference. He did not dare express that resentment, for he knew it would be scorned, but nor did he really wish to express it, for he had discovered that he wanted Sharpe's admiration rather than his deference. Lawford wanted to prove that he was as tough as the Private, and that desire kept him stoically walking on toward the horrid unknown.

Sharpe was equally worried. He liked Lawford, but suspected he would have to work hard to keep the Lieutenant out of trouble. He was a quick study, the Lieutenant, but so ignorant of the world's ways that he could easily betray the fact that he was no common soldier. As for the Tippoo, he was an unknown danger, but Sharpe was canny enough to know that he would have to do whatever the Tippoo's men wanted. He worried about Mary, too. He had persuaded her to come on this fool's errand, and she had not taken much persuading, but now she was here Sharpe was concerned that he could not protect both her and Lawford. But despite his worries he still felt free. He was, after all, off the army's leash and he reckoned he could survive so long as Lawford made no mistake, and if Sharpe survived he knew how to prosper. The rules were simple: trust no one, be ever watchful, and if trouble came hit first and hit hard. It had worked for him so far.

Mary too had doubts. She had persuaded herself she was in love with Sharpe, but she sensed a restlessness in him that made her think he might not always be in love with her. Still, she was happier here than back with the army, and that was not just because of Sergeant Hakeswill's threat but because, although the army was the only life Mary had ever known, she sensed the world could offer her more. She had grown up in Calcutta and, though her mother had been Indian, Mary had never felt at home in either the army or in India. She was neither one thing nor the other. To the army she was a *bibbi*, while to the Indians she was outside their castes, and she was acceptable to neither. She was a half-breed, suspended in a purgatory of distrust, with only her looks to help her survive, and though the army was the place that provided the friendliest company, it hardly offered a secure future. Ahead of her stretched a succession of husbands, each one succeeding as the previous one was killed in battle or else died of a fever, and when she was too old to attract another man she would be left with her children to fend as best she could. Mary, just like Sharpe, wanted to find some way up and out of that fate, but how she was to do it she did not know, though this expedition at least gave her a chance to break temporarily out of the trap.

Lawford led them to a slight hill from where, screened by flowering bushes, he scanned the country ahead. He thought he could see a gleam of water to the south and the small glimpse was sufficient to persuade him that it must be the River Cauvery. "That way," he said, "but we'll have to avoid the villages." There were two in sight, both barring the direct path to the river.

"The villagers will see us anyway," Mary said. "They don't miss much."

"We're not here to trouble them," Lawford said, "so perhaps they'll leave us alone?"

"Turn our coats, Bill," Sharpe suggested.

"Turn our coats?"

"We're running, aren't we? So put your coat on back to front as a sign that you're on the run."

"The villagers will hardly realize the significance of that," Lawford observed tartly.

"Bugger the villagers," Sharpe said. "It's the Tippoo's bloody men I'm worried about. If those bastards see red coats, they'll shoot before they ask questions." Sharpe had already undone his crossbelts and was shrugging off the wool coat, grunting with the pain that the exertion gave to his back. Lawford, watching, saw that blood had seeped through the thick bandages to stain the dirty shirt.

Lawford was reluctant to turn his coat. A turned coat was a sign of disgrace. Battalions that had let the army down in battle were sometimes forced to turn their coats as a badge of shame, but once again the Lieutenant saw the wisdom of Sharpe's argument and so he stripped and turned his coat so that its gray lining was outermost. "Maybe we shouldn't carry the muskets?" he suggested.

"No deserter would throw away his gun," Sharpe answered. He buckled his belt over the turned coat and picked up his gun and pack. He had carried the pack in his hand all night rather than have its weight press on his wounds. "Are you ready?"

"In a moment," Lawford said, then, to Sharpe's surprise, the Lieutenant went on one knee and said a silent prayer. "I don't pray often," Lawford admitted as he stood, "but maybe some help from on high would be providential today." For today, Lawford guessed, would be the day they would meet the Tippoo's patrols.

They walked south toward the gleam of water. All three were tired, and Sharpe was plainly weakened by the loss of blood, but anticipation gave them all a nervous energy. They skirted the nearest village, watched by cows with pendulous folds of skin hanging beneath their necks, then they walked through groves of cocoa trees as the sun climbed. They saw no one. A deer skittered away from their path in the late morning and an hour later an excited troupe of small monkeys scampered beside them. At midday they rested in the small shade offered by a grove of bamboos, then pressed on again beneath the baking sun. By early afternoon the river was in sight and Lawford suggested they should rest on its bank. Mary's eye had swollen and blackened, giving her the grotesque look she believed would protect her.

"I could do with a rest now," Sharpe admitted. The pain was terrible and every step was now an agony. "And I need to wet the bandages."

"Wet them?" Lawford asked.

"That's what that bastard Micklewhite said. Said to keep the bandages damp or else the stripes won't heal."

"We'll wet them at the river," Lawford promised.

But they never reached the riverbank. They were walking beside some beech trees when a shout sounded behind them and Sharpe turned to see horsemen coming from the west. They were fine-looking men in tiger-striped tunics and with spiring brass helmets who couched their lances and galloped hard toward the three fugitives. Sharpe's heart pounded. He stepped ahead of his companions and held up a hand to show they meant no harm, but the leading lancer only grinned in reply and lowered his lance point as he pricked back his spurs.

Sharpe shook his head and waved, then realized the man intended to skewer the spear into his belly. "Bastard!" Sharpe shouted, and dropped his pack and put both hands on his musket as though it was a quarterstaff. Mary screamed in terror.

"No!" Lawford shouted at the galloping lancers. "No!"

The lancer thrust his blade at Sharpe who knocked the spear point aside with the muzzle of the gun, then swung the gun fast back so that its butt smacked hard onto the horse's head. The beast whinnied and reared, throwing its rider backward. The other lancers laughed, then sawed their reins to swerve past the fallen man. Mary was shouting at them in a language Sharpe did not understand, Lawford was waving his hands desperately, but the lancers bored on in, concentrating on Sharpe who stepped backward from their wicked-looking spearpoints. He slashed a second lance aside, then a third man rammed his spurs back and attempted to drive his spear hard into Sharpe's belly. Sharpe half managed to edge away from the blow and, instead of skewering his stomach, the lance sliced through the skin of his waist, through his coat, and into the tree behind him. The lancer left his spear buried in the beech and wheeled his horse away. Sharpe was pinned to the bark, his back a sheet of agony where it was forced against the tree. He tugged at the lance, but his loss of blood had made him far too weak and the weapon would not budge, and then another lancer spurred toward him with his spearpoint aimed at Sharpe's eyes. Mary shouted frantically.

The spearpoint paused an inch from Sharpe's left eyeball. The lancer looked at Mary, grimaced at her filthy state, then said something.

Mary answered.

The lancer, who was evidently an officer, looked back to Sharpe and seemed to be debating whether to kill or to spare him. Finally he grinned, leaned down, and grasped the spear pinning Sharpe to the tree. He dragged it free.

Sharpe swore foully, then collapsed at the foot of the tree.

There were a score of horsemen and they all now gathered around the fugitives. Two of them held their razor-sharp lances at Lawford's neck while the officer spoke to Mary. She answered defiantly, and to Sharpe, who was struggling to stand, it seemed that the conversation went on for a long time. Nor did the lancers seem friendly. They were magnificent-looking men and Sharpe, despite his pain, noted how well they maintained their weapons. There was no rust on the lanceheads, and the shafts were oiled smooth. Mary argued with the officer, and he seemed indifferent to her pleading, but at last she must have made her point for she turned and looked at Lawford. "He wants to know if you're willing to serve in the Tippoo's forces," she told the Lieutenant.

The lance tips were tickling Lawford's neck, and as a recruiting device they worked wonders. The Lieutenant nodded eagerly. "Absolutely!" he said. "Just what we want! Volunteers! Tell him we're ready to serve! Both of us! Long live the Tippoo!"

The officer did not need the enthusiastic reply translated. He smiled and ordered his lancers to take their weapons from the redcoat's neck.

And thus Sharpe joined the enemy's army.

CHAPTER 5

Sharpe was near to exhausted despair by the time he reached the city. The lancers had driven the three fugitives westward at an unrelenting pace, but had offered none of them a saddle, and so the three had walked and by the time he stumbled through the ford that took them south across the Cauvery to the island on which Seringapatam was built Sharpe's back burned like a sheet of fire. The city itself still lay a mile to the west, but the whole island had been ringed with new earthworks inside which thousands of refugees were gathered. The refugees had brought their livestock, obedient to the Tippoo's orders that all food stocks should be denied to the slowly advancing British army. A half-mile from the city wall a second earthwork had been thrown up to protect a sprawling encampment of thatched, mud-brick barracks in which thousands of the Tippoo's infantry and cavalry lived. None of the troops were idle. Some were drilling, others were heightening the mud wall around the encampment, and still more were firing their muskets at targets of straw men propped against the city's stone wall. The straw men were all dressed in makeshift red coats and Lawford watched aghast as the muskets knocked the targets over or else exploded great chunks from their straw-stuffed torsos. The soldiers' families lived inside the encampment and the women and children flocked to see the two white men pass. They assumed Sharpe and Lawford were prisoners and some jeered as they went by and others laughed when Sharpe staggered in pain.

"Keep going, Sharpe," Lawford said encouragingly.

"Call me Dick, for Christ's sake," Sharpe snapped.

"Keep going, Dick," Lawford managed to say, albeit angrily for having been reproved by the Private.

"Not far now," Mary said in Sharpe's ear. She was helping Sharpe walk, though at times, when the jeering became raucous, she clung to Sharpe for support. Ahead of them were the city walls and Lawford, seeing them, wondered how anyone could hope to blast through such massive works. The great ramparts were limewashed so that they seemed to shine in the sun, and Lawford could see cannon muzzles showing in every embrasure. Cavaliers, jutting out like small square bastions, had been built everywhere along the face of the wall so that yet more guns could be brought to bear on any attacker. Above the walls, on which the Tippoo's flags stirred in the small warm wind, the twin white minarets of the city's mosque towered in the sunlight. Beyond the minarets Lawford could see the intricate tower of a Hindu temple, its stone layers elaborately carved and gorgeously painted, while just north of the temple there shone the gleaming green tiles of what Lawford supposed was the Tippoo's palace. The city was all much bigger and grander than Lawford had expected, while the white-painted wall was higher and stronger than he had ever feared. He had expected a mud wall, but as he drew closer to the ramparts he could see that these eastern walls were made from massive stone blocks that would need to be chipped away by the siege guns if a breach were ever to be made. In places, where the wall had been damaged by previous sieges, there were patches where the stone had been repaired by brickwork, but nowhere did the wall look weak. It was true that the city had not had time to build itself a modern European type of

defense with star-shaped walls and outlying forts and awkward bastions and confusing ravelins, but even so the place
looked dauntingly strong, and even now vast ant-like gangs
of laborers, some of them naked in the heat, were carrying
baskets of deep-red earth on their backs and piling the soil
to heighten the glacis that lay directly in front of the limewashed walls. The growing earthen glacis, that was separated
from the walls by a ditch that could be flooded with river
water, was designed to deflect the besiegers' shots up and
over the ramparts. Lawford consoled himself that Lord
Cornwallis had managed to smash into this formidable city
seven years before, but the heightening of the glacis demonstrated that the Tippoo had learned from that defeat and
suggested that General Harris would not find it nearly so
easy.

The lancers ducked their spired helmets as they clattered
through the tunnel of the city's Bangalore Gate and so led
the fugitives into the stinking tangle of crowded streets. The
spears forged the lancers' path, driving civilians aside and
forcing wagons and handcarts into hasty retreats up any con-
venient alley. Even the sacred cows that wandered freely
inside the city were forced aside, though the lancers did it
gently, not wanting to offend the sensibilities of the Hindus.
They passed the mosque, then turned down a street lined
with shops, their open fronts thickly hung with cloth, silk,
silver jewelery, vegetables, shoes, and hides. In one alley
Lawford caught a glimpse of bloodsoaked men butchering
two camels and the sight almost made him gag. A naked child
hurled a bloody camel's tail at the two white men, and soon
a horde of tattered, chanting children were dodging through
the lancers' horses to mock the prisoners and pelt them with
animal dung. Sharpe cursed them, Lawford hunched low as
he walked, and the children only ran away when two Euro-

pean soldiers, both dressed in blue jackets, chased them away. *"Prisonniers?"* one of the two men called cheerfully.

"Non, monsieur," Lawford answered in his best schoolboy French. *"Nous sommes déserteurs."*

"C'est bon!" The man tossed Lawford a mango. *"La femme aussi?"*

"La femme est notre prisonnière." Lawford tried a little wit and was rewarded with a laugh and a farewell shout of *bonne chance*.

"You speak French?" Sharpe asked.

"A little," Lawford claimed modestly. "Really only a little."

"Bloody amazing," Sharpe said and Lawford was obscurely pleased that he had at last succeeded in impressing his companion. "But not many private soldiers speak Frog," Sharpe dashed Lawford's pleasure, "so don't show yourself as being too good at it. Stick to bloody English."

"I didn't think of that," Lawford said ruefully. He looked at the mango as though he had never seen such a piece of fruit before, and it was plain that his hunger was tempting him to bite into the sweet flesh, but then his manners prevailed and he gallantly insisted that Mary eat the fruit instead.

The lancers turned into a delicately sculpted archway where two sentries stood guard. Once inside the archway the cavalrymen slid down from their saddles and, lances in hand, led their horses down a narrow passage between two high brick walls. Sharpe, Mary, and Lawford were more or less abandoned just inside the gateway where the two sentries ignored them, but did chase away the more curious townsfolk who had gathered to stare at the Europeans. Sharpe sat on a mounting block and tried to ignore the pain in his back. Then the lancer officer returned and shouted at them to follow him. He led them through another arch, then under an arcade where flowers twined round pillars, and so to a guardroom. The officer said something to Mary, then locked the door. "He says we're to wait," Mary said. She still had the mango, and though the lancers had stripped Sharpe and Lawford of their coats and packs and had searched the two men for coins and hidden weapons, they had not searched Mary and she took a small folding penknife from an inside pocket of her skirt and cut the fruit into three portions. Lawford ate his share, then wiped juice from his chin. "Did you ever get that picklock, Sharpe?" he asked, saw Sharpe's furious glare, and colored. "Dick," he corrected himself.

"Had it all along," Sharpe said. "Mary's got it. And she's got the guinea." He grinned despite his pain.

"You mean you lied to General Baird?" Lawford asked sternly.

"'Course I bloody lied!" Sharpe snarled. "What kind of a fool admits to having a picklock?"

For a moment Lawford looked as though he would reprove Sharpe for dishonesty, but the Lieutenant controlled the urge. He merely shook his head in mute disapproval, then sat with his back against the bare brick wall. The floor was made of small green tiles on which Sharpe lay on his belly. In minutes he was asleep. Mary sat beside him, sometimes stroking his hair and Lawford found himself embarrassed by her display of affection. He felt he ought to talk with Mary, but found he had nothing to say and so decided it was better not to speak in case he woke Sharpe. He waited. Somewhere deep in the palace a fountain splashed. Once there was a great clatter of hooves as cavalrymen led their horses out from the inner stables, but most of the time it was quiet in the room. It was also blessedly cool.

Sharpe woke after dark. He groaned as the pains in his back registered and Mary hushed him. "What time is it, love?" Sharpe asked her.

"Late."

"Jesus," Sharpe said as a stab of agony tore down his spine. He sat up, whimpering with the effort, and tried to prop himself against the wall. A wan moonlight came through the small barred window and Mary, in its dim light, could see the bloodstains spreading through the bandages and onto Sharpe's shirt. "Have they forgotten us?" Sharpe asked.

"No," Mary said. "They brought us some water while you were asleep. Here." She lifted the jug toward him. "And they gave us a bucket." She gestured across the dim cell. "For . . ." she faltered.

"I can smell what the bucket's for," Sharpe said. He took the jug and drank. Lawford was slumped against the far wall and there was a small open book face down on the floor beside the sleeping Lieutenant. Sharpe grimaced. "Glad the bugger's brought something useful," he said to Mary.

"You mean this?" Lawford said, indicating the book. He had not been asleep after all.

Sharpe wished he had not used the insult, but did not know how to retrieve it. "What is it?" he asked instead.

"A Bible."

"Bloody hell," Sharpe said.

"You don't approve?" Lawford asked icily.

"I had a bellyful of the good book when I was in the foundlings' home," Sharpe said. "If they weren't reading it to us they were hitting us round the head with it, and it wasn't some little book like that one, but a bloody great big thick thing. Could have stunned an ox, that Bible."

"Did they teach you to read it?" Lawford asked.

"We weren't reckoned good enough to read. Good enough to pick hemp, we were, but not read. No, they just read it to us at breakfast. It was the same every morning: cold porridge, tin of water, and an earful of Abraham and Isaac."

"So you can't read?" Lawford asked.

"Of course I can't read!" Sharpe laughed scornfully. "What the bloody hell's the use of reading?"

"Don't be a fool, Dick," Lawford said patiently. "Only a fool takes pride in pretending that a skill he doesn't possess is worthless." For a second Lawford was tempted to launch himself on a panegyric of reading; how it would open a new world to Sharpe, a world of drama and story and information and poetry and timeless wisdom, then he thought better of it. "You want your sergeant's stripes, don't you?" he asked instead.

"A man doesn't have to read to be a sergeant," Sharpe said stubbornly.

"No, but it helps, and you'll be a better sergeant if you can read. Otherwise the company clerks tell you what the reports say, and what the lists say, and what the punishment book says, and the quartermasters will rob you blind. But if you can read then you'll know when they're lying to you."

There was a long silence. Somewhere in the palace a sentry's footsteps echoed off stone, then came a sound so familiar that it almost made Lawford weep for homesickness. It was a clock striking the hour. Twelve o'clock. Midnight. "Is it hard?" Sharpe finally asked.

"Learning to read?" Lawford said. "Not really."

"Then you and Mary had better teach me, Bill, hadn't you?"

"Yes," Lawford said. "Yes. We had."

They were taken out of the guardroom in the morning. Four tiger-striped soldiers fetched them and pushed them down the arcade, then into a narrow corridor that seemed to run beside the kitchens, and afterward through a shadowed tangle of stables and storerooms that led to a double gate which opened into a large courtyard where the bright sun made them blink. Then Sharpe's eyes adjusted to the brilliant daylight and he saw what waited for them in the courtyard, and he swore. There were six tigers, all of them huge beasts with yellow eyes and dirty teeth. The animals stared at the three newcomers, then one of the tigers rose, arched its back, shook himself, and slowly padded toward them. "Jesus Christ!" Sharpe said, but just then the tiger's chain lifted from the dusty ground, stretched taut, and the tiger, cheated of its breakfast, growled and went back to the shadows. Another beast scratched itself, a third yawned. "Look at the size of the bastards!" Sharpe said.

"Just big pussycats," Lawford said with an insouciance he did not entirely feel.

"Then you go and scratch their chins," Sharpe said, "and see if they purr. Bugger off, you." This was to another curious beast that was straining toward him from the end of its chain. "Need a big mouse to feed one of those bastards."

"The tigers can't reach you." A voice spoke in English from behind them. "Unless their keepers release them from their chains. Good morning." Sharpe turned. A tall, middle-aged officer with a black mustache had come into the courtyard. He was a European and wore the blue uniform of France. "I am Colonel Gudin," the officer said, "and you are?"

For a moment none of them spoke, then Lawford straightened to attention. "William Lawford, sir."

"His name's Bill," Sharpe said. "I'm called Dick, and this is my woman." He put an arm round Mary's shoulder.

Gudin grimaced as he looked at Mary's swollen black eye and her filthy skirts. "You have a name"—he paused— "*Mademoiselle*?" He finally decided that was the most appropriate way to address Mary.

"Mary, sir." She made a small curtsey and Gudin returned the courtesy with an inclination of his head. "And your name?" he asked Sharpe.

"Sharpe, sir. Dick Sharpe."

"And you are deserters?" the Colonel asked with a measure of distaste.

"Yes, sir," Lawford said.

"I am never certain that deserters are to be trusted," Gudin said mildly. He was accompanied by a burly French sergeant who kept giving the tigers nervous glances. "If a man can betray one flag," Gudin observed, "why not another?"

"A man might have good reason to betray his flag, sir," Sharpe said defiantly.

"And your reason, Sharpe?"

Sharpe turned round so that the blood on his back was visible. He let Gudin stare at the stains, then turned back. "Is that good enough, sir?"

Gudin shuddered. "I never understand why the British flog their soldiers. It is barbarism." He waved irritably at the flies which buzzed about his face. "Sheer barbarism."

"You don't flog in the French army, sir?"

"Of course not," Gudin said scornfully. He put a hand on Sharpe's shoulder and turned him around again. "When was this done to you?"

"Couple of days ago, sir."

"Have you changed the bandages?"

"No, sir. Wetted them, though."

"You'll still be dead in a week unless we do something," Gudin said, then turned and spoke to the sergeant who walked briskly out of the courtyard. Gudin turned Sharpe around again. "So what had you done to deserve such barbarism, Private Sharpe?"

"Nothing, sir."

"Beyond nothing," Gudin said tiredly, as though he had heard every excuse imaginable.

"I hit a sergeant, sir."

"And you?" Gudin challenged Lawford. "Why did you run?"

"They were going to flog me, sir." Lawford was nervous telling the lie, and the nervousness intrigued Gudin.

"For doing nothing?" Gudin asked with amusement.

"For stealing a watch, sir." Lawford reddened as he spoke. "Which I did steal," he added, but most unconvincingly. He had made no effort to hide the accent that betrayed his education, though whether Gudin's ear was sufficiently attuned to English to detect the nuance was another matter.

The Frenchman was certainly intrigued by Lawford. "What did you say your name was?" the Colonel asked.

"Lawford, sir."

Gudin gave Lawford a long scrutiny. The Frenchman was tall and thin, with a lugubrious and tired face, but his eyes, Sharpe decided, were shrewd and kind. Gudin, Sharpe reckoned, was a gentleman, a proper type of officer. Like Lawford, really, and maybe that was the trouble. Maybe Gudin had already seen through Lawford's disguise. "You do not seem to me, Private Lawford, to be a typical British soldier," Gudin said, thus fulfilling Sharpe's fears. "In France, now, you would be nothing strange for we must insist that every young man serve his country, but in Britain, am I not right, you only accept the dregs of the streets? Men from the gutter?"

"Men like me," Sharpe said.

"Quiet," Gudin reproved Sharpe with a sudden authority. "I did not speak to you." The Frenchman took one of Lawford's hands and mutely inspected the soft, uncallused fingers. "How is it that you are in the army, Lawford?"

"Father went bankrupt, sir," Lawford said, conjuring the worst disaster that he could ever imagine.

"But the son of a bankrupt father can take employment, can he not?" Gudin looked again at the soft fingers, then released Lawford's hand. "And any job, surely, is better than the life of a British soldier?"

"I got drunk, sir," Lawford said miserably, "and I met a recruiting sergeant." The Lieutenant's misery was not at the imagined memory, but at the difficulty he was having in telling the lie, but his demeanor impressed Gudin. "It was in a pub, sir, in Sheffield," Lawford went on. "The Hawse in the Lake, sir. In Sheffield, sir. In Pond Lane, sir, on market day." His voice trailed away as he suddenly realized he did not know which day of the week the market was held.

"In Sheffield?" Gudin asked. "Is that not where they make iron? And—what is the word? —cutlery! You don't look like a cutler, Lawford."

"I was a lawyer's apprentice, sir." Lawford was blushing violently. He knew he had mixed up the name of the pub, though it was doubtful that Colonel Gudin would ever know the difference, but the Lieutenant was certain his lies were as transparent as a pane of glass.

"And your job in the army?" Gudin asked.

"Company clerk, sir."

Gudin smiled. "No ink on your breeches, Lawford! In our army the clerks spatter ink everywhere."

For a moment it seemed as though Lawford was about to abandon his lie and, in his misery, confess the whole truth to the Frenchman, but then the Lieutenant had a sudden inspiration. "I wear an apron, sir, when I'm writing. I don't want to be punished for a dirty uniform, sir."

Gudin laughed. In truth he had never doubted Lawford's story, mistaking the Lieutenant's embarrassment for shame at his family's bankruptcy. If anything, the Frenchman felt sorry for the tall, fair-haired, and fastidious young man who should plainly never have become a soldier, and that, to Gudin, was enough to explain Lawford's nervousness. "You're a clerk, eh? So does that mean you see paperwork?"

"A lot, sir."

"So do you know how many guns the British are bringing here?" Gudin asked. "How much ammunition?"

Lawford shook his head in consternation. For a few seconds he was speechless, then managed to say that he never saw that sort of paperwork. "It's just company papers I see, sir. Punishment books, that sort of thing."

"Bloody thousands," Sharpe interjected. "Beg pardon for speaking, sir."

"Thousands of what?" Gudin asked.

"Bullocks, sir. Six eighteen-pounder shot strapped on apiece, sir, and some of the buggers have got eight. But it's thousands of round shot."

"Two thousand? Three?" Gudin asked.

"More than that, sir. I ain't seen a herd the size of it, not even when the Scots drive the beeves down from Scotland to London."

Gudin shrugged. He very much doubted whether these two could tell him anything useful, certainly nothing that the Tippoo's scouts and spies had not already discovered, but the questions had to be asked. Now, waving flies from his face, he told the two deserters what they might expect. "His Majesty the Tippoo Sultan will decide your fate, and if he is merciful he will want you to serve in his forces. I assume you are willing?"

"Yes, sir," Sharpe said eagerly. "It's why we came, sir."

"Good," Gudin said. "The Tippoo might want you in one of his own *cushoons*. That's the word they use for a regiment here, a *cushoon*. They're all good soldiers and well-trained, and you'll be made welcome, but there is one disadvantage. You will both have to be circumcised."

Lawford went pale, while Sharpe just shrugged. "Is that bad, sir?"

"You know what circumcision is, Private?"

"Something the army does to you, sir? Like swear you in?"

Gudin smiled. "Not quite, Sharpe. The Tippoo is a Muslim and he likes his foreign volunteers to join his religion. It means one of his holy men will cut your foreskin off. It's quite quick, just like slicing the top from a soft-boiled egg, really."

"My prick?" Sharpe was as aghast as Lawford now.

"It's over in seconds," Gudin reassured them, "though the bleeding can last for a while and you cannot, how shall I say . . . ?" He glanced at Mary, then back to Sharpe. "You can't let the egg become hard boiled for a few weeks."

"Bloody hell, sir!" Sharpe said. "For religion? They do that?"

"We Christians sprinkle babies with water," Gudin said, "and the Muslims chop off foreskins." The Frenchman paused, then smiled. "However, I cannot think that a man with a bleeding prick will make a good soldier, and your armies will be here in a few days, so I will suggest to His Majesty that the two of you serve with my men. We are few, but none of us are Muslims, and all of our soft-boiled eggs retain their full shells."

"Quite right too, sir," Sharpe said enthusiastically. "And it'll be an honor to serve you, sir," he added.

"In a French battalion?" Gudin teased him.

"If you don't flog, sir, and you don't carve up pricks, then it'll be more than an honor."

"If the Tippoo allows it," Gudin warned them, "which he may not. But I think he might. I have other Britishers in the battalion, and some Germans and Swiss. I'm sure you will be happy there." He looked at Mary. "But what of you, *Mademoiselle*?"

Mary touched Sharpe's elbow. "I came with Richard, sir."

Gudin inspected her black eye. "How did that happen, *Mademoiselle*?"

"I fell, sir," Mary said.

Gudin's face flickered with a smile. "Or did Private Sharpe hit you? So that you would not appear attractive?"

"I fell over, sir."

Gudin nodded. "You hit hard, Private Sharpe."

"No point else, sir."

"That is true," Gudin said, then shrugged. "My men have their women. If His Majesty allows it I don't see why the two of you should not stay together." He turned as his sergeant reappeared, bringing with him an elderly Indian who carried a cloth-covered basket. "This is Doctor Venkatesh," Gudin said, greeting the doctor with a bow, "and he is quite as good as any physician I ever found in Paris. I imagine, Sharpe, that removing those filthy bandages will hurt?"

"Not as much as circumscribing, sir."

Gudin laughed. "All the same, I think you had better sit down."

Removing the bandages hurt like buggery. Mister Micklewhite, the surgeon, had put a salve on the lashes, but no army surgeon ever wasted too much precious ointment on a common soldier, and Micklewhite had not used enough salve to stop the bandages from crusting to the wounds and so the cloth had become one clotted mass of linen and dried blood that tore the scabs away from the wounds as the Indian peeled the bandages away. Doctor Venkatesh was indeed skillful and gentle and his voice was ever-soothing in Sharpe's ear as he delicately prized the horrid mess away from the torn flesh, but even so Sharpe could not forbear from whimpering as the bandages were lifted. The tigers, smelling fresh blood, lunged at their chains so that the courtyard was filled with the clank and snap of stretching links.

The Indian doctor plainly disapproved of both the injury and the treatment. He tutted and muttered and shook his head as the carnage was revealed. Then, when he had picked the last filthy scrap of bandage away with a pair of ivory tweezers, he poured an unguent over Sharpe's back and the cool liquid was wonderfully soothing. Sharpe sighed with relief, then suddenly the doctor sprang away from him, stood, clasped his hands, and bowed low.

Sharpe twisted round to see that a group of Indians had come into the courtyard. At their head was a shortish plump man, maybe fifty years old, with a round face and a neatly trimmed black mustache. He was dressed in a white silk tunic above white silk leggings and black leather boots, but the simple clothes glittered with jewels. He wore rubies on his turban, diamond-studded bangles on his arms, and pearls were sewn onto his blue silk sash from which there hung a sapphire-studded scabbard in which rested a sword with a golden hilt fashioned into the face of a snarling tiger. Doctor Venkatesh backed hurriedly away, still bowing, while Gudin stood respectfully at attention. "The Tippoo!" Gudin warned Sharpe and Lawford in a whisper, and Sharpe struggled to his feet and, like the Frenchman, stood to attention.

The Tippoo stopped a half-dozen paces short of Sharpe and Lawford. He stared at them for a few seconds, then spoke softly to his interpreter. "Turn around," the interpreter ordered Sharpe.

Sharpe obediently turned, showing his back to the Tippoo, who, fascinated by the open wounds, stepped close so he could inspect the damage. Sharpe could feel the Tippoo's breath on the back of his neck, he could smell the man's subtle perfume, and then he felt a spider-soft touch as the Tippoo fingered a strip of hanging skin.

Then a sudden pain like the blow of a red-hot poker slammed through Sharpe. He almost cried aloud, but instead he stiffened and flinched. The Tippoo had thrust the tiger hilt of his sword against the deepest wound to see Sharpe's reaction. He ordered Sharpe to turn around and peered up to see whether there were any tears showing. Tears were pricking at Sharpe's eyes, but none spilt onto his cheeks.

The Tippoo nodded approval and stepped back. "So tell me about them," he ordered Gudin.

"Ordinary deserters," Gudin said in French to the interpreter. "That one"—he indicated Sharpe—"is a tough soldier who'd probably be a credit to any army. The other one's just a clerk."

Lawford tried not to show his disapproval of the judgement. The Tippoo glanced at him, saw nothing to interest him, and looked at Mary instead. "The woman?" he asked Gudin.

"She's with the tall one," Gudin said, again indicating Sharpe, then waited as the interpreter turned his answer into Persian.

The Tippoo gave Mary a brief inspection. She was slouching, trying to accentuate her drab, bruised, and dirty appearance, but when she saw his pensive gaze she became flustered and tried to make a curtsy. The Tippoo seemed amused by the gesture, then looked back to Gudin. "So what do they know of the British plans?" he asked, gesturing at Lawford and Sharpe.

"Nothing."

"They say they know nothing," the Tippoo corrected Gudin. "And they're not spies?"

Gudin shrugged. "How can one tell? But I think not."

"I think we can tell," the Tippoo said. "And I think we can discover what kind of soldiers they are too." He turned and rapped some orders to an aide, who bowed, then ran out of the courtyard.

The aide returned with a pair of hunting muskets. The long-barrelled weapons were like no guns Sharpe had ever seen, for their stocks were crusted with jewels and inlaid with a delicate ivory filigree. The jewelled butts had an extravagant flair at their shoulder pieces and the two guns' trigger guards were rimmed with small rubies. The dogheads that held the flints had been fashioned into tiger heads with diamonds for the tigers' eyes. The Tippoo took the guns, made sure their flints were properly seated within the tiger jaws, then tossed one gun to Lawford and the other to Sharpe. The aide then placed a pot filled with black powder on the ground and beside it a pair of musket balls that Sharpe could have sworn were made of silver. "Load the guns," the interpreter said.

A British soldier, like any other, learned to load with a paper cartridge, but there was no mystery about using naked powder and ball. Plainly the Tippoo wished to see how proficient the two men were and, while Lawford hesitated, Sharpe stooped to the pot and took out a handful of powder. He straightened up and let the black powder trickle down the gun's chased barrel. The powder was extraordinarily fine and a fair bit blew away on the small wind, but he had enough to spare and, once the charge was safe inside the barrel, he stooped again, picked up the bullet, shoved it into the muzzle, and scraped the ramrod out of its three golden hoops. He twirled the ramrod, let it slide through his hand onto the bullet, and then slammed the missile hard down onto the powder charge. The Tippoo had provided no wadding, but Sharpe guessed it did not matter. He pulled the ramrod out, reversed it, and let it fall into the precious loops beneath the long barrel. Then he stooped again, took a pinch of powder, primed the gun, closed the frizzen, and stood to attention with the gun's jeweled butt grounded beside him. "Sir!" he said, signifying he was done.

Lawford was still trying to trickle powder into the muzzle. The Lieutenant was just as proficient at loading a gun as Sharpe, but being an officer he was never required to do it quickly, for that was the one indispensable skill of a private soldier. Lawford only loaded guns while hunting, but in the army he had a servant who loaded his pistols and never in his life had he needed to be quick with a gun and now he demonstrated a lamentable slowness. "He was a clerk, sir," Sharpe explained to Gudin. He paused to lick the powder residue off his fingers. "He never needed to fight, like."

The interpreter translated the words for the Tippoo who waited patiently as Lawford finished loading the musket. The Tippoo, like his entourage, was amused at the Englishman's slowness, but Sharpe's explanation that Lawford had been a clerk seemed to convince them. Lawford at last finished and, very self-consciously, stood to attention.

"You can evidently load," the Tippoo said to Sharpe, "but can you shoot?"

"Aye, sir," Sharpe answered the interpreter.

The Tippoo pointed over Sharpe's shoulder. "Then shoot him."

Sharpe and Lawford both turned to see an elderly British officer being escorted through the courtyard's gate. The man was weak and pale, and he stumbled as the bright sunlight struck his eyes. He cuffed with a manacled hand at his face, then looked up and recognized Lawford. For a second an expression of disbelief crossed his face, then he managed to hide whatever emotion he was feeling. The officer was white-haired and dressed in a kilt and red jacket, both garments stained with dust and damp, and Sharpe, horrified to see a British officer so dishevelled and humiliated, presumed this had to be Colonel McCandless.

"You can't shoot . . . " Lawford began.

"Shut up, Bill," Sharpe said and brought the musket up to his shoulder and swung its muzzle to face the horrified Scots officer.

"Wait!" Gudin shouted, then spoke urgently to the Tippoo.

The Tippoo laughed away Gudin's protest. Instead he had his interpreter ask Sharpe what he thought about British officers.

"Scum, sir," Sharpe said loudly enough for Colonel McCandless to hear. "Goddamn bloody scum, sir. Think they're better than us because the bastards can read and were born with a bit of money, but there ain't one I couldn't beat in a fight."

"You are willing to shoot that one?" the interpreter asked.

"I'd pay for the chance," Sharpe said vengefully. Lawford hissed at him, but Sharpe ignored the warning. "Pay for it," he said again.

"His Majesty would like you to do it very close," the interpreter said. "He wants you to blow the man's head off."

"It'll be a bloody pleasure," Sharpe said enthusiastically. He cocked the gun as he walked toward the man he presumed he had been sent to save. He stared at McCandless as he approached and there was nothing but brute pleasure on Sharpe's hard face. "Stuck-up Scotch bastard," Sharpe spat at him. He looked at the two guards who still flanked the Colonel. "Move out the way, you stupid sods, else you'll be smothered in the bastard's blood." The two men stared blankly at him, but neither moved and Sharpe guessed that neither man spoke any English. Doctor Venkatesh, who had been trying to hide in the gateway's shadows, shook his head in horror at what was about to happen.

Sharpe raised the musket so that its muzzle was no more than six inches from McCandless's face. "Any message for General Harris?" he asked softly.

McCandless again hid his reaction, other than sparing one glance at Lawford. Then he looked back to Sharpe and spat at him. "Attack anywhere but from the west," the Scotsman said quietly, and then, much louder, "May God forgive you."

"Bugger God," Sharpe said, then pulled the trigger. The

flint fell, it snapped its spark on the frizzen, and nothing else happened. McCandless's face jerked back as the flint sparked, then an expression of pure relief crossed his face. Sharpe hesitated a second, then drove the gun's muzzle into the Colonel's belly. The blow looked hard, but he checked it at the last moment. McCandless still doubled over, gasping, and Sharpe raised the jeweled butt to bring it hard down on the officer's gray head.

"Stop!" Gudin shouted.

Sharpe paused and turned. "I thought you wanted the bugger dead."

The Tippoo laughed. "We need him alive for a while. But you passed your test." He turned and spoke to Gudin, and Gudin answered vigorously. It seemed to Sharpe that they were discussing his fate, and he prayed he would be spared a painful initiation into one of the Tippoo's *cushoons*. Another Indian officer, a tall man in a silk tunic decorated with the Tippoo's tiger stripes, was talking to Mary while Sharpe still stood above the crouching McCandless.

"Did Harris send you?" McCandless asked softly.

"Yes," Sharpe hissed, not looking at the Colonel. Mary was shaking her head. She glanced at Sharpe, then looked back to the tall Indian.

"Beware the west," McCandless whispered. "Nothing else." The Scotsman groaned, pretending to be in much more pain than he was. He retched dryly, tried to stand, and instead toppled over. "You're a traitor," he said loudly enough for Gudin to hear him, "and you'll die a traitor's death."

Sharpe spat on McCandless. "Come here, Sharpe!" Gudin, disapproval plain in his voice, ordered him.

Sharpe marched back to Lawford's side where one of the Tippoo's attendants took back the two muskets. The Tippoo gestured at McCandless's guards, evidently signifying that the Scotsman was to be returned to his cell. The Tippoo then gave Sharpe an approving nod before turning and leading his entourage out of the courtyard. The tall Indian in the silk tiger stripes beckoned to Mary.

"I'm to go with him, love," she explained to Sharpe.

"I thought you were staying with me!" Sharpe protested.

"I'm to earn my keep," she said. "I'm to teach his little sons English. And sweep and wash, of course," she added bitterly.

Colonel Gudin intervened. "She will join you later," he told Sharpe. "But for now you are both, how do you say it? On test?"

"Probation, sir?" Lawford offered.

"Exactly," Gudin said. "And soldiers on probation are not permitted wives. Don't worry, Sharpe. I'm sure your woman will be safe in General Rao's house. Now go, *Mademoiselle*."

Mary stood on tiptoe and kissed Sharpe's cheek. "I'll be all right, love," she whispered, "and so will you."

"Look after yourself, lass," Sharpe said, and watched her follow the tall Indian officer out of the courtyard.

Gudin gestured toward the archway. "We must let Doctor Venkatesh finish your back, Sharpe, then give you both new uniforms and muskets. Welcome to the Tippoo Sultan's army, gentlemen. You earn a *haideri* each every day."

"Good money!" Sharpe said, impressed. A *haideri* was worth half a crown, far above the miserable tuppence a day he received in the British army.

"But doubtless in arrears," Lawford said sarcastically. He was still angry at Sharpe for having tried to shoot McCandless, and the musket's misfire had not placated him.

"The pay is always in arrears," Gudin admitted cheerfully, "but in what army is the pay ever on time? Officially you earn a *haideri* a day, though you will rarely receive it, but I can promise you other consolations. Now come." He summoned

Doctor Venkatesh who retrieved his basket and followed Gudin out of the palace.

Thus Sharpe went to meet his new comrades and readied himself to face a new enemy: his own side.

General David Baird did not feel guilty about Sharpe and Lawford, for they were soldiers and were paid to take risks, but he did feel responsible for them. The fact that neither the British nor Indian cavalry patrols had discovered the two men suggested that they might well have reached Seringapatam, but the more Baird thought about their mission the less sanguine he was about its successful completion. It had seemed a good idea when he had first thought of it, but two days' reflection had diluted that initial hope with a score of reservations. He had always suspected that even with the help of Ravi Shekhar their chances of rescuing McCandless were woefully small, but at the very least he had hoped they might learn McCandless's news and succeed in bringing it out of the city, but now he feared that neither man would even survive. At best, he thought, the two men could only hope to escape execution by joining the Tippoo's forces, which would mean that both Sharpe and Lawford would be in enemy uniform when the British assaulted the city. There was little Baird could do about that, but he could prevent a dreadful miscarriage of justice following the city's fall, and so that night, when the two armies' great encampment was established just a few days' march from their goal, Baird sought out the lines of the 33rd.

Major Shee seemed alarmed at the General's sudden appearance, but Baird soothed the Major and explained he had a little business with the Light Company. "Nothing to trouble you, Major. Just an administrative matter. A triviality."

"I'll take you to Captain Morris, sir," Shee said, then

clapped on his hat and led the General down the line of officers' tents. "It's the end one, sir," he said nervously. "Do you need me at all?"

"I wouldn't waste your time, Shee, on trifles, but I'm obliged for your help, though."

Baird found a shirt-sleeved Captain Morris frowning at his paperwork in the company of an oddly malevolent-looking sergeant who, at the General's unannounced arrival, sprang to quivering attention. Morris hastily placed his cocked hat over a tin mug that Baird suspected was full of arrack. "Captain Morris?" the General asked.

"Sir!" Morris upset his chair as he stood up, then he plucked his red coat off the floor where it had fallen with the chair.

Baird waved to show that Morris need not worry about donning a coat. "There's no need for formality, Captain. Leave your coat off, man, leave it off. It's desperately hot, isn't it?"

"Unbearable, sir," Morris said nervously.

"I'm Baird," Baird introduced himself. "I don't think we've had the pleasure?"

"No, sir." Morris was too nervous to introduce himself properly.

"Sit you down, man," Baird said, trying to put the Captain at his ease. "Sit you down. May I?" Baird gestured at Morris's cot, asking permission to use it as a chair. "Thank you kindly," Baird said, then he sat, took off his plumed hat, and fanned his face with its brim. "I think I've forgotten what cold weather is like. Do you think it still snows anywhere? My God, but it saps a man, this heat. Saps him. Do relax, Sergeant."

"Thank you, sir." Sergeant Hakeswill's stiff posture unbent a fraction.

Baird smiled at Morris. "You lost two men this week, Captain, did you not?"

"Two men?" Morris frowned. That bastard Sharpe had run, taking his *bibbi* with him, but who else? "Oh!" Morris said. "You mean Lieutenant Lawford, sir?"

"The very fellow. A lucky fellow too, eh? Carrying the dispatch to Madras. It's quite an honor for him." Baird shook his head ruefully. "Myself, I'm not so certain that little scrap the other day was worth a dispatch, but General Harris insisted and your Colonel chose Lawford." Baird was using the excuse the army had invented to explain Lawford's disappearance. The excuse had provoked some resentment in the 33rd for Lawford was one of the most junior of the battalion's lieutenants and most men who carried dispatches could expect a promotion as a reward for the task which, in turn, was usually only given to men who had distinguished themselves in battle. It seemed to Morris, as to every other officer in the battalion, that Lawford had neither distinguished himself nor deserved promotion, but Morris could hardly admit as much to Baird.

"Very glad for him," Morris managed to say.

"Found a replacement, have you?" Baird asked.

"Ensign Fitzgerald, sir," Morris said. "Lieutenant Fitzgerald now, sir, by brevet, of course." Morris managed to sound disapproving. He would have much preferred Ensign Hicks to have received the temporary promotion, but Hicks did not have the hundred and fifty pounds needed to purchase up from ensign to lieutenant, whereas Fitzgerald did, and if Lawford's reward for carrying the dispatches was a promotion to captain then Fitzgerald must replace him. In Morris's opinion the newly breveted Lieutenant was altogether too easy with the men, but a money draft was a money draft, and Fitzgerald was the monied candidate and so had been given the temporary rank.

"And the other fellow you lost?" Baird asked, trying hard to sound casual. "The private? In the book, is he?"

"He's in the book all right, sir." The Sergeant answered for Morris. "Hakeswill, sir," he introduced himself. "Sergeant Obadiah Hakeswill, sir, man and boy in the army, sir, and at your command, sir."

"What was the rogue's name?" Baird asked Morris.

"Sharpe, sir." Hakeswill again answered. "Richard Sharpe, sir, and as filthy horrible a little piece of work as ever I did see, sir, in all my born days, sir."

"The book?" Baird asked Morris, ignoring Hakeswill's judgement.

Morris frantically searched the mess on his desk for the Punishment Book, at the back of which were kept the army's official forms for deserters. Hakeswill eventually found it, and, with a crisp gesture, handed it to the General. "Sir!"

Baird leafed through the front pages, finally discovering the entry for Sharpe's court martial. "Two thousand strokes!" the Scotsman said in horror. "It must have been a grave offence?"

"Struck a sergeant, sir!" Hakeswill announced.

"You, perhaps?" Baird asked drily, noting the Sergeant's swollen and bruised nose.

"Without any provocation, sir," Hakeswill said earnestly. "As God is my judge, sir, I never treated young Dick Sharpe with anything but kindness. Like one of my own children he was, sir, if I had any children, which I don't, at least not so as I knows of. He was a very lucky man, sir, to be let off at two hundred lashes, and you see how he rewards us?" Hakeswill sniffed indignantly.

Baird did not respond, but just turned to the last page of the book where he found the name Richard Sharpe filled in at the top of the printed form, and beneath it Sharpe's age which was given as twenty-two years and six months, though

Captain Morris, if indeed it had been Morris who had filled
in the form, had placed a question mark beside the age.
Sharpe's height was reported at six feet, only four inches less
than Baird himself who was one of the tallest men in the
army. "Make or Form" was the next question, to which Morris had answered "well built," and there followed a list of
headings: Head, Face, Eyes, Eyebrows, Nose, Mouth, Neck,
Hair, Shoulders, Arms, Hands, Thighs, Legs, and Feet. Morris had filled them all in, thus offering a comprehensive
description of the missing man. "Where Born?" was
answered simply by "London," while beside "Former Trade
or Occupation" was written "Thief." The form then gave the
date and place of desertion and offered a description of the
clothes the deserter had been wearing when last seen. The
final item on the form was "General Remarks," beside which
Morris had written "Back scarred from flogging. A dangerous
man." Baird shook his head. "A formidable description, Captain," the general said.

"Thank you, sir."

"It's been distributed?"

"Tomorrow, sir." Morris blushed. The form should have
been copied out four times. One copy went to the General
commanding the army, who would have it copied again and
distributed to every unit under his command. A second copy
would go to Madras in case Sharpe ran there. A third copy
went to the War Office in London to be copied again and
given to all recruiting officers in case the man succeeded in
reaching Britain and tried to rejoin the army, while the last
copy was supposedly sent to the man's home parish to alert
his neighbors to his treachery and the local constables to his
crime. In Sharpe's case, there was no home parish, but once
Morris caught up with his paperwork and the company clerk
had made the necessary copies, Sharpe's description would
be broadcast throughout the army. If Sharpe was then found

in Seringapatam, which Baird suspected he would be, he was supposed to be arrested, but it was far more likely that he would be killed. Most soldiers resented deserters, not because of their crime, but because they had dared to do what so many others never had the courage to try, and no officer would punish a man for killing a deserter.

Baird put the open book onto Morris's table. "I want you to add a note under 'General Remarks,'" Baird told the Captain.

"Of course, sir."

"Just say that it is vital that Private Sharpe be taken alive. And that if he is captured he must be brought either to me or to General Harris."

Morris gaped at Baird. "You, sir?"

"Baird, B-A-I-R-D. Major General."

"Yes, sir, but . . ." Morris had been about to ask what possible business a major general had with a deserter, then realized that such a question would never fetch a civil answer, so he just dipped a quill in ink and hurriedly added the words Baird had requested. "You think we might see Sharpe again, sir?" he asked.

"I do hope so, Captain." Baird stood. "I even pray as much. Now may I thank you for your hospitality?"

"Yes, sir, of course, sir." Morris half stood as the General left, then dropped back onto his chair and stared at the words he had just written. "What in God's name is all that about?" he asked when Baird was safely out of earshot.

Hakeswill sniffed. "No good, sir, I'll warrant that."

Morris uncovered the arrack and took a sip. "First the bastard is summoned to Harris's tent, then he runs, and now Baird says we'll see him again and wants him kept alive! Why?"

"He's up to no good, sir," Hakeswill said. "He took his woman and vanished, sir. Ain't no general who can condone that behavior, sir. It's unforgivable, sir. The army's going to the dogs, sir."

"I can't disobey Baird," Morris muttered.

"But you don't wants Sharpie back here either, sir," Hakeswill said fervently. "A soldier who's a general's pet? He'll be given a sergeant's stripes next!" The thought of such an affront struck Hakeswill momentarily speechless. His face quivered with indignation, then, with a visible effort, he controlled himself. "Who knows, sir," he suggested slyly, "but the little bastard might be reporting on you and me, sir, like the traitor what he is. We don't need snakes in our bosoms, sir. We don't want to disturb the happy mood of the company, not by harboring a general's pet, sir."

"General's pet?" Morris repeated softly. The Captain was a venal man and, though no worse than many, he nevertheless dreaded official scrutiny, but he was far too lazy to correct the malfeasances half-concealed in the closely-penned columns of the pay books. Worse, Morris feared that Sharpe could somehow reveal his complicity in the false charge that had resulted in Sharpe's flogging, and though it seemed impossible for a mere private to carry that much weight in the army, so it seemed equally impossible that a major general should make a special errand to discuss that private. There was something very odd going on, and Morris disliked strange threats. He merely asked for the quiet life, and he wanted Sharpe out of it. "But I can't leave those words off the form," he complained to Hakeswill, gesturing at the new addition on Sharpe's page.

"Don't need to, sir. With respect, sir. Ain't no form being distributed here, sir, not in the 33rd, sir. Don't need a form, do we? We knows what the bugger looks like, we does, so they won't give us no form, sir. They never do, sir. So I'll let it be known that if anyone sees Sharpie they're to oblige the army by putting a goolie in his back." Hakeswill saw Morris's nervousness. "Won't be no fuss, sir, not if the bugger's in Seringapatam and we're pulling the bloody place to pieces. Kill him quick, sir, and that's more than he deserves. He's up to no good, sir, I can feel it in my waters, and a bugger up to no good is a bugger better off dead. Says so in the scriptures, sir."

"I'm sure it does, Sergeant, I'm sure it does," Morris said, then closed the Punishment Book. "You must do whatever you think is best, Sergeant. I know I can trust you."

"You do me honor, sir," Hakeswill said with feigned emotion. "You do me honor. And I'll have the bastard for you, sir, have him proper dead."

In Seringapatam.

"What in God's name did you think you were doing, Sharpe?" Lawford demanded furiously. The lieutenant was much too angry to go along with the pretence of being a private, and, besides, the two men were now alone for the first time that day. Alone, but not unguarded, for though they were standing sentry in one of the south wall cavaliers there were a dozen men of Gudin's battalion within sight, including the burly Sergeant, called Rothière, who watched the two newcomers from the next cavalier along. "By God, Private," Lawford hissed, "I'll have you flogged for that display when we're back! We're here to rescue Colonel McCandless, not to kill him! Are you mad?"

Sharpe stared south across the landscape, saying nothing. To his right the shallow river flowed between shelving green banks. Once the monsoon came the river would swell and spread and drown the wide flat rocks that dotted its bed. He was feeling more comfortable now, for Doctor Venkatesh had placed some salve on his back which had taken away a lot of the pain. The doctor had then put on new bandages and warned Sharpe that they must not be dampened, but ought to be changed each day until the wounds healed.

Colonel Gudin had then taken the two Englishmen to a barracks room close by the city's southwestern corner. Every man in the barracks was a European, most of them French, but with a scattering of Swiss, Germans and two Britishers. They all wore the blue coats of French infantry, but there were none to spare for the two new men, and so Sergeant Rothière had issued Sharpe and Lawford with tiger tunics like those the Tippoo's men wore. The tunics did not open down the front like a European coat, but had to be pulled over the head. "Where you boys from?" an English voice asked Sharpe as he pulled down the dyed-cotton tunic.

"33rd," Sharpe had said.

"The Havercakes?" the man said. "Thought they were up north, in Calcutta?"

"Brought down to Madras last year," Sharpe said. He gingerly sat on his cot, an Indian bed made from ropes stretched between a simple wooden frame. It proved surprisingly comfortable. "And you?" he asked the Englishman.

"Royal bleeding Artillery, mate, both of us. Ran three months back. Name's Johnny Blake and that's Henry Hickson."

"I'm Dick Sharpe and that's Bill Lawford," Sharpe said, introducing the Lieutenant who looked desperately awkward in his knee-length tunic of purple and white stripes. Over the tunic he wore two crossbelts and an ordinary belt from which hung a bayonet and a cartridge pouch. They had been issued with heavy French muskets and warned they would have to do their share of sentry duty with the rest of the small battalion.

"Used to be a lot more of us," Blake told Sharpe, "but men die here like flies. Fever mostly."

"But it ain't bad here," Henry Hickson offered. "Food's

all right. Plenty of *bibbis* and Gudin's a real decent officer. Better than any we ever had."

"Right bastards we had," Blake agreed.

"Aren't they all?" Sharpe had said.

"And the pay's good, when you get it. Five months over-due now, but maybe we'll get it when we beat the stuffing out of the British." Blake laughed at the suggestion.

Blake and Hickson were not required to stand guard, but instead manned one of the big tiger-mouthed guns that crouched behind a nearby embrasure. Sharpe and Lawford stood their watch alone and it was that privacy which had encouraged Lawford into his furious attack. "Have you got nothing to say for yourself, Private?" he challenged Sharpe who still stared serenely over the green landscape through which the river curled south about the city's island. "Well?" Lawford snapped.

Sharpe looked at him. "You loaded the musket, didn't you, Bill?"

"Of course!"

"You ever felt gunpowder that smooth and fine?" Sharpe gazed into the Lieutenant's face.

"It could have been gunpowder dust!" Lawford insisted angrily.

"That shiny?" Sharpe said derisively. "Gunpowder dust is full of rat shit and sawdust! And did you really think, Bill"—he pronounced the name sarcastically—"that the bleeding Tippoo would let us have loaded guns before he was sure he could trust us? And with him standing not six feet away? And did you bother to taste the powder? I did, and it weren't salty at all. That weren't gunpowder, Lieuten-ant, that were either ink powder or black pigment, but what-ever it was it was never going to spark."

Lawford gaped at Sharpe. "So you knew all along the gun wouldn't fire?"

"Of course I bloody knew! I wouldn't have pulled the trigger else. You mean you didn't realize that weren't powder?"

Lawford turned away. Once again he had been made to look like a fool and he blushed at the realization. "I'm sorry," he said. He was crestfallen, and again he felt a galling sense of inadequacy compared to this common soldier.

Sharpe stared at a patrol of the Tippoo's lancers who were riding back toward the city. Three of them were wounded and were being supported in their saddles by their comrades, which suggested the British were not so very far away now. "I'm sorry, sir," he said very softly, and deliberately using the word "sir" to mollify Lawford, "but I'm not trying to be insolent. I'm just trying to keep you and me alive."

"I know. I'm sorry too. I should have known it wasn't powder."

"It was confusing, weren't it?" Sharpe said, trying to console his companion. "What with the Tippoo being there. Fat little bugger, ain't he? But you're doing all right, sir." Sharpe spoke feelingly, knowing that the young Lieutenant desperately needed encouragement. "And you were clever as hell, sir, saying you wore an apron. I should have splashed some ink on your uniform, shouldn't I? But I never thought of it, but you got us out of that one."

"I was thinking of Private Brookfield," Lawford said, not without some pride at the memory of his inspired lie. "You know Brookfield?"

"The clerk of Mister Stanbridge's company, sir? Fellow who wears spectacles? Does he wear a pinny?"

"He says it keeps the ink off him."

"He always was an old woman," Sharpe said scornfully, "but you did well. And I'll tell you something else. We have to get out of here soon because I know why we came now. We don't have to find your merchant fellow, we just have to get out. Unless you think we ought to rescue your uncle, but if you don't, then we can just run, because I know why we came now."

Lawford gaped at him. "You know?"

"The Colonel spoke to me, sir, while we was going through that pantomime back there in the palace. He says we're to tell General Harris to avoid the west wall. Nothing else, just that."

Lawford stared at Sharpe, then glanced across the angle of the city walls toward the western defenses, but nothing he could see there looked strange or suspicious. "You'd better stop calling me 'sir,'" he said. "Are you sure about what he said?"

"He said it twice. Avoid the west wall."

A bellow from the next cavalier made them turn. Rothière was pointing south, suggesting that the two Englishmen watch that direction as they were supposed to instead of gaping like yokels toward the west. Sharpe obediently stared southward, though there was nothing to be seen there except some women carrying loads on their heads and a thin naked boy herding some scrawny cattle along the riverbank. His duty now, Sharpe thought, was to escape this place and get back to the British army, but how in God's name was he ever to do that? If he were to jump off the wall now, Sharpe reckoned, he would stand a half-chance of breaking a leg, and even if he survived the jump he would only land in the glacis ditch, and if he managed to cross the glacis he would merely reach the military encampment that was built hard around the city's southern and eastern walls, and if he was lucky enough to escape the hundreds of soldiers who would converge on him, he would still need to cross the river, and meanwhile every gun on the encampment wall would be hammering at his heels, and once he had crossed the river, if he ever did, the Tippoo's lancers would be waiting on the far bank. The sheer impossibility of escaping the city made him smile. "God knows how we'll ever get out of here," he said to Lawford.

"Maybe at night?" Lawford suggested vaguely.

"If they ever let us stand guard at night," Sharpe said dubiously, then thought of Mary. Could he leave her in the city?

"So what do we do?" Lawford asked.

"What we always do in the army," Sharpe said stoically. "Hurry up and do nothing. Wait for the opportunity. It'll come, it'll come. And in the meantime, maybe we can find out just what the devils are doing in the west of the city, eh?"

Lawford shuddered. "I'm glad I brought you, Sharpe."

"You are?" Sharpe grinned at that compliment. "I'll tell you when I'll be glad. When you take me back home to the army." And suddenly, after weeks of thinking about desertion, Sharpe realized that what he had just said was true. He did want to go back to the army, and that knowledge surprised him. The army had bored Richard Sharpe, then done its best to break his spirits. It had even flogged him, but now, standing on Seringapatam's battlements, he missed the army.

For at heart, as Richard Sharpe had just discovered for himself, he was a soldier.

CHAPTER 6

The armies of Britain and Hyderabad reached Seringapatam four days later. The first evidence of their coming was a cloud of dust that thickened and rose to obscure the eastern horizon, a great fog of dust kicked up by thousands of hooves, boots, and wheels. The two armies had crossed the river well to the city's east and were now on its southern bank and Sharpe climbed with the rest of Gudin's men to the firestep above the Mysore gate to watch the first British cavalry patrols appear in the distance. A torrent of lancers clattered out of the gate to challenge the invaders. The Tippoo's men rode with green and scarlet pennants on their lanceheads and beneath silk banners showing the golden sun blazoned against a scarlet field. Once the lancers had passed through the gate a succession of painted ox carts squealed and ground their way into the city, each loaded with rice, grain, or beans. There was plenty of water inside Seringapatam, for not only did the River Cauvery wash beneath two of the walls, but each street had its own well, and now the Tippoo was making certain that the granaries were filled to overflowing. The city's magazines were already crammed with ammunition. There were guns in every embrasure and, behind the walls, spare guns waited to replace any that were dismounted. Sharpe had never seen so many guns. The Tippoo Sultan had great faith in artillery and he had collected cannon of every shape and size. There were guns with barrels disguised as crouching tigers, and guns inscribed with flowing Arabic letters, and guns supplied from France, some still with the ancient Bourbon cipher incised close to their touchholes. There were huge guns with barrels over twenty feet long that fired stone balls close to fifty pounds in weight and small guns, scarce longer than a musket, that fired individual balls of grape. The Tippoo intended to meet any British assault with a storm of cannon fire.

And not just cannon fire, for as the two enemy armies marched closer to the city the rocketmen brought their strange weapons to the firesteps. Sharpe had never seen rockets before and he gaped as the missiles were stacked against the parapets. Each was an iron tube some four or five inches wide and about eighteen inches long that was attached by leather thongs to a bamboo stick that stood higher than a man. A crude tin cone tipped the iron cylinder, and inside the cone was either a small solid shot or else an explosive charge that was ignited by the rocket's own gunpowder propellant. The missiles were fired by lighting a twist of paper that emerged from the base of the iron cylinders. Some of the rocket tubes had been wrapped with paper, then painted with either snarling tigers or verses from the Koran. "There's a man in Ireland working on a similar weapon," Lawford told Sharpe, "though I don't think he puts tigers on his rocket heads."

"How do you aim the bloody things?" Sharpe asked. Some of the rockets had been placed ready to fire, but there was no gun barrel to direct them; instead they were simply laid on the parapet and pointed in the general direction of the enemy.

"You don't really aim them," Lawford said, "at least I don't think you do. They're just pointed in the right direction and fired. They are notoriously inaccurate," he added, "at least I hope they are."

"We'll see soon enough," Sharpe said as another handcart of the strange missiles was heaved up the ramp to the fire-step.

Sharpe looked forward to seeing the rockets fired, but then it became apparent that the British and Hyderabad armies were not approaching the city directly and thus bringing themselves into range, but instead planned to march clear around Seringapatam's southern margin. The progress of the two armies was painfully slow. They had appeared at dawn, but by nightfall they had still not completed their half-circuit of the island on which Seringapatam sat. A crowd of spectators thronged the city ramparts to watch the enormous sprawl of herds, battalions, cavalry squadrons, guns, civilians, and wagons that filled the southern landscape. Dust surrounded the armies like an English fog. From time to time the fog thickened as a group of the Tippoo's lancers attacked some vulnerable spot, but each time the lancers were met by a countercharge of allied cavalry and more dust would spew up from the horses' hooves as the riders charged, clashed, circled, and fought. One lancer rode back to the city with a British cavalryman's hat held aloft on his spearpoint and the soldiers on the walls cheered his return, but gradually the greater number of allied cavalry gained the upper hand and the cheers died away as more and more of the Tippoo's horsemen splashed back wounded through the South Cauvery's ford. Some of the enemy, when the Tippoo's cavalry was driven away, ventured closer to the city. Small groups of officers trotted their horses toward the river so that they could examine the city walls, and it was one such group that drew the first rocket fire.

Sharpe watched fascinated as an officer turned one of the long weapons on the flat top of the parapet so that its tin cone pointed directly toward the nearest group of horsemen. The rocketman waited beside his officer, swinging a length of slow match to keep its burning end bright and hot. The officer fussed with the rocket's alignment, then, satisfied at last, he stepped back and nodded to the rocketman who grinned and touched his slow match to the twist of paper at the rocket's base.

The fuse paper, Sharpe guessed, had been soaked in water diluted with gunpowder, then dried, because it immediately caught the glowing fire which ate its way swiftly up the fuse as the rocketman stepped hurriedly away. The glowing trail vanished into the iron cylinder, there was silence for a second, then the rocket twitched as a bright flame abruptly choked and spat from the tube's base. The twitch of the igniting powder charge threw the heavy rocket out of its careful alignment, but there was no chance to correct the weapon's aim for a jet of flame was spitting fiercely enough from the cylinder to scorch the rocket's quivering bamboo stick, and then, very suddenly, the bright flame roared into a furnace-like intensity with a noise like a huge waterfall, only instead of water it was spewing sparks and smoke, as the rocket began to move. It trembled for an instant, scraped an inch or two across the parapet, then abruptly accelerated away into the air, leaving a thick cloud of smoke and a scorch mark on the parapet's coping. For a few seconds it seemed as if the rocket was having trouble staying aloft, for the long scorched tail wobbled as the fiery tube fought against gravity and as the smoke trail stitched a crazy whorl above the ditch at the foot of the wall, but then at last it gained momentum and raced away across the glacis, the encampment, and the river. It spewed a tail of sparks, fire, and smoke as it flew, then, as the powder charge began to be exhausted, the rocket fell earthward. Beneath the missile the group of horsemen had collapsed their spyglasses and were fleeing in every direction as the fire-tailed demon came shrieking out of the sky. The rocket struck the ground, bounced, tumbled, then exploded with a small crack of noise and a burst of flame and white smoke. None of the horsemen had been touched, but their panic delighted the Tippoo's men on the bastions who gave the rocketmen a cheer. Sharpe cheered with them. Farther up the wall a cannon fired at a second group of horsemen. The smoke of the gun billowed out across the encampment beneath the walls and the heavy round shot screamed across the river to disembowel a horse a half-mile away, but no one cheered the gunners. Guns were not so spectacular as rockets.

"He's got thousands of those bloody things," Sharpe told Lawford, indicating a pile of the rockets.

"They really aren't very accurate," Lawford said with pedantic disapproval.

"But fire enough at once and you wouldn't know if you were in this world or the next. I wouldn't fancy being on the wrong end of a dozen of those things."

Behind them, from one of the tall white minarets of the city's new mosque, the muezzin was chanting the summons for the evening prayer and the Muslim rocketmen hastened to unroll their small prayer mats and face westward toward Mecca. Sharpe and Lawford also faced west, not out of any respect for the Tippoo's religion, but because the vanguard of British and Indian cavalry was scouting the flat land beyond the South Cauvery which was plainly visible from the summit of the Mysore Gate. The main body of the two armies was making camp well to the south of the city, but the horsemen had ridden ahead to reconnoiter the western country in preparation for the next day's short march. Sharpe could even see officers pacing out and marking where the lascars would pitch the armies' tents. It seemed that General Harris had decided to attack from the west, the one direction that McCandless had warned against.

"Poor bloody fools," Sharpe said, though neither he nor

Lawford yet knew what was dangerous about the western defenses. Nor had they been given the slightest chance to escape from the city. They were never unwatched, they were never allowed to stand guard at night, and Sharpe knew that even the smallest attempt to break away from the city would lead to immediate death, yet they were not otherwise treated badly. They had been accepted well enough by their new comrades, but Sharpe could detect a reserve and he supposed that until he and Lawford proved their reliability there would always be an undercurrent of suspicion. "It ain't that they don't trust you," Henry Hickson had explained on their first night, "but till they've actually seen you bang a few balls off at your old mates, they won't really know whether you're stout." Hickson was sewing up the frayed edge of his leather thumbstall which protected his hand when a cannon was swabbed out. The gunner had to stop the touchhole so that the rammer could not drive a jet of fresh air down the barrel and so ignite any scraps of remaining powder, and Hickson's old and blackened thumbstall betrayed how long he had been an artilleryman. "Had this in America," Hickson said, flourishing the ancient scrap of leather. "Stitched for me by a little girl in Charleston. Lovely little thing she was."

"How long have you been in the artillery?" Lawford had asked the gray-haired Hickson.

"Bleeding lifetime, Bill. Joined in '76." Hickson laughed. "King and country! Go and save the colonies, eh? And all I did was march up and down like a little lost lamb and only ever fired a dozen shots. I should have stayed there, shouldn't I, when they kicked us out, but, like a fool, I didn't. Went to Gibraltar, polished cannon for a couple of years, then got posted out here."

"So why did you run?" Lawford asked.

"Money, of course. The Tippoo might be a black heathen bastard, but he pays well for gunners. When he pays at all, of course, which isn't precisely frequent, but all the same he ain't done bad by me. And if I'd stayed in the gunners I wouldn't have met Suni, would I?" He had jerked his callused thumb toward his Indian woman who was cooking the evening meal with the wives of the other soldiers.

"Don't you ever worry that you'll be recaptured?" Lawford asked him.

"Of course I bloody worry! All the bleeding time!" Hickson held the thumbstall close to his right eye to judge the neatness of his stitching. "Christ, Bill, I don't want to be stood up against a bleeding post with a dozen bastards staring down their musket barrels at me. I want to die in Suni's bed." He grinned. "You do ask the most stupid questions, Bill, but what do you expect of a bleeding clerk! All that reading and writing, mate, it doesn't do a man any bleeding good." He had shaken his head in despair of Lawford ever seeing sense. Like all of Gudin's soldiers, Hickson was more suspicious of Lawford than of Sharpe. They all understood Sharpe, for he was one of them and good at his trade, but Lawford was patently uncomfortable. They put it down to his having come from a comfortable home that had fallen on hard times, and while they were sympathetic to that misfortune they nevertheless expected him to make the best of it. Others in Gudin's small battalion despised Lawford for his clumsiness with weapons, but Sharpe was his friend and so far no man had been willing to risk Sharpe's displeasure by needling Lawford.

Sharpe and Lawford watched the invading armies make their camp well out of cannon range to the south of the city. A few Mysorean cavalrymen still circled the armies, watching for a chance to snap up a fugitive, but most of the Tippoo's men were now back on the city's island. There was an excited buzz in the city, almost a relief that the enemy was in sight and the waiting at last was over. There was also a feeling of confidence, for although the enemy horde looked vast, the Tippoo had formidable defenses and plenty of men. Sharpe could detect no lack of enthusiasm among the Hindu troops. Lawford had told him there was bad blood between them and the Muslims, but on that evening, as the Tippoo's men hung more defiant banners above their limewashed walls, the city seemed united in its defiance.

Sergeant Rothière shouted at Sharpe and Lawford from the inner wall of the Mysore Gate, pointing to the big bastion at the city's south-western corner. "Colonel Gudin wants us," Lawford translated for Sharpe.

"*Vite!*" Rothière bellowed.

"Now," Lawford said nervously.

The two men threaded their way through the spectators who crowded the parapets until they found Colonel Gudin in a cavalier that jutted south from the huge square bastion. "How's your back?" the Frenchman greeted Sharpe.

"Mending wonderfully, sir."

Gudin smiled, pleased at the news. "It's Indian medicine, Sharpe. If I ever go back to France I've a mind to take a native doctor with me. Much better than ours. All a French doctor would do is bleed you dry, then console your widow." The Colonel turned and gestured south across the river. "Your old friends," he said, indicating where the British and Indian cavalry were exploring the land between the army's encampment and the city. Most were staying well out of range of Seringapatam's cannon, but a few braver souls were galloping closer to the city, either to tempt the Tippoo's cavalry to come out and dare single combat, or else to provoke the gunners on the city wall. One especially flamboyant group was shouting toward the city, and even waving, as though inviting cannon fire, and every now and then a cannon would boom or a rocket scream across the river, though somehow the jeering cavalrymen always remained untouched. "They're distracting us," Gudin explained, "drawing attention away from some others. There, see? Some bushes. Beside the cistern." He was pointing across the river. "There are some scouts there. On foot. They are trying to see what defenses we have close to the river. You see them? Look in the bushes under the two palm trees."

Sharpe stared, but could see nothing. "You want us to go and get them, sir?" he offered.

"I want you to shoot them," Gudin said.

The bushes under the twin palms were nearly quarter of a mile away. "Long bloody range for a musket, sir," Sharpe said dubiously.

"Try this, then," Gudin said and held out a gun. It must have been one of the Tippoo's own weapons, for its stock was decorated with ivory, its tiger-head lock was chased with gold, and its barrel engraved with Arabic writing.

Sharpe took and hefted the gun. "Might be pretty, sir," he said, "but no amount of fancy work on the outside will make it more accurate than that plain old thing." He patted his heavy French musket.

"You're wrong," Gudin said. "That's a rifle."

"A rifle!" Sharpe had heard of such weapons, but he had never handled one, and now he peered inside the muzzle and saw that the barrel was indeed cut in a pattern of spiraling grooves. He had heard that the grooves spun the bullet which somehow made a rifle far more accurate than a shot from a smoothbore musket. Why that should be the case he had not the slightest idea, but every man he had ever spoken to about rifles had sworn it was true. "Still," he said dubiously, "near a quarter-mile? Long ways for a bullet, sir, even if it is spinning."

"That rifle can kill at four hundred paces, Sharpe," Gudin said confidently. "It's loaded, by the way," the Colonel added, and Sharpe, who had been peering down the muzzle again, jerked back. Gudin laughed. "Loaded with the best powder and with its bullet wrapped in oiled leather. I want to see how good a shot you are."

"No, you don't, sir," Sharpe said, "you want to see if I'm willing to kill my own countrymen."

"That too, of course," Gudin agreed placidly, and laughed at having had his small ploy discovered. "At that range you should aim about six or seven feet above your target. I have another rifle for you, Lawford, but I don't suppose we can expect a clerk to be as accurate as a skirmisher like Sharpe?"

"I'll do my best, sir," Lawford said and took the second rifle from Gudin. Lawford might be clumsy at loading a gun, but he was a practiced shot in the hunting field and had been firing rifled fowling pieces since he was eight years old.

"Some men find it hard to shoot at their old comrades," Gudin told Lawford mildly, "and I want to make sure you're not among them."

"Let's hope the bastards are officers," Sharpe said, "begging your presence, sir."

"There they are!" Gudin said, and, sure enough, just beside the cistern beneath the two palm trees across the river, were a pair of red coats. The men were examining the city walls through telescopes. Their horses were picketed behind them.

Sharpe knelt in a gun embrasure. He instinctively felt that the range was much too long for any firearm, but he had heard about the miracle of rifles and he was curious to see if the rumors were true. "You take the one on the left, Bill," he said, "and fire just after me." He glanced at Gudin and saw that the Colonel had moved a few feet down the cavalier to watch the effect of the shots from a place where the rifles' smoke would not obscure his glass. "And aim well, Bill," Sharpe said in a low voice. "They're probably only bloody cavalrymen, so who cares if we plug them with a pair of bloody goolies." He crouched behind the rifle and aligned its well-defined sights that were so much more impressive than the rudimentary stub that served a musket as a foresight. A man could stand fifty feet in front of a well-aimed musket and still stand a better than evens chance of walking away unscathed, but the delicacy of the rifle's sights seemed to confirm what everyone had told Sharpe. This was a long-range killer.

He settled himself firmly, keeping the sights lined on the distant man, then gently raised the barrel so that the rifle's muzzle obscured his target but would give the ball the needed trajectory. There was no wind to speak of, so he had no need to offset his aim. He had never fired a rifle, but it was just common sense really. Nor was he unduly worried about killing one of his own side. It was a sad necessity, something that needed to be done if he was to earn Gudin's trust and thus the freedom that might let him escape from the city. He took a breath, half let it out, then pulled the trigger. The gun banged into his shoulder, its recoil much harder than an ordinary musket's blow. Lawford fired a half-second later, the smoke of his gun joining the dense cloud pumped out by Sharpe's rifle.

"The clerk wins!" Gudin exclaimed in astonishment. He lowered his spyglass. "Yours went six inches past the man's head, Sharpe, but I think you killed your man, Lawford. Well done! Well done indeed!"

Lawford reddened, but said nothing. He looked very troubled and Gudin put his evident confusion down to a natural shyness. "Is that the first man you've ever killed?" he asked gently.

"Yes, sir," Lawford said, truthfully enough.

"You deserve to be better than a clerk. Well done. Well done both of you." He took the rifles from them and laughed at Sharpe's rueful expression. "You expected to do better, Sharpe?"

"Yes, sir."

"You will. Six inches off at that distance is very good shooting. Very good indeed." Gudin turned to watch as the uninjured redcoat dragged his companion back toward the horses. "I think, maybe," Gudin went on, "that you have a natural talent, Lawford. I congratulate you." The Colonel fished in his pouch and brought out a handful of coins. "An advance on your arrears of pay. Well done! Off you go, now!"

Sharpe glanced behind him, hoping to see what devilment the western walls held, but he could see nothing strange there and so he turned and followed Lawford down the ramp. Lawford was shaking. "I didn't mean to kill him!" the Lieutenant said when he was out of Gudin's earshot.

"I did," Sharpe muttered.

"God, what have I done? I was aiming left!"

"Don't be a bloody fool," Sharpe said, "what you've done is earned our freedom. You did bloody well." He dragged Lawford into a tavern. The Tippoo might be a Muslim, and the Muslims might preach an extraordinary hatred of alcohol, but most of the city was Hindu and the Tippoo was sensible enough to keep the taverns open. This one, close to Gudin's barracks, was a big room, open to the street, with a dozen tables where old men played chess and young men boasted of the slaughter they would inflict on the besiegers. The tavern-keeper, a big woman with hard eyes, sold a variety of strange drinks: wine and arrack mostly, but she also kept a weird-tasting beer. Sharpe could still hardly speak a word of the local language, but he pointed to the arrack barrel and held up two fingers. Now that he and Lawford were dressed in the tiger-striped tunics and carried muskets they attracted little attention in the city and no hostility. "Here." He put the arrack in front of Lawford. "Drink that."

Lawford drank it in one go. "That was the first man I've killed," he said, blinking from the harshness of the liquor.

"Worry you?"

"Of course it does! He was British!"

"Can't skin a cat without making a bloody mess," Sharpe said comfortingly.

"Jesus!" Lawford said angrily.

Sharpe poured half his liquor into Lawford's glass, then beckoned to one of the serving girls who circled the tables refilling glasses. "You had to do it," he said.

"If I'd have missed like you," Lawford said ruefully, "Gudin would have been just as impressed. That was a fine shot of yours."

"I was aiming to kill the bugger."

"You were?" Lawford was shocked.

"Jesus Christ, Bill! We have to convince these buggers!" Sharpe smiled as the girl poured more liquor, then he tipped a handful of small brass coins into a wooden bowl on the table. Another bowl held a strange spice which the other drinkers nibbled between sips, but Sharpe found the stuff too pungent. Once the girl was gone he looked at the troubled Lieutenant. "Did you think this was going to be easy?"

Lawford was silent for a few seconds, then gave a shrug. "In truth I thought it would be impossible."

"So why did you come?"

Lawford cradled the glass in both hands and stared at Sharpe as if weighing up whether or not to answer. "To get away from Morris," he finally confessed, "and for the excitement." He seemed embarrassed to admit as much.

"Morris is a bastard," Sharpe said feelingly.

Lawford frowned at the criticism. "He's bored," he said chidingly, then he steered the conversation away from the danger area of criticizing a superior officer. "And I also came because I owe gratitude to my uncle."

"And because it would get you noticed?"

Lawford looked up with some surprise on his face, then he nodded. "That too."

"Same as me then," Sharpe said. "Exact same as me. Except till the General said you was coming with me I had half a mind to run proper."

Lawford was shocked by the admission. "You really wanted to desert?"

"For Christ's sake! What do you think it's like in the ranks if you've got an officer like Morris and a sergeant like Hakeswill? Those bastards think we're just bleeding cattle, but we're not. Most of us want to do a decent job. Not too decent, maybe. We want a bit of money and a *bibbi* from time to time, but we don't actually enjoy being flogged. And we can fight like the bloody devil. If you bastard lot started trusting us instead of treating us like the enemy, you'd be bloody amazed what we could do."

Lawford said nothing.

"You've got some good men in the company," Sharpe insisted. "Tom Garrard is a better soldier than half the officers in the battalion, but you don't even notice him. If a man can't read and doesn't speak like a bleeding choirboy you think he can't be trusted."

"The army's changing," Lawford said defensively.

"Like hell it is. Why do you make us powder our hair like bleeding women? Or wear that bloody stock?"

"Change takes time," Lawford said weakly.

"Too much bloody time," Sharpe said fervently, then leaned against the wall and eyed the girls who were cooking at the tavern's far end. Were they whores, he wondered? Hickson and Blake had told him they knew where the best whores were, then he remembered Mary and suddenly felt guilty. He had not seen her once since their arrival in Seringapatam, but nor had he thought that much about her. In truth he was having too good a time here; the food was good, the liquor cheap, and the company acceptable, and to that was added the heady spice of danger. "After that brilliant piece of sharpshooting," he encouraged Lawford, "we're going to be all right. We'll have a chance to get out of here."

"What about Mrs. Bickerstaff?" Lawford asked.

"I was just thinking of her. And maybe you were right. Maybe I shouldn't have brought her. Couldn't leave her with the army though, could I? Not with Hakeswill planning to sell her to a *kin*."

"A *kin*?"

"A pimp."

"He really planned that?" Lawford asked.

"Him and Morris. In it together, they were. Bloody Hakeswill told me as much, the night he got me to hit him. And Morris was there with that little bastard Hicks, just waiting for me to do it. I was a bloody fool to fall for it, but there it is."

"Can you prove it?"

"Prove it!" Sharpe asked derisively. "Of course I can't prove it, but it's true." He blew out a rueful breath. "Just what am I going to do with Mary?"

"Take her with you, of course," Lawford said sternly.

"Might not have a chance," Sharpe said.

Lawford stared at him for a few seconds. "God, you're ruthless," he finally said.

"I'm a soldier. It fits." Sharpe said it proudly, but he was not proud, merely defiant. What was he to do with Mary? And where was she? He drank the rest of his arrack and clapped his hands for more. "You want to find a *bibbi* tonight?" he asked Lawford.

"A whore?" Lawford asked in horror.

"I don't suppose a respectable woman will help us out much. Not unless you want a spot of polite conversation."

Lawford stared aghast at Sharpe. "What we should do," the Lieutenant said softly, "is find this man Ravi Shekhar. He may have a way of getting news out of the city."

"And how the hell are we supposed to find him?" Sharpe asked defiantly. "We can't wander the bloody streets asking for this fellow in English. No one will know what the heck we're doing! I'll ask Mary to find him when we see her." He grinned. "Bugger Shekhar. How about a *bibbi* instead?"

"Maybe I'll read."

"Your choice," Sharpe said carelessly.

Lawford hesitated, his face reddening. "It's just that I've seen men with the pox," he explained.

"Christ! You've seen men vomit, but it don't stop you drinking. Besides, don't worry about the pox. That's why God gave us mercury. The stuff worked for bloody Hakeswill, didn't it? Though God knows why. Besides, Harry Hickson says he knows some clean girls, but of course they always say that. Still, if you want to ruin your eyes reading the Bible, go ahead, but there ain't no mercury that will give you your sight back."

Lawford said nothing for a few seconds. "Maybe I will come with you," he finally said shyly, staring down at the table.

"Learning how the other half lives?" Sharpe asked with a grin.

"Something like that," Lawford mumbled.

"Well enough, I tell you. Give us some cash and a willing couple of frows and we can live like kings. We'll make this the last drink, eh? Don't want to lower the flag, do we?"

Lawford was now deep red. "You won't, of course, tell anyone about this when we're back?"

"Me?" Sharpe pretended to be astonished at the very idea. "My lips are gummed together. Not a word, promise."

Lawford worried that he was letting his dignity slide, but

he did not want to lose Sharpe's approval. The Lieutenant was becoming fascinated by the younger man's confidence, and envied the way in which Sharpe so instinctively negotiated a wicked world and he wished he could find the same easy ability in himself. He thought briefly of the Bible waiting back in the barracks, and of his mother's advice to read it diligently, but then he decided to hell with them both. He drained his arrack, picked up his musket, and followed Sharpe into the dusk.

Every house in the city was prepared for the siege. Storehouses were filled with food and valuables were being hastily concealed in case the enemy armies broke through the wall. Holes were dug in gardens and filled with coins and jewelry, and in some of the wealthier houses whole rooms were concealed by false walls so that the women could be hidden away when the invaders rampaged through the streets.

Mary helped General Appah Rao's household prepare for that ordeal. She felt guilty, not because she came from the army that was imposing this threatened misery on the city, but because she had unexpectedly found herself happy in Rao's sprawling home.

When General Appah Rao had first taken her away from Sharpe she had been frightened, but the General had taken her to his own house and there reassured her of her safety. "We must clean you," the General told her, "and let that eye heal." He treated her gently, but with a measure of reserve that sprang from her disheveled looks and her presumed history. The General did not believe that Mary was the most suitable addition to his household, but she spoke English and Appah Rao was shrewd enough to reckon that a command of English would be a profitable accomplishment in Mysore's future and he had three sons who would have to survive in that future. "In time," Rao told Mary, "you can join your man, but it's best he should settle in first."

But now, after a week in the General's household, Mary did not want to leave. For a start the house was filled with women who had taken her into their care and treated her with a kindness that astonished her. The General's wife, Lakshmi, was a tall plump woman with prematurely gray hair and an infectious laugh. She had two grown unmarried daughters and, though there was a score of female servants, Mary was surprised to discover that Lakshmi and her daughters shared the work of the big house. They did not sweep it or draw water—those tasks were for the lowest of the servants—but Lakshmi loved to be in the kitchen from where her laughter rippled out into the rest of the house.

It had been Lakshmi who had scolded Mary for being so dirty, had stripped her from her western clothes, forced her into a bath, and there untangled and washed her filthy hair. "You'd be beautiful if you took some trouble," Lakshmi had said.

"I didn't want to draw attention to myself."

"When you're my age, my dear, no one pays you any attention at all, so you should take all you can get while you're young. You say you're a widow?"

"He was an Englishman," Mary said nervously, explaining the lack of the marriage mark on her forehead and worried lest the older woman thought she should have thrown herself onto her husband's pyre.

"Well, you're a free woman now, so let's make you expensive." Lakshmi laughed and then, helped by her daughters, she first brushed and then combed Mary's hair, drawing it back and then gathering it into a bun at the nape of her neck. A cheerful maid brought in an armful of clothes and the women tossed *cholis* at her. "Choose one," Lakshmi said. The *choli* was a brief blouse that covered Mary's breasts, shoulders and upper arms, but left most of her back naked and Mary instinctively selected the most modest, but Lakshmi would have none of it. "That lovely pale skin of yours, show it off!" she said, and chose a brief *choli* patterned in extravagant swirls of scarlet flowers and yellow leaves. Lakshmi tugged the short sleeves straight. "So why did you run with those two men?" Lakshmi asked.

"There was a man back in the army. A bad man. He wanted to . . ." Mary stopped and shrugged. "You know."

"Soldiers!" Lakshmi said disapprovingly. "But the two men you ran away with, did they treat you well?"

"Yes, oh yes." Mary suddenly wanted Lakshmi's good opinion, and that opinion would not be good if she thought that Mary had run from the army with a lover. "One of them"—she told the lie shyly—"is my half-brother."

"Ah!" Lakshmi said as though everything was clear now. Her husband had told her that Mary had run with her lover, but Lakshmi decided to accept Mary's story. "And the other man?" she asked.

"He's just a friend of my brother's." Mary blushed at the lie, but Lakshmi did not seem to notice. "They were both protecting me," Mary explained.

"That's good. That's good. Now, this." She held out a white petticoat that Mary stepped into. Lakshmi laced it tight at the back, then began hunting through the pile of saris. "Green," she said, "that'll suit you," and she unfolded a vast bolt of green silk that was four feet wide and over twenty feet long. "You know how to wear a sari?" Lakshmi asked.

"My mother taught me."

"In Calcutta?" Lakshmi hooted. "What do they know of saris in Calcutta? Skimpy little northern things, that's all they are. Here, let me." Lakshmi wrapped the first length of sari about Mary's slender waist and tucked it firmly into the petticoat's waistband, then she wrapped a further length about the girl, but this she skillfully flicked into pleated folds that were again firmly anchored in the petticoat's waistband. Mary could easily have done the job herself, but Lakshmi took such pleasure in it that it would have been cruel to have denied her. By the time the pleats were tucked in about half of the sari had been used up, and the rest Lakshmi looped over Mary's left shoulder, then tugged at the silk so that it fell in graceful folds. Then she stepped back. "Perfect! Now you can come and help us in the kitchens. We'll burn those old clothes."

In the mornings Mary taught the General's three small boys English. They were bright children and learned quickly and the hours passed pleasantly enough. In the afternoons she helped in the household chores, but in the early evening it was her job to light the oil lamps about the house and it was that duty that threw Mary into the company of Kunwar Singh who, at about the same time as the lamps were lit, went around the house ensuring that the shutters were barred and the outer doors and gates either locked or guarded. He was the chief of Appah Rao's bodyguard, but his duties were more concerned with the household than with the General who had enough soldiers surrounding him wherever he went in the city. Kunwar Singh, Mary learned, was a distant relation of the General, but there was something oddly sad about the tall young man whose manners were so courteous but also so distant.

"We don't talk about it," Lakshmi said to Mary one afternoon when they were both hulling rice.

"I'm sorry I asked."

"His father was disgraced, you see," Lakshmi went on enthusiastically. "And so the whole family was disgraced. Kunwar's father managed some of our land near Sedasseer, and he stole from us! Stole! And when he was found out, instead of throwing himself on my husband's mercy, he became a bandit. The Tippoo's men caught him in the end and cut his head off. Poor Kunwar. It's hard to live down that sort of disgrace."

"Is it a worse disgrace than having been married to an Englishman?" Mary asked miserably, for somehow, in this lively house, she did feel obscurely ashamed. She was half English herself, but under Lakshmi's swamping affection, she kept remembering her mother who had been rejected by her own people for marrying an Englishman.

"A disgrace? Married to an Englishman? What nonsense you do talk, girl!" Lakshmi said, and the next day she took care to send Mary to deliver a present of food to the young deposed Rajah of Mysore who survived at the Tippoo's mercy in a small house just east of the Inner Palace. "But you can't go alone," Lakshmi said, "not with the streets full of soldiers. Kunwar!" And Lakshmi saw the blush of happiness on Mary's face as she set off in the tall Kunwar Singh's protective company.

Mary was happy, but she felt guilty. She knew she ought to try and find Sharpe for she suspected he must be missing her, but she was suddenly so content in Appah Rao's household that she did not want to disturb that happiness by returning to her old world. She felt at home and, though the city was surrounded by enemies, she felt oddly safe. One day, she supposed, she would have to find Sharpe, and perhaps everything would turn out well on that day, but Mary did nothing to hasten it. She just felt guilty and made sure that she did not start lighting the lamps until she heard the first shutter bar fall.

And Lakshmi, who had been wondering just where she might find poor disgraced Kunwar Singh a suitable bride, chuckled.

❖   ❖   ❖

Once the British and Hyderabad armies had made their permanent encampment to the west of Seringapatam the siege settled into a pattern that both sides recognized. The allied armies stayed well out of the range of even the largest cannon on the city's wall and far beyond the reach of any rocket, but they established a picquet line facing an earth-banked aqueduct that wended its way through the fields about a mile west of the city and there they posted some field artillery and infantry to cover the land across which they would dig their approach ditches. The sooner those ditches were begun the sooner the breaching batteries could be built, but to the south of that chosen ground the steeply banked aqueduct made a deep loop that penetrated a half-mile westward and the inside of that bend was filled by a *tope*, a thick wood, and from its leafy cover the Tippoo's men kept up a galling musket fire on the British picquet line, while his rocketmen rained an erratic but troublesome barrage of missiles onto the forward British works. One lucky rocket streaked a thousand yards to hit an ammunition limber and the resultant explosion caused a cheer to sound from the distant walls of the city.

General Harris endured the rocket bombardment for two days, then decided it was time to capture the whole length of the aqueduct and clear the *tope*. Orders were written and trickled down from general to colonel to captains, and the captains sought out their sergeants. "Get the men ready, Sergeant," Morris told Hakeswill.

Hakeswill was sitting in his own tent, a luxury he alone enjoyed among the 33rd's sergeants. The tent had belonged to Captain Hughes and should have been auctioned with the rest of the Captain's belongings after Hughes died of the fever, but Hakeswill had simply claimed the tent and no one had liked to cross him. His servant Raziv, a miserable half-witted creature from Calcutta, was polishing Hakeswill's boots so the Sergeant had to come barefooted from his tent to face Morris. "Ready, sir?" he said. "They are ready, sir." He stared suspiciously about the Light Company's lines. "Better be ready, sir, or we'll have the skin off the lot of them." His face jerked.

"Sixty rounds of ammunition," Morris said.

"Always carry it, sir! Regulations, sir!"

Morris had drunk the best part of three bottles of wine at luncheon and was in no mood to deal with Hakeswill's equivocations. He swore at the sergeant, then pointed south to where another rocket was smoking up from the *tope*. "Tonight, you idiot, we're cleaning those bastards out of those trees."

"Us, sir?" Hakeswill was alarmed at the prospect. "Just us, sir?"

"The whole battalion. Night attack. Inspection at sundown. Any man who looks drunk gets flogged."

Officers excepted, Hakeswill thought, then quivered as he offered Morris a cracking salute. "Sir! Inspection at sundown, sir. Permission to carry on, sir?" He did not wait for Morris's permission, but turned back into his tent. "Boots! Give 'em here! Come on, you black bastard!" He gave Raziv a cuff round the ear and snatched his half-cleaned boots. He tugged them on, then dragged Raziv by the ear to where the halberd was planted like a banner in front of the tent. "Sharpen!" Hakeswill bawled in the unfortunate boy's bruised ear. "Sharpen! Understand, you toad-witted heathen? I want it sharp!" Hakeswill gave the boy a parting slap as an encouragement, then stumped off through the lines. "On your bleeding feet!" he shouted. "Look lively now! Time to earn your miserable pay. Are you drunk, Garrard? If you're drunk, boy, I'll have your bones given a stroking."

The battalion paraded at dusk and, to its surprise, found itself being inspected by its Colonel, Arthur Wellesley. There was a feeling of relief in the ranks when Wellesley appeared, for by now every man knew that they were due for a fight and none wished to go into battle under the uncertain leadership of Major Shee who had drunk so much arrack that he was visibly swaying on his horse. Wellesley might be a coldhearted bastard, but the men knew he was a careful soldier and they even looked cheerful as he trotted down their ranks on his white horse. Each man had to demonstrate possession of sixty cartridges, and those who failed had their names taken for punishment. Two sepoy battalions from the East India Company's forces paraded behind the 33rd and, just as the sun disappeared behind them, all three battalions marched southeastward toward the aqueduct. Their colors were flying and Colonel Wellesley led them on horseback. Other King's battalions marched to their left, going to attack the northern stretch of the aqueduct.

"So what are we doing, Lieutenant?" Tom Garrard asked the newly promoted Lieutenant Fitzgerald.

"Silence in the ranks!" Hakeswill bawled.

"He was talking to me, Sergeant," Fitzgerald said, "and you will do me the honor of not interfering in my private conversations." Fitzgerald's retort improved the Irishman's stock with the company twentyfold. He was popular anyway, for he was a cheerful and easygoing young man.

Hakeswill growled. Fitzgerald claimed his brother was the Knight of Kerry, whatever the holy hell that was, but the claim did not impress Sergeant Obadiah Hakeswill. Proper officers left discipline to sergeants, they did not curry favor with the men by telling jokes and chatting away like magpies. It was also plain that Brevet-Lieutenant bloody Fitzgerald did not like Sergeant Hakeswill for he took every chance he could to countermand Hakeswill's authority, and Hakeswill was determined to change that. The Sergeant's face twitched. There was nothing he could do at this moment, but

Mister Fitzgerald, he told himself, would be taught his lesson, and the sooner it was taught the better.

"You see those trees ahead?" Fitzgerald explained to Garrard. "We're going to clear the Tippoo's boys out of them."

"How many of the bastards, sir?"

"Hundreds!" Fitzgerald answered cheerfully. "And all of them quaking at the knees to think that the Havercakes are coming to give them a thrashing."

The Tippoo's boys might be quaking, but they could clearly see the three battalions approaching and their rocketmen sent up a fiery barrage in greeting. The missiles climbed through the darkening sky, their exhaust flames unnaturally bright as they spewed volcanoes of sparks into the smoke trails that mingled as the rockets reached their apogee and then plunged toward the British and Indian infantry. "No breaking ranks!" an officer shouted, and the three battalions marched stolidly on as the opening barrage plunged down to explode all around them. Some jeers greeted the barrage's inaccuracy, but the officers and sergeants shouted for silence. More rockets climbed and fell. Most screamed erratically off course, but a few came close enough to make men duck, and one exploded just a few feet from the 33rd's Light Company so that the sharp-edged scraps of its shattered tin nose cone whistled about their ears. Men laughed at their narrow escape, then someone saw that Lieutenant Fitzgerald was staggering. "Sir!"

"It's nothing, boys, nothing," Fitzgerald called. A scrap of the rocket's cylinder had torn open his left arm, and there was a gash on the back of his head that was dripping blood from the ends of his hair, but he shook off any help. "Takes more than a black man's rocket to knock down an Irishman," he said happily. "Ain't that right, O'Reilly?"

"It is, sir," the Irish Private answered.

"Got skulls like bloody buckets, we have," Fitzgerald said,

and crammed his tattered shako back on his head. His left arm was numb, and blood had soaked his sleeve to the wrist, but he was determined to keep going. He had taken worse injuries on the hunting field and still been in his saddle at the death of the fox.

Hakeswill's resentment of Fitzgerald seethed. How dare a mere lieutenant overrule him? A bloody child! Not nineteen years old yet, and still with the bog water wet behind his ears. Hakeswill slashed at a cactus with his halberd, and the savagery of the gesture dislodged the musket that was slung on his left shoulder. The Sergeant never usually carried a musket, but tonight he was armed with the halberd, the musket, a bayonet, and a brace of pistols. Except for the brief fight at Malavelly it had been years since Hakeswill had been in a battle and he was not sure he wanted to fight another this night, but if he did then he would make damned sure that he carried more weapons than any heathen enemy he might meet.

The sun had long gone by the time Wellesley halted the three battalions, though a lambent light still suffused the western sky and, under its pale glow, the 33rd formed line. The two sepoy battalions waited a quarter of a mile behind the 33rd. The rocket trails seemed brighter now as they climbed into a cloudless twilight sky where the first few stars pricked the dark. The missiles hissed as they streaked overhead, their smoke trails made lurid by the spitting flames. Spent rockets lay on the ground with small pale flames flickering feebly from their exhausts. The weapons were spectacular, but so inaccurate that even the inexperienced 33rd no longer feared them, but their relief was tempered by a sudden display of bright sparks at the lip of the aqueduct's embankment. The sparks were instantly extinguished by a cloud of powder smoke, and the sound of musketry followed a few seconds later, but the range was too great and the balls spent themselves harmlessly.

Wellesley galloped his horse to Major Shee's side, spoke briefly, then spurred on. "Flank companies!" the Colonel shouted. "Advance in line!"

"That's us, boys," Fitzgerald said and drew his sabre. His left arm was throbbing now, but he did not need it to fight with a blade. He would keep going.

The Grenadier and Light companies advanced from the two flanks of the battalion. Wellesley halted them, formed them into a line of two ranks, and ordered them to load their muskets. Ramrods rattled into barrels. "Fix bayonets!" the Colonel called and the men drew out their seventeen-inch blades and slotted them onto the musket muzzles. It was full night now, but the heat was still like a wet blanket. The sound of slaps echoed through the ranks as men swatted at mosquitoes. The Colonel curbed his white horse at the front of the two ranks. "We're going to chase the enemy off the embankment," he said in his cold, precise voice, "and once we've cleared them away Major Shee will bring on the rest of the battalion to drive the enemy out of the trees altogether. Captain West?"

"Sir!" Francis West, the commander of the Grenadier Company, was senior to Morris and so was in charge of the two companies.

"You may advance."

"At once, sir," West said. "Detachment! Forward!"

"I'm in your hands, Mother," Hakeswill said under his breath as the two companies began their advance. "Look after me now! Oh God in his heaven, but the black bastards are firing at us. Mother! It's your Obadiah here, Mother!"

"Steady in the line!" Sergeant Green's voice called. "Don't hurry! Keep your ranks!"

Morris had discarded his horse and drawn his sabre. He

felt distinctly unwell. "Give them steel when we get there," he called to his company.

"We should give the buggers some bleeding artillery," someone muttered.

"Who said that?" Hakeswill shouted. "Keep your bleeding tongues still!"

The first balls were whistling past their ears now and the crackle of the enemy's musketry filled the night. The Tippoo's men were firing from the aqueduct's embankment and the flames of their fusillade sparked bright against the dark background of the *tope*. The two companies instinctively spread out as they advanced and the corporals, charged to be file-closers, bawled at them to close up. The ground was night dark, but the skyline above the trees still showed clearly enough. Lieutenant Fitzgerald glanced behind once and was appalled to see that the western sky was still touched by a blazing streak and he knew that crimson glow would silhouette the company once it climbed the embankment, but there was no going back now. He stretched his long legs, eager to be first into the enemy lines. Wellesley was advancing behind the companies and Fitzgerald wanted to impress the Colonel.

The musketry fire blazed along the embankment's lip, each shot a spark of brightness that glowed briefly in the dark smoke, but the fire was wildly inaccurate for the attackers were still in the night-shadowed low ground and concealed by the defenders' own powder smoke. Far off to their left other battalions were assaulting the northern stretch of the embankment and Fitzgerald heard a cheer as those men charged home, then Captain West gave the order to charge and the men of the 33rd's two flank companies let loose their own cheer as they were released from the leash.

They ran hard toward the embankment. Musket balls whipped overhead. All the redcoats wanted now was to get this attack over and done. Kill a few bastards, loot a few bodies, then get the hell back to the camp. They cheered as they reached the embankment and clambered up its short steep slope. "Kill them, boys!" Fitzgerald shouted as he reached the crest, but there was suddenly no enemy there, only a still stretch of dark gleaming water and, as the attackers joined him, they all checked rather than plunge into the aqueduct.

A blast of musketry erupted from the farther bank. The Light Company, poised on the lip of the western bank, was silhouetted against the remnants of the daylight while the Tippoo's men were shrouded by the *tope*'s night-dark trees.

Redcoats fell as the bullets thumped home. The aqueduct was only about ten paces wide and, at that range, the Mysorean infantry could not miss. One man was lifted right off his feet and thrown back onto the ground behind the embankment. Rockets slashed across the dark water, their fiery trails slicing just inches above the twin embankments. For a few seconds no one knew what to do. A man gasped as a rocket snatched off his foot, then he slid down into the weed-thick water where his blood swirled dark. Some redcoats fired back at the trees, but they fired blind and their bullets hit nothing. The wounded stumbled back down the embankment, the dead twitched as they were struck by bullets, while the living were dazed by the noise and dazzled by the rockets' dreadful red tails. Captain Morris stared in confusion. He had somehow not expected to cross the aqueduct. He had thought the trees were on this side of the water and he did not know what to do, but then Lieutenant Fitzgerald gave a shout of defiance and jumped down into the waterway. The black water came up to his waist. "Come on, boys! Come on! There's not so many of the bastards!" He waded forward, his naked sabre bright in the starlight. "Let's flush them out! Come on, Havercakes!"

"Follow him, lads!" Sergeant Green shouted and about

half the Light Company jumped into the green-scummed water. The others crouched, waiting for Morris's orders, but Morris was still confused and Sergeant Hakeswill was crouching at the foot of the embankment out of the enemy's sight.

"Go on!" Wellesley shouted, angered at their hesitation. "Go on! Don't let them stand there! Captain West! On! On! Captain Morris, move!"

"Oh Jesus, Mother!" Hakeswill called as he scrambled up the embankment. "Mother, Mother!" he shouted as he dropped into the warm water. Fitzgerald and the first half of the company was already across the farther embankment and inside the *tope* now and Hakeswill could hear shouts and shots and a chilling clash as steel scraped on steel.

Wellesley saw his two flank companies at last advance across the aqueduct and he sent an aide back to summon Major Shee and the rest of the battalion. The musket fire in the *tope* was dense, an unending crackle of shots, each flash momentarily illuminating the fog of powder smoke that spread between the leaves. It looked like something from hell: flash after flash of fire blooming in the dark, rocket trails blazing among the trees, and always the moans of dying men and shrieks of pain. A sergeant yelled at his men to close up, another man shouted desperately, wanting to know where his comrades were. Fitzgerald was cheering his men forward, but too many of the redcoats were being penned back against the embankment where they were in danger of being overwhelmed. Wellesley sensed he had done this all wrong. He should have used the whole battalion instead of just the two flank companies, and the realization of his mistake annoyed him. He took pride in his profession, but if a professional soldier could not hurl a few enemy infantry and rocketmen out of a small wood, then what good was he? He thought about spurring Diomed, his horse, across the aqueduct and into the flaring smoke patches among the *tope*, but he resisted the impulse for then he would be among the trees and out of touch with the rest of the 33rd and he knew he needed Shee's remaining eight companies to reinforce the attackers. If necessary he could summon the two sepoy battalions as reinforcements, but he was sure the remainder of the 33rd would be sufficient to retrieve victory from confusion and so he turned and galloped back to hurry the battalion forward.

Hakeswill slithered down the farther embankment into the black shadows among the trees. He held the musket in his left hand and the halberd in his right. He crouched beside a tree trunk and tried to make sense of the chaos around him. He could see muskets flashing, their garish flames momentarily suffusing the smoke with light and glinting off the leaves, he could hear a man crying and he could hear shouts, but he had no idea what was happening. A handful of his men had stayed close to him, but Hakeswill did not know what to tell them; then a terrible war cry sounded close to his left and he whirled round to see a group of tiger-striped infantry charging toward him. He screamed in pure panic, fired the musket one-handed, and dropped the weapon immediately as he fled into the trees to avoid the assault. Some of the redcoats scattered blindly, but others were too slow and were overrun by the Indians. Their shouts were cut short as bayonets did their work, and Hakeswill, knowing that the Tippoo's men were slaughtering the small group of redcoats, blundered desperately through the tangling trees to get clear. Captain Morris was calling Hakeswill's name, a note of panic in his voice. "I'm here, sir!" Hakeswill called back. "I'm here, sir!"

"Where?"

"Here, sir!" A volley of musketry crashed in the trees and the balls slashed through leaves and thumped into trunks.

Rockets screamed up to clatter among the high branches. Their fiery exhausts blinded the men and the explosions of their powder-filled cones rained down shards of hot metal and fluttering scraps of leaves. "Mother!" Hakeswill shouted and shrank down beside a tree.

"Form line!" Morris shouted. "Form line!" He had a dozen men with him and they formed a nervous line and crouched among the trees. The reflected flames of the burning rockets flickered red on their bayonets. Somewhere nearby a man panted as he died, the blood bubbling in his gullet at the end of every labored breath. A volley crackled and splintered a few yards away, but it was fired away from Morris who nevertheless ducked. Then, for a few blessed seconds, the confusing noise of battle diminished and in the comparative silence Morris looked around to try and find some bearings. "Lieutenant Fitzgerald!" he shouted.

"I'm here, sir!" Fitzgerald called confidently from the darkness ahead. "Up afront of you. Cleared the buggers out of here, sir, but some of the rascals are working about your flank. Watch the left, sir." The Irishman sounded indecently cheerful.

"Ensign Hicks!" Morris called.

"I'm here, sir, right beside you, sir," a small voice said from almost beneath Morris.

"Jesus Christ!" Morris swore. He had been hoping that Hicks could have brought reinforcements, but it seemed that no one except Fitzgerald had any control in the chaos. "Fitzgerald!" Morris shouted.

"Still here, sir! Got the buggers worried, we have."

"I want you here, Lieutenant!" Morris insisted. "Hakeswill! Where are you?"

"Here, sir," Hakeswill said, but not moving from his hiding place among the bushes. He guessed he was a few paces north of Morris, but Hakeswill did not want to risk being ambushed by a tiger-striped soldier as he blundered about in search of his Captain and so he stayed put. "Coming to join you, sir," he called, then crouched even lower among the shrouding leaves.

"Fitzgerald!" Morris shouted irritably. "Come here!"

"The bloody man," Fitzgerald said under his breath. His left arm was useless now, and he sensed it had been injured more badly than he had supposed. He had ordered a man to tie a handkerchief around the wound and hoped the pressure would staunch the blood. The thought of gangrene was nagging at him, but he pushed that worry away to concentrate on keeping his men alive. "Sergeant Green?"

"Sir?" Green responded stoically.

"Stay with the men here, Sergeant," Fitzgerald ordered. The Irishman had led a score of the Light Company deep into the *tope* and he saw no point in surrendering the ground just because Morris was nervous. Besides, Fitzgerald was fairly sure that the Tippoo's troops were just as confused as the British and if Green stayed steady and used volley fire he should be safe enough. "I'll bring the rest of the company back here," Fitzgerald promised Sergeant Green, then the Lieutenant turned and called back through the trees. "Where are you, sir?"

"Here!" Morris called irritably. "Hurry, damn you!"

"Back in a minute, Sergeant," Fitzgerald reassured Green, and headed off through the trees in search of Morris.

He strayed too far north, and suddenly a rocket flared up from the *tope*'s eastern edge to lodge with a tearing crash among the tangling branches of a tall tree. For a few seconds the trapped missile thrashed wildly, startling scared birds up into the dark, then it became firmly wedged in the crook of a branch. The exhaust poured an impotent torrent of fire and smoke to illuminate a whole patch of the thick woodland, and in the sudden blaze Hakeswill saw the Lieutenant stumbling toward him. "Mister Fitzgerald!" Hakeswill called.

"Sergeant Hakeswill?" Fitzgerald asked.

"It's me, sir. Right here, sir. This way, sir."

"Thank God." Fitzgerald crossed the clearing at a run, his left arm hanging useless at his side. "No one knows what the hell they're doing. Or where they are."

"I know what I'm doing, sir," Hakeswill said, and as the fierce crackling fire in the high leaves died away he lunged upward with the halberd's spear point at the Lieutenant's belly. His face twitched as the newly sharpened blade ripped through the Lieutenant's clothes and into his stomach. "It isn't the soldierly thing, sir, to contradict a sergeant in front of his men, sir," he said respectfully. "You do understand that, sir, don't you, sir?" Hakeswill said, and grinned with joy for the pleasure of the moment. The spear point was deep in Fitzgerald's belly, so deep that Hakeswill was certain he had felt its razor-sharp point lodge against the man's backbone. Fitzgerald was on the ground now and his body was jerking like a gaffed and landed fish. His mouth was opening and closing, but he seemed unable to speak, only to moan as Hakeswill gave the spear a savage twist in an effort to free its blade. "We is talking about proper respect, sir," Hakeswill hissed at the Lieutenant. "Respect! Sergeants must be supported, sir, says so in the scriptures, sir. Don't worry, sir, won't hurt, sir. Just a prick," and he jerked the bloodied blade free and thrust it down again, this time into the Lieutenant's throat. "Won't be showing me up again, sir, will you, sir? Not in front of the men. Sorry about that, sir. And good night, sir."

"Fitzgerald!" Morris shouted frantically. "For Christ's sake, Lieutenant! Where the hell are you?"

"He's gone to hell." Hakeswill chuckled softly. He was searching the Lieutenant's body for coins. He dared not take anything that might be recognized as the Lieutenant's property, so he left the dead man's sabre and the gilded gorget he had worn about his throat, but he did find a handful of unidentifiable small change which he pushed into his pouch before scrambling a few feet away to make sure no one saw him with his victim.

"Who's that?" Morris called as he heard Hakeswill pushing through the undergrowth.

"Me, sir!" Hakeswill called. "I'm looking for Lieutenant Fitzgerald, sir."

"Come here instead!" Morris snapped.

Hakeswill ran the last few yards and dropped down between Morris and a frightened Ensign Hicks. "I'm worried about Mister Fitzgerald, sir," Hakeswill said. "Heard him up in the bushes, and there was heathens there, sir. I know, sir, 'cos I killed a couple of the black bastards." He flinched as some muskets flamed and banged some yards away, but he could not tell who fired, or at what.

"You think the bastards found Fitzgerald?" Morris asked.

"I reckon so," Hakeswill said. "Poor little bastard. I tried to find him, sir, but there was just heathens there."

"Jesus." Morris ducked as a volley of bullets flicked through the leaves overhead. "What about Sergeant Green?"

"Probably skulking, sir. Hiding his precious hide, I don't wonder."

"We're all bloody skulking," Morris answered truthfully enough.

"Not me, sir. Not Obadiah Hakeswill, sir. Got me halberd proper wet, sir. Want to feel it, sir?" Hakeswill held out the spearpoint. "Heathen blood, sir, still warm."

Morris shuddered at the thought of touching the spear, but took some comfort in having Hakeswill at his side. The *tope* was filled with shouts as a group of the Tippoo's troops charged. Muskets hammered. A rocket exploded nearby, while another, this one with a solid shot in its cone, ripped through bushes and crashed into a tree. A man screamed, then the scream was abruptly chopped off. "Jesus," Morris cursed uselessly.

"Maybe we should go back?" Ensign Hicks suggested. "Back across the aqueduct?"

"Can't, sir," Hakeswill said. "Buggers are behind us."

"You're sure?" Morris asked.

"Fought the black buggers there myself, sir. Couldn't hold them. A whole tribe of the bastards, sir. Did my best. Lost some good men." Hakeswill sniffed with pretended emotion.

"You're a brave man, Hakeswill," Morris said gruffly.

"Just following your lead, sir," Hakeswill said, then ducked as another enemy volley whipped overhead. A huge cheer sounded, followed by the screaming roar of rockets as the Tippoo's reinforcements, sent from the city, came shouting and fighting through the trees to drive every last infidel from the *tope*. "Bleeding hell," Hakeswill said. "But not to worry! I can't die, sir! I can't die!"

Behind him there was another cheer as the rest of the 33rd at last crossed the aqueduct.

"Forward!" a voice shouted from somewhere behind the Light Company's scattered fugitives. "Forward!"

"Bloody hell!" Morris snapped. "Who the hell is that?"

"33rd!" the voice shouted. "To me! To me!"

"Stay where you are!" Morris called to a few eager men, and so they crouched in the warm dark that was loud with the ripping of bullets and filled by the whimpers of dying men and bright with the glare of rockets and foul with the stench of blood that was being spilt in a black place where only chaos and fear prevailed.

· CHAPTER 7 ·

Sharpe! Sharpe!" It was Colonel Gudin who, at nightfall, burst into the barracks room. "Come, quick! As you are, hurry!"

"What about me, sir?" Lawford asked. The Lieutenant had been idly reading his Bible as he lay on his cot.

"Come on, Sharpe!" Gudin did not wait to answer Lawford, but just ran across the barracks' courtyard and out into the street which separated the European soldiers' quarters from the Hindu temple. "Quick, Sharpe!" the Frenchman called back as he hurried past a pile of mud bricks that were stacked at the street corner. Sharpe, dressed in tiger-striped tunic and boots, but with no hat, crossbelt, pouches, or musket, ran after the Colonel. He leapt over a half-naked man who was sitting cross-legged beside the temple wall, shoved a cow out of his way, then turned the corner and hurried after Gudin toward the Mysore Gate. Lawford had paused to tug on his boots and by the time he reached the street beside the temple, Sharpe had already vanished.

"Can you ride a horse?" Gudin shouted at Sharpe when the two men reached the gate.

"I did a couple of times," Sharpe said, not bothering to explain that the beasts had been unsaddled draught horses that had ambled docilely around the inn yard.

"Get on that one!" Gudin said, pointing to a small excited mare that was being held by an Indian infantryman along with Gudin's own horse. "She belongs to Captain Romet, so for God's sake take care," Gudin shouted as he swung himself up into the saddle. Captain Romet was one of Gudin's two deputies, but as both the junior French officers spent most of their lives in the city's most expensive brothel, Sharpe had yet to meet either of them. He climbed gingerly onto the mare's back, then kicked back his heels and clung desperately to the horse's mane as she followed Gudin's gelding into the gateway. "The British are attacking a wood just north of Sultanpetah," the Colonel explained as he pushed his horse through the crowded archway.

Sharpe could hear the distant fight. Muskets snapped and shells exploded dully to flicker red bursts of light far to the city's west. It was very nearly night in the city. The first house lamps had long been lit and flaming torches smoked in the archway of the Mysore Gate through which a stream of men was hurrying. Some were infantry, others carried rockets. Gudin bellowed at them for passage, used his gelding to force the slower rocketmen aside, and then, once through the gate, he sawed on his reins to turn westward.

Sharpe followed, more intent on staying on the mare than watching the excitement that seethed around him. A narrow bridge led across the South Cauvery just outside the gate and Gudin shouted at its guards to clear the roadway. Rocketmen shrank back against the balustrades as Sharpe and Gudin hurried between the bridge's small forts and then over the shallow, shrunken river. Once on the far bank they galloped hard across a stretch of muddy grass, then splashed through another small branch of the river. Sharpe clung to the mare's neck as she lurched up out of the stream. Rockets were flaring in the sky ahead which still glowed from the last rays of the invisible sun.

"Your old friends are trying to clear the *tope*," Gudin explained, pointing at the thick wood that showed black against the eastern skyline. He had slowed down, for now they were crossing more uneven ground and the Colonel did not want to break a horse's leg by being too reckless. "I want you to confuse them."

"Me, sir?" Sharpe slipped half out of the saddle, gripped the pommel desperately, and somehow dragged himself upright. He could hear the snapping crack of muskets, and see the small muzzle flames flickering all across the land ahead. It seemed to him like a major attack, especially when a British field gun fired in the distance and its muzzle flame lit the twilight like sheet lightning.

"Shout orders at them, Sharpe," Gudin said, when the report of the gun had rolled past them. "Confuse them!"

"Lawford would have done better, sir," Sharpe said. "He's got a voice like an officer."

"Then you'll have to sound like a sergeant," Gudin said, "and if you do it right, Sharpe, I'll make you up to corporal."

"Thank you, sir."

Gudin had slowed his horse to a walk as they neared the wood. It was too dark to trot now and there was a danger they could lose their way. To Sharpe's north, where the field gun had fired, the musketry was regular, suggesting that the British soldiers or sepoys were steadily taking their objectives, but in the wood in front, there seemed to be nothing but confusion. Muskets crackled irregularly, rockets streaked fire amongst the branches, and smoke boiled from small brush fires. Sharpe could hear men shouting, either in fear or triumph. "I wouldn't mind a gun, sir," he said to Gudin.

"You don't need one. We're not here to fight, just to mix them up. That's why I came back to get you. Dismount here." The Colonel tied both horses' reins to an abandoned handcart that must have been used to bring more rockets forward. The two men were a hundred yards short of the *tope* now and Sharpe could hear officers shouting orders. It was hard to tell who was giving the orders, for the Tippoo's army used English words of command, but as Sharpe and Gudin hurried closer to the fight Sharpe could tell that it was Indian voices that shouted the commands to fire, to advance, and to kill. Whatever British or Indian troops were trying to capture the wood were evidently in trouble, and it had been Gudin's inspiration to snatch the first Englishman he could find in the barracks and use him to sow even more confusion among the attackers. Gudin drew a pistol. "Sergeant Rothière!" he called.

"*Mon Colonel!*" The big Sergeant, who had first used Captain Romet's horse to reach the fight, materialized out of the gloom. He gave Sharpe a suspicious glowering look, then cocked his musket.

"Let's enjoy ourselves," Gudin said in English.

"Aye, sir," Sharpe said and wondered what the hell he should do now. In the dark, he reckoned, there should be no trouble in slipping away from the Colonel and Rothière and joining the beleaguered attackers, but how would that leave Lieutenant Lawford? The trick of it, Sharpe decided, was not to make it look as though he was deliberately trying to get back to the British, but rather to make it seem as though he was captured accidentally. That still might make things very awkward for Lawford, but Sharpe knew that his overriding duty was to carry McCandless's warning to General Harris, just as he knew that he might never get another opportunity as good as this one that Gudin had dropped so unexpectedly into his lap.

Gudin paused at the edge of the *tope*. Rocketmen were enthusiastically blasting their weapons through the trees where the missiles were being deflected off branches to tumble erratically through the leaves. Muskets sounded deep inside the wood. Wounded men lay at the trees' edge, and somewhere not far off a dying man alternately screamed and panted. "So far," Gudin said, "we seem to be beating them. Let's go forward."

Sharpe followed the two Frenchmen. Off to his right there was a sudden blast of gunfire and the sound of bayonets clashing, and Gudin swerved toward the sound, but the fight was over before they ever reached it. The Tippoo's men had encountered a small group of redcoats and had killed one and chased the others deeper into the wood. Gudin saw the redcoat's body in the fast-dying flame light of an exhausted rocket and knelt beside the man. The Colonel took out a tinderbox, struck a spark, blew the charred linen in the box alight, then held the tiny flame down beside the redcoat's chest. The man was not quite dead, but he was unconscious, blood was bubbling slow in his throat, and his eyes were closed. "Recognize the uniform?" Gudin asked Sharpe. The tinderbox's flickering glow revealed that the redcoat's turn-backs and facings were scarlet piped with white.

"Bloody hell," Sharpe said. "Excuse me, sir," he added, then he gently moved Gudin's hand up to the dying man's face. Blood had poured out of the man's mouth to soak his powdered hair, but Sharpe recognized him all the same. It was Jed Mallinson who usually paraded in the rearmost rank of Sharpe's file. "I know the uniform and the man, sir," Sharpe told Gudin. "It's the 33rd, my old battalion. West Riding, Yorkshire."

"Good." Gudin snapped the tinderbox shut, extinguishing the small flame. "And you don't mind confusing them?"

"That's why I'm here, sir," Sharpe said with a suitable bloodthirstiness.

"I think the British army lost a good man in you, Sharpe," Gudin said, standing and guiding Sharpe deeper into the trees. "If you don't want to stay in India you might think of coming home with me."

"To France, sir?"

Gudin smiled at Sharpe's surprised tone. "It isn't the devil's country, Sharpe; indeed I suspect it's the most blessed place on God's earth, and in the French army a good man can be very easily raised to officer rank."

"Me, sir? An officer?" Sharpe laughed. "Like making a mule into a racehorse."

"You underestimate yourself." Gudin paused. There were feet trampling to the right, and a sudden blast of musketry off to the left. The musketry attracted an excited rush of the Tippoo's infantry who blundered through the trees. Sergeant Rothière bellowed at them in a mix of French and Kanarese, and his sudden authority calmed the men who gathered around Colonel Gudin. Gudin smiled wolfishly. "Let's see if we can mislead some of your old comrades, Sharpe. Shout at them to come this way."

"Forward!" Sharpe obediently bellowed into the dark trees. "Forward!" He paused, listening for an answer. "33rd! To me! To me!"

No one responded. "Try a name," Gudin suggested.

Sharpe invented an officer's name. "Captain Fellows! This way!" He called it a dozen times, but there was no response. "Hakeswill!" he finally shouted. "Sergeant Hakeswill!"

Then, from maybe thirty paces away, the hated voice called back, "Who's that?" The Sergeant sounded suspicious.

"Come here, man!" Sharpe snapped.

Hakeswill ignored the order, but the fact that a man had replied at all cheered Gudin who had quietly formed the stray unit of the Tippoo's infantry into a line that waited to kill whoever came in response to Sharpe's hailing. Chaos reigned ahead. Rockets banged into branches, musket flames flared in the drifting smoke, while bullets thumped into trees or crackled through the thick leaves. A bloodthirsty cheer sounded a long way off, but whether it was Indian or British troops who cheered, Sharpe could not tell.

One thing was plain to Sharpe. The 33rd was in trouble. Poor Jed Mallinson should never have been abandoned to die, and that sad death, along with the scattered sounds of firing, suggested that the Tippoo's men had succeeded in splitting the attacking force and was now picking it off piece by piece. It was now or never, Sharpe reckoned. He had to get away from Gudin and somehow rejoin his battalion. "I need to get closer, sir," he told the Colonel and, without waiting for Gudin's consent, he ran deeper into the trees. "Sergeant Hakeswill!" he shouted as he ran. "To me, now! Now! Come on, you miserable bastard! Move your bloody self! Come on!" He could hear Gudin following him, so Sharpe fell silent and, suddenly deep in shadow, dodged off to his right.

"Sharpe!" Gudin hissed, but Sharpe was well away from the Colonel now and he reckoned he had done it without looking like a deserter.

"Sergeant Hakeswill!" Sharpe bellowed, then ran on again. There was a danger that by shouting he would keep Gudin on his heels, but it was a greater danger to let the Frenchman think that he was deliberately trying to rejoin the British, for then Lawford might suffer, and so Sharpe ran the risk as he worked his way still farther into the dense trees. "Hakeswill! To me! To me!" He pushed through thick foliage, tripped over a bush, picked himself up, and ran on into a clearing. "Hakeswill!" he shouted.

A rocket crashed into a branch high above Sharpe and slashed straight down into the clearing ahead of him. Once on the ground the missile circled furiously like a mad dog chasing its own tail and the brilliant light of the exhaust lit the trees all around. Sharpe flinched away from the lash of the fiery tail and almost ran straight into Sergeant Hakeswill who had suddenly appeared from the bushes to his left.

"Sharpie!" Hakeswill shouted. "You bastard!" He slashed

wildly at Sharpe with his bloody halberd. Morris, hearing Hakeswill's name shouted, had ordered the Sergeant to find whoever was summoning him and Hakeswill had unwillingly obeyed. Now, suddenly, Hakeswill was alone with Sharpe and the Sergeant slammed the spear forward again. "Traitorous little bastard!" Hakeswill said.

"For Christ's sake, drop it!" Sharpe shouted, retreating before the quick lunges of the spear head.

"Running off to the enemy, Sharpie?" Hakeswill said. "I should take you in, shouldn't I? It'll be another court martial and a firing party this time. But I won't risk that. I'm going to put your gizzards on a skewer, Sharpie, and send you back to your maker. And wearing a frock, too?" The Sergeant stabbed again, and Sharpe leapt back once more, but then the dying rocket fizzed across the clearing and its long bamboo stick tangled Sharpe's legs. He fell backward and Hakeswill gave a shout of triumph as he sprang toward him with the halberd poised ready to lunge downward.

Sharpe felt the rocket's iron tube under his right hand, gripped it and threw it up at Hakeswill's face. The rocket's gunpowder fuel was almost gone, but there was just enough left to spurt one last sudden flame that licked across Hakeswill's blue-eyed face. The Sergeant screamed, dropped the halberd, and clapped his hands to his eyes. To his surprise he discovered he could still see and that his face was not badly burned, but in his panic he had stumbled past Sharpe and so now he turned back and, as he did so, he dragged a pistol out of his belt.

Just then a squad of redcoats burst into the clearing. The burning carcass of the rocket showed that they were men from the 33rd's Grenadier Company who were as lost as every other redcoat on this night of chaos. One of the grenadiers saw Sharpe who, in his tiger-striped tunic, was scrambling to his feet. The grenadier raised his gun. "Leave the bastard!" Hakeswill screamed. "He's mine!"

Then a volley of musketry flamed from the trees and half of the grenadiers spun around or were hurled backward. Blood hissed in the fiery remnants of the rocket as a company of tiger-striped troops burst out of the trees. Colonel Gudin and Sergeant Rothière led them. Hakeswill turned to run at the sight of the enemy, but one of the Tippoo's men lunged forward with a bayonet-tipped musket and succeeded in driving the Sergeant down to the ground where he first twisted frantically aside, then screamed for mercy. Gudin ran past the fallen Hakeswill. "Well done, Sharpe," Gudin called. "Well done! Stop that! Stop that!" These last orders were to the Tippoo's men who had enthusiastically begun to bayonet the surviving grenadiers. "We take prisoners!" Gudin roared. "Prisoners!" Rothière knocked a bayonet aside to stop the soldier from slaughtering Hakeswill.

Sharpe was cursing. He had so nearly got clean away! If Hakeswill had not attacked him he might have run another fifty yards through the trees, discarded the tiger-striped tunic, and discovered some of his old friends. Instead he had become a hero to Gudin who believed that Sharpe had lured all the grenadiers into the clearing where the twelve who had survived the enthusiastic attack were now prisoners along with the twitching and cursing Hakeswill.

"You took a terrible risk, Corporal!" Gudin said, coming back to Sharpe and sheathing his sword. "You could have been shot by your old friends. But it worked, eh? And now you are a corporal!"

"Aye, sir. It worked," Sharpe said, though he took no pleasure in it. It had all gone so disastrously wrong, indeed the whole night had gone disastrously wrong for the British. The Tippoo's men were now clearing the *tope* yard by yard, and chasing British survivors back across the aqueduct. They pursued the beaten fugitives with jeers, volleys of musket fire, and salvoes of rockets. Thirteen prisoners had been taken, all by Sharpe and Gudin, and those unfortunate men were herded back toward the city while the redcoat dead were looted for weapons and valuables.

"I'll make sure the Tippoo hears of your bravery, Sharpe," Gudin said as he retrieved his horse. "He's a brave man himself and he admires it in others. I don't doubt he'll want to reward you!"

"Thank you, sir," Sharpe said, though without enthusiasm.

"You're not wounded, are you?" Gudin asked anxiously, struck by the forlorn tone of Sharpe's voice.

"Burned my hand, sir," Sharpe said. He had not realized it when he snatched up the rocket tube to fend off Hakeswill, but the metal cylinder had scorched his hand, though not badly. "Nothing much," he added. "I'll live."

"Of course you'll live," Gudin said, then laughed delightedly. "Gave them a beating, didn't we?"

"Trounced 'em proper, sir."

"And we'll trounce them again, Sharpe, when they attack the city. They don't know what's waiting for them!"

"What is waiting for them, sir?" Sharpe asked.

"You'll see. You'll see," Gudin said, then hauled himself up into his saddle. Sergeant Rothière wanted to stay in the *tope* to retrieve British muskets, so the Colonel insisted that Sharpe ride the second horse back to the city with the disconsolate prisoners who were under the guard of a gleeful company of the Tippoo's troops.

Hakeswill looked up at Sharpe and spat. "Bloody traitor!"

"Ignore him," Gudin said.

"Snake!" Hakeswill hissed. "Piece of no-good shit, that's what you are, Sharpie. Jesus Christ!" This last imprecation was because one of the escorting soldiers had hit the back of Hakeswill's head with a musket barrel. "Black bastard," Hakeswill muttered.

"I'd like to kick his bloody teeth in, sir," Sharpe said to Gudin. "In fact, if you've no objection, sir, I'll take the bastard into the dark and finish him off."

Gudin sighed. "I do object," the Colonel said mildly, "because it's rather important we treat prisoners well, Sharpe. I sometimes fear the Tippoo doesn't understand the courtesies of war, but so far I've managed to persuade him that if we treat our prisoners properly then our enemies will treat theirs properly in return."

"I'd still like to kick the bastard's teeth in, sir."

"I assure you the Tippoo might do that without any help from you," Gudin said grimly.

Sharpe and the Colonel spurred ahead of the prisoners to cross the bridge back to the city where they dismounted at the Mysore Gate. Sharpe handed the mare's reins to Gudin who thanked him yet again and tossed him a whole golden *haideri* as a reward. "Go and get drunk, Sharpe," the Colonel said, "you deserve it."

"Thank you, sir."

"And believe me, I'll tell the Tippoo. He admires bravery!"

Lieutenant Lawford was among the curious crowd who waited just inside the gate. "What happened?" he asked Sharpe.

"I buggered up," Sharpe said bitterly. "I bloody well buggered it up. Come on, let's spend some money. Get drunk."

"No, wait." Lawford had seen the redcoats coming through the flame light of the gate torches and he pulled away from Sharpe to watch as the thirteen prisoners were pushed at bayonet point into the city. The crowd began jeering.

"Come away!" Sharpe insisted and he tugged at Lawford's elbow.

Lawford shook off the tug and stared at the prisoners, unable to hide his chagrin at the sight of British soldiers being herded into captivity. Then he recognized Hakeswill who, at the same instant, stared into the Lieutenant's face, and Sharpe saw Hakeswill's look of utter astonishment. For a second the world seemed to pause in its turning. Lawford appeared unable to move, while Hakeswill was gaping with disbelief and seemed about to shout his recognition. Sharpe was reaching to snatch a musket from one of the Tippoo's infantrymen, but then Hakeswill turned deliberately away and composed his features as though sending a silent message that he would not remark on Lawford's presence. The twelve grenadier prisoners were still a few yards behind and Lawford, suddenly realizing that yet more men of his battalion might recognize him, at last turned away. He pulled Sharpe with him. Sharpe protested. "I want to kill Hakeswill!"

"Come on!" Lawford hurried down an alley. The Lieutenant had gone pale. He stopped beside the arched doorway of a small temple that was surmounted by a carving of a cow resting beneath a parasol. Little flames sputtered inside the sanctuary. "Will he say anything?" Lawford asked.

"That bastard?" Sharpe said. "Anything's possible."

"Surely not. He wouldn't betray us," Lawford said, then shuddered. "What happened, for God's sake?"

Sharpe told him of the night's events and how close he had come to making a clean break back to the British lines. "It were bloody Hakeswill that stopped me," he complained.

"He could have misunderstood you," Lawford said.

"Not him."

"But what happens if he does betray us?" Lawford asked.

"Then we join your uncle in the bloody cells," Sharpe said

gloomily. "You should have let me shoot the bastard back at the gate."

"Don't be a fool!" Lawford snapped. "You're still in the army, Sharpe. So am I." He suddenly shook his head. "God Almighty!" he swore. "We need to find Ravi Shekhar."

"Why?"

"Because if we can't get the news out, then maybe he can!" Lawford said angrily. His anger was at himself. He had been so beguiled by exploring the existence of a common soldier that he had forgotten his duty, and that dereliction now filled him with guilt. "We have to find him, Sharpe!"

"How? We can't ask in the streets for him!"

"Then find Mrs. Bickerstaff," Lawford said urgently. "Find her, Sharpe!" He lowered his voice. "And that's an order."

"I outrank you," Sharpe said.

Lawford turned on him furiously. "What did you say?"

"I'm a corporal now, Private." Sharpe grinned.

"This is not a joke, Sharpe!" Lawford snapped. There was a sudden authority in his voice. "We're not here to enjoy ourselves. We're here to do a job."

"We've done it bloody well so far," Sharpe said defensively.

"No, we haven't," Lawford said firmly. "Because we haven't got the news out, have we? And until we do that, Sharpe, we've achieved nothing. Absolutely nothing. So talk to your woman and tell her what we know and get her to find Shekhar. That's an order, Private Sharpe. So do it!" Lawford abruptly turned and stalked away.

Sharpe felt the comforting weight of the *haideri* in his tunic pocket. He thought about following Lawford, then decided to hell with it. Tonight he could afford the best and life was too short to pass up that sort of chance. He decided he would go back to the brothel. He had liked the place, a house filled with curtains, rugs and shaded oil lamps where two giggling girls had given Lawford and Sharpe baths before letting them go up the stairs to the bedrooms. A *haideri* would buy a whole night in one of those rooms, perhaps with Lali, the tall girl who had left Lieutenant Lawford exhausted and guilt-ridden.

So he went to spend his gold.

The 33rd marched unhappily back to the encampment. The wounded were carried or limped back and one man cried out every time he put his left foot down, but otherwise the battalion was silent. They had been whipped, and the distant jeers of the Tippoo's men rubbed salt into their wounds. A last few rockets pursued them, their flames streaking wildly askew across the stars.

The Grenadier and Light Companies had taken the casualties. Men were missing and Wellesley knew that some of those missing were dead and he feared that others were prisoners or else still lying wounded among the dark trees. The remaining eight companies of the battalion had marched to support the flank companies, but in the dark they had crossed the aqueduct too far to the south and, while Wellesley had tried to find his beleaguered flank companies, Major Shee had stolidly marched straight through the *tope* and out across the aqueduct on the far side without encountering the enemy or firing a shot. The two sepoy battalions could easily have turned the night's disaster into a victory, but they had received no orders, though one of the battalions, fearing disaster, had fired a panicked volley that had killed their own commanding officer while, a half-mile to their front, the 33rd had floundered about in unsoldierlike chaos.

It was that lack of professionalism that galled Wellesley. He had failed. The northern stretch of the aqueduct had been efficiently captured by other battalions, but the 33rd had blundered. Wellesley had blundered, and he knew it. General Harris was sympathetic enough when the young Colonel reported his failure; Harris murmured about the uncertainty of night attacks and how everything could be put right in the morning, but Wellesley still felt the failure keenly. He knew only too well that experienced soldiers like Baird despised him, believing that his promotion to second-in-command was due solely to the fact that his elder brother was Governor-General of the British regions in India, and Wellesley's shame had been made worse because Major General Baird had been waiting with Harris when Wellesley arrived to report his failure and the tall Scotsman seemed to smirk as Wellesley confessed to the night's disasters. "Difficult things, night attacks," Harris said yet again while Baird said nothing and Wellesley smarted under the Scotsman's telling silence.

"We'll clear the *tope* in the morning," Harris tried to console Wellesley.

"My men will do it," Wellesley promised quickly.

"No, no. They won't be rested," Harris said. "Better if we use fresh troops."

"My fellows will be quite ready." Baird spoke for the first time. He smiled at Wellesley. "The Scotch Brigade, I mean."

"I request permission to command the attack, sir," Wellesley said very stiffly, ignoring Baird. "Whatever troops you use, sir, I'll still be duty officer."

"I'm sure, I'm sure," Harris said vaguely, neither granting nor denying Wellesley's request. "You must get some sleep," he said to the young Colonel, "so let me wish you a restful night." He waited till Wellesley was gone, then shook his head mutely.

"A whippersnapper," Baird said loudly enough for the retreating Colonel to hear him, "with his nursery maid's apron strings still trapped in his sword belt."

"He's very efficient," Harris said mildly.

"My mother was efficient, God rest her soul," Baird retorted vigorously, "but you wouldn't want her running a damned battle. I tell you, Harris, if you let him lead the assault on the city you'll be asking for trouble. Give the job to me, man, give it to me. I've got a score to settle with the Tippoo."

"So you have," Harris agreed, "so you have."

"And let me take the damned *tope* in the morning. God, man, I could do it with a corporal's guard!"

"Wellesley will still be officer of the day tomorrow morning, Baird," Harris said, then pulled off his wig as a sign that he wanted to go to bed. One side of his scalp was curiously flattened where he had been wounded at Bunker Hill. He scratched at the old injury, then yawned. "I'll bid you good night."

"You know how to spell Wellesley's name for the dispatch, Harris?" Baird asked. "Three L's!"

"Good night," Harris said firmly.

At dawn the Scotch Brigade and two Indian battalions paraded east of the encampment, while a battery of four twelve-pounder guns unlimbered to their south. As soon as the sun was up the four guns began throwing shells into the *tope*. The missiles left filmy smoke traces in the air from their burning fuses, then plunged into the trees where their explosions were muffled by the thick foliage. One shell fell short and a great gout of water spurted up from the aqueduct. Birds wheeled above the smoking *tope*, squawking their protests at the violence that had once again disturbed their nests.

Major General Baird waited in front of the Scotch Brigade. He itched to take his countrymen forward, but Harris insisted it was Wellesley's privilege. "He's officer of the day till noon," Harris said.

"He ain't up," Baird said. "He's sleeping it off. If you wait for him to wake up it'll be past noon anyway. Just let me go, sir."

"Give him five minutes," Harris insisted. "I sent an aide to wake him."

Baird had intercepted the aide to make certain Wellesley did not wake in time, but just before the five minutes expired the young Colonel came racing across the ground on his white horse. He looked disheveled, like a man who had made too hasty a toilet. "My sincerest apologies, sir," he greeted Harris.

"You're ready, Wellesley?"

"Indeed, sir."

"Then you know what to do," Harris said curtly.

"Look after my Scots boys!" Baird called to Wellesley, and received, as he expected, no answer.

The Scots colors were unfurled, the drummer boys sounded the advance, the pipers began their fierce music and the brigade marched into the rising sun. The sepoys followed. Rockets streaked up from the *tope*, but the missiles were no more accurate in the morning than they had been at night. The four brass field guns fired shell after shell, only stopping when the Scotsmen reached the aqueduct. Harris and Baird watched as the brigade attacked in a four-deep line that climbed the nearer embankment, dropped out of sight into the aqueduct, briefly reappeared on the farther embankment, then finally disappeared into the trees beyond. For a few moments there was the disciplined sound of musket volleys, then silence. The sepoys followed the Scots, spreading left and right to attack the fringes of the battered woodland. Harris waited, then a galloper came from the northern stretch of the aqueduct, which had been captured during the night, to report that the land between the *tope* and the city was thick with enemy fugitives running back to

Seringapatam. That news was proof that the *tope* was at last taken and that the whole aqueduct was now in allied hands. "Time for breakfast," Harris said happily. "You'll join me, Baird?"

"I'll hear the butcher's bill first, sir, if you don't mind," Baird answered, but there was no butcher's bill, for none of the Scots or Indian troops had died. The Tippoo's men had abandoned the *tope* once the artillery shells began to fall among the trees and they left behind only the plundered British dead of the previous night. Lieutenant Fitzgerald was among them, and he was buried with honors. Killed by an enemy bayonet, the report said.

And now, with the approach ground west of the city in Harris's hands, the siege proper could begin.

It did not prove difficult to find Mary. Sharpe merely asked Gudin and, after the night's events in the *tope*, the Colonel was eager to give Sharpe whatever he wanted. The loss of the *tope* the following dawn had in no way diminished the Frenchman's delight at the nighttime victory, nor the optimism inside the city, for no one had seriously expected the *tope* to resist for more than a few minutes and the previous night's victory, with its catch of prisoners and its tales of British defeat, had convinced the Tippoo's forces that they would prove more than a match for the enemy armies.

"Your woman, Sharpe?" Gudin teased. "You become a corporal and all you want is your woman back?"

"I just want to see her, sir."

"She's in Appah Rao's household. I'll have a word with the General, but first you're to go to the palace at midday."

"Me, sir?" Sharpe felt an instant pang of alarm, fearing that Hakeswill had betrayed him.

"To get an award, Sharpe," Gudin reassured him. "But don't worry, I'll be there to steal most of your glory."

"Yes, sir." Sharpe grinned. He liked Gudin, and he could not help contrasting the kind and easy-going Frenchman with his own Colonel who always appeared to treat common soldiers as if they were a nuisance that had to be endured. Of course Wellesley was sheltered from his ranks by his officers and sergeants, while Gudin had such a small battalion that in truth he was more like a captain than a colonel. Gudin did have the assistance of a Swiss adjutant and the occasional help of the two French captains when they were not drinking in the city's best brothel, but the battalion had no lieutenants or ensigns, and only three sergeants, which meant that the rank and file had an unprecedented access to their Colonel. Gudin liked it that way for he had little else to occupy him. Officially he was France's adviser to the Tippoo, but the Tippoo rarely sought anyone's advice. Gudin confessed as much as he walked with Sharpe to the palace at midday. "Knows it all, does he, sir?" Sharpe asked.

"He's a good soldier, Sharpe. Very good. What he really wants is a French army, not a French adviser."

"What does he want a French army for, sir?"

"To beat you British out of India."

"But then he'd just be stuck with you French instead," Sharpe pointed out.

"But he likes the French, Sharpe. You find that strange?"

"I find everything in India strange, sir. Haven't had a proper meal since I got here."

Gudin laughed. "And a proper meal is what?"

"Bit of beef, sir, with some potatoes and a gravy thick enough to choke a rat."

Gudin shuddered. *"La cuisine anglaise!"*

"Sir?"

"Never mind, Sharpe, never mind."

A half-dozen men waited to be presented to the Tippoo, all of them soldiers who had somehow distinguished themselves in the defense of the *tope* the previous night. There was also one prisoner, a Hindu soldier who had been seen to run away when the attackers had first crossed the aqueduct. All of them, coward and heroes alike, waited in the courtyard where Sharpe and Lawford had been tested by the Tippoo, though today five of the six tigers had been taken away, leaving only a big old docile male. Gudin crossed to the beast and tickled its chin, then scratched it between the ears. "This one's tame as a cat, Sharpe."

"I'll let you stroke it, sir. Wild horses wouldn't get me near a beast like that."

The tiger liked being scratched. It closed its yellow eyes and for a few seconds Sharpe could almost persuade himself the big beast was purring, then it yawned hugely, displaying a massive mouth with old worn teeth, and when it had yawned it stretched out its long forepaws and, from its furry pads, two sets of long, hooked claws emerged. "That's how it kills," Gudin said, gesturing at the claws as he backed away. "Holds you down with its teeth, then slits your belly open with the claws. Not this one, though. He's just an old soft pet. Flea-bitten too." Gudin picked a flea off his hand, then turned as a doorway to the courtyard was opened and a procession of palace attendants filed into the sunlight. It was led by two robed men who carried staffs tipped with silver tiger heads. They served as chamberlains, mustering the heroes into line and pushing the coward to one side, and behind them came two extraordinary men.

Sharpe gaped at them. They were both huge; tall and muscled like prizefighters. Their dark skin, naked to their waists, was oiled to a glistening shine, while their long black hair had been twisted round and round their heads and then tied with white ribbons. They had bristling black beards and wide mustaches that had been stiffened into points with wax. "*Jettis*," Gudin whispered to Sharpe.

"*Jettis*? What are they, sir?"

"Strongmen," Gudin said, "and executioners." The soldier who had fled from the attacking British dropped to his knees and shouted an appeal to the chamberlains. They ignored him.

Sharpe stood at the left-hand end of the line of heroes, who straightened proudly when the Tippoo himself entered the courtyard. He was escorted by six more servants, four of whom held a tiger-striped canopy above his head. The silken canopy was supported by poles with tiger finials and had a fringe of pearl drops. The Tippoo was in a green robe hung with more pearls and with his tiger-hilted sword hanging in its jeweled scabbard from a yellow silk sash. His broad turban was also green and wrapped about with more pearls, while in a plume at its crown there glittered a ruby so huge that Sharpe at first assumed it must be made of glass for surely no precious stone could be that massive, except perhaps for the big yellow-white diamond that formed the pommel of a dagger that the Tippoo wore in his yellow sash.

The Tippoo glanced at the quivering soldier, then nodded at the *jettis*.

"This is not pleasant, Sharpe," Colonel Gudin warned softly from just behind Sharpe.

One of the *jettis* seized the terrified prisoner and dragged him upright, then half carried and half led him so that he stood directly in front of the Tippoo. There the *jetti* forced the man to make a half-turn, then pushed him down to his knees, knelt behind him and wrapped his arms around the prisoner's arms and torso so that he could not move. The condemned man called piteously to the Tippoo who ignored the plea as the second *jetti* stood in front of the prisoner. The Tippoo nodded and the standing *jetti* placed his big hands on either side of the doomed man's head. The man screamed, then the scream was cut off as the *jetti* tightened his grip.

"God almighty!" Sharpe said in wonderment as he watched the man's head being wrung like a chicken. He had never seen such a thing, nor dreamed it was even possible. Behind him Colonel Gudin made a small noise of disapproval, but Sharpe had been impressed. It was a quicker death than being flogged, and quicker too than most hangings where the prisoners were left to dangle and dance as the rope choked them. The Tippoo applauded the *jetti*'s display, rewarded him, then ordered the dead man to be dragged away.

Then, one by one, the night's heroes were led up to the tiger-striped canopy and to the short plump man who stood in its shade. Each soldier knelt as he was named, and each time the Tippoo leaned down and used both hands to lift the man up before talking to him and presenting the hero with a large medallion. The medallions looked as if they were gold, but Sharpe guessed they had to be made of polished brass, for surely no one would give away that much gold! Each of the men kissed the gift, then shuffled backward to his place in the line.

At last it was Sharpe's turn. "You know what to do," Gudin said encouragingly.

Sharpe did. He disliked going on his knees to any man, let alone this plump little monarch who was his country's enemy, but there was no future in unnecessary defiance and so he obediently went down on one knee. The yellow-white stone in the dagger's hilt glinted at him, and Sharpe could have sworn it was a real diamond. A huge diamond. Then the Tippoo smiled, leaned forward and raised Sharpe by putting his hands under his armpits. He was surprisingly strong.

Gudin had come forward with Sharpe and now spoke to the Tippoo's interpreter in French, and the interpreter translated into Persian, which left Sharpe none the wiser. So far as he was concerned the events of the previous night had been a shambles, but it was evident that Gudin was telling a tale of high heroics for the Tippoo kept giving Sharpe appreciative glances. Sharpe stared back in fascination. The Tippoo had gray eyes, a dark skin, and a finely trimmed black mustache. At a distance he looked plump, even soft, but closer there was a grimness to his face which persuaded Sharpe that Colonel Gudin had been right when he claimed that this man was a fine soldier. Sharpe towered over the Tippoo so much that if he looked straight ahead he found himself gazing at the huge stone in the Tippoo's plume. It did not look like glass. It looked like one giant ruby, the size of a piece of grapeshot. It was held in a delicate gold clasp, and had to be worth a bloody fortune. Sharpe remembered his promise to give Mary a proper ruby on the day he married her, and he almost grinned at the thought of stealing the Tippoo's stone. Then he forgot the stone as the Tippoo asked some questions, but Sharpe was not required to answer for Colonel Gudin did all his speaking for him. Once the questions were answered the Tippoo looked up into Sharpe's eyes and spoke directly to him. "He says," Gudin translated the interpreter's words, "that you have proved yourself a worthy soldier of Mysore. He is proud to have you in his forces, and he looks forward to the day when, with the infidel beaten back from the city, you can become a full and proper member of his army."

"Does that mean I'll have to be circumvented, sir?" Sharpe asked.

"It means you are extraordinarily grateful to His Majesty, as I shall now tell him," Gudin said and duly did so, and when that statement had been translated, the Tippoo smiled and turned to an attendant, took the last of the medallions from its silk-lined basket, and reached up to put it round

Sharpe's neck. Sharpe stooped to make it easier, and blushed as the Tippoo's face came close. He could smell a pungent perfume on the monarch, then Sharpe stepped back and, just like the other soldiers, he lifted the medallion to his lips. He almost swore as he did so, for the thing was not made of brass at all, but of heavy gold.

"Back away," Gudin muttered.

Sharpe bowed to the Tippoo and backed clumsily to his place in the line. The Tippoo spoke again, though this time no one bothered to translate for Sharpe, and then the small ceremony was over and the Tippoo turned and went back into his palace.

"You are now officially a hero of Mysore," Gudin said drily, "one of the Tippoo's beloved tigers."

"Don't deserve to be, sir," Sharpe said, peering at the medallion. One side was patterned with an intricate design, while the other showed a tiger's face, though the face seemed to be cunningly constructed from the whorls of an intricate script. "Does it say something, sir?" he asked Gudin.

"It says, Sharpe, '*Assad Allah al-ghalib*,' which is Arabic and it means "The Lion of God is victorious.'"

"Lion, not tiger?"

"It's a verse from the Koran, Sharpe, the Muslim Bible, and I suspect the holy book does not mention tigers. It can't, otherwise I'm sure the Tippoo would use the quotation."

"Funny, isn't it?" Sharpe said, peering at the heavy gold medallion.

"What is?"

"The British beast is the lion, sir." Sharpe chuckled, then hefted the gold in his hand. "Is he a rich bugger, the Tippoo?"

"As rich as can be," Gudin said drily.

"And those are real stones? That ruby in his hat and the diamond in his dagger?"

"Both worth a king's ransom, Sharpe, but be careful. The diamond is called the Moonstone and is supposed to bring ill luck to anyone who steals it."

"I wasn't thinking of thieving it, sir," Sharpe said, though he had been thinking exactly that. "But what about this?" He lifted the heavy medallion again. "Do I get to keep it?"

"Of course you do. Though I might say you only received it because I somewhat exaggerated your exploits."

Sharpe unlooped the medallion. "You can have it, sir." He pushed the heavy gold toward the Frenchman. "Really, sir! Go on."

Gudin backed away and held up his hands in horror. "If the Tippoo discovered you had given it away, Sharpe, he would never forgive you! Never! That's a badge of honor. You must wear it always." The Colonel pulled out a Breguet watch and clicked open its lid. "I have duties, Sharpe, and that reminds me. Your woman will be waiting for you in the small temple beside Appah Rao's house. You know where that is?"

"No, sir."

"Go to the north side of the big Hindu temple," the Colonel said, "and keep walking. You will come almost to the city wall. Turn left there and you will see the temple on your left. It has one of those cows over the gate."

"Why do they put cows over the gates, sir?"

"For the same reason we put images of a tortured man in our churches. Religion. You ask too many questions, Sharpe." The Colonel smiled. "Your woman will meet you there, but remember, Corporal, guard duty at sundown!" With those words Gudin strode away and Sharpe, with one final glance at the somnolent tiger, followed.

It was not hard to find the small temple that lay opposite

an old gateway that led through the western defenses. It was these walls that McCandless had warned against, but Sharpe, staring at them from the temple entrance, could see nothing strange about them. A long ramp ran up to the firestep and a pair of soldiers were struggling to push a handcart loaded with rockets to the ramparts where a dozen great guns stood unattended in their embrasures, but he could see nothing sinister, no trap to destroy an army. One of the Tippoo's sun-blazoned flags flew on a tall staff above the gatehouse itself, flanked by two smaller green flags that showed a silver device. The wind lifted one of the flags and Sharpe saw it was the same calligraphic tiger head that was engraved on his medal. He grinned. That was something to show Mary.

He went into the temple, but Mary had not yet arrived. Sharpe found a patch of shade in a niche to one side of the open courtyard from where he watched a stark-naked man with a white stripe painted across his bald pate who was sitting cross-legged in front of an idol that had a man's body, a monkey's head, and was painted red, green, and yellow. Another god, this one with seven cobra heads, stood in a niche that was littered with fading flowers. The cross-legged man did not move, Sharpe could swear he did not even blink, not even when two other worshipers came to the temple. One was a tall slim woman in a pale-green sari with a small diamond glinting in the side of her nose. Her companion was a tall man dressed in the Tippoo's tiger-striped tunic with a musket slung on one shoulder and a silver-hilted sword hanging at his side. He was a fine-looking man, a fitting companion for the elegant woman who crossed to a third idol, this one a seated goddess with four sets of arms. The woman touched her joined hands to her forehead, bowed low, then reached forward and rang a tiny handbell to attract the goddess's attention. It was only then that Sharpe recognized her. "Mary!" he called, and she turned in alarm to see Sharpe standing in the deep shadows at the side of the shrine. The look of terror on Mary's face checked Sharpe. The tall young soldier had put a hand on the hilt of his sword. "Mary," Sharpe called again, "lass."

"Brother!" Mary called aloud, and then, almost in a panic, she repeated the word. "Brother!"

Sharpe grinned, disguising his confusion. Then he saw there were tears in Mary's eyes and he frowned. "Are you all right, lass?"

"I'm very well," she said deliberately, and then, in an even more stilted voice, "brother."

Sharpe glanced at the Indian soldier and saw that the man had a fiercely protective look. "Is that the General?" he asked Mary.

"No. It's Kunwar Singh," Mary said, and she turned and gestured toward the soldier and Sharpe saw a look of tenderness on her face, and all at once he understood what was happening.

"Does he speak English?" Sharpe asked, and then, with a grin, "sister?"

Mary threw him a look of pure relief. "Some," she said. "How are you? How's your back?"

"Mending all right, it is. That Indian doctor does magic, he does. I still feel it now and then, but not like it was. No, I'm doing all right. I even won a medal, look!" He held the gold toward Mary. "But I need to talk to you privately," he added as she leaned close to peer at the medallion. "It's urgent, love," he hissed.

Mary fingered the gold, then looked up at Sharpe. "I'm sorry, Richard," she whispered.

"There's nothing to be sorry for, lass," Sharpe said, and he spoke truthfully, for ever since he had seen Mary in her sari he had sensed that she was not for him. She looked too sophisticated, too elegant, and the wives of common soldiers were usually neither. "You and him, eh?" he asked, glancing at the lean and handsome Kunwar Singh.

Mary gave a tiny nod.

"Good for you!" Sharpe called to the Indian and gave him a smile. "Good girl, my sister!"

"Half-sister," Mary hissed.

"Make up your bloody mind, lass."

"And I've taken an Indian name," she said. "Aruna."

"Sounds good. Aruna." Sharpe smiled. "I like it."

"It was my mother's name," Mary explained, then fell into an awkward silence. She glanced at the man with the white stripe on his head, then tentatively touched Sharpe's elbow and so led him back into the shaded niche where he had been waiting. A ledge ran round the niche and Mary sat on it, facing Sharpe with her hands held modestly on her lap. Kunwar Singh watched them, but did not try to come close.

For a second neither Sharpe nor Mary had anything to say. "I've been watching that naked fellow," Sharpe said, "and he ain't moved an inch."

"It's one way to worship," Mary said softly.

"Bloody odd though. The whole thing's odd." Sharpe gestured around the decorated shrine. "Looks like a circus, don't it? Can't imagine it at home. Painted clowns in church, eh? Can you imagine that?" Then he remembered Mary had never seen England. "It ain't the same," he said weakly, then jerked his head toward the ever watchful Kunwar Singh. "You and him, eh?" Sharpe said again.

Mary nodded. "I'm sorry, Richard. Truly."

"It happens, lass," Sharpe said. "But you don't want him to know about you and me, is that it?"

She nodded and again looked fearful. "Please?" she begged him. Sharpe paused, not to keep Mary on tenterhooks, but because the naked man had at last moved. He had slowly clasped his hands together, but that seemed the extent of his exertions for he went quite still again. "Richard?" Mary pleaded. "You won't tell him, will you?"

He looked back to her. "I want you to do something for me," he said.

She looked wary, but nodded. "Of course. If I can."

"There's a fellow in this city called Ravi Shekhar. Got the name? He's a merchant, God knows what he sells, but he's here right enough and you've got to find him. Do they ever let you out of the house?"

"Yes."

"Then you get out, lass, and find this Ravi Shekhar and tell him to get a message to the British. And the message is this. They mustn't attack the west wall. That's it, just that. The daft buggers are setting themselves to attack it right now, so it's urgent. Will you do that?"

Mary licked her lips, then nodded. "And you won't tell Kunwar about us?"

"I wouldn't have told him anyway," Sharpe said. "Of course I wouldn't. I wish you joy of the fellow, sister, eh?" He smiled. "Sister Aruna. It's nice to have some family and you're all I've got. And I hate to ask you to find this Shekhar fellow, but the Lieutenant and me, we just can't manage to escape so someone else has to send the message out. Looks like you." Sharpe grinned. "But it looks like you've changed sides now and I don't blame you. So you don't mind doing this for me?"

"I'll do it for you. I promise."

"You're a good lass." He stood. "Do brothers kiss sisters in India?"

Mary half smiled. "I think they do, yes."

Sharpe gave her a very respectable kiss on the cheek, smelling her perfume. "You look grand, Mary," he said. "Too grand for me, eh?"

"You're a good man, Richard."

"That won't get me very far in this world, will it?" He backed away from Mary then grinned at Kunwar Singh who offered him a stiff, slight bow. "You're a lucky man!" Sharpe said, and then, with a backward glance at the tall elegant woman who now called herself Aruna, he walked away from Mary Bickerstaff. Easy come, easy go, he thought, but there was also a pang of jealousy for the tall good-looking Indian. But what the hell? Mary was doing her best to survive and Sharpe could never blame someone for doing that. He was doing the same himself.

He had turned back toward the barracks where Gudin's battalion was quartered. He was thinking about Mary and about how graceful, even unapproachable, she had looked, and he was hardly looking where he was going when a cheerful shout warned him of an approaching bullock cart that was loaded with great barrels. Sharpe stepped hastily aside as the bullocks, their horns painted yellow and blue and tipped with small silver bells, lumbered past. He saw that the brightly painted cart was heading down a narrow alley which led toward the gatehouse in the western wall and the sentries at the gate, seeing the cart approach, heaved back the huge double doors.

And Sharpe instinctively knew something was amiss. He stood watching and suspected he was on the edge of solving the city's mystery. The guards were opening the gates, yet so far as Sharpe knew there were no gates in the city's western wall which faced the South Cauvery river. He knew of the Bangalore Gate to the east, the Mysore Gate to the south, and the much smaller Water Gate to the north, but no one had ever spoken of a fourth gate, yet there it was. Once, plainly, there had been another water gate here, a gate that opened onto the South Cauvery, and presumably that entrance to the city had long ago been sealed up, yet now Sharpe was watching the gates being opened and he impul-

sively turned and followed the cart down the alley. The cart
had already vanished into the deep gloom inside the gate's
tunnel and the two guards were dragging the big double
doors closed, but then they saw the bright gold medallion on
Sharpe's chest and maybe that rare token convinced them
that he had the authority to enter. "Looking for Colonel
Gudin!" Sharpe offered in brazen explanation when one of
the two men nervously moved to intercept him. "Got a message for the Colonel, see?"

Then he was through the gate and he saw that it was not a
passage out of the city at all, but was rather a long tunnel
that led only to a blank stone wall. It had once been a gateway, that much was obvious, but at some time the old outer
gate had been walled shut to leave this gloomy tunnel that
was now stacked with barrels. They had to be powder barrels, for Sharpe could see pale lengths of fuses coming from
their stoppered bungholes. The whole northern side of the
tunnel was crammed with the powder barrels. Just the northern side.

An officer saw him and shouted angrily. Sharpe played the
innocent. "Colonel Gudin?" he asked. "Have you seen Colonel Gudin, sahib?"

The Indian officer ran toward him and, as he came, he
drew a pistol, but then, in the tunnel's dim dusty light, he
saw the gold medal on Sharpe's chest and he pushed the
pistol back into his sash. "Gudin?" he asked Sharpe.

Sharpe smiled eagerly. "He's my officer, sahib. I've got a
message for him."

The Indian did not understand, but he did know the significance of the medal and it was enough to make him
respectful. But he was still firm. He pointed Sharpe toward
the door and gestured that he was to leave.

"Gudin?" Sharpe insisted.

The man shook his head and Sharpe, with a grin, left the tunnel.

He had forgotten Mary now for he knew he was on the verge of understanding what was being kept so secret. He went back down the alley and at its end he turned and looked at the wall above and he wondered why there were no gunners standing by the brass guns, and why no sentries stood in the embrasures and why no flags were hung on the battlements. Everywhere else on the walls there were flags and sentries and gunners, but not here. He waited until the tunnel gates had been closed, then he hurried up the nearby ramp that led to the wall's firestep. The wall here was made of red mud bricks and was not nearly so formidable as the southern wall which was constructed from massive granite blocks. Nor was this wall more than twenty feet thick, whereas the tunnel had been nearer a hundred feet long. He ran up to the parapet where the big guns waited and, when he reached the firestep, he understood everything.

For there was not one wall here, but two. The one he was standing on was the inner wall and it was new, so new that some short stretches of the wall were still festooned with scaffolding and ropes where the Tippoo's laborers hastened to complete the work. And sixty feet away, beyond an empty inner ditch, was the city's outer wall where the flags were hung and where the gunners and sentries stood guard. That old outer wall was a couple of feet higher than this new inner wall, but opposite Sharpe, and close to where he had seen the powder-crammed tunnel, those older ramparts had crumbled at their top. That decay would surely serve as a beacon to the British, enticing them to aim their guns at that stretch of decayed wall in the certainty that they could soon finish its destruction with their bombardment. The big eighteen- and twenty-four-pounder guns would hammer away until the older outer wall collapsed to leave a ramp-like breach. The British, staring across the river at that breach, would doubtless see the new inner wall, but they might well think it was nothing but the flank of a warehouse or a temple. And so the assault would come storming across the shallow river and up the ramp of the breach in the outer wall, and then spill down into the space between the two walls. More and more men would come, those behind forcing the ones in front ever onward, and slowly the crush between the walls would grow. The guns and rockets on the inner wall would rain down death, but after a while, when the attackers filled the space between the walls, the huge charge of powder, stored in what remained of the old elaborate gateway, would be detonated. And that explosion, its force funnelled by the old and new walls, would tear into the narrow gap and flood the ditch between the walls with blood. Sharpe looked to his left and saw that the tunnel was built beneath a squat gate tower. That ancient tower would surely collapse, spilling stones onto any troops who might survive the terrible blast.

"Bloody hell," Sharpe said, and then he slipped back down the inner wall's ramp and went to find Lawford. If Mary did not get the news out, he thought, there would be slaughter when the assault came. It would be pure slaughter, and it seemed that only Mary, who was now in love with the enemy, could prevent it.

CHAPTER 8

The siege works advanced steadily, hampered only by the Tippoo's guns and by a shortage of the heavy timber needed to shore up the trenches and construct the batteries where the big siege guns would be emplaced. Colonel Gent, an engineer of the East India Company, supervised the work, and he agreed wholeheartedly with General Harris that the decayed stretch of the city's western walls was the obvious and opportune target. Then, just days after the construction of the siege works had begun, a local farmer revealed the existence of a new second wall behind the first. The man insisted the new wall was unfinished, but Harris was worried enough by the farmer's news to call his deputies to his tent where Colonel Gent delivered the gloomy intelligence about the new inner ramparts. "The fellow says his sons were taken away to help build the walls," the engineer reported, "and he seems to be telling the truth."

Baird broke the brief silence that followed Gent's words. "They can't surely garrison both walls," the Scotsman insisted.

"The Tippoo has no shortage of men," Wellesley pointed out. "Thirty or forty thousand, we hear. More than enough to defend both walls, I should think."

Baird ignored the young Colonel, while Harris, uncomfortably aware of the bad feeling between his two deputies, stared fixedly at his map of the city in the hope that some new inspiration would strike. Colonel Gent sat beside Harris. The engineer unfolded a pair of wire-framed spectacles and hooked them over his ears as he peered down at the map.

Harris sighed. "I still think it has to be the west," he said, "despite this new wall."

"The north?" Wellesley asked.

"According to our farmer fellow," Gent answered, "the new inner wall goes all the way round the north." He picked up a pencil and sketched the line of the new inner wall on the map to show that wherever the river flowed close to the city there was now a double rampart. "And the west is infinitely preferable to the north," Gent added. "The South Cauvery's shallow, while the main river can still be treacherous at this time of year. If our fellows have to wade through the Cauvery, let them do it here." He tapped the city's western approach. "Of course," he added optimistically, "maybe that fellow was right, and maybe that inner wall ain't finished."

Harris wished to God that McCandless was still with the army. That subtle Scotsman would have dispatched a dozen disguised sepoys and discovered within hours the exact state of the new inner wall, but McCandless was lost and so, Harris suspected, were the two men sent to rescue him.

"We could cross the Arrakerry Ford," Baird suggested, "then blast our way in from the east like Cornwallis did."

Harris lifted the hem of his wig and scratched at his old scalp wound. "We discussed all this before," he said wearily. He offered Baird a wan smile to take the sting from his mild reproof, then explained his reasons for not assaulting from the east. "First we have to force the crossing, and the enemy has the riverbanks entrenched. Then we must get through the new wall around their encampment"—he touched the map, showing where the Tippoo had constructed a stout mud wall, well served with guns, that surrounded the encampment which lay outside the city's southern and eastern walls—"and after that we have to lay siege to the city proper, and we know that both the east and south ramparts already have inner walls. And to breach those walls every round shot and pound of powder will have to be carried across the river."

"And one good rainfall will make the ford impassable," Gent put in gloomily, "not to mention bringing those damned crocodiles back." He shook his head. "I wouldn't want to be carrying three tons of supplies a day across a half-flooded river full of hungry teeth."

"So wherever we attack," Wellesley asked, "we have to pierce two walls?"

"That's what the man said," Baird growled.

"This new inner wall," Wellesley asked Gent, ignoring Baird, "what do we know of it?"

"Mud," Gent said, "red mud bricks. Just like Devon mud."

"Mud will crumble," Wellesley pointed out.

"If it's dry, it will," Gent agreed, "but the core of the wall won't be dry. Thoroughly good stuff, mud. Soaks up the cannon fire. I've seen twenty-four-pounder shots bounce off mud like currants off a suet pudding. Give me a good stone wall to break down any day. Break its crust and the guns turn the rubble core into a staircase. But not mud." Gent stared at the map, picking his teeth with the sharpened nib of a quill. "Not mud," he added in a gloomy undertone.

"But it will yield?" Harris asked anxiously.

"Oh, it'll yield, sir, it'll yield, I can warrant you that, but how much time do we have to persuade it to yield?" The engineer peered over his spectacles at the bewigged General. "The monsoon ain't so far off, and once the rains begin we might as well go home for all the good we'll ever do. You want a path through both walls? It'll take two weeks more, and even then the inner breach will be perilously narrow.

Perilously narrow! Can't enfilade it, you see, and the breach in the outer wall will serve as a glacis to protect the base of the inner wall. Straight on fire, sir, and all aimed a deal higher than any respectable gunner would want. We can make you a breach of sorts, but it'll be narrow and high, and God only knows what'll be waiting on the other side. Nothing good, I dare say."

"But we can breach this outer wall quickly enough?" Harris asked, tapping the place on his map.

"Aye, sir. It's mostly mud again, but it's older so the center will be drier. Once we break through the crust the thing should fall apart in hours."

Harris stared down at the map, unconsciously scratching beneath his wig. "Ladders," he said after a long pause.

Baird looked alarmed. "You're not thinking of an escalade, God save us?"

"We've no timber!" Gent protested.

"Bamboo scaling ladders," Harris said, "just a few." He smiled as he leaned back in his chair. "Make me a breach, Colonel Gent, and forget the inner wall. We'll assault the breach, but we won't go through it. Instead we'll attack the shoulders of the breach. We'll use ladders to climb off the breach onto the walls, then attack around the ramparts. Once those outer walls are ours, the beggars will have to surrender."

There was silence in the tent as the three officers considered Harris's suggestion. Colonel Gent tried to clean his spectacle lenses with a corner of his sash. "You'd better pray our fellows get up on the walls damned fast, sir." Gent broke the silence. "You'll be sending whole battalions across the river, General, and the lads behind will be pushing the fellows in front, and if there's any delay they'll spill into the space between the walls like water seeking its level. And God knows what's in between those walls. A flooded ditch?

Mines? But even if there's nothing there, the poor fellows will still be trapped between two fires."

"Two Forlorn Hopes," Harris said, thinking aloud and ignoring Gent's gloomy comments, "instead of one. They both attack two or three minutes ahead of the main assault. Their orders will be to climb off the breach and onto the walls. One Hope turns north along the outer ramparts, the other south. That way they don't need to go between the walls."

"It'll be a desperate business," Gent said flatly.

"Assaults always are," Baird said stoutly. "That's why we employ Forlorn Hopes." The Forlorn Hope was the small band of volunteers who went first into a breach to trigger the enemy's surprises. Casualties were invariably heavy, though there was never a shortage of volunteers. This time, though, it did promise to be desperate, for the two Forlorn Hopes were not being asked to fight through the breach, but rather to turn toward the walls either side of the breach and fight their way up onto the ramparts. "You can't take a city without shedding blood," Baird went on, then stiffened in his chair. "And once again, sir, I request permission to lead the main assault."

Harris smiled. "Granted, David." He spoke gently, using Baird's Christian name for the first time. "And God be with you."

"God be with the damned Tippoo," Baird said, hiding his delight. "He's the one who'll need the help. I thank you, sir. You do me honor."

Or I send you to your death, Harris thought, but kept the sentiment silent. He rolled up the city map. "Speed, gentlemen," he said, "speed. The rains will come soon enough, so let's get this business done."

The troops went on digging, zigzagging their way across the fertile fields between the aqueduct and the south branch of the Cauvery. A second British army, six and a half thousand men from Cannanore on India's western Malabar coast, arrived to swell the besiegers' ranks. The newcomers camped north of the Cauvery and placed gun batteries that could sweep the approach to the proposed breach so that the city, with its thirty thousand defenders, was now besieged by fifty-seven thousand men, half of whom marched under British colors and half under the banners of Hyderabad. Six thousand of the British troops were actually British, the rest were sepoys, and behind all the troops, in the sprawling encampments, more than a hundred thousand hungry civilians waited to plunder the supplies rumored to be inside Seringapatam.

Harris had men enough for the siege and assault, but not enough to ring the city entirely and so the Tippoo's cavalry made daily sallies from the unguarded eastern side of the island to attack the foraging parties who ranged deep into the country in search of timber and food. The Nizam of Hyderabad's horsemen fought off the daily attacks. The Nizam was a Muslim, but he had no love for his coreligionist, the Tippoo, and the men of Hyderabad's army fought fiercely. One horseman came back to the camp with the heads of six enemies tied by their long hair to his lance. He held the bloody trophies aloft and galloped proudly along the tent lines to the cheers of the sepoys and redcoats. Harris sent the man a purse of guineas, while Meer Allum, the commander of the Nizam's forces, more practically ordered a concubine to express his gratitude.

The trenches made ground daily, but one last formidable obstacle prevented their approach close enough to the city for the siege guns to begin their destructive work. On the southern bank of the Cauvery, a half-mile west of the city, stood the ruins of an old watermill. Built of stone, the ancient walls were thick enough to withstand the artillery fire from

Harris's camp and from the new British positions across the river. The ruined buildings had been converted into a stout fort that was equipped with a deep defensive ditch and was strongly garrisoned by two of the Tippoo's finest *cushoons*, reinforced by cannon and rocketmen, and so long as the mill fort existed no British gun could be dragged within battering range of the city's walls. The two flags that flew over the mill fort were shot away every day, but each dawn the flags would be hoisted again, albeit on shorter staffs, and once again the British and Indian gunners would blaze away with round shot and shell, and once again the sun flag and the banner of the Lion of God would be felled, but whenever skirmishers went close to the fort to discover if any defender survived, there would be a blast of cannon, rockets, and musketry to prove that the Tippoo's men were still dangerous. The Tippoo could even reinforce the garrison thanks to a deep trench that ran close to the south branch of the Cauvery and up which his men could creep through the night to relieve the fort's battered garrison.

The fort had to be taken. Harris ordered a dusk attack that was led by Indian and Scottish flank companies supported by a party of engineers whose job was to bridge the mill's deep ditch. For an hour before the assault the artillery on both banks of the river rained shells into the mill. The twelve-pounder guns were loaded with howitzer shells and the wispy trails of their burning fuses sputtered across the darkening sky to plunge into the smoke which churned up from the battered fort. To the waiting infantry who would have to wade through the Little Cauvery, cross the ditch, and assault the mill it seemed as if the small fort was being obliterated, for there was nothing to be seen but the boiling smoke and dust amongst which the shells exploded with dull red flashes, but every few moments, as if to belie the destruction that seemed so complete, an Indian gun would flash back its response and a round shot would scream across the fields toward the British batteries. Or else a rocket would flare up from the defenders and snake its thicker smoke trail across the delicate tracery left by the fuses of the howitzer shells. The largest guns on the city wall were also firing, trying to bounce their shot up from the ground so that the ricochets would reach the besiegers' artillery. Sharpe, inside the city, heard the vast hammering of the guns and wondered if it presaged an assault on the city's walls, but Sergeant Rothière assured the men that it was only the British wasting ammunition on the old mill.

The bombardment suddenly ceased and the Tippoo's men came scrambling out of the mill's damp cellars to take their places at their fire-scorched ramparts. They reached their broken firesteps just in time, for the leading engineers were already hurling lit carcasses into the ditch. The carcasses were bundles of damp straw tight wrapped about a paper-cased shell of saltpeter, corned gunpowder, and antimony. The carcasses burned fiercely, consuming the straw from the inside to billow choking streams of smoke through vents left in the casings so that within seconds the ditch was filled with a dense fog of gray smoke into which the frightened defenders poured a badly aimed musket volley. More carcasses were hurled, adding to the blinding smoke, and under this cover a dozen planks were thrown across the ditch and screaming attackers charged across with fixed bayonets. Only a few of the Tippoo's men still had loaded muskets. Those men fired, and one of the attackers fell through the smoke to fall on the hissing carcasses, but the rest were already scrambling over the walls. Half the attackers were Macleod's Highlanders from Perthshire, the others were Bengali infantry, and both came into the mill like avenging furies. The Tippoo's men seemed stunned by the suddenness of the assault, or else they had been so shaken by the shelling and were so con-

fused by the choking smoke that they were incapable of resistance, and incapable, too, of surrender. Bengalis and
Highlanders hunted through the ruins, their war cries shrill
as they bayoneted and shot the garrison, while behind them,
before the smoke of the carcasses had even begun to fade or
the fighting in the mill die down, the engineers were con-
structing a stouter bridge across which they could haul their
siege guns so they could turn the old mill into a breaching
battery.

The smoke of the carcasses at last died and drifted away,
its remnants touched red by the setting sun, and in the lurid
light a Highlander capered on the ramparts with the captured sun banner at the end of his bayonet while a Bengali
havildar waved the Tippoo's lion flag in celebration. The
assault had turned into a massacre and the officers now tried
to calm the attackers down as they pierced ever deeper into
the mill's vaults. The innermost cellar was grimly defended
by a group of the Tippoo's infantry, but an engineer brought
the last remaining carcass into the mill, lit its fuse, waited
until the smoke began to pour from the vents and then
hurled it down the steps. There were a few seconds of
silence, then dazed and gasping defenders came scrambling
up the steep stairs. The mill fort was taken, and astonishingly
only one of the attackers had been killed, but a shocked
Highlander lieutenant counted two hundred dead bodies
dressed in the Tippoo's tiger-striped tunic, and still more
enemy dead were piled bloodily in every embrasure. The rest
of the garrison was either taken prisoner or else had managed to flee down the connecting trench to the city. A Scottish sergeant, finding one of the Tippoo's rockets in a
magazine, stuck it vertically between two of the ruin's bigger
stones, then lit the fuse. There were cheers as the rocket
flamed and smoked, then louder cheers as it screamed up
into the sky. It began to corkscrew, leaving a crazy trail of

smoke in the twilight air, and then, reaching its apogee, and by now almost invisible, it tumbled and fell into the Cauvery.

Next morning the first eighteen-pounders were already emplaced in the mill. The range to the city was long, but not impossible, and Harris gave the order for the guns to open fire. The eighteen-pounder cannon were among the heavy siege guns that would make the breach, but for now they were employed to batter the enemy's own guns. Seringapatam's outer wall was protected by a glacis, but there was not enough distance between the river and the wall to construct a full glacis with a gently sloping outer face high enough to bounce cannon shot over the city's walls, and so the low glacis could only protect the wall's base, not the parapet, and the eighteen-pounders' first shots were aimed to scour that parapet of its guns. The good fortune that had accompanied the Bengalis and the Highlanders in their assault on the old mill now seemed to settle on the shoulders of the gunners for their very first shot cracked apart an embrasure and the second dismounted the gun behind it, and after that every shot seemed to have an equally destructive effect. British and Indian officers watched through spyglasses as embrasure after embrasure was destroyed and as gun after gun was thrown down. A dozen heavy cannon were tumbled forward into the flooded ditch between the city wall and the glacis, and every tumbling fall was greeted by a cheer from the besiegers. The city's western wall was being stripped of guns, and the artillerymen's prowess seemed to promise an easy assault. Spirits in the allied ranks soared.

While inside the city, watching his precious cannon being destroyed, the Tippoo fumed. The mill fort, on which he had pinned such high hopes of delaying the enemy till the monsoon washed them away, had fallen like a child's wooden toy. And now his precious guns were being obliterated.

It was time, the Tippoo decided, to show his soldiers that

these red-coated enemies were not invulnerable demons, but mortal men, and that like any other mortal men, they could be made to whimper. It was time to unsheath the tiger's claws.

A half-hour's walk east of the city, just outside the embrasured wall that protected the Tippoo's encampment, lay his Summer Palace, the Daria Dowlat. It was much smaller than the Inner Palace within the city, for the Inner Palace was where the Tippoo's enormous harem lived and where his government had its offices and his army its headquarters, and so it was a sprawl of stables, storehouses, courtyards, state rooms, and prison cells. The Inner Palace seethed with activity, a place where hundreds of folk had their daily living, while the Summer Palace, set in its wide green gardens and protected by a thick hedge of aloe, was a haven of peace.

The Daria Dowlat had not been built to impress, but rather for comfort. Only two stories high, the building was made from huge teak beams over which stucco had been laid, then modeled and painted so that every surface glittered in the sunlight. The whole palace was surrounded by a two-storied verandah and on the western outer wall, under the verandah where the sun could not fade it, the Tippoo had ordered painted a vast mural showing the battle of Pollilur at which, fifteen years before, he had destroyed a British army. That great victory had extended Mysore's dominion along the Malabar Coast and, in honor of the triumph, the palace had been built and received its name, the Daria Dowlat or Treasure of the Sea. The palace lay on the road leading to the island's eastern tip, the same road on which was built the fine, elegant mausoleum in which the Tippoo's great father, Hyder Ali, and his mother, the Begum Fatima, were buried. There too, one day, the Tippoo prayed he would lie at rest.

The Daria Dowlat's garden was a wide lawn dotted with

pools, trees, shrubs, and flowers. Roses grew there, and mangoes, but there were also exotic strains of indigo and cotton mixed with pineapples from Africa and avocados from Mexico, all of them plants that the Tippoo had encouraged or imported in the hope that they would prove profitable for his country, but on this day, the day after the mill fort had been swamped with smoke, fire, and blood, the garden was filled with two thousand of the Tippoo's thirty thousand troops. The men paraded in three sides of a hollow square to the north of the palace, leaving the Daria Dowlat's shadowed facade as the fourth side of their square.

The Tippoo had ordered entertainment for his troops. There were dancers from the city, two jugglers and a man who charmed snakes, but, best of all, the Tippoo's wooden tiger organ had been fetched from the Inner Palace and the soldiers laughed as the life-size model tiger raked its claws across the redcoat's blood-painted face. The bellow-driven growl did not carry very far, any more than did the pathetic cry of the tiger's victim, but the action of the toy alone was sufficient to amuse the men.

The Tippoo arrived in a palanquin just after midday. None of his European advisers accompanied him, nor were any of his European troops present, though Appah Rao was in attendance, for two of the five *cushoons* parading in the palace gardens came from Rao's brigade, and the Hindu General stood tall and silent just behind the Tippoo on the palace's upper verandah. Appah Rao disapproved of what was about to happen, but he dared not make a protest, for any sign of disloyalty from a Hindu was enough to rouse the Tippoo's suspicions. Besides, the Tippoo could not be dissuaded. His astrologers had told him that a period of ill luck had arrived and that it could only be averted by sacrifice. Other sages had peered into the smoke-misted surface of a pot of hot oil, the Tippoo's favorite form of divination, and had deciphered the strange-colored and slow-moving swirls to declare that they told the same grim tale: a season of bad fortune had come to Seringapatam. That bad luck had caused both the fall of the mill fort and the destruction of the guns on the outer western wall and the Tippoo was determined to avert this sudden ill fortune.

The Tippoo let his soldiers enjoy the tiger for a few moments longer, then he clapped his hands and ordered his servants to carry the model back to the Inner Palace. The tiger's place was taken by a dozen *jettis* who strode onto the forecourt with their bare torsos gleaming. For a few moments they amused the soldiers with their more common-place tricks: they bent iron rods into circles, lifted grown men on both hands or juggled with cannonballs.

Then a goatskin drum sounded and the *jettis*, obedient to its strokes, went back to the shadows under the Tippoo's balcony. The watching soldiers fell into an expectant silence, then growled as a sorry party of prisoners was herded onto the forecourt. There were thirteen prisoners, all in red coats, all of them men of the 33rd who had been captured during the night battle at the Sultanpetah *tope*.

The thirteen men stood uncertainly amidst the ring of their enemies. The sun beat down. One of the prisoners, a sergeant, twitched as he stared at the ranks of tiger-striped soldiers, and still his face twitched as he turned around and gazed with a curious intensity when the Tippoo stepped to the rail of the upper verandah and, in a clear high voice, spoke to his troops. The enemy, the Tippoo said, had been fortunate. They had gained some cheap victories to the west of the city, but that was no reason to fear them. The British sorcerers, knowing they could not defeat the tigers of Mysore by force alone, had made a powerful spell, but with the help of Allah that spell would now be confounded. The soldiers greeted the speech with a long and approving sigh while the prisoners, unable to understand any of the Tippoo's words, looked anxiously about, but could make no sense of the occasion.

Guards surrounded the prisoners and pushed them back to the palace, leaving just one man alone on the forecourt. That man tried to go with his companions, but a guard thrust him back with a bayonet and the uneven contest between a confused prisoner and an armed guard sparked a gust of laughter. The prisoner, driven back to the center of the forecourt, waited nervously.

Two *jettis* walked toward him. They were big men, formidably bearded, tall and with their long hair bound and tied about their heads. The prisoner licked his lips, the *jettis* smiled, and suddenly the redcoat sensed his fate and took two or three hurried steps away from the strongmen. The watching soldiers laughed as the redcoat tried to escape, but he was penned in by three walls of tiger-striped infantry and there was nowhere to run. He tried to dodge past the two *jettis*, but one of them reached out and snatched a handful of his red coat. The prisoner beat at the *jetti* with his fists, but it was like a rabbit cuffing at a wolf. The watching soldiers laughed again, though there was a nervousness in their amusement.

The *jetti* drew the soldier in to his body, then hugged him in a terrible last embrace. The second *jetti* took hold of the redcoat's head, paused to take breath, then twisted.

The prisoner's dying scream was choked off in an instant. For a second his head stared sightlessly backward, then the *jettis* released him and, as the twisted neck grotesquely righted itself, the man collapsed. One of the *jettis* picked up the corpse in one huge hand and contemptuously tossed it high into the air like a terrier tossing a dead rat. The watching soldiers were silent for a second, then cheered. The Tippoo smiled.

A second redcoat was driven to the *jettis*, and this man was forced to kneel. He did not move as the nail was placed on his head. He uttered one curse, then died in seconds as his blood spurted out onto the gravel forecourt. A third man was killed with a single punch to his chest, a blow so massive that it drove him back a full twelve paces before, shuddering, his ruptured heart gave up. The watching soldiers shouted that they wanted to see another man's neck wrung like a chicken, and the *jettis* obliged. And so, one by one, the prisoners were forced to their killers. Three of the men died abjectly, calling for mercy and weeping like babes. Two died saying prayers, but the rest died defiantly. Three put up a fight, and one tall grenadier raised an ironic cheer from the watching troops by breaking a *jetti*'s finger, but then he too died like the rest. One after the other they died, and those who came last were forced to watch their comrades' deaths and to wonder how they would be sent to meet their Maker; whether they would be spiked through the skull or have their necks twisted north to south or simply be beaten to bloody death. And all of the prisoners, once dead, were decapitated by a sword blow before the two parts of their bodies were wrapped in reed mats and laid aside.

The *jettis* saved the Sergeant till last. The watching soldiers were in a fine mood now. They had been nervous at first, apprehensive of cold-blooded death on a sun-drenched afternoon, but the strength of the *jettis* and the desperate antics of the doomed men trying to escape had amused them and now they wanted to enjoy this last victim who promised to provide the finest entertainment of the day. His face was twitching in what the spectators took to be uncontrollable fear, but despite that terror he proved astonishingly agile, forever scuttling out of the *jettis*' way and shouting up toward the Tippoo. Again and again he would appear to be cornered, but somehow he would always slide or twist or duck his way free and, with his face shuddering, would call desperately to the Tippoo. His shouts were drowned by the cheers of the soldiers who applauded every narrow escape. Two more *jettis* came to help catch the elusive man and, though he tried to twist past them, they at last had the Sergeant trapped. The *jettis* advanced in a line, forcing him back toward the palace, and the watching soldiers fell silent in expectation of his death. The Sergeant feinted to his left, then suddenly twisted and ran from the advancing *jetti* toward the palace. The guards moved to drive him back toward his executioners, but the man stopped beneath the verandah and stared up at the Tippoo. "I know who the traitors are here!" he shouted in the silence. "I know!"

A *jetti* caught the Sergeant from behind and forced him to his knees.

"Get these black bastards off me!" the Sergeant screamed. "Listen, Your Honor, I know what's going on here! There's a British officer in the city wearing your uniform! For God's sake! Mother!" This last cry was torn from Obadiah Hakeswill as a second *jetti* placed his hands on the Sergeant's head. Hakeswill wrenched his face round and bit down hard on the ball of the *jetti*'s thumb and the astonished man jerked his hands away, leaving a scrap of flesh in the Sergeant's mouth.

Hakeswill spat the morsel out. "Listen, Your Grace! I know what the bastards are up to! Traitors. On my oath. Get away from me, you heathen black bastard! I can't die! I can't die! Mother!" The *jetti* with the bitten hand had gripped the Sergeant's head and begun to turn it. Usually the neck was wrung swiftly, for a huge explosion of energy was needed to break a man's spine, but this time the *jetti* planned a slow and exquisitely painful death in revenge for his bitten hand. "Mother!" Hakeswill screamed as his face was forced farther around, and then, just as it was twisted back past his shoulder, he made one last effort. "I saw a British officer in the city! No!"

"Wait," the Tippoo called.

The *jetti* paused, still holding Hakeswill's head at an unnatural angle.

"What did he say?" the Tippoo asked one of his officers who spoke some English and who had been translating the Sergeant's desperate words. The officer translated again.

The Tippoo waved one of his small delicate hands and the aggrieved *jetti* let go of Hakeswill's head. The Sergeant cursed as the agonizing tension left his neck, then rubbed at the pain. "Bleeding heathen bastard!" he said. "You murdering black bugger!" He spat at the *jetti*, shook himself out of the grip of the man holding him, then stood and walked two paces toward the palace. "I saw him, didn't I? With my own eyes! In a frock, like them." He gestured at the watching soldiers in their tiger-striped tunics. "A lieutenant, he is, and the army says he went back to Madras, but he didn't, did he? 'Cos he's here. 'Cos I saw him. Me! Obadiah Hakeswill, Your Highness, and keep that bleeding heathen darkie away from me." One of the *jettis* had come close and Hakeswill, his face twitching, turned on the looming man. "Go on, bugger off back to your sty, you bloody great lump."

The officer who spoke English called down from the verandah. "Who did you see?" he asked.

"I told you, Your Honor, didn't I?"

"No, you didn't. Give us a name."

Hakeswill's face twitched. "I'll tell you," he wheedled, "if you promise to let me live." He dropped to his knees and stared up at the verandah. "I don't mind being in your dungeons, my Lord, for Obadiah Hakeswill never did mind a rat or two, but I don't want these bleeding heathens screwing me neck back to front. It ain't a Christian act."

The officer translated for the Tippoo who, at last, nodded

and so prompted the officer to turn back to Hakeswill. "You will live," he called down.

"Word of honor?" Hakeswill asked.

"Upon my honor."

"Cross your heart and hope to die? Like it says in the scriptures?"

"You will live!" the officer snapped. "So long as you tell us the truth."

"I always do that, sir. Honest Hakeswill, that's my name, sir. I saw him, didn't I? Lieutenant Lawford, William he's called. Tall lanky fellow with fair hair and blue eyes. And he ain't alone. Private bleeding Sharpe was with him."

The officer had not understood everything that Hakeswill had said, but he had understood enough. "You are saying this man Lawford is a British officer?" he asked.

"'Course he is! In my bleeding company, what's more. And they said he'd gone back to Madras on account of carrying dispatches, but he never did, 'cos there weren't no dispatches to be carried. He's here, Your Grace, and up to no bleeding good and, like I said, dolled up in a stripy frock."

The officer seemed sceptical. "The only Englishmen we have here, Sergeant, are prisoners or deserters. You're lying."

Hakeswill spat on the gravel that was soaked with the blood from the decapitated prisoners. "How can he be a deserter? Officers don't desert! They sell their commissions and bugger off home to Mummy. I tell you, sir, he's an officer! And the other one's a right bastard! Flogged, he was, and quite right too! He should have been flogged to bleeding death, only the General sent for him."

The mention of the flogging woke a memory in the Tippoo. "When was he flogged?" The officer translated the Tippoo's question.

"Just before he ran, sir. Raw, he must have been, but not raw enough."

"And you say the General sent for him?" The officer sounded disbelieving.

"Harris, sir, the bugger what lost a lump out of his skull in America. He sent our Colonel, he did, and Colonel Wellesley stopped the flogging. Stopped it!" Hakeswill's indignation was still keen. "Stopping a flogging what's been properly ordered! Never seen anything so disgraceful in all me born days! Going to the dogs, the army is, going to the dogs."

The Tippoo listened to the translation, then stepped back from the railing. He turned to Appah Rao who had once served in the East India Company's army. "Do British officers desert?"

"None that I've ever heard of, Your Majesty," Appah Rao said, glad that the shadows of the balcony were hiding his pale and worried face. "They might resign and sell their commission, but desert? Never."

The Tippoo nodded down to the kneeling Hakeswill. "Put that wretch back in the cells," he ordered, "and tell Colonel Gudin to meet me at the Inner Palace."

Guards dragged Hakeswill back to the city. "And he had a *bibbi* with him!" Hakeswill shouted as he was pulled away, but no one took any notice. The Sergeant was shedding tears of pure happiness as he was taken back through the Bangalore Gate. "Thank you, Mother," he called to the cloudless sky, "thank you, Mother, for I cannot die!"

The twelve dead men were hidden in a makeshift grave. The troops marched back to their encampment while the Tippoo, being carried to the Inner Palace beneath the tiger-striped canopy of his palanquin, reflected that the sacrifice of the twelve prisoners had not been in vain for it had revealed the presence of enemies. Allah be thanked, he reflected, for his luck had surely turned.

❖   ❖   ❖

"You think Mrs. Bickerstaff has gone over to the enemy?" Lawford asked Sharpe for the third or fourth time.

"She's gone to his bed," Sharpe said bleakly, "but I reckon she'll still help us." Sharpe had washed both his and Lawford's tunics and now he patted the cloth to see if it had dried. Looking after kit in this army, he reflected, was a deal easier than in the British. There was no pipeclay here to be caked onto crossbelts and musket slings, no blackball to be used on boots and no grease and powder to be slathered on the hair. He decided the tunics were dry enough and tossed one to the Lieutenant, then pulled his own over his head, carefully freeing the gold medallion so that it hung on his chest. His tunic also boasted a red cord on his left shoulder, the Tippoo's insignia of a corporal. Lawford seemed to resent Sharpe bearing these marks of rank that were denied to him.

"Suppose she betrays us?" Lawford asked.

"Then we're in trouble," Sharpe said brutally. "But she won't. Mary's a good lass."

Lawford shrugged. "She jilted you."

"Easy come, easy go," Sharpe said, then belted the tunic. Like most of the Tippoo's soldiers he now went bare-legged beneath the knee-length garment, though Lawford insisted on keeping his old British trousers. Both men wore their old shakos, though George III's badge had been replaced by a tin tiger with an upraised paw. "Listen," Sharpe said to a still worried Lawford, "I've done what you asked, and the lass says she'll find this Ravi whatever his name is, and all we have to do now is wait. And if we get a chance to run, we run like buggery. You reckon that musket's ready for inspection?"

"It's clean," Lawford said defensively, hefting his big French firelock.

"Christ, you'd be on a charge for that musket back in the proper army. Give it here."

Sergeant Rothière's daily inspection was not for another

half-hour, and after that the two men would be free until mid afternoon when it would be the turn of Gudin's battalion to stand guard over the Mysore Gate. That guard duty ended at midnight, but Sharpe knew there would be no chance of an escape, for the Mysore Gate did not offer an exit from the Tippoo's territory, but rather led into the city's surrounding encampment which, in turn, had a strong perimeter guard. The previous night Sharpe had experimented to see whether his red cord and gold medallion would be authority enough for him to wander through the encampment, maybe allowing him to find a shadowed and quiet stretch of its earthworks over which he could scramble in the dark, but he had been intercepted within twenty yards of the gate and politely but firmly ushered back. The Tippoo, it seemed, was taking no chances.

"I already had Wazzy clean that," Lawford said, nodding at the musket in Sharpe's hands. Wazir was one of the small boys who hung around the barracks to earn pice for washing and cleaning equipment. "I paid him," Lawford said indignantly.

"If you want a job done properly," Sharpe said, "you do it yourself. Hell!" He swore because he had pinched his finger on the musket's mainspring which he had uncovered by unscrewing the lock plate. "Look at that rust!" He managed to unseat the mainspring without losing the trigger mechanism, then began to file the rust off the spring's edge. "Bloody rubbish, these French muskets," he grumbled. "Nothing like a proper Birmingham bundook."

"Do you clean your own musket like that?" Lawford asked, impressed that Sharpe had unscrewed the lock plate.

" 'Course I do! Not that Hakeswill ever cares. He only looks at the outside." Sharpe grinned. "You remember that day you saved my skin with the flint? Hakeswill had changed

it for a bit of stone, but I caught it before he could do any
damage. He's a fly bastard, that one."

"He changed it?" Lawford seemed shocked.

"Bloody snake, that Obadiah. How much did you pay
Wazzy?"

"An anna."

"He robbed you. You want to pass me that oil bottle?"

Lawford obliged, then settled back against the stone water
trough in which Sharpe had washed the tunics. He felt
strangely content, despite the apparent failure of his mission.
There was a pleasure in sharing this intimacy with Sharpe,
indeed it felt oddly like a privilege. Many young officers were
frightened of the men they commanded, fearing their scorn,
and they concealed their apprehension with a display of care-
less arrogance. Lawford doubted he could ever do that now,
for he no longer felt any fear of the crude, hard men who
formed the ranks of Britain's army. Sharpe had cured him of
that by teaching him that the crudity was unthinking and the
hardness a disguise for conscientiousness. Not that every
man was conscientious, any more than all Britain's soldiers
were crude, but too many officers assumed they were all
brutes and treated them as such. Now Lawford watched as
Sharpe's capable fingers forced the cleaned mainspring back
into its cavity, using his picklock as a lever.

"Lieutenant?" a voice called respectfully across the yard.
"Lieutenant Lawford?"

"Sir?" Lawford responded without thinking, turning
toward the voice and rising to his feet. Then he realized what
he had done and blanched.

Sharpe swore.

Colonel Gudin walked slowly across the yard, rubbing his
long face as he approached the two Englishmen. "Lieutenant
William Lawford," he enquired gently, "of His Majesty's
33rd Regiment of Foot?"

Lawford said nothing.

Gudin shrugged. "Officers are supposedly men of honor, Lieutenant. Are you going to continue to lie?"

"No, sir," Lawford said.

Gudin sighed. "So are you a commissioned officer or not?"

"I am, sir." Lawford sounded ashamed, though whether it was because he had been accused of dishonorable behavior or because he had betrayed his true rank, Sharpe could not tell.

"And you, *Caporal* Sharpe?" Gudin asked sadly.

"I ain't an officer, Colonel."

"No," Gudin said, "I did not think you were. But are you a true deserter?"

"Of course I am, sir!" Sharpe lied.

Gudin smiled at Sharpe's confident tone. "And you, Lieutenant," he asked Lawford, "are you truly a deserter?" Lawford made no reply and Gudin sighed. "Answer me on your honor, Lieutenant, if you would be so kind."

"No, sir," Lawford admitted. "Nor is Private Sharpe, sir."

Gudin nodded. "That is what the sergeant said."

"The Sergeant, sir?" Lawford asked.

Gudin grimaced. "I fear the Tippoo executed the prisoners taken the other night. He spared just one, because that man told him of you."

"The bastard!" Sharpe said, throwing the musket down in disgust. Bloody Hakeswill! He swore again, far more viciously.

"Sir?" Lawford said to Gudin, ignoring Sharpe's anger.

"Lieutenant?" Gudin responded courteously.

"We were captured by the Tippoo's men while wearing our red coats, sir. That means we should be protected as legitimate prisoners of war."

Gudin shook his head. "It means nothing of the sort, Lieutenant, for you lied about your rank and your intentions." He sounded disapproving. "But I shall still plead for your lives." Gudin sat on the water trough's edge and flapped a hand at a persistent fly. "Will you tell me why you came here?"

"No, sir," Lawford said.

"I suppose not, but I warn you that the Tippoo will want to know." Gudin smiled at Sharpe. "I had come to the conclusion, Sharpe, that you are one of the best soldiers I have ever had the pleasure to command. But only one thing worried me about you, and that was why a good soldier would desert from his allegiance, even if he had been flogged, but now I see you are a better man than I thought." He frowned because Sharpe, while this elegant compliment was being paid, had lifted the back of his tunic and seemed to be scratching his bottom.

"Sorry, sir," Sharpe said, noticing the Colonel's distaste and dropping his tunic's hem.

"I'm sorry to be losing you, Sharpe," Gudin went on. "I'm afraid there is an escort waiting for you outside the barracks. You're to be taken to the palace." Gudin paused, but must have decided there was nothing he could add that might ameliorate the implied threat of his words. Instead he turned and snapped his fingers to bring a disapproving Sergeant Rothière into the courtyard. Rothière carried their red coats and Sharpe's white trousers. "They may help a little," Gudin said, though without any real hope in his voice. The Colonel watched as they discarded their newly cleaned tunics and pulled on their red coats. "About your woman," he said to Sharpe, then hesitated.

"She had nothing to do with this, sir," Sharpe said hurriedly as he pulled on the trousers. He buttoned his old jacket and the red coat felt strangely confining after the looser tunic. "On my honor, sir. And besides," he added, "she gave me the push."

"Twice unlucky, Sharpe. Bad in a soldier, that." Gudin

smiled and reached out a hand. "Your muskets, gentlemen, if you please."

Sharpe handed over both guns. "Sir?"

"Private Sharpe?"

Sharpe reddened and became awkward. "It was an honor to serve you, sir. I mean that. I wish we had more like you in our army."

"Thank you, Sharpe," Gudin gravely acknowledged the compliment. "Of course," he added, "if you tell me now that your experiences here have changed your loyalties and that you would truly like to continue serving the Tippoo, then you might be spared whatever is in store for you. I think I could persuade His Majesty of your change of heart, but you'd need to tell me why you came here in the first place."

Lawford stiffened as this offer was made to Sharpe. Sharpe hesitated, then shook his head. "No, sir," he said. "I reckon I'm a proper redcoat."

Gudin had expected the reply. "Good for you, Sharpe. And by the way, Private, you might as well hang the medallion around your neck. They'll find it anyway."

"Yes, sir." Sharpe retrieved the gold from his trouser pocket where he had optimistically concealed it, and looped the chain over his head.

Gudin stood and gestured toward the barracks room. "This way, gentlemen."

That was the end of the pleasantries.

And Sharpe suspected it would be the last pleasantry for a very long time.

For now they were the Tippoo's prisoners.

Appah Rao had Mary fetched to a room off the courtyard of his house. Kunwar Singh was waiting there, but Mary was frightened and dared not look at Kunwar Singh for fear of seeing a hint of bad news on his handsome face. Mary had no particular reason to expect bad news, but she was ever wary, and something about Appah Rao's stiff demeanor told her that her presentiments were justified. "Your companions," Appah Rao told her when the servant had closed the door behind her, "have been arrested. Lieutenant Lawford and Private Sharpe, the one you say is your brother."

"My half-brother, sir," Mary whispered.

"If you say so," Appah Rao conceded. Kunwar Singh spoke a little English, though not enough to follow the conversation, which was why Appah Rao had chosen to question Mary in that language even though his mastery of it was uncertain. Appah Rao doubted whether Sharpe and Mary were related, but he liked the girl nevertheless and he approved of her as Kunwar Singh's bride. The gods alone knew what the future would bring to Mysore, but it was likely that the British would be involved, and if Kunwar Singh had a wife who spoke English there would be an advantage for him. Besides, Appah Rao's wife Lakshmi was convinced that the girl was a good modest creature and that her past, like the past of Kunwar Singh's family, was best forgotten. "Why did they come here?" the General asked.

"I don't know, sir."

Appah Rao took a pistol from his belt and began loading it. Both Mary and Kunwar Singh watched with alarm as the General carefully measured powder from a silver horn into the pistol's chased barrel. "Aruna," he said, using the name Mary had taken from her mother, "let me tell you what will happen to Lieutenant Lawford and Private Sharpe." He paused to tap the horn's spout against the pistol's muzzle to shake loose the last specks of powder. "The Tippoo will have them questioned and doubtless the questioning will be painful. In the end, Aruna, they will confess. All men do. Maybe they will live, maybe not, I cannot tell." He looked up at her, then pushed a scrap of wadding into the pistol. "The Tippoo," he went on as he selected a bullet from the pistol's wooden case, "will want to know two things. First, why they came here, and, second, whether they were told to make contact with any person inside the city. Do you understand me?"

"Yes, sir."

The General placed the bullet in the barrel, then pulled out the pistol's short ramrod. "They're going to tell him, Aruna. However brave they are, they will talk in the end. Of course"—he paused as he rammed the bullet hard down—"the Tippoo might remember your existence. And if he does, Aruna, then he will send for you and you will be questioned too, but not so gently as I am questioning you now."

"No, sir," Mary whispered.

Appah Rao slotted the short ramrod back in its hoops. He primed the gun, but did not cock it. "I want no harm to come to you, Aruna, so tell me why the two men came to Seringapatam."

Mary stared at the pistol in the General's hand. It was a beautiful weapon with a butt inlaid with ivory and a barrel chased with silver whorls. Then she looked up into the General's eyes and saw that he had no intention of shooting her. She did not see threat in those eyes, just fear, and it was that fear which decided her to tell the truth. "They came, sir," she said, "because they had to reach a man called McCandless."

It was the answer Rao had feared. "And did they?"

"No, sir."

"So what did they find out?" Rao asked, laying the pistol down on the table. "What did they find out?" he asked in a harder voice.

"Private Sharpe told me that the British shouldn't attack in the west, sir," Mary said, forgetting to describe Sharpe as her brother. "That's all he said, honestly, sir."

"All?" Rao asked. "Surely not. Why would he tell you that? Did he think you could get the news out of the city?"

Mary stared down at the pistol. "I was to find a man, sir," she said at last.

"Who?"

She looked up at the General, fear in her eyes. "A merchant, sir, called Ravi Shekhar."

"Anyone else?"

"No, sir! Truly."

Rao believed her, and felt a wash of relief. His greatest fear was that Sharpe and Lawford might have been given his own name, for although Colonel McCandless had promised to keep Rao's treachery a secret Rao could not be certain that the promise had been kept. McCandless himself had not been questioned under torture, for the Tippoo seemed convinced that the elderly Colonel "Ross" had indeed been foraging when he had been captured, but Rao still felt the threat of discovery moving insidiously closer. Lawford and Sharpe could not identify Rao himself as a traitor, but they very well might identify McCandless and then the Tippoo's *jettis* would turn their attentions to the elderly Scotsman, and how long would he endure their merciless treatment? The General wondered if he should make a dash from the city to the British lines, but rejected the thought almost as soon as it occurred to him. Such an escape might secure Appah Rao's own safety, but it would sacrifice his large family and all the faithful servants who were in his employment. No, he decided, this dangerous game must be seen to its finish. He pushed the pistol closer to Mary. "Take it," he ordered her.

Mary looked astonished. "The pistol, sir?"

"Take it! Now listen, girl. Ravi Shekhar is dead and his body was fed to the tigers. It's possible the Tippoo will forget you even existed, but if he remembers then you might need that pistol." Appah Rao wondered if he could smuggle the girl clean out of the city. It was a tempting thought, but every civilian was stopped at the gates and had to produce a pass stamped by the Tippoo himself, and very few received that pass. A soldier might succeed in escaping the city, but not a civilian. Appah Rao gazed into Mary's dark eyes. "I am told that placing it in your mouth and pointing it slightly upwards is the most effective." Mary shuddered and the General nodded to Kunwar Singh. "I give her to your care," he said.

Kunwar Singh bowed his head.

Mary went back to the women's quarters while Appah Rao made an offering at his household shrine. He lingered there, thinking how he envied the certainty of men like the Tippoo or Colonel McCandless. Neither man seemed to have any doubts, but rather believed that destiny was whatever they themselves made of it. They were not subject to other men's wills and Appah Rao would have liked such certainty for himself. He would have liked to live in a Mysore ruled by its ancient Hindu house, and a Mysore in which no other nations intruded: no British, no French, no Mahrattas, and no Muslims, but instead he found himself caught between two armies and somehow he had to keep his wife, his children, his servants, and himself alive. He closed his eyes, touched his hands to his forehead, and bowed to Ganesh, the elephant-headed god who guarded Appah Rao's household. "Just keep us alive," he prayed to the god, "just keep us alive."

The Tippoo himself came to the courtyard where the tigers had been restored to their long chains. Four infantrymen guarded the two Englishmen. The Tippoo did not come in state, with chamberlains and courtiers, but was accompanied by only one officer and two *jettis* who watched impassively as the Tippoo strode to Sharpe and tugged the medallion from around his neck. He pulled so hard that the chain cut into the back of Sharpe's neck before it snapped. Then the Tippoo spat into Sharpe's face and turned away.

The officer was a suave young Muslim who spoke good English. "His Majesty," he said when the Tippoo turned back to face the prisoners, "wishes to know why you came to the city."

Lawford stiffened. "I am an officer in His Britannic Majesty's . . ." he began, but the Indian cut him off with a gesture.

"Quiet!" the officer said wearily. "You are nothing except what we make you. So why are you here?"

"Why do you think?" Sharpe said.

The officer looked at him. "I think," he said judiciously, "that you came here to spy."

"So now you know," Sharpe said defiantly.

The officer smiled. "But maybe you were given the name of a man who might help you inside the city? That is the name we want."

Sharpe shook his head. "Didn't give us any names. Not one."

"Maybe," the officer said, then nodded at the two *jettis* who seized hold of Sharpe, then ripped the coat down his back so that its buttons tore off one by one as it was dragged down. He wore no shirt beneath, only the bandages that still covered the wounds caused by his flogging. One of the *jettis* drew a knife and unceremoniously sliced through the bandages, making Sharpe flinch as the blade cut into the almost healed wounds. The bandages were tossed aside, and the smell of them made one of the tigers stir. The other *jetti* had crossed to the four soldiers where he had drawn out one of their muskets' ramrods. Now he stood behind Sharpe and, when the Tippoo nodded, he gave Sharpe's back a vicious cut with the metal rod.

The sudden pain was every bit as bad as the flogging. It stabbed up and down Sharpe's spine and he gasped with the effort not to scream aloud as the force of the blow threw him forward. He broke his fall with his hands and now his back faced the sky and the *jetti* slashed down three more times, opening the old wounds, cracking a rib, and spurting blood onto the courtyard's sand. One of the tigers growled and the links of its chain jangled as the beast lunged toward the smell of fresh blood. "We shall beat him until we have the name," the officer told Lawford mildly, "and when he is dead we shall beat you until you are dead."

The *jetti* struck down again, and this time Sharpe rolled onto his side, but the second *jetti* pushed him back onto his belly. Sharpe was grunting and panting, but was determined not to cry aloud.

"You can't do this!" Lawford protested.

"Of course we can!" the officer answered. "We shall start splintering his bones now, but not his spine, not yet. We want the pain to go on." He nodded, and the *jetti* slashed down again and this time Sharpe did cry aloud as the stab of pain brought back all the agony of the flogging.

"A merchant!" Lawford blurted out.

The officer held up his hand to stop the beating. "A merchant, Lieutenant? The city is full of merchants."

"He deals in metals," Lawford said. "I don't know more than that."

"Of course you do," the officer said, then nodded at the *jetti* who raised the ramrod high in the air.

"Ravi Shekhar!" Lawford shouted. The Lieutenant was bitterly ashamed for giving the name away, and the shame was obvious on his face, but nor could Lawford stand by and watch Sharpe beaten to death. He believed, or he wanted to believe, that he could have endured the pain of the beating himself without betraying the name, but it was more than he could bear to watch another man pounded into a bloody pulp.

"Ravi Shekhar," the officer said, checking the *jetti*'s stroke. "And how did you find him?"

"We didn't," Lawford said. "We didn't know how! We were waiting till we spoke some of your language, then we were going to ask for him about the city, but we haven't tried yet."

Sharpe groaned. Blood trickled down his sides and dripped onto the stones. One of the tigers staled beside the wall and the smell of urine filled the courtyard with its thin sour stench. The officer, who was wearing one of the prized gold tiger medallions about his neck, talked with the Tippoo who stared dispassionately at Sharpe, then asked a question.

"And what, Lieutenant," the officer translated, "would you have told Ravi Shekhar?"

"Everything we'd discovered about the defenses," Lawford said miserably. "That's why we were sent."

"And what did you discover?"

"How many men you have, how many guns, how many rockets."

"That's all?"

"It's enough, isn't it?" Lawford retorted.

The officer translated the answers. The Tippoo shrugged, glanced at Lawford, then took a small brown leather bag from inside a pocket of his yellow silk tunic. He unlaced the bag's mouth, stepped to Sharpe's side, then trickled salt onto the beaten man's open wounds. Sharpe hissed with the pain.

"Who else would you have told in the city?" the officer asked.

"There was no one else!" Lawford pleaded. "In the name of God, there was no one else. We were told Ravi Shekhar could get a message out. That was all!"

The Tippoo believed him. Lawford's chagrin was so clear and his shame so palpable that he was utterly believable.

Besides, the story made sense. "And so you've never seen Ravi Shekhar?" the officer asked.

"Never."

"You're looking at him now," the officer said, gesturing at the tigers. "His body was fed to the tigers weeks ago."

"Oh, God," Lawford said, and he closed his eyes as he realized just what an utter failure he had been. For a moment he wanted to retch, then he controlled the impulse and opened his eyes to watch as the Tippoo picked up Sharpe's red coat and dropped it onto the bloody back.

For a second the Tippoo hesitated, wondering whether to release the tigers onto the two men. Then he turned away. "Take them to the cells," he ordered.

The sacrifice of prisoners had yielded up the traitors and turned the Tippoo's luck. There was no need for a further sacrifice, not yet, but the Tippoo knew that fortune was ever capricious and so the prisoners could wait until another sacrifice was needed and then, to guarantee victory or to stave off defeat, they would die. And till then, the Tippoo decided, they could just rot.

· CHAPTER 9 ·

The dungeons lay in one of the palace's northern court-yards, hard under the city's inner mud wall. The court-yard stank of sewage, the smell powerful enough to make Sharpe half retch as he staggered beside Lawford at the point of a bayonet. The courtyard was a busy place. The families of the palace servants lived in low thatched buildings surrounding the yard where their lives were spent cheek by jowl with the Tippoo's stables and the small enclosure where he kept eight cheetahs he used for hunting gazelles. The cheetahs were taken to the hunt in wheeled cages and at first Sharpe thought they were to be placed inside one of the barred vehicles, but then one of the escorts pushed him past the ponderous carts toward a flight of stone steps that descended to a long narrow trench of stone that lay open to the sky. A tall fence of iron bars surrounded the pit that was guarded by a pair of soldiers. One of them used a key to open a padlock the size of a mango, then the escort shoved Sharpe and Lawford through the open gate.

The dungeon guards did not carry muskets, but instead had coiled whips in their belts and bell-mouthed blunder-busses on their shoulders. One of them pointed mutely down the steps and Sharpe, following Lawford down the stairs, saw that the trench was a stone-flagged, dead-end corridor lined on either side with barred cells. There were eight cells in the pit, four on each side, and each separated from its neighbors, and from the central trench-like corridor, by iron bars alone, but bars that were as thick as a man's wrist. The turnkey indicated that they should wait while he unlocked a cell, but the first padlock he attempted to open had become stiff, or else had rusted, for it would not budge, and then he could not find a key to fit another of the big old locks. Something stirred in the straw of the cell that lay at the far right-hand end of the corridor. Sharpe, waiting as the guard sorted through his keys, heard the straw rustle again, then there was a growl as a huge tiger heaved up from its bed to stare at them with blank yellow eyes.

More straw stirred in the first cell on the left, close by where Sharpe and Lawford were standing. "Look who it isn't!" Hakeswill had come to the bars. "Sharpie!"

"Be quiet, Sergeant," Lawford snapped.

"Yes, sir, Mister Lieutenant Lawford, sir, quiet it is, sir." Hakeswill clung to the bars of his cage, staring wide-eyed at the two newcomers. His face twitched. "Quiet as the grave, sir, but no one talks to me down here. He won't." He nodded toward the cell opposite that the guard was now unlocking. "Likes it quiet, he does," Hakeswill went on. "Like a bleeding church. Says his prayers, too. Always quiet it is here, except when the darkies are having a shout at each other. Dirty bastards they are. Smell the sewage, can you? One giant jakes!" Hakeswill's face twisted in rictus and, in the gloom of the shadowed cells, his eyes seemed to glitter with an unholy delight. "Been missing company, I have."

"Bastard," Sharpe muttered.

"Quiet! Both of you," Lawford insisted and then, with his innate politeness, the Lieutenant nodded thanks to the guard who had finally opened the cell directly opposite Hakeswill's lair. "Come on, Sharpe," Lawford said, then stepped fastidiously into the filthy straw. The cell was eight foot deep and ten foot long and a little over the height of a man. The sewage smell was rank, but no worse than in the courtyard above. The barred door clashed shut behind them and the key was turned.

"Willie," a tired voice said from the shadows of the cell, "how very good of you to visit me." Sharpe, his eyes accustoming themselves to the dimness of the dungeons, saw that Colonel McCandless had been crouching in one corner, half shrouded by straw. The Colonel now stood to greet them, but he was weak for he tottered as he stood, though he shook off Lawford's attempt to help him. "A fever," he explained. "It comes and it goes. I've had it for years. I suspect the only thing that will cure it will be some soft Scottish rain, but that seems an ever more unlikely prospect. It is good to see you, Willie."

"You too, sir. You've met Private Sharpe, I think."

McCandless gave Sharpe a grim look. "I have a question for you, young man."

"It wasn't gunpowder, sir," Sharpe said, remembering his first confrontation with the Colonel and thus anticipating the question. "It tasted wrong, sir. Wasn't salty."

"Aye, it didn't look like powder," the Scotsman said. "It was blowing in the wind like flour, but that wasn't my question, Private. My question, Private, is what would you have done if it had been gunpowder?"

"I'd have shot you, sir," Sharpe said, "begging your pardon, sir."

"Sharpe!" Lawford remonstrated.

"Quite right, man," McCandless said. "The wretched fellow was testing you, wasn't he? He was giving you a recruitment test, and you couldn't fail it. I'm glad it wasn't powder, but I don't mind saying you had me worried for a brief while. Do you mind if I sit, Willie? I'm not in my usual good health." He sank back into his straw from where he frowned up at Sharpe. "Nor are you, Private. Are you in pain?"

"Bastards cracked a rib, sir, and I'm bleeding a bit. Do you mind if I sit?" Sharpe gingerly sat against the side bars of the cell and carefully lifted away the coat that had been draped over his back. "Bit of fresh air will heal it, sir," he said to Lawford who was insisting on examining the newly opened wounds, though there was nothing he could do to help them mend.

"You won't get fresh air here," McCandless said. "You smell the sewage?"

"You can't miss that smell, Uncle," Lawford said.

"It's the new inner wall," McCandless explained. "When they built it they cut the city drains, so now the night soil can't reach the river and the sewage puddles just east of here. Some of it seeps away through the Water Gate, but not enough. One learns to pray for a west wind." He smiled grimly. "Among other things."

McCandless wanted news, not only of what had brought Lawford and Sharpe into Seringapatam, but of the siege's progress and he groaned when he heard where the British had placed their works. "So Harris is coming from the west?"

"Yes, sir."

"Straight into the Tippoo's loving arms." The Scotsman sat quietly for a moment, sometimes shivering because of his fever. He had wrapped himself in straw again, but he was still cold, despite the day's intense damp heat. "And you couldn't get a message out? No, I suppose not. Those things are never easy." He shook his head. "Let's hope the Tippoo doesn't finish his mine."

"It's near finished, sir." Sharpe delivered yet more bad news. "I saw it."

"Aye, it would be. He's an efficient man, the Tippoo," McCandless said, "efficient and clever. Cleverer than his father, and old Hyder Ali was canny enough. I never met him, but I think I'd have liked the old rogue. This son, now,

I never met him either until I was captured, and I wish I hadn't. He's a good soldier but a bad enemy." McCandless closed his eyes momentarily as a shudder racked his body.

"What will he do with us?" Lawford asked.

"That I cannot say," Colonel McCandless replied. "It depends, probably, on his dreams. He's not as good a Muslim as he'd like us to think, for he still believes in some older magic and he sets great store by his dreams. If his dreams tell him to kill us then doubtless we'll have our heads turned back to front like the unfortunate gentlemen who shared these cells with me until quite recently. You heard about them?"

"We heard," Lawford said.

"Murdered to amuse the Tippoo's troops!" McCandless said disapprovingly. "And there were some good Christian men among them too. Only that thing over there survived." He jerked his head toward Hakeswill's cell.

"He survived, sir," Sharpe said vengefully, "because he betrayed us."

"It's a lie, sir!" Hakeswill, who had been avidly listening to Sharpe and Lawford's tale, snapped indignantly from across the corridor. "A filthy lie, sir, as I'd expect from a gutter soldier like Private Sharpe."

McCandless turned to gaze at the Sergeant. "Then why were you spared?" he asked coldly.

"Touched by God, sir. Always have been, sir. Can't be killed, sir."

"Mad," McCandless said quietly.

"You can be killed, Obadiah," Sharpe said. "Christ, if it wasn't for you, you bastard, I'd have taken our news to General Harris."

"Lies, sir! More lies," Hakeswill insisted.

"Quiet, both of you," McCandless said. "And Private Sharpe?"

"Sir?"

"I'd be grateful if you did not blaspheme. Remember that 'Thou shalt not take the name of the Lord thy God in vain; for the Lord will not hold him guiltless that taketh his name in vain.' Exodus twenty, verse seven."

"Amen, sir," Hakeswill called, "and praise the Lord, sir."

"Sorry, sir," Sharpe muttered.

"You do know your Ten Commandments, don't you, Sharpe?" McCandless asked.

"No, sir."

"Not one of them?" McCandless asked, shocked.

"Thou shalt not be found out, sir? Is that one of them?" Sharpe asked guilelessly.

McCandless stared at him in horror. "Do you have any religion, Sharpe?"

"No, sir. Never found a need for it."

"You were born with a hunger for it, man." The Colonel spoke with some of his old energy.

"And for a few things else, sir."

McCandless shivered under his mantle of straw. "If God spares me, Sharpe, I may attempt to repair some of the damage to your immortal soul. Do you still have the Bible your mother gave you, Willie?"

"They took it from me, sir," Lawford said. "But I did manage to save one page." He took the single page from his trouser pocket. He was blushing, for both he and Sharpe knew why the page had been torn from the holy book, and it was not for any purpose that Colonel McCandless would have approved. "Just the one page, sir," Lawford said apologetically.

"Give it here, man," McCandless said fiercely, "and let us see what the good Lord has to say to us." He took the crumpled page, smoothed it and tipped it to the light. "Ah! The

Revelation!" He seemed pleased. "'Blessed are the dead which die in the Lord,'" he read aloud. "Amen to that."

"Not very cheerful, sir," Sharpe ventured.

"It is the most cheerful thing I can contemplate in this place, Private. A promise from the Lord God Almighty Himself that when I die I shall be carried into His glory." The Colonel smiled for that consolation. "Might I assume, Private, that you cannot read?"

"Me, sir? No, sir. Never taught, sir."

"Pig stupid, sir, he is, sir," Hakeswill offered from across the corridor. "Always was, sir. Dumb as a bucket."

"We must teach you your letters," McCandless said, ignoring the Sergeant's comments.

"Mister Lawford was going to do that, sir," Sharpe said.

"Then I suggest he begin now," McCandless said firmly.

Lawford smiled diffidently. "It's difficult to know where to begin, Uncle."

"Why not with T for tiger?" McCandless suggested.

The beast growled, then settled in its straw. And Sharpe, some years late, began his lessons.

The siege works advanced fast. Redcoats and sepoys worked day and night, sapping forward and shoring up the trench sides with bamboo mats. Rockets continually harassed the work, and the Tippoo succeeded in remounting some of his guns on the western walls, though their fire did little to disturb the work and the gunners suffered grievously from the counterfire of the British eighteen-pounders emplaced in the captured mill fort. Smaller guns, twelve-pounders and short-barreled howitzers, joined the bombardment of the ramparts and their shells and round shot seared above the ground where yard by yard the red earth was broken until, at last, the big short-range breaching batteries were dug and the rest of the massive siege guns were rolled forward in the night and concealed in their gun pits. To the Tippoo's troops, watching from the battered summit of the western wall, the approaches to the city were now a maze of newly turned earth. Approach trenches angled their way across the farmland, ending in larger mounds of earth thrown up from the deeper pits that held the breaching guns. Not all those bigger mounds concealed guns, for some of the spoil heaps were deliberately thrown up as deceptions so that the Tippoo could not guess where the real guns were emplaced until they opened fire. The Tippoo only knew that the British would aim at his western wall, but he did not yet know the exact stretch of wall that the enemy engineers had chosen, and it suited General Harris that the Tippoo should not learn that spot until it was necessary for the breaching batteries to open fire. If the defenders had too much warning of the place chosen for the storm then they would have time to build elaborate new defenses behind it.

But the Tippoo was gambling that he already knew where the British would choose to make their breach, and in the old gatehouse where the massive mine was concealed his engineers finished their preparations. They stacked stone around the vast powder charge so that its explosion would be directed northward into the space between the walls. For the mine to be effective the British had to site their breach in the short stretch of wall between the old gatehouse and the city's northwest bastion, and the Tippoo's gamble was not an outrageous risk for it was not difficult to forecast that the breach would indeed be blasted in that section of wall. The site was dictated by the outer wall's decay, and by the shortcomings of the low glacis that lay outside that inviting wall. The rudimentary glacis half protected most of the city's western battlements, its raw earth slope designed to deflect cannonballs up from the wall's base, but where the city wall was most decayed the river ran very close to the defenses and there had been no room to construct even the pretence of a glacis. Instead a low mud wall continued the line of the glacis, and that wall penned in the water that had been pumped into the ditch between the outer ramparts and the glacis. That low wall was no obstacle compared to a glacis and the Tippoo reckoned it would be an irresistible target for the enemy engineers.

He did not put all his faith in the single massive mine. That mine could well kill or maim hundreds of the assaulting troops, but there were thousands more enemy soldiers who could be sent against the city and so the Tippoo prepared his army for its test. The western walls would be crammed with men when the time came, and those men would each have at least three loaded muskets, and behind each fighting soldier would be men trained to reload the discharged weapons. The British storm would thus be met with a blistering hail of musket fire, and mixed with that maelstrom of lead would be round shot and canister fired from the cannons that had replaced the destroyed guns and which were now concealed behind the mutilated ramparts. Thousands of rockets were also ready. At long range the weapon was erratic, but in the close confines of a breach, where men were crammed as tight as sheep in a pen, the rockets could inflict a dreadful slaughter. "We shall stuff hell with infidel souls," the Tippoo boasted, though at every prayer time he took care to beseech Allah for an early monsoon and every dawn he would look at the sky in hope of seeing some signs of rain, but the skies remained obstinately clear. An early monsoon would drown the British in torrential rain before the rockets and guns could cut them to bloody shreds, but it seemed the rains would not come early to Mysore this year.

The skies might be clear, but every other omen was good. The ill luck that had led to the loss of the mill fort had been diverted by the sacrifice of the British prisoners and now the

Tippoo's dreams and auguries spoke only of victory. The Tippoo recorded his dreams each morning, writing them down in a large book before discussing their portents with his advisers. His diviners peered into pots of heated oil to read the shifting colored swirls on the surface, and those shimmering signs, like the dreams, forecast a great victory. The British would be destroyed in southern India and then, when the French sent troops to reinforce Mysore's growing empire, the redcoats would be scoured from the north of the country. Their bones would bleach on the sites of their defeats and their silken colors would fade on the walls of the Tippoo's great palaces. The tiger would rule from the snowy mountains of the north to the palm-edged beaches of the south, and from the Coromandel Coast to the seas off Malabar. All that glory was foretold by the dreams and by the glistening auguries of the oil.

But then, one dawn, it seemed the auguries might be deceiving, for the British suddenly unmasked four of their newly made breaching batteries and the great guns crashed back on their trails and the intricate network of trenches and earthworks was shrouded by the giant gusts of smoke that were belched out with every thunderous recoil.

The balls were not aimed where the Tippoo had hoped, at the vulnerable part of the wall behind the missing section of glacis, but at the city's mighty northwest bastion: a complex of battlements that loomed high above the river and, from its topmost ramparts, dominated both the northern and western walls. The whole city seemed to shake as the balls slammed home again and again and every strike sprang dust from the old masonry until at last the first stones fell. From the north bank of the river, where the smaller British camp was sited, more guns added their fire and still more stones tumbled down into the ditches as the gunners gnawed away at the great bastion.

Next day more of the siege guns opened fire, but these new weapons were aimed at the cavaliers at the very southern end of the western wall. There were small cannon mounted in those cavaliers, but their embrasures were destroyed in less than a morning's work and the defenders' guns were hurled back off their carriages. And still the batteries hammered at the northwest bastion until, an hour after midday, the great fortification collapsed. At first the sound of the bastion's fall was like the creak and groan of a deep earthquake, then it turned into a rumble like thunder as the massive battlements disintegrated beneath a huge cloud of dust that slowly drifted to settle on the Cauvery so that, for almost a mile downstream, the water was turned as white as milk. There was an eerie silence after the bastion had been toppled, for the besiegers' guns had fallen silent. The Tippoo's troops rushed to the walls, their muskets and rockets ready, but no attackers stirred from the British lines. Their impudent flags flapped in the breeze, but the redcoats and their native allies stayed in their trenches.

A brave man of the Tippoo's army ventured up the mound of rubble that had been the northwest corner of the city's defenses. Dust coated the tiger stripes of his tunic as he clambered across the unsteady ruins to find the green flag that had been flying from the bastion's topmost rampart. He retrieved the flag, shook the dust from its folds, and waved it in the air. One enemy gunner saw the movement on top of the rubble heap and fired his huge gun. The ball screamed through the dust, ricocheted from a boulder, and bounced on up over the northern defenses to fall into the whitened river. The soldier, unscathed, waved the flag again, then planted its broken staff at the summit of the bastion's ruins.

The Tippoo inspected the damage to his western defenses. The guns were gone from the southern cavaliers, and the northwest bastion was untenable, but there was no breach in either place and both the outer and inner walls were undamaged. The low glacis had protected the bottom part of the walls, and though some of the northwest bastion's stones had fallen into the flooded ditch there was no ramp up which a storming party could climb. "What they were doing," the Tippoo announced to his entourage, "was destroying our flanking guns. Which means they still plan to attack in the center of the wall. Which is where we want them to attack."

Colonel Gudin agreed. For a time, like the Tippoo, he had been worried that the British bombardment meant that they planned to enter the city at its northwestern corner, but now, in the lull after the collapse of the towers, the enemy's strategy seemed plain. They had not been trying to make a breach, but instead had knocked down the two places where the Tippoo could mount high guns to plunge their fire onto the flanks of the storming troops. The breach would be made next. "It will be where we want it to be, I'm sure," Gudin confirmed the Tippoo's guess.

The man who had planted the flag on the crest of the fallen bastion was brought to the Tippoo on the western wall close to where the towers had fallen. The Tippoo rewarded him with a purse of gold. The man was a Hindu, and that pleased the Tippoo who worried about such men's loyalties. "Is he one of yours?" he asked Appah Rao who was accompanying the Tippoo on the inspection.

"No, Your Majesty."

The Tippoo suddenly turned and gazed up into the tall Appah Rao's face. He was frowning. "Those wretched men of Gudin's," the Tippoo said, "wasn't there a woman with them?"

"Yes, Your Majesty."

"And didn't she go to your house?" the Tippoo charged Appah Rao.

"She did, Highness, but she died." Appah Rao told the lie smoothly.

The Tippoo was intrigued. "Died?"

"She was a drab sick creature," Appah Rao said carelessly, "and just died. As should the men who brought her here." He still feared that the arrest of Sharpe and Lawford could lead to his own betrayal and, though he did not truly wish them dead, nor did he wish the Tippoo to believe that he desired them to live.

"Those two will die," the Tippoo promised grimly, his query about Mary apparently forgotten. "They will surely die," he promised again as he clambered up the ruins of the northwestern bastion. "We shall either offer their black souls to avert ill fortune, or we shall sacrifice them as thanks for our victory." He would prefer the latter, and he imagined killing the two men on the very same day that he first ascended the silver steps of his tiger throne, the throne he had sworn never to use until his enemies were destroyed. He felt a fierce pang of anticipation. The redcoats would come to his city and there they would be seared by the fires of vengeance and crushed by falling stone. Their groans would echo through the days of their dying, and then the rains would come and the sluggish Cauvery would swell into its full drowning spate and the remaining British, who were already low on food, would have no choice but to withdraw. They would leave their guns behind and begin their long journey across Mysore and every mile of their retreat would be dogged by the Tippoo's lancers and sabremen. The vultures would grow fat this year, and a trail of sun-whitened bones would be left across India until the very last red-coated man died. And there, the Tippoo decided, where the last Englishman died, he would erect a high pillar of marble, white and gleaming and crowned with a snarling tiger's head.

The muezzin's call echoed across the city, summoning the

faithful to prayer. The sound was beautiful in the silence after the guns. The Tippoo, obedient to his God, hurried toward his palace with one last backward glance at the damned. They could make their breach, they could cross the river, and they could come to his walls. But once at the walls they would die.

''P-I-K,'' Sharpe said, scratching the letters in the dust of the cell's floor where he had cleared a patch of straw. "L-O-K."

"Picklock," Lawford said. "Very good, but you've left out two C's."

"But I've got the picklock, sir," Sharpe said, and produced it from his coat pocket. It was a small cluster of metal shafts, some curiously bent at their tips, which he quickly hid once he had shown it to Lawford.

"Why didn't they find it?" Lawford asked. Both men had been searched when they had been taken to the palace after their arrest, and though the guards had left the page of the Bible in Lawford's pocket, they had taken everything else of value.

"I had it somewhere it couldn't be found, sir," Sharpe said. "Colonel Gudin thought I was scratching my arse, if you follow me, but I was hiding it."

"I'd rather not know," Lawford said primly.

"A good picklock like that can take care of those old padlocks in seconds, sir," Sharpe said, nodding at the lock on their cell door. "Then we just have to rush the guards."

"And get a bellyful of lead?" Lawford suggested.

"When the assault comes," Sharpe said, "the guards will like as not be at the top of the steps, trying to see what's happening. They won't hear us." Sharpe's back was still painful, and the wounds inflicted by the *jetti* were crusted with dried blood and pus that tore whenever he moved too quickly, but there was no gangrene and he had been spared any fever, and that good fortune was restoring his confidence.

"When the assault comes, Sharpe," Colonel McCandless intervened, "our guards are more likely to be on the walls, leaving our security to the tiger."

"Hadn't thought of that, sir." Sharpe sounded disappointed.

"I don't think even you can rush a tiger," McCandless said.

"No, sir. I don't suppose I can," Sharpe admitted. Each night, at dusk, the guards left the cells, but first they released the tiger. It was a difficult process, for the tiger had to be held away from the guards with long spears as they retreated up the steps. It had evidently tried to charge the guards once for it bore a long scar down one muscular striped flank, and these days, to prevent another such attack, the guards tossed down a great chunk of raw goat meat to satisfy the tiger's hunger before they released it, and the prisoners would spend the night hours listening to the creature grinding and slavering as it ripped the last pieces of flesh from the bones. Each dawn the tiger was herded back to its cell where it slept through the heat of the day until its time for guard duty came again. It was a huge and mangy beast, not nearly so sleek as the six tigers kept in the palace yard, but it had a hungrier look and sometimes, in the moonlight, Sharpe would watch it pacing up and down the short corridor, the fall of its pads silent on the stone as it endlessly went up and down, up and down, and he wondered what tiger thoughts brewed behind its night-glossed yellow eyes. Sometimes, for no reason, it would roar in the night and the hunting cheetahs would call back and the night would be loud with the sound of the animals. Then the tiger would leap lithely up the steps and roar another challenge from the bars at the head of the staircase.

It always came back down, its approach silent and its gaze malevolent.

By day, when the tiger twitched in its sleep, the guards would watch the cells. Sometimes there were just two guards, but at other times there were as many as six. Each morning a pair of prisoners from the city's civilian jail arrived in leg irons to take away the night-soil buckets, and when these had been emptied and returned, the first meal was served. It was usually cold rice, sometimes with beans or scraps of fish in it, with a tin jug of water. A second pail of rice was brought in the afternoon, but otherwise the prisoners were left alone. They listened to the sounds above them, ever fearful that they might be summoned to face the Tippoo's dreaded killers, and while they waited McCandless prayed, Hakeswill mocked, Lawford worried, and Sharpe learned his letters.

At first the learning was hard and it was made no easier by Hakeswill's constant scoffing. Lawford and McCandless would tell the Sergeant to be quiet, but after a while Hakeswill would chuckle again and start talking, ostensibly to himself, in the far corner of his cage. "Above himself, ain't he?" Hakeswill would mutter just loud enough for Sharpe to hear. "Got hairs and bleeding graces. That's what Sharpie's got. Hairs and graces. Learning to read! Might as well teach a stone to fart! It ain't natural, ain't right. A private soldier should know his place, says so in the scriptures."

"It says nothing of the sort, Sergeant!" McCandless would always snap after such an assertion.

And always, every daylight hour of every day, there was the sound of the besiegers' guns. Their thunderous percussions filled the sky and were echoed by the crack of iron on sun-dried mud as the eighteen-pound round shots struck home, while, nearer, the Tippoo's own guns answered. Few such cannon had survived on the western walls, but closer to

298 · BERNARD CORNWELL

the dungeons, on the northern rampart, the Tippoo's gunners traded shot for shot with the batteries across the Cauvery and the sound of the weapons punched the warm air incessantly.

"Working hard, them gunners!" Hakeswill would say. "Doing a proper job, like real soldiers should. Working up a proper muck sweat. Not wasting their time with bleeding letters. C-A-T? Who the hell needs to know that? It's still a bleeding pussycat. All you needs to know is how to skin the thing, not how to spell it."

"Quiet, Sergeant," McCandless would growl.

"Yes, sir. I shall be quiet, sir. Like a church mouse, sir." But a few moments later the Sergeant could be heard grumbling again. "Private Morgan, I remembers him, and he could read and he wasn't nothing but trouble. He always knew more than anyone else, but he didn't know better than to be flogged, did he? Would never have happened if he hadn't had his letters. His mother taught him, the silly Welsh bitch. He read his Bible when he should have been cleaning his musket. Died under the lash, he did, and good riddance. A private soldier's got no business reading. Bad for the eyes, sends you blind."

Hakeswill even talked at night. Sharpe would wake to hear the Sergeant talking in a low voice to the tiger, and one night even the tiger stopped to listen. "You're not such a bad puss, are you?" Hakeswill crooned. "Down here all alone, you are, just like me." The Sergeant reached a tentative hand through the bars and gave the beast's back a swift pat. He was rewarded with a low snarl. "Don't you growl at me, puss, or I'll have your bleeding eyes out. And how will you catch mouses then? Eh? You'll be a hungry blind pussycat, that's what you'll be. That's it. Lay you down now and rest your big head, see? Doesn't hurt, does it?" And the Sergeant reached out and, with remarkable tenderness, scratched the big cat's flank and, to Sharpe's wonder, the huge beast settled itself comfortably against the bars of the Sergeant's cell. "You're awake, aren't you, Sharpie?" Hakeswill called softly as he scratched the tiger. "I knows you are, I can tell. So what happened to little Mary Bickerstaff, eh? You going to tell me, boy? Some heathen darkie got his filthy hands on her, has he? She'd have done better lifting her skirts to me. Instead she's being rogered by some blackie, ain't she? Is that what happened? Still now, still!" he soothed the tiger. Sharpe pretended to be asleep, but Hakeswill must have sensed his attention. "Officer's pet, Sharpie? Is that what you are? Learning to read so you can be like them, is that what you want? It won't do you no good, boy. There's only two sorts of officers in this army, and the one sort's good and the other sort ain't. The good sort knows better than to get their hands dirty with you rankers; they leave it all to the sergeants. The bad sort interfere. That young Mister Fitzgerald, he was an interferer, but he's gone to hell now and hell's the best place for him, seeing as how he was an upstart Irishman with no respect for sergeants. And your Mister Lawford, he ain't no good either, no good at all." Hakeswill suddenly quieted as Colonel McCandless groaned.

The Colonel's fever was growing worse, though he tried hard not to complain. Sharpe, abandoning his pretence of sleep, carried the water bucket to him. "Drink, sir?"

"That's kind of you, Sharpe, kind."

The Colonel drank, then propped his back against the stone wall at the back of the cell. "We had a rainstorm last month," he said, "not a severe one, but these cells were flooded all the same. And not all of the flooding was rain, a good deal was sewage. I pray God gets us out of here before the monsoon."

"No chance of us still being here then, is there, sir?"

"It depends, Sharpe, whether we take the city or not."

"We will, sir," Sharpe said.

"Maybe." The Colonel smiled at Sharpe's serene confidence. "But the Tippoo might decide to kill us first." McCandless fell silent for a while, then shook his head. "I wish I understood the Tippoo."

"Nothing to understand, sir. He's just an evil bastard, sir."

"No, he's not that," the Colonel said severely. "He's actually rather a good ruler. Better, I suspect, than most of our Christian monarchs. He's certainly been good for Mysore. He's fetched it a deal of wealth, given it more justice than most countries enjoy in India and he's been tolerant to most religions, though I fear he did persecute some unfortunate Christians." The Colonel grimaced as a shudder racked his body. "He's even kept the Rajah and his family alive, not in comfort, but alive, and that's more than most monarchs would ever do. Most usurpers kill their country's old ruler, but not here. I can't forgive him for what he did to those poor prisoners of ours, of course, but I suppose some capricious cruelty is probably necessary in a ruler. All in all, I think, and judging him by the standards of our own monarchy, we should have to give the Tippoo fairly high marks."

"So why the hell are we fighting him, sir?"

McCandless smiled. "Because we want to be here, and he doesn't want us to be here. Two dogs in a small cage, Sharpe. And if he beats us out of Mysore he'll bring in the French to chase us out of the rest of India and then we can bid farewell to the best part of our eastern trade. That's what it's about, Sharpe, trade. That's why you're fighting here, trade."

Sharpe grimaced. "It seems a funny thing to be fighting about, sir."

"Does it?" McCandless seemed surprised. "Not to me, Sharpe. Without trade there's no wealth, and without wealth there's no society worth having. Without trade, Private Sharpe, we'd be nothing but beasts in the mud. Trade is indeed worth fighting for, though the good Lord knows we don't appreciate trade much. We celebrate kings, we honor great men, we admire aristocrats, we applaud actors, we shower gold on portrait painters and we even, sometimes, reward soldiers, but we always despise merchants. But why? It's the merchant's wealth that drives the mills, Sharpe; it moves the looms, it keeps the hammers falling, it fills the fleets, it makes the roads, it forges the iron, it grows the wheat, it bakes the bread, and it builds the churches and the cottages and the palaces. Without God and trade we would be nothing."

Sharpe laughed softly. "Trade never did 'owt for me, sir."

"Did it not?" McCandless asked gently. The Colonel smiled. "So what do you think is worth fighting for, Private?"

"Friends, sir. And pride. We have to show that we're better bastards than the other side."

"You don't fight for King or country?"

"I've never met the King, sir. Never even seen him."

"He's not much to look at, but he's a decent enough man when he's not mad." McCandless stared across at Hakeswill. "Is he mad?"

"I think so, sir."

"Poor soul."

"He's evil, too," Sharpe said, speaking too softly for Hakeswill to hear him. "Takes a joy, sir, in having men punished. He thieves, he lies, he rapes, he murders."

"And you've done none of those things?"

"Never raped, sir, and as for the others, only when I had to."

"Then I pray God you'll never have to again," McCandless said fervently, and with that he leaned his gray head against the wall and tried to sleep.

Sharpe watched the dawn light seep into the dungeon pit. The last bats of the night wheeled in the patch of sky above, but soon they were gone and the first gun of the day spoke. It was clearing its throat, as the gunners liked to say, for the city and its besiegers were waking and the fight would go on.

The opening shot of the day was aimed at the low mud wall that plugged the gap in the glacis and kept the water dammed in the ditch behind. The wall was thick and the shot, which fell low and so lost much of its force as it ricocheted up from the riverbank, did little more than shiver dust from the wall's crevices.

One by one the other siege guns woke and had their throats blasted clear. The first few shots were often lackadaisical as the gun barrels were still cool and thus caused the balls to fly low. A handful of guns answered the fire from the city walls, but none of them was large. The Tippoo was hiding his big guns for the assault, but he permitted his gunners to mount and fire their small cannon, some of which discharged a ball no bigger than a grapeshot. The defenders' fire did no damage, but even the sound of their guns gave the citizens a feeling that they were fighting back.

This morning the British guns seemed erratic. Every battery was at work, but their fire was uncoordinated. Some aimed at the wall in the glacis while others targeted the higher ramparts, but an hour after dawn they all fell silent and, a moment later, the Tippoo's gunners also ceased firing. Colonel Gudin, staring through a spyglass from the western ramparts, distinctly saw the sepoy gunners in one breaching battery heaving at the trail of their piece. Gudin reckoned that the big guns were at last being carefully aligned on the section of wall that had been chosen for the breach. The guns were hot now, they would fire true, and soon they would concentrate a dreadful intensity of iron against the chosen spot in the city's defenses. With his spyglass he could see men straining at the gun, but he could not see the gun itself for the embrasure had been momentarily stopped up with wicker baskets filled with earth. Gudin prayed that the British would take the Tippoo's bait and aim their pieces at the weakest section of the wall.

He trained his glass on the nearest battery which was scarce four hundred yards from the vulnerable section of wall. The gunners were stripped to the waist, and no wonder, for the temperature would soon be well over ninety degrees and the humidity was already stifling and these men had to handle enormous weights of gun and shot. An eighteen-pounder siege gun weighed close to twelve tons, and all that mass of hot metal was hurled back with each shot and the gun then had to be manhandled back into its firing position. The shot of such a gun measured a little over five inches across, and each gun could fire perhaps one such ball every two minutes and the Tippoo's spies had reported that General Harris now had thirty-seven of these heavy guns, and two more cannon, even heavier, that each fired a twenty-four-pound missile. Gudin, waiting for the gunfire to start again, made a simple computation in his head. Each minute, he reckoned, about three hundred and fifty pounds of iron, traveling at unimaginably high velocities, would hammer into the city wall. And to that hefty weight of metal the British could add a score of howitzers and several dozen twelve-pounders that would be used to bombard the walls either side of the place General Harris had chosen to make his breach.

Gudin knew that the serious business of making the breach was about to begin and he almost held his breath as he waited for the first shot, for that opening gun would tell him whether or not the Tippoo's gamble had succeeded. The waiting seemed to stretch for ever, but at last one of the batteries unmasked a gun and the great brute belched a jet of smoke fifty yards in front of its embrasure. The sound came a half-second later, but Gudin had already seen the shot fall.

The British had swallowed the bait. They were coming straight for the trap.

The rest of the breaching guns now opened fire. For a moment a rumbling thunder filled the sky that was flapping with the wings of startled birds. The shots seared over the dry land, across the river and slammed into the brief curtain wall that joined the sections of glacis. The wall lasted less than ten minutes before an eighteen-pounder shot pierced through it and suddenly the water of the inner ditch was gushing out into the South Cauvery. For a few seconds the water was a clear, thin spurt arcing out to the river, then the force of the flow abraded the remaining mud and the wall collapsed so that a murky flood washed irresistibly down the riverbank.

The guns scarcely paused, only now they raised their aim very slightly so that the balls could strike against the base of the outer rampart which had been completely unmasked by the collapse of the glacis's brief connecting wall. Shot after shot slammed home, their impacts reverberating down the whole length of the ancient battlements, and each shot punched out a handful of mud bricks. The water from the punctured ditch kept flowing out, and the shots kept slamming home as the gunners sweated and hauled and spiked and sponged out and rammed and fired again.

All day long they fired, and all day long the old wall crumbled. The shots were kept low, aimed to strike at the foot of the wall so that the bricks above would collapse to make a ramp of rubble that would lead up and through the gap that the guns were making.

By nightfall the wall still stood, but at its base there was a crumbling, dusty cavern that had been carved deep into the rampart. A few British guns fired in the night, mostly scattering canister or grapeshot in an attempt to stop the Tippoo's men from repairing the cavern, but in the dark it was difficult to keep the guns aimed true and most of the shots went wild, and in the morning the British gunners pointed their telescopes and saw that the cavern had been plugged with earth-filled wicker gabions and baulks of timber. The first few shots made short shrift of those repairs, scattering the timber and soil in huge gouts as the balls bit home, and once the cavern was reexposed the gunners went to work on it. The land between the aqueduct and the river became shrouded with a mist of powder smoke as the artillery poured in their fire until, at midday, a cheer from the British lines marked the wall's collapse.

It crumpled slowly, jetting a cloud of dust into the air, a cloud so thick that at first no man could see the extent of the damage, but as the small wind cleared the smoke away from the guns and the dust from the wall they could see that a breach had been made. The limewashed wall now had a gap twenty yards wide, and the gap was filled with a mound of rubble up which a man could climb so long as he was unencumbered by anything other than a musket, a bayonet, and his cartridge box. That made the breach practicable.

Yet still the guns fired. Now the gunners were trying to flatten the slope of the breach and some of their shots ricocheted up to the inner wall and for a time Gudin feared that the British were planning to blast a passage clean through that new inner rampart, but then the gunners lowered their aim to keep their balls hammering at the newly made breach or else to gnaw at the shoulders of the outer wall's gap.

A half-mile away from Gudin, in the British lines, General Harris and General Baird stared at the breach through their telescopes. Now, for the first time, they could inspect a short stretch of the new inner wall. "It isn't as high as I feared," Harris commented.

"Let's pray it's unfinished," Baird growled.

"But still I think it's better to ignore it," Harris decreed. "Capture the outer wall first."

Baird turned to stare at some clouds that lay heavy and low on the western horizon. He feared the clouds presaged rain. "We could go tonight, sir," he suggested. Baird was remembering the forty-four months he had endured in the Tippoo's dungeons, some of them spent chained to the wall of his cell, and he wanted revenge. He was also eager to get the bloody business of storming the city done.

Harris collapsed his glass. "Tomorrow," he said firmly, and scratched beneath the edge of his wig. "We risk more by rushing things. We'll do it properly, and we'll do it tomorrow."

That night a handful of British officers crept out from the leading trenches with small white cotton flags attached to bamboo poles. The sky was laced with a tracery of thin clouds that intermittently hid the waning moon, and in the cloud shadows the officers explored the South Cauvery to find the river's treacherous deep pools. They marked the shallows with their flags and so pointed the path toward the breach.

And all through that night the assault troops filed down the long trenches. Harris was determined that his assault would be overwhelming. He would not tickle the city, he told Baird, but swamp it with men, and so Baird would lead two columns of troops, half of them British and half sepoys, but nearly all of them prime men from the army's elite flanking companies. The six thousand attackers would either be grenadiers, who were the biggest and strongest men, or else from the light companies who were the quickest and cleverest soldiers, and those picked men would be accompanied by a detachment of Hyderabad's finest warriors. The attackers would also be accompanied by engineers carrying fascines to fill in any ditches that the defenders might have dug on the breach's summit and bamboo ladders to scale the edges of the breach. Volunteer gunners would follow the leading troops up onto the ramparts and there turn the Tippoo's own cannon against the defenders on the inner wall. Two Forlorn Hopes would go ahead of the columns, each Hope composed solely of volunteers and each led by a sergeant who would be made an officer if he survived. Both the Forlorn Hopes would carry the British colors into the breach, and those color bearers would be the very first men to climb into the enemy's guns. Once on the breach the Forlorn Hopes were ordered not to go on into the space between the walls, but to climb the broken stumps of the shoulders either side of the breach's ramp and from there lead the fight north and south around the whole ring of Seringapatam's ramparts.

"God knows," Harris said that night at supper, "but I can think of nothing left undone. Can you, Baird?"

"No, sir, I can't," Baird said. "Upon my soul, I can't." He was trying to sound cheerful, but it was still a subdued meal, though Harris had done his best to make it festive. His table was spread with a linen cloth and was lit by fine spermaceti candles that burned with a pure white light. The General's cooks had killed their last chickens to provide a change from the usual half-ration of beef, but none of the officers around the table had much appetite, nor, it seemed, any enthusiasm for conversation. Meer Allum, the commander of the Hyderabad army, did his best to encourage his allies, but only Wellesley seemed capable of responding to his remarks.

Colonel Gent, who as well as being Harris's chief engineer, had taken on himself the collation of what intelligence came out of the city, poured himself some wine. It was rancid stuff, soured by its long journey from Europe and by the heat of India. "There's a rumor," he said heavily when a break in the desultory conversation had stretched for too long, "that the heathen bastards have planted a mine."

"There are always such rumors," Baird said curtly.

"A bit late to tell us, surely?" Harris remonstrated mildly.

"Only heard of it today, sir," Gent said defensively. "One of their cavalry fellows deserted. He could be making up tales, of course, these people do. Maybe the Tippoo sent him. Wants to scare us into delay, I daresay." He fell silent, toying with a blue-glass saltcellar. The salt was crusted from the humidity, and he attacked it with the small silver spoon, crumbling it as the city wall had crumbled under the onslaught of the guns. "But the fellow seemed sure of himself," he said after a while. "Says it's a big mine."

Baird grimaced. "So the bastards will blow it when the Forlorn Hopes attack. That's why we have Forlorn Hopes. To die." He had not meant to sound so callous, but he had wanted to silence the engineer.

Somewhere in the far distance there was a grumble of thunder. Everyone around the table waited for the patter of rain on the tent's canvas, but no such sound came. "My worry," Gent said, apparently unmoved by Baird's brusqueness, "is that they'll blow their mine once we're on the ramparts, and if it's a big enough brute it'll clear our fellows clean off the walls." He thrust the spoon hard down into the salt. "Clean off."

"Then let us hope the rumors are untrue," Harris said firmly, squashing the engineer's pessimism. "Colonel Wellesley, can I persuade you to another glass?"

Wellesley shook his head. "I've drunk enough, sir, thank you." But then the young Colonel looked down the table to where his rival Baird was sitting. "Though maybe, sir, I should accept a glass and drink to your success and renown."

Baird, whose distaste for the young Colonel had only increased over the last few days, managed to look pleased. "Obliged to you, Wellesley." He forced himself to be courteous. "Greatly obliged to you."

Harris was grateful for Wellesley's generosity. He disliked having his deputies at odds, especially as Harris had decided that it should be Wellesley, the younger and more junior man, who should be made Governor of Mysore if the city fell. Baird would undoubtedly be displeased, for the Scotsman would regard the appointment as a slight, yet in truth Baird's hatred of all things Indian disqualified him from such a post. Britain needed a friendly Mysore, and Wellesley was a tactful man who harbored no prejudice against natives. "Good of you, Wellesley," Harris said when the toast had been drunk. "Very good of you, I'm sure."

"This time tomorrow," Meer Allum said in his odd English accent, "we shall all dine in the Tippoo's palace. Drink from his silver and eat from his gold."

"I pray that we do," Harris said, "and I pray we manage it without grievous loss." He scratched his old wound beneath his wig.

The officers were still somber when the meal ended. Harris bade them a good night, then stood for a while outside his tent staring at the moon-glossed walls of the distant city. The limewashed ramparts seemed to glow white, beckoning him, but to what? He went to his bed where he slept badly and, in his waking moments, found himself rehearsing excuses for failure. Baird also stayed awake for a while, but drank a good measure of whisky and, afterward, in full uniform and with his big claymore propped beside his cot, he slipped in and out of a restless sleep. Wellesley slept well. The men crammed in the trenches hardly slept at all.

Bugles greeted the dawn. The storm clouds had thickened in the west, but there was no rain, and the rising sun soon burned the small wispy clouds from above the city. The assaulting troops crouched in the trenches where they could not be seen from Seringapatam's walls. The small white flags fluttered in the river. The siege guns kept firing, some attempting to open the breach wider, but most just trying to discourage the defenders from making any attempt to repair the breach or place obstacles on its forward slope. The undamaged ramparts gleamed white in the sun, while the breach appeared as a red-brown scar in the long city wall.

The Tippoo had spent the night in a small sentry shelter on the north walls. He woke early for he expected an attack at dawn and he had ordered that all his soldiers should be ready on the walls, but no assault came and, as the sun climbed higher, he allowed some of the defenders back to their barracks to rest while he himself went to the Inner Palace. He sensed a nervous expectancy in the crowded streets, and he himself was a troubled man for during his restless night he had dreamed of monkeys, and monkeys were ever a bad omen, and the Tippoo's mood was not helped when his diviners reported that the oil in their pots had been clouded. Today, it seemed, was an inauspicious day, but luck, as the Tippoo knew, was malleable and he attempted to change the day's ill-starred beginning by giving gifts. He summoned a Hindu priest and presented the man with an elephant, a sack of oilseed, and a purse of gold. To the Brahmins who accompanied the priest he gave a bullock, a nanny goat, two buffalo, a black hat, a black coat, and one of his precious pots of divining oil. Then he washed his hands and donned a cloth-padded war helmet that had been dipped in a sacred fountain to make its wearer invulnerable. On his right arm, his sword arm, he wore a silver amulet inscribed with verses from the Koran. A servant pinned the great red ruby onto the helmet's plume, the Tippoo slung the gold-hilted sword at his waist, then went back to the western walls.

Nothing had changed. Beyond the gently flowing South Cauvery the sun baked the ground where the British guns still fired. Their massive round shots churned up the rubble ramp, but no redcoats stirred from their trenches and the only signs that an assault might be imminent were the small pennants stuck in the riverbed.

"They want another day to widen the breach," an officer opined.

Colonel Gudin shook his head. "They'll come today," he insisted.

The Tippoo grunted. He was standing just north of the breach from where he watched the enemy trenches through a spyglass. Some of the British round shot struck dangerously close to where he stood, and his aides tried to persuade him to move to a safer place, but even when a stone shard thrown up by a cannonball flicked at his white linen tunic, he would not move. "They would have come at dawn," he finally said, "if they were coming today."

"They want us to think that," Gudin protested, "to lull us. But they will come today. They won't give us another night to make preparations. And why plant the flags?" He pointed at the river.

The Tippoo stepped back from the remains of the parapet. Was his luck changed? He had given gifts to the enemies of his God in the hope that his God would then reward him with victory, but he still felt an unease. He would much have preferred that the storming should be delayed another day so that another set of auspices could be taken, but perhaps Allah willed it otherwise. And nothing would be lost by assuming that the attack would come this day. "Assume they will come this afternoon," he ordered. "Every man back to the walls."

The walls, already thick with troops, now became crowded with defenders. One company of Muslims had volunteered to face the first enemy who came into the breach and those brave men, armed with swords, pistols, and muskets, crouched just inside the breach, but hidden from the enemy's guns by the mound of rubble. Those volunteers would almost certainly die, if not at the hands of the attackers then when the great mine blew, but each man had been assured of his place in paradise and so they went gladly to their deaths. Rockets were piled on the ramparts, and guns that had stayed hidden from the bombardment were manhandled into position to take the attackers in the flanks.

Others of the Tippoo's finest troops were posted on the outer wall above the edges of the breach. Their job was to defend the shoulders of the breach, for the Tippoo was determined to funnel the attackers into the space between the walls where his mine could destroy them. Let the British come, the Tippoo prayed, but let them be shepherded across the breach and into the killing ground.

The Tippoo had decided to lead the fight on the wall north of the breach. Colonel Gudin's battalion would fight south of the breach, but Gudin himself had responsibility for blowing the great mine. It was ready now, a hoard of powder crammed into the old gate passage and shored up by stones and timber so that the blast of the explosion would be forced northward between the walls. Gudin would watch the killing space from his place on the inner rampart, then signal to Sergeant Rothière to light the fuse. Rothière and the fuse were guarded by two of Gudin's steadiest men and by six of the Tippoo's *jettis*.

The Tippoo assured himself that all had been done that could be done. The city was ready and, in honor of the slaughter of infidels, the Tippoo had arrayed himself in jewels, then consigned his soul and his kingdom into Allah's keeping. Now he could only wait as the late-morning sun climbed higher and yet higher to become a burning whiteness in the Indian sky where the vultures circled on their wide ragged wings.

The British guns fired on. In the mosque some men prayed, but all of them were old men, for any man young enough to fight was waiting on the walls. The Hindus prayed to their gods while the women of the city made themselves ragged and dirty so that, should the city fall, they would not attract the enemy's attention.

Midday came. The city baked in the heat. It seemed strangely silent, for the fire of the siege guns was desultory now. The sound of each shot echoed dully from the walls and each strike would start a trickle of stone and a small cloud of dust and afterward there would be silence again. On the walls a horde of men crouched behind their firesteps, while in the trenches across the river an opposing horde waited for the order that would send them against an expectant city.

The Tippoo had a prayer mat brought to the walls and there, facing toward the enemy, he knelt and bowed in prayer. He prayed that Colonel Gudin was wrong and that his enemies would give him one more day, and then, as in a waking dream, a message came to him. He had given gifts, and gifts of charity were blessed, but he had not made sacrifice. He had been saving his sacrifice for the celebration of victory, but perhaps victory would not come unless he made his offerings now. Luck was malleable, and death was a great changer of fortune. He made a last obeisance, touching his forehead to the mat's weave, then climbed to his feet. "Send for three *jettis*," he ordered an aide, "and tell them to bring me the British prisoners."

"All of them, Your Majesty?" the aide asked.

"Not the Sergeant," the Tippoo said. "Not the one who twitches. The others. Tell the *jettis* to bring them here." For his victory needed one last sacrifice of blood before the Cauvery was made dark with it.

CHAPTER 10

Appah Rao was an able man, otherwise he would not have been promoted to the command of one of the Tippoo's brigades, but he was also a discreet man. Discretion had kept Rao alive and discretion had enabled him to preserve his loyalty to the unthroned Rajah of the house of Wodeyar while still serving the Tippoo.

Now, ordered to take his men to the walls of Seringapatam and there fight to preserve the Muslim dynasty of the Tippoo, Appah Rao at last questioned his discretion. He obeyed the Tippoo, of course, and his *cushoons* filed dutifully enough onto the city ramparts, but Appah Rao, standing beneath one of the sun banners above the Mysore Gate, asked himself what he wanted of this world. He possessed family, high rank, wealth, and ability, yet he still bowed his head to a foreign monarch and some of the flags above his men's heads were inscribed in Arabic to celebrate a god who was no god of Appah Rao's. His own monarch lived in poverty, ever under the threat of execution, and it was possible, more than possible, Rao allowed, that victory this day would raise the Tippoo so high that he would no longer need the small advantage of the Rajah's existence. The Rajah was paraded like a doll on Hindu holy days to placate the Tippoo's Hindu subjects, but if Mysore had no enemies in southern India, why should the Hindus of Mysore need to be placated? The Rajah and all his family would be secretly strangled and their corpses, like the bodies of the twelve murdered British prisoners, would be wrapped in reed mats and buried in an unmarked grave.

But if the Tippoo lost then the British would rule in Mysore. True, if they kept their word, the Rajah would be restored to his palace and to his ancient throne, but the power of the palace would still rest with the British advisers, and the Rajah's treasury would be required to pay for the upkeep of British troops. But if the Tippoo won, Appah Rao thought, then the French would come and what evidence was there that the French were any better than the British?

He stood above the southern gate, waiting for an unseen enemy to erupt from their trenches and assault the city, and he felt like a man buffeted between two implacable forces. If he had been less discreet he might have considered rebelling openly against the Tippoo and ordering his troops to help the invading British, but such a risk was too great for a cautious man. Yet if the Tippoo lost this day's battle, and if Appah Rao was perceived to be loyal to the defeated man, then what future did he have? Whichever side won, Appah Rao thought, he lost, but there was one small act that might yet snatch survival from defeat. He walked out to the end of a jutting cavalier, waved the gunners posted there away from their cannon, and beckoned Kunwar Singh to his side. "Where are your men?" he asked Singh.

"At the house, Lord." Kunwar Singh was a soldier, but not in any of the Tippoo's *cushoons*. His loyalty was to his kinsman, Appah Rao, and his duty was to protect Appah Rao and his family.

"Take six men," the General said, "and make sure they are not dressed in my livery. Then go to the dungeons, find Colonel McCandless, and take him back to my house. He speaks our tongue, so gain his trust by reminding him that you came with me to the temple at Somanathapura, and tell him that I am trusting him to keep my family alive." The General had been staring southwards as he spoke, but he now turned to look into Kunwar Singh's eyes. "If the British do get into the city then McCandless will protect our women." Appah Rao added this last assurance as though to justify the order he was giving, but Kunwar Singh still hesitated. Singh was a loyal man, but that loyalty was being dangerously stretched for he was being asked to rebel against the Tippoo. He might need to kill the Tippoo's men to free this enemy soldier, and Appah Rao understood his hesitation. "Do this for me, Kunwar Singh," the General promised, "and I shall restore your family's land."

"Lord," Kunwar Singh said, then stepped back, turned and was gone. Appah Rao watched him go, then stared past the city's southwestern corner to where he could see a portion of the enemy trenches. It was past noon and there were still no signs of life from the British lines except for a desultory gunshot once in a while. If the Tippoo won this day, Appah Rao thought, then his anger at McCandless's disappearance would be terrible. In which case, Appah Rao decided, McCandless must die before he could ever be discovered and have the truth beaten out of him. But if the Tippoo lost, then McCandless was Appah Rao's best guarantor of survival. And a Hindu living in a Muslim state was an expert at survival. Appah Rao, despite the risk he was running, knew he had acted for the best. He drew his sword, kissed its blade for luck, then waited for the assault.

It took only a minute for Kunwar Singh to reach the General's house. He ordered six of his best men to discard their tunics which bore Appah Rao's badge and to put on tiger-striped tunics instead. He changed his own coat, then borrowed a gold chain with a jeweled pendant from the General's treasure chest. Such a jewel was a sign of authority in the city and Kunwar Singh reckoned he might need it. He armed himself with a pistol and a sword, then waited for his picked squad.

Mary came to the courtyard and demanded to know what was happening. There was a strange stillness in the city, and the tempo of the British guns, which had been firing so hard and fast for days, was now muted and the ominous silence had made Mary nervous.

"We think the British are coming," Kunwar Singh told her, then blurted out that she would be safe for he had been ordered to free the British Colonel from the dungeons and bring him to the house where McCandless's presence would protect the women. "If the British even get through the wall," he added dubiously.

"What about my brother?" Mary asked.

Kunwar Singh shrugged. "I have no orders for him."

"Then I shall come with you," Mary declared.

"You can't!" Kunwar Singh insisted. He was often shocked by Mary's defiance, though he also found it appealing.

"You can stop me," she said, "by shooting me. Or you can let me come. Make up your mind." She did not wait to hear his answer, but hurried to her quarters where she snatched up the pistol that Appah Rao had given her. Kunwar Singh made no further protest. He was confused by what was happening, and, though he sensed that his master's loyalties were wavering, he still did not know which way they would ultimately fall.

"I can't let your brother come back here," he warned Mary when she came back to the courtyard.

"We can free him," Mary insisted, "and after that he can look after himself. He's good at that."

The streets of the city were oddly deserted. Most of the Tippoo's soldiers were on the ramparts, and anyone who had no business in the coming battle had taken care to lock their

318 · BERNARD CORNWELL

doors and stay hidden. A few men still trundled handcarts of ammunition and rockets toward the walls, but there were no bullock carts and no open shops. A few sacred cows wandered the city with sublime unconcern, but otherwise it was like a place of ghosts and it only took Kunwar Singh's small party five minutes to reach the complex of small courtyards that lay to the north of the Inner Palace. No one questioned Kunwar Singh's right to be in the palace precincts, for he wore the Tippoo's uniform and the jewels hanging about his neck were glittering proof of his authority.

The difficulty, Kunwar Singh had anticipated, would lie in persuading the guards to unlock the gate of the dungeon's outer cage. Once that gate was open the rest should be easy, for his men could swiftly overwhelm the guards and so find the key to McCandless's cell. Kunwar Singh had decided that his best course was simply to pretend to an authority he did not have and claim to bear a summons from the Tippoo himself. Arrogance went far in Mysore and he would give it a try. Otherwise he must order his men to use their muskets to blast the cage doors down and he feared that such a commotion would bring guards running from the nearby Inner Palace.

But when he reached the cells he found there were no guards. The space within the outer cage and around the stone steps was empty. A soldier on the inner wall above the cells saw the small group standing uncertainly beside the dungeon gate and assumed they had come to fetch the guards. "They've already gone!" the man shouted down. "Ordered to the walls. Gone to kill some Englishmen."

Kunwar Singh acknowledged the man, then rattled the gate, vainly hoping that the padlock would fall off. "You don't want to go inside," the helpful man called down, "the tiger's on duty."

Kunwar Singh instinctively stepped back. The soldier

above him lost interest and went back to his post as Kunwar Singh stepped back to the gate and tugged a second time at the huge padlock. "Too big to shoot open," he said. "That lock will take five or six bullets, at least."

"We can't get inside?" Mary asked.

"No. Not without attracting the guards." He gestured toward the palace. The thought of the tiger had made him nervous and he was wondering whether he would do better to wait until the assault started and then, under the cover of its huge noise, try to shoot the padlock away from the gate, then kill the tiger. Or else just give up the errand. The courtyard stank of sewage, and the smell only reinforced Kunwar Singh's presentiments of failure.

Then Mary stepped to the bars. "Richard?" she called. "Richard!"

There was a momentary pause. "Lass?" The answer came at last.

Kunwar Singh's nervousness increased. There were a dozen soldiers on the inner wall immediately above him, and a score of other people were peering through windows or above stable doors. No one was yet taking a suspicious interest in his party, but it seemed likely that someone of true authority would soon pass by the dungeons. "We should leave," he hissed to Mary.

"We can't get inside!" Mary called to Sharpe.

"Have you got a gun, lass?" Sharpe called back. Mary could not see him, for the outer cage was far enough back from the dungeon steps to hide the cells.

"Yes."

"Chuck it down here, lass. Chuck it as close to the bottom of the steps as you can. Make sure the bugger's not cocked."

Kunwar Singh rattled the gate again. The sound of the clangorous iron prompted a growl from the pit and a moment later the tiger loped up the steps, stared blank-eyed at Kunwar Singh, then turned and went back to the remnants of a half-carcass of goat. "We can't wait!" Kunwar Singh insisted to Mary.

"Throw us a gun, love!" Sharpe shouted.

Mary groped inside the folds of her sari to find the ivory-inlaid pistol that Appah Rao had given to her. She pushed it through the bars and then, very nervously, she tried to gauge how much effort would be needed to toss the gun into the pit, but not too far from the bottom of the steps. Kunwar Singh hissed at her, but made no move to stop her.

"Here, Richard!" she called, and she tossed the gun underarm. It was a clumsy throw, and the pistol fell short of the steps, but its momentum carried it over the edge and Mary heard the gun clattering down the stone stairs.

Sharpe cursed, for the pistol had lodged three steps up. "Have you got another one?" he shouted.

"Give me your pistol," Mary said to Kunwar Singh.

"No! We can't get in." Kunwar Singh was close to panic now and his six men had been infected by his fear. "We can't help them," he insisted.

"Mary!" Sharpe called.

"I'm sorry, Richard."

"Not to worry, lass," Sharpe said, staring at the pistol. He did not doubt he could pick the lock open, but could he reach the gun before the tiger reached him? And even if he did, would one small pistol ball stop eight feet of hungry tiger? "Jesus Christ!" he swore.

"Sharpe!" McCandless chided him.

"I was praying, sir. Because this is a right bugger-up, sir, a right bugger-up." Sharpe took out the picklock and unfolded one of the shafts. He put his hands through the bars and grabbed hold of the padlock, then explored the big keyhole with the hooked shaft. It was a crude lock that ought to be easy to open, but the mechanism was not properly oiled and

Sharpe feared that the picklock might snap rather than move the levers aside. Lawford and McCandless watched him, while from across the corridor Hakeswill stared with huge blue eyes.

"Go on, boy, good boy," Hakeswill said. "Get us out of here, boy."

"Shut your ugly face, Obadiah," Sharpe muttered. He had moved one lever, now only the second remained, but it was much stiffer than the first. Sweat was pouring down Sharpe's face. He was working half blind, unable to pull the padlock to an angle where he could see the keyhole. The tiger had paused in its eating to watch him, intrigued by the hands protruding through the bars. Sharpe maneuvered the picklock, felt the hook lodge against the lever, and gently pressed. He pressed harder, and suddenly the hook scraped off the lever's edge and Sharpe swore.

And just as he swore the tiger twisted and sprang. It attacked with appalling speed, a sudden unleashing of coiled muscles that ended with a swipe of one unsheathed paw as it tried to hook a claw into the protruding hands. Sharpe recoiled, dropping the picklock, and cursing as the tiger's slash missed him by inches. "Bastard," he swore at the beast, then he stooped and reached through the bars for the fallen picklock that lay a foot away. He moved fast, but the tiger was faster, and this time Sharpe got a deep scratch on the back of his hand.

"Sergeant Hakeswill," Sharpe hissed. "Get the beast over on your side."

"Nothing I can do!" Hakeswill protested, his face twitching. The tiger was watching Sharpe. It was only two feet away from him, its teeth were bared and its claws unsheathed, and there was a glint in its yellow eyes. "You want to fight a tiger, Sharpie," Hakeswill said, "that's your business, not mine.

Man doesn't have to fight pussycats, says so in the scriptures."

"You say that one more time," McCandless roared in sudden and unexpected fury, "and I'll make sure you never wear stripes again! Do you understand me, man?"

Hakeswill was taken aback by the Colonel's anger. "Sir," he said weakly.

"So do as Private Sharpe says," Colonel McCandless ordered. "And do it now."

Hakeswill beat his hands against the bars. The tiger turned its head and Sharpe immediately snatched the picklock back into the cell and stood again. The tiger leapt at Hakeswill, shaking the bars of his cell with its violence, and Hakeswill backed hurriedly away.

"Keep provoking it, man!" McCandless ordered Hakeswill, and the Sergeant spat at the tiger, then threw a handful of straw toward its face.

Sharpe worked on the lock. He had the hook against the lever again. The tiger, roused to a petulant fury, stood with its paws against the bars of Hakeswill's cell as Sharpe pressed on the lever and at last felt it move. His hands trembled and the hook grated as it slipped across the lever's face, but he steadied himself and pressed harder. He was holding his breath, willing the lever to unlatch. Sweat stung his eyes, then suddenly the lever clicked across and the lock sprang open in his hands.

"That was the easy part," he said grimly. He folded the picklock and put it back in his pocket. "Mary!" he called. There was no answer. "Mary!" he shouted again, but still there was no reply. Kunwar Singh had pulled his men away from the cells and was now in a deep gateway on the courtyard's far side, trapped between his wish to obey Appah Rao and the apparent impossibility of that obedience.

"What do you need her for?" Colonel McCandless asked.

"I don't even know if the bloody gun's loaded, sir. I never asked her."

"Assume it is," McCandless said.

"Easy for you, sir," Sharpe said respectfully, "being as you ain't the one who's got to go out and kill the beast."

"I'll do it," Lawford offered.

Sharpe grinned. "It's either you or me, sir," he said, "and being honest, sir, who do you think will do the best job?"

"You," Lawford admitted.

"Which is what I reckoned, sir. But one thing, sir. How do you shoot a tiger? In the head?"

"Between the eyes," McCandless said, "but not too high up. Just below the eyes."

"Bloody hell," Sharpe said. He had eased the padlock out of its hasp and he could now move the door outwards, though he did it gingerly, unwilling to attract the tiger's attention. He pulled the door shut again and stooped for his red jacket that lay on the straw. "Let's hope the bugger's a stupid pussycat," he said, then he gently pushed the door open again. The hinges squealed alarmingly. He had the door in his left hand and his red coat was bundled in his right. When the door was open a foot he tossed the coat as hard as he could toward the remains of the goat at the corridor's farther end.

The tiger saw the motion, twisted away from Hakeswill's cage, and sprang toward the coat. The red jacket had flown the best part of twenty feet and the tiger covered the distance in one powerful leap. It batted the coat with its claws, then batted it again, but found no flesh and blood inside the cloth.

Sharpe had slipped through the door, turned to the steps, and snatched up the pistol. He turned back, hoping to regain the safety of the cell before the tiger noticed him, but his foot slipped on the lowest step and he fell backward against the stone stairs. The tiger heard him, turned, and went still. The yellow eyes stared at Sharpe, Sharpe gazed back, then slowly thumbed the cock of the pistol. The tiger heard the click and its tail lashed once. The merciless eyes watched Sharpe, then, very slowly, the tiger crouched. Its tail swung back and forth once more.

"Don't shoot now!" McCandless called softly. "Get close!"

"Yes, sir," Sharpe said. He kept his eyes on the tiger's eyes as he slowly, slowly climbed to his feet and edged toward the beast. The fear was like a mad wild thing inside him. Hakeswill was spitting encouragement, but Sharpe heard nothing and he saw nothing but the tiger's eyes. He wondered if he should attempt to duck back into the cell, but guessed that the tiger would spring while he was still trying to open the door. Better to face the beast and shoot it in the open pit, he decided. He held the pistol at arm's length, keeping the muzzle aimed at a patch of black fur just beneath the animal's eyes. Fifteen feet away, twelve. His boots grated on the stone floor. How accurate was the pistol? It was a pretty enough thing, all ivory and silver, but did it fire true? And how tightly was the ball sized to the barrel? Even a gap between barrel and ball the width of a sheet of paper was enough to throw a bullet wide as it spat out of the muzzle. Even at twelve feet a pistol could miss a man-size target, let alone a small patch of matted fur between a man-eating tiger's eyes.

"Kill the bugger, Sharpie!" Hakeswill urged.

"Careful, man!" McCandless hissed. "Make sure of your shot. Careful now!"

Sharpe edged forward. His eyes were still fixed on the tiger's eyes. He was willing the beast to stay still, to receive its death gracefully. Ten feet. The tiger was motionless, just watching him. Sweat stung Sharpe's eyes and the weight of the pistol was making his hand tremble. Do it now, he thought, do it now. Pull the trigger, put the bugger down, and run like shit. He blinked, his eyes stinging with the sweat. The tiger did not even blink. Eight feet. He could smell the beast, see its unsheathed claws on the stone, see the glint in its eyes. Seven feet. Close enough, he reckoned, and he straightened his arm to line up the pistol's rudimentary sights.

And the tiger sprang. It came from the ground so fast that it was almost on top of Sharpe before he even realized that the beast had moved. He had a wild glimpse of huge claws stretched far out of their pads and of feral yellow teeth in a snarling mouth, and he was unaware that he called aloud in panic. He was unaware, too, that he had pulled the trigger, not smoothly as he had planned, but in a desperate, panicked jerk. Then, instinctively, he dropped to the ground and curled tight so that the tiger's leap would pass over him.

Lawford gasped. The echo of the pistol shot was hugely loud in the confines of the dungeon pit which suddenly reeked with the sulfurous smell of powder smoke. Hakeswill was crouching in a corner of his cell, scarce daring to look, while McCandless was mouthing a silent prayer. Sharpe was on the ground, waiting for the agony of the claws to rip him apart.

But the tiger was dying. The bullet had struck the back of the tiger's mouth. It was only a small bullet, but the force of it was sufficient to pierce through the throat's tissues and into the brain stem. Blood spattered the cell bars as the tiger's graceful leap slumped into death's collapse. It had fallen at the foot of the steps, but some terrible instinct of surging life still animated the beast and it tried to stand. Its paws scrabbled against stone and its head jerked up for a snarling second as the tail lashed, then blood surged out of its mouth, the head fell back, and the beast went still.

There was silence.

The first flies came down to explore the blood spilling

from the tiger's mouth. "Oh, sweet suffering Christ," Sharpe said, picking himself up. He was shaking. "Jesus bloody wept."

McCandless did not reprove him. The Colonel knew a prayer when he heard one.

Sharpe fetched his torn jacket, pulled the cell door wide open, then gingerly sidled past the dead tiger as though he feared the beast might come back to life. McCandless and Lawford followed him up the stone stairs. "What about me?" Hakeswill called. "You can't leave me here. It ain't Christian!"

"Leave him," McCandless ordered.

"I was planning on it, sir," Sharpe said. He found his picklock again and reached for the padlock on the outer gate. This lock was much simpler, merely a crude one-lever mechanism, and it took only seconds to snap the ancient lock open. "Where are we going?" Lawford asked.

"To ground, man," McCandless said. The sudden freedom seemed to have lifted the Colonel's fever. "We must find somewhere to hide."

Sharpe pushed the gate outward, then saw Mary gazing at him from a doorway across the courtyard and he smiled, then saw she was not smiling back, but was instead looking terrified. There were men with her, and they too were unmoving with fear. Then Sharpe saw why.

Three *jettis* were crossing the courtyard toward the dungeon cage. Three monsters. Three men with bare oiled chests and muscles like tiger thews. One carried a coiled whip while the other two were armed with hugely long spears with which they had planned to subdue the tiger before opening the prisoners' cell. Sharpe swore. He dropped his coat and picklock.

"Can you lock us in again?" McCandless asked.

"Those buggers are strong enough to tear the padlocks

clean away, sir. We have to kill the bastards." Sharpe darted through the gate and ran to his right. The *jettis* followed him, but more slowly. They were not fast men, though their massive strength gave them an easy confidence as they spread out into a line to trap Sharpe in a corner of the courtyard. "Throw me a musket!" Sharpe called to Mary. "Quick, lass, quick!"

Mary snatched a musket from one of Kunwar Singh's men and, before the astonished man could protest, she tossed it to Sharpe. He caught it, held it at his waist, but did not cock the weapon. Then he advanced on the middle *jetti*. The man had seen that the musket was uncocked and he smiled, anticipating an easy victory, then slashed out his whip so that its coiled end wound round Sharpe's throat. He tugged, planning to pull Sharpe off balance, but Sharpe was already running toward him, cheating the whip's tension, and the *jetti* had never faced a man as quick as Sharpe. Nor as lethal. The *jetti* was still recovering from his surprise when the muzzle of the musket rammed into his Adam's apple with the force of a sledgehammer. He choked, his eyes widened, then Sharpe kicked him in the crotch and the huge man staggered and collapsed. One big muscle-bound brute was down, gasping desperately for breath, but the long spears were turning toward Sharpe who, with the whip still trailing from his throat, turned fast to his right. He knocked the next *jetti*'s spear aside with his musket barrel, then reversed the weapon and charged. The *jetti* abandoned his spear and reached for the musket, but Sharpe checked his rush so that the big man's hands closed on nothing, and then Sharpe swung the musket by its barrel so that its brass-bound butt slammed into the man's temple with the sound of an axe biting into soft wood.

Two of the bastards were down. The soldiers on the inner ramparts' battery were watching the fight, but not interfering. They were confused, for Kunwar Singh was standing right beside the fight and doing nothing, and his jewels made him appear a man of high authority, and so they followed his example and did not try to intervene. Some of the watching soldiers were even cheering, for, though the *jettis* were admired, they were also resented because they received privileges far above any ordinary soldier's expectations.

Lawford had moved to help Sharpe, but his uncle held him back. "Let him be, Willie," McCandless said quietly. "He's doing the Lord's work and I've rarely seen it done better."

The third *jetti* lumbered at Sharpe with his spear. He advanced warily, confused by the ease with which this foreign demon had downed his two companions.

Sharpe smiled at the third *jetti*, shouldered the musket, pulled back the cock, and fired.

The bullet drummed into the *jetti*'s chest, making all his huge muscles shudder with the force of its impact. The *jetti* slowed, then tried to charge again, but his knees gave way and he fell forward onto his face. He twitched, his hands scrabbled for an instant, then he was still. From the ramparts above the soldiers cheered.

Sharpe uncoiled the whip from his neck, picked up one of the clumsy spears, and finished off the two *jettis* who still lived. One had been stunned and the other was almost unable to breathe, and both now had their throats cut. From the windows of the low buildings around the courtyard men and women stared at Sharpe in shock.

"Don't just stand there!" Sharpe snarled at Lawford. "Sir," he added hastily.

Lawford and McCandless came through the gate, while Kunwar Singh, as if released from a spell, suddenly hurried to meet them. Mary crossed to Sharpe. "Are you all right?"

"Never better, lass," he said. In truth he was shaking as he picked up his red coat and as Kunwar Singh's six men stared at him as though he was a devil come from nightmare. Sharpe wiped sweat from his eyes. He was oblivious of most of what had just happened for he had fought as he had always fought, fast and with a lethal skill, but it was instinct that led him, not reason, and the fight had left him with a seething hate. He wanted to slake that hate by killing more men, and perhaps Kunwar Singh's soldiers picked up that ferocity, for none of them dared move.

Lawford crossed to Sharpe. "We think the assault is about to come, Sharpe," the Lieutenant said, "and Colonel McCandless is being taken to a place of safety. He's insisted that we go with him. The fellow in the jewels isn't happy about that, but McCandless won't go without us. And well done, by the way."

Sharpe glanced up into the Lieutenant's eyes. "I'm not going with him, sir, I'm going to fight."

"Sharpe!" Lawford reproved him.

"There's a bloody great mine, sir!" Sharpe raised his voice angrily. "Just waiting to kill our lads! I ain't letting that happen. You can do what you bloody well like, but I'm going to kill some more of these bastards. You can come with me, sir, or stay with the Colonel, I don't care. You, lad!" This was to one of Kunwar Singh's uncomprehending soldiers. "Give me some cartridges. Come on, hurry!" Sharpe crossed to the man, pulled open his pouch, and helped himself to a handful of cartridges that he shoved into a pocket. Kunwar Singh made no move to stop him. Indeed, everyone in the court-yard seemed to be stunned by the ferocity that had reduced three of the Tippoo's prized *jettis* to dead meat, though the officer commanding the troops on the inner wall did now call down to demand to know what was happening. Kunwar Singh shouted back that they were doing the Tippoo's bidding.

McCandless had overheard Sharpe talking to Lawford. "If I can help, Private . . ." the Colonel said.

"You're weak, sir, begging your pardon, sir. But Mister Lawford will help me."

Lawford said nothing for a moment, then nodded. "Yes, of course I will."

"What will you do?" McCandless asked. He spoke to Sharpe, not Lawford.

"Blow the bloody mine, sir, blow it to kingdom come."

"God bless you, Sharpe. And keep you."

"Save your prayers for the bloody enemy, sir," Sharpe said curtly. He rammed a bullet home, then plunged into an alleyway that led southward. He was loose in his enemy's rear, he was angry, and he was ready to give the bastards a taste of hell on earth.

Major General Baird hauled a huge watch from his fob pocket, sprang open the lid, and stared at the hands. One o'clock. On the fourth of May, 1799. A Saturday. A drop of sweat landed on the watch crystal and he carefully wiped it away with a tassel of his red sash. His mother had made the sash. "You'll not let us down, young Davy," she had said sternly, giving him the strip of tasseled silk and then saying no more as he had walked away to join the army. The sash was over twenty years old now, and it was frayed and threadbare, but Baird reckoned it would last him. He would take it back to Scotland one day.

It would be good, he thought, to go home and see the new century. Maybe the eighteen hundreds would bring a different world, even a better one, but he doubted that the new era would manage to dispense with soldiers. Till time ended, Baird suspected, there would be uses for a man and his sword. He took off his mildewed hat and wiped the sweat from his forehead with his sleeve. Almost time.

He peered between two sandbags that formed the forward lip of the trench. The South Cauvery rippled prettily between its flat boulders, the paths across its bed marked with the little white flags on their bamboo sticks. In a moment he would launch men across those paths, then through the gap in the glacis and up that mound of stone, brick, mud, and dust. He counted eleven cannonballs stranded on the breach, looking for all the world like plums stuck in a pudding. Three hundred yards of ground to cover, one river to cross, and one plum pudding to climb. He could see men peering from between the city's battered crenellations. Flags flew there. The bastards would have guns mounted crosswise to the breach and perhaps a mine buried in the rubble. God preserve the Forlorn Hopes, he thought, though God was not usually merciful in such matters. If Colonel Gent was right, and there was a massive mine waiting for the attackers, then the Forlorn Hopes would be slaughtered, and then the main attack would have to assault the breach and climb its shoulders to where the enemy was massed on the outer ramparts. So be it. Too late to worry now.

Baird pushed through the waiting men to find Sergeant Graham. Graham would lead one of the two Forlorn Hopes and, if he lived, would be Lieutenant Graham by nightfall. The Sergeant was scooping a last ladleful of water from one of the barrels that had been placed in the trenches to slake the thirst of the waiting men. "Not long now, Sergeant," Baird said.

"Whenever you say, sir." Graham poured the water over his bare head, then pulled on his shako. He would go into the breach with a musket in one hand and a British flag in the other.

"Whenever the guns give their farewell volley, Sergeant." Baird clicked open the watch again and it seemed to him the

332 · BERNARD CORNWELL

hands had scarcely moved. "In six minutes, I think, if this is accurate." He held the watch to his ear. "It usually loses a minute or two every day."

"We're ready, sir," Graham said.

"I'm sure you're ready," Baird said, "but wait for my order."

"Of course, sir."

Baird looked at the volunteers, a mix of British and sepoys. They grinned back at him. Rogues, he thought, every last man jack of them, but what splendid rogues, brave as lions. Baird felt a pang of sentimentality for these men, even for the sepoys. Like many soldiers the Scotsman was an emotional man, and he instinctively disliked those men, like Colonel Wellesley, who seemed passionless. Passion, Baird reckoned, was what would take men across the river and up the breach. Damn scientific soldiering now. The science of siege warfare had opened the city, but only a screaming and insane passion would take men inside. "God be with you all, boys," he said to the Forlorn Hope and they grinned again. Like every man who would cross the river today none of them was encumbered with a pack. They had all stripped off their stocks, too. They carried weapons and cartridges and nothing else, and if they succeeded they would be rewarded with General Harris's thanks and maybe a pittance of coins.

"Is there food in the city, sir?" one of the volunteers asked.

"Plenty, boys, plenty." Baird, like the rest of the army, was on half-rations.

"And some *bibbi*, sir?" another man asked.

Baird rolled his eyes. "Running over with it, lads, and all of them just panting for you. The place is fair crammed with *bibbi*. Even enough for us old generals."

They laughed. General Harris had given strict orders that the inhabitants were not to be molested, but Baird knew that the terrible savagery of an assault on a breach almost demanded that the men's appetites be satisfied afterward. He did not care. So far as Major General David Baird was concerned the boys could play to their loins' content so long as they first won.

He edged his way through the crush of men to a point midway between the two Forlorn Hopes. The watch still ticked, but again the minute hand seemed scarcely to have moved since he last looked at the face. Baird closed the lid, pushed the watch into his fob, then peered again at the city. The undamaged parts of the wall glowed white in the sun. It was, with its towers and shining roofs and tall palms, a beautiful place, yet it was there that Baird had spent close to four years as a prisoner of the Tippoo. He hated the place as he hated its ruler. Revenge had been a long time coming, but it was here now.

He drew his claymore, a brutal Scottish blade that had none of the finesse of more modern swords, yet Baird, at six feet four inches tall, had little need of finesse. He would carry his butcher's blade into a breach of blood to pay back the Tippoo for forty-four months of hell.

In the batteries behind Baird the gunners blew on their linstocks to keep the fire burning. General Harris pulled out his watch. Colonel Arthur Wellesley, who would lead the second wave of attackers through the breach, adjusted his cravat, and thought of his responsibilities. The bulk of his men were from the Régiment de Meuron, a Swiss battalion that had once fought for the Dutch, but which had put itself under the command of the East India Company when the British had captured Ceylon. The men were mostly Swiss, but with a leavening from the German states, and they were a sober, steady battalion that Wellesley planned to lead to the Inner Palace to protect its contents and its harem from the ravages of the attackers. Seringapatam might fall, and the Tippoo might die, but the important thing was to gain

Mysore's friendship and Wellesley was determined to make certain that no unnecessary atrocities soured its citizens' new allegiance. He adjusted the silver-gilt gorget about his neck, drew his sword an inch or two, then let it fall back into its scabbard before momentarily closing his eyes to say a prayer beseeching God's protection on his men.

The Forlorn Hopes, their muskets loaded and tipped with steel, crouched in the trenches. The officers' watches ticked on, the river ran gentle across its stones, and the silent city waited.

''Coat off,'' Sharpe said to Lawford, instinctively lapsing back into the relationship that had existed between them when they had served in Gudin's battalion. "No point in showing a red coat till we have to," Sharpe explained, turning his own coat inside out. He did not put it back on, but knotted its sleeves about his neck so that the claw-torn jacket hung down against his scarred and naked back. The two men were crouched in a byre off the alley that led from the courtyard. Colonel McCandless had gone, led away to Appah Rao's house, and Sharpe and Lawford were alone. "I don't even have a gun," the Lieutenant said nervously.

"Soon remedy that," Sharpe said confidently. "Come on now."

Sharpe led, plunging into the intricate maze of small streets that surrounded the palace. A white man's face was not so unusual as to attract attention in Seringapatam, for there were plenty of Europeans serving the Tippoo, but even so Sharpe did not fancy his chances in a red coat. He did not fancy his chances much at all, but he would be damned before he abandoned his fellow soldiers to the Tippoo's mine.

He hurried past a shuttered goldsmith's shop and half glimpsed, deep in its shadowed entrance, an armed man who was standing guard on the property. "Stay here," he told Lawford, then slung the musket on his shoulder and doubled back. He pushed a wandering cow out of his way and ducked into the goldsmith's entrance. "How are you feeling today?" he said pleasantly to the man who, speaking no English, just frowned in confusion. He was still frowning when Sharpe's left fist buried itself in his belly. He grunted, but then the right fist smacked him on the bridge of his nose and he was in no state to resist as Sharpe stripped him of musket and cartridge box. For good measure Sharpe gave the man a tap on the skull with the butt end of the musket, then went back to the street. "One musket, sir, filthy as hell, but she'll fire. Cartridges too."

Lawford opened the musket's pan to check that it was loaded. "Just what do you plan to do, Sharpe?" the Lieutenant asked.

"Don't know, sir. Won't know till we get there."

"You're going to the mine?"

"Aye, sir."

"There'll be guards."

"Like as not."

"And only two of us."

"I can count, sir." Sharpe grinned. "It's reading I find hard. But my letters are coming on, aren't they?"

"You're reading well," Lawford said. Probably, the Lieutenant thought, as well as most seven-year-olds, but it had still been gratifying to see the pleasure Sharpe took from the process, even if his only reading matter was a crumpled page of the Revelation full of mysterious beasts with wings that covered their eyes. "I'll get you some more interesting books when we're out of here," Lawford promised.

"I'd like that, sir," Sharpe said, then ran across a street junction. The fear of an imminent assault had served to empty the streets of their usual crowds, but the alleys were clogged with parked carts. Stray dogs barked as the two men hurried southward, but there were few people to remark their presence. "There, sir, there's our bloody answer," Sharpe said. He had run from a street into a small square, and now jerked back into the shadows. Lawford peered about the corner to see that the small open space was filled with handcarts, and that the handcarts were piled with rockets. "Waiting to take them up to the wall, I daresay," Sharpe said. "Got so many up there already they have to store the rest down here. What we do, sir, is take one cart, go down that next street, and have a private Guy Fawkes day."

"There are guards."

"Of course there are."

"I mean on the rocket carts, Sharpe."

"They're nothing," Sharpe said scornfully. "If those fellows were any good they'd be up on the walls. Can't be nothing but maimed men and grandfathers. Rubbish. All we have to do is shout at the buggers. Are you ready?"

Lawford looked into his companion's face. "You're enjoying this, aren't you, Sharpe?"

"Aye, sir. Aren't you?"

"I'm scared as hell," Lawford admitted.

Sharpe smiled. "You won't be when we're through, sir. We're going to be all right. You just behave as though you owned the bloody place. You officers are supposed to be good at that, aren't you? So I'll grab a cart and you shout at the rubbish. Tell them Gudin sent us. Come on, sir, time's wasting. Just walk out there as though we owned the place."

Sharpe brazenly walked into the sunlight, his musket slung on his shoulder, and Lawford followed him. "You won't tell anyone that I confessed to being scared?" the Lieutenant asked.

"Of course not, sir. You think I'm not scared myself? Jesus, I almost fouled my breeches when that bloody tiger jumped at me. I've never seen a thing move so bloody fast. But I wasn't going to show I was scared in front of bloody Hakeswill. Hey, you! Are you in charge?" Sharpe shouted imperiously at a man who squatted beside one of the carts. "Move your bloody self, I want the cart."

The man sprang aside as Sharpe jerked up the handles. There must have been fifty rockets in the cart, more than enough for Sharpe's purpose. Two other men shouted protests at Sharpe, but Lawford waved them down. "Colonel Gudin sent us. Understand?" Lawford said. "Colonel Gudin. He sent us." The Lieutenant followed Sharpe down the street leading south from the square. "Those two men are coming after us," he said nervously.

"Shout at the buggers, sir. You're an officer!"

"Back!" Lawford shouted. "To your duties! Go on! Now! Do as I say, damn your eyes! Go!" He paused, then gave a delighted chuckle. "Good God, Sharpe, it worked."

"Works with us, sir, should work with them," Sharpe said. He turned a corner and saw the towering sculptures of the big Hindu temple. He recognized where he was now and he knew the alley leading to the mine was only a few yards away. It would be filled with guards, but Sharpe now had a whole arsenal of his own.

"We can't do anything if there isn't an attack," Lawford said.

"I know that, sir."

"So what do we do if there isn't an assault?"

"Hide, sir."

"Where, for God's sake?"

"Lali will take us in, sir. You remember Lali, don't you, sir?"

Lawford blushed at the memory of his introduction to Seringapatam's brothels. "You really believe she'll hide us?"

"She thinks you're sweet, sir." Sharpe grinned. "I've seen

her a couple of times since that first night, sir, and she always asks after you. I reckon you made a conquest there, sir."

"Good God, Sharpe, you won't tell anyone?"

"Me, sir?" Sharpe pretended to be shocked. "Not a word, sir."

Then, very suddenly, and far off, muffled by distance so that it was thin and wavering, a trumpet sounded.

And every gun in creation seemed to fire at once.

Baird clambered up the trench wall, climbed over the sandbags and turned to face his men. "Now, my brave fellows," he shouted in his broad Scottish accent, waving his sword toward the city, "follow me and prove yourselves worthy of the name British soldiers!"

The Forlorn Hopes were already on their way. The moment Baird had climbed out of the trench the seventy-six men of the two Hopes had scrambled over the lip and begun running. They splashed through the Little Cauvery, then sprinted toward the larger river. The air about them churned with noise. Every siege gun had fired at almost the same instant and the breach was a boiling mass of dust, while the huge sound of the guns was echoing back from the walls. The banners of Britain streamed as the leading men ran into the South Cauvery. The first bullets plucked at the water, throwing up small fountains, but the Forlorn Hopes did not notice the firing. They were screaming their challenge and racing each other to be first up the breach.

"Fire!" the Tippoo shouted, and the walls of the city were rimmed with flame and smoke as a thousand muskets poured lead down into the South Cauvery and out toward the trenches. Rockets hissed off the walls, their trails twisting madly as they tangled in the hot air. The trumpet was still sounding. The musketry of the defenders was unending as men simply dropped their empty guns, snatched up loaded ones, and fired into the smoke cloud that edged the city. The sound of their guns was like a giant fire crackling, the river was foaming with bullets and a handful of redcoats and sepoys were jerking and thrashing as they drowned or bled to death.

"Come on!" Sergeant Graham roared as he stumbled over the remains of the mud wall that had penned in the water behind the glacis. A foot of muddy water still lay in the old ditch, but Graham ran through it as though he had wings. A bullet plucked at the flag in his left hand. "Come on, you bastards!" he shouted. He was on the lower slope of the breach now, and his whole world was nothing but noise and smoke and whipsawing bullets. It was a tiny place, that world, a hell of dust and fire above a rubble slope. He could see no enemy, for those above him were hidden by their own musket smoke, but then the defenders on the inner wall, who could stare straight down the throat of the breach in the outer wall, saw the redcoats clambering up the ramp and opened fire. A man behind Graham collapsed backward with blood gurgling from his throat. Another pitched forward with a shattered knee.

Graham reached the breach's summit. His real goal was the wall to his left, but the summit of the breach felt like triumph enough and he rammed the flagstaff deep into the stones and dust. "Lieutenant Graham now!" he shouted exultingly, and a bullet immediately snatched him off the summit and hurled him back toward his men.

It was just then that the Tippoo's own volunteers struck. Sixty men swarmed up from behind the wall with sabres and muskets to meet the two Forlorn Hopes on the crest of the rubble breach. These were the Tippoo's best men, his tigers, the warriors of Allah who had been promised a favored place in paradise, and they screamed with exultation as they attacked. They fired a musket volley as they climbed, then threw down the empty guns to attack the redcoats with bright curved swords. Musket barrels parried swords, bayonets lunged and were cut aside. Men swore and killed, swore and died. Some men fought with hands and boots, they gouged and bit each other as they grappled hand to hand on the dusty summit. One Bengali sepoy snatched up a fallen sword and carved a way to the foot of the wall where it climbed up from the breach to the northern ramparts. A Mysorean volunteer sliced at him, the sepoy instinctively parried, then cut down through the man's brass helmet so violently that the blade was buried and trapped in his enemy's skull. The Bengali left it there and, so fevered by battle that he did not realize he was weaponless, tried to scale the broken wall's flank to attack the defenders waiting on the firestep above. A musket shot from the top of the wall hurled him backward and he slid, dying and bleeding, to lodge against the wounded Graham.

Baird was still west of the river. His job was not to die with the Forlorn Hopes, but to lead the main attack up the path they had cleared. That main attack now formed itself into two columns of platoons.

"Forward!" Baird shouted, and led the twin columns toward the river. The ground ahead was being pitted by bullets as if an invisible hail fell. Behind him the drummer boys were sounding the advance while the engineers, laden with their fascines and ladders, walked alongside the platoons. Rockets screamed above Baird, their trails stitching ropes of smoke above the river. Men struggled hand to hand in the breach and the walls of the city spat flame through the churning rill of smoke.

Hell had come to Seringapatam and Baird hurried toward it.

*　*　*

''Jesus Christ!" Sharpe swore, for he could hear the sudden sound of battle swelling just beyond the western walls. Men were dying there. Men were storming a breach and the Tippoo's mine waited for them, its tons of powder cunningly crammed into a stone tunnel and poised to annihilate a whole brigade.

He stopped at a corner of the alley which led to the ancient gateway that had been filled with the explosives. He peered round the corner and saw Sergeant Rothière and two Frenchmen from Gudin's battalion. All three were standing beside a barrel, staring up at the inner ramparts, and around the Europeans was a guard of a half-dozen *jettis*, all armed with muskets and swords. He ducked back and blew the priming out of his musket's pan. "Only nine or ten of the bastards," he told Lawford, "so let's give them a headache."

The rockets were stacked nose first on the cart so that their long bamboo tails stuck out toward the cart's handles. Sharpe went to the front of the cart, seized the thin boards that were painted with gods and elephants, and wrenched them off. They came away easily, their nails pulling out of the cart's sides. He beat off the last slivers of wood so that now there was no obstacle in front of the lethal cargo, then he turned the cart so that the rockets' tin cones were pointing toward the alley, though he took care to make sure that the cart and its contents were still hidden from the men waiting beside the mine's fuse.

Lawford said nothing, but just watched as Sharpe tore the fuse paper from one of the rockets. He twisted the paper into a spill, then pushed it into the musket's empty lock, cocked the gun and pulled the trigger. The powder-impregnated paper immediately caught the spark and started burning.

Sharpe dropped the musket and began lighting the fuses of the topmost row of rockets. The paper in his hand burned fiercely, but he managed to light eight of the weapons before he was forced to tear off another fuse and use it to light more. It was difficult to reach between the rocket's bamboo sticks, but he lit another ten while the first few fuses were fizzing and smoking. Lawford, seeing what Sharpe was doing, had taken the single page of the Bible from his pocket and twisted it into a spill that he used to light still more of the missiles. Then the first rocket to be lit suddenly coughed and spat out a gout of smoke and Sharpe immediately snatched up the cart's handles and shoved it around the corner so that the missiles were pointing straight down the alley. He crouched beside it, sheltered from the men in the alley by the corner of the building, and pulled his musket toward him. He used the musket to raise the cart's handles so that the vehicle's bed, and the rockets it contained, were horizontal.

The first rocket shuddered, then streaked away. The second went an instant later, then two more, and suddenly the whole cart was shaking and jerking as the rockets seethed away. A musket bullet hit the cart, another flicked dust from the corner of the building, but then there were no more shots, just shouts of terror as the missiles screamed between the alley's close walls. Some of the rockets had solid shot in their nose cones, others had small charges of black powder, and those now began to explode. A man screamed. More rockets exploded, the sound of their blasts cramming the alley with noise while the missiles' fierce trails filled the small street with smoke and flame. Sharpe waited till the last lit rocket flamed off the cart. "Now's the hard bit," he warned Lawford. He replaced the priming in his musket with a pinch from a fresh cartridge, then seized the handcart and pushed it in front of him down the alley. At least thirty of the rockets had fired, and the alley was now an inferno of boiling smoke amongst which a handful of live rockets still ricocheted or spun crazily while the carcasses of the spent weapons burned bright in the gloom. Sharpe charged into that chaos, hoping that the half-loaded cart would serve as a shield if any man still lived in the alley.

Lawford charged with him. At least four men were still on their feet, while another had found shelter in a deep doorway, but they were all dazed by the violence of the rockets and half blinded by the thick smoke. Sharpe gave the cart a huge push to send it clattering toward them. One of the *jettis* saw the cart, dodged aside, and charged at Sharpe with a drawn sabre, but Lawford shot him with his musket, taking the huge man in the throat as quickly and cleanly as if he had been a pheasant rising from a brake. The cart struck two of the standing men and sent them reeling. Sharpe stamped on the head of one and kicked the other in the crotch. He slammed the butt of the musket onto the back of a Frenchman's skull, then drove the weapon's muzzle deep into a *jetti*'s belly and, as the man folded, he rammed the barrel into his face. The *jetti* screamed and staggered away, his hands clutched tight to one eye. Lawford had seized a fallen sword and sliced it savagely across another *jetti*'s neck and was so inspired and elated by battle that he did not even feel any revulsion when the man's blood gushed out to hiss in the burning remnants of a rocket. Sergeant Rothière was on the ground with one of his legs broken by the strike of a rocket, but he cocked his musket and aimed the gun at Lawford, then the Sergeant heard Sharpe behind him and tried to swing the musket round. Sharpe was too close and too fast. He felled Rothière with a huge swing of his gun. He felt the butt break the Sergeant's skull. The gun was still loaded, so he reversed it and snarled a challenge as he peered through the choking smoke. He could see no danger now, just wounded men, dead men, and flickering rocket cases. The mine's trail, a snaking length of quick fuse, had somehow escaped the fire of the rockets and lay discarded beside the toppled barrel in which Rothière had been keeping a lit linstock. Sharpe moved toward the barrel, then heard the click of a gun being cocked.

"That's far enough, Sharpe." It was Colonel Gudin who spoke. He was behind Sharpe. The Colonel had been waiting for the Tippoo's signal on the inner ramparts just beside the gatehouse, but he had jumped down onto a rooftop and then into the alley and now he aimed his pistol at Sharpe. Lawford, sabre in hand, was a half-dozen paces away, too far to help. Gudin jerked the pistol. "Put the musket down, Sharpe." Gudin spoke calmly.

Sharpe had turned with the musket at his hip. The Colonel was only three or four paces away. "Put your pistol down, sir," Sharpe said.

A slight look of regret crossed the Colonel's face as he straightened his arm to take more careful aim. Sharpe fired as soon as he saw the small movement and though he had not aimed the musket, but fired it from the hip, his bullet struck the Colonel high on his right shoulder so that Gudin's pistol arm flew into the air. "Sorry, sir," Sharpe said, and then he ran to where one of the spent rockets still had weak flames burning from its exhaust. He carried the flaming carcass to the end of the quick fuse and there paused to listen. He could hear cannons firing, and knew they must be the Tippoo's guns, for no British artilleryman would dare fire now for fear of hitting the assaulting troops. He could hear musket fire, but he could not hear the massive, deep-throated roar of men coming into the breach. The Forlorn Hope alone must be fighting, and that meant the space between the walls must still be clear of British soldiers. He stooped to put the rocket's feeble flames to the waiting fuse, but Lawford pushed his arm aside. Sharpe looked up at the Lieutenant. "Sir?"

"Best to leave the mine alone, I think, Sharpe. Our men might be too close."

Sharpe still held the burning tube. "Just you and me, sir, eh?"

"You and me, Sharpe?" Lawford asked, puzzled.

"In five minutes, sir, when the Tippoo wonders why his fireworks aren't going off? And he sends a dozen men to find out what's happening. You and me? We're going to fight all those buggers off alone?"

Lawford hesitated. "I don't know," he said uncertainly.

"I do, sir," Sharpe said, and he pushed the burning rocket onto the fuse and immediately a quick and bitter fire began to fizzle and spark down the powder-impregnated rope. Gudin tried to stub it out with his foot, but Sharpe unceremoniously shoved the Frenchman aside. "Are you hurt bad, sir?" he asked Gudin.

"Broken shoulder, Sharpe." Gudin looked close to tears, not because of his wound, but because he had failed in his duty. "I've no doubt Doctor Venkatesh will mend it. How did you escape?"

"Killed a tiger, sir, and some more of those *jetti* buggers."

Gudin smiled sadly. "The Tippoo should have killed you when he had the chance."

"We all make mistakes, sir," Sharpe said as he watched the fire burn through the stone barricade that had been piled up in front of the ancient archway's gates. "I reckon we'd better get you into cover, sir," he said, and he pulled an unwilling Gudin into a doorway where Lawford was already crouching. The smoke was thinning from the alley. A wounded *jetti* was crawling blindly against the farther wall, another was vomiting, and Sergeant Rothière was groaning. There was blood bubbling at the Sergeant's nostrils, and the back of his head was black with gore.

"I reckon you've just made Sergeant, Sharpe," Lawford said.

Sharpe smiled. "I reckon I have, sir."

"Well done, Sergeant Sharpe." Lawford held out a hand. "A good day's work."

Sharpe shook his officer's hand. "But the day's work ain't done yet, sir."

"It isn't?" Lawford asked. "For God's sake, man, what else are you planning?"

But Lawford never heard what Sergeant Sharpe answered, for at that moment the mine blew.

· CHAPTER 11 ·

The Tippoo's engineers had done their work well. Not all the mine's force was directed northwards, but the greater part of it was, and that part was devastating. The explosion scoured the space between the inner and outer walls, a space that should have been packed with British soldiers.

To Sharpe, peering around the doorway, it at first looked as though the whole squat gatehouse disintegrated; not into rubble and dust, but into its constituent stones, for the dressed granite blocks all jarred slightly apart as the ancient building bulged from the terrible pressure of the fire within. Dust sprang from every opened crevice as the big stones separated cleanly along their mortared joints, then Sharpe lost sight of the collapsing gatehouse because there was suddenly nothing but dust, smoke, flame, and noise. He jerked back into shelter and covered his head with his arms when the noise boomed past him just an instant after he had seen the dust whip past the doorway as the gases escaped from the expanding fire.

The noise seemed to go on forever. First there was the swelling bang of the powder exploding, then the grinding crash of stones cracking and tumbling and the whistle of shards whirling away across the city, and then there was a ringing in Sharpe's ears and above the ringing, but sounding as far away and as thin as the trumpet that had heralded the assault, the screams of men caught by fire or blast or stone. After that came the sound of a wind, an unnatural wind that scoured thatch off houses, threw down tiles, and raised dust devils in streets a quarter of a mile away from the explosion.

The men on the walls nearest the gatehouse saw nothing, unless it was the flash that ended their lives, for the explosion plucked the Tippoo's defenders clean off the ramparts south of the breach. The wall itself was undamaged, even where it ran past the gatehouse, for there the old outer archway was blown out like a bung and a monstrous jet of smoky flame jetted from the city wall to vent the explosive's power safely beneath the ramparts, but the squat tower over the old gateway fell. It collapsed slowly, sliding down into the space between the inner and outer walls. Scraps of brick and stone arched up and outward, splashing in the river just ahead of Baird's advancing columns. More scraps of stone rained down on the city.

The noise slowly faded. The ringing in Sharpe's ears diminished until he could hear a man whimpering somewhere in the horror. He peered out again and saw that the explosion had scoured the alley of dead and wounded men. There was no sign of the handcart. There was nothing except broken stone, burning thatch, and smears of blood.

North of the breach, where the lick of flame and blast had been lessened by distance, the defenders were dizzied by noise. Their banners of gold and scarlet and green silk whipped stiff in the blast as men crouched in embrasures or reeled like drunks before the hot wind. The Tippoo's heroes who had volunteered to fight the Forlorn Hopes on the breach were killed almost to a man, for they were on the inner side of the breach where nothing could save them, while the survivors of the Forlorn Hopes, thrust back by the first charge of the Tippoo's men, had been shielded by the southern shoulder of the broken wall.

In the breach itself there was a vast veil of swirling dust. A huge boiling pyre of smoke churned above the walls, but the breach, for a moment at least, was undefended. The Tippoo's men who should have been guarding the shoulders of the breach were either dead or so shocked as to be unable to respond, while the men on the inner wall had ducked down as the terrible noise and heat and dust pounded about them. Most of them still crouched, fearful of the strange silence that followed the explosion.

"Now, boys, now!" a man shouted on the breach, and the survivors of the Forlorn Hopes climbed into the smoke, then up the broken stonework of the walls. They choked on the airborne dust and their red coats were whitened by it, but they were men who had steeled themselves to the worst ordeal of war, the storming of a breach, and the steel was hard and cold in their souls so that they were scarcely aware of the horror of the last few seconds, only of the need to climb the shoulders of the breach and start their killing. Those who went south found an empty wall, while those who went north climbed to meet dazed men. The redcoats and sepoys had expected no mercy in this assault and were prepared to show none, and so they began their slaughter. "Pig-sticking time, lads!" one corporal shouted. He stabbed his bayonet into a wild-eyed man and rid his blade of the body's encumbrance by shaking the corpse over the inner ramparts' edge. His comrades stormed past him, their blood whipped into rage by the fear of being the first men into the enemy citadel. Now, up on the ramparts, they killed in a frenzy to let their fear escape in a torrent of enemy blood.

Baird had still been west of the river when the explosion occurred and he had felt a momentary pang of horror as the great blast blossomed in the city. For a terrible second he thought the whole city, all its houses and temples and palaces, was about to disintegrate before his eyes, but he had kept moving, indeed he had quickened his pace so that he splashed into the South Cauvery while the debris was still falling. He waded the shallows as all around him the river foamed with falling stone, and he shouted incomprehensibly, desperate to take his heavy sword to the enemy that had once imprisoned him. The dust obscuring the breach shifted as a snatch of wind caught and whirled it northwards and Baird saw that his Forlorn Hopes were on the walls now. He saw some red coats, oddly whitened, moving north, then he glimpsed a rush of the enemy coming from the southern bastions to replace the defenders who had been scoured from the ramparts by the explosion. Those reinforcements were running past a great roiling gray-white plume of smoke amongst which pale flames licked the sky. Baird assumed the explosion had been the Tippoo's feared mine, but his horror at its force turned to exultation as he realized that the blast had been premature and that, instead of slaughtering his men, it had opened the city to storm. But he also recognized that the enemy was now waking from his nightmare and rushing men to face the attack, and so Baird hurried out of the river, through the shattered glacis, and up the breach that was now vividly slicked with great splashes of fresh blood. He chose to turn southward to help that Forlorn Hope face the rush of the Tippoo's reinforcements.

Behind Baird the twin columns of redcoats splashed through the river. Each column had three thousand men, and their task was to encircle the city and so capture the whole ring of Seringapatam's walls and bastions and towers and gates, but the Tippoo's men were recovering their wits now and the invading streams were at last being opposed. Muskets blasted down from ramparts, concealed guns were unmasked, and rockets streaked away from the parapets. Canister and round shot slashed down at the two columns, the missiles exploding high gouts of water as they struck the river. Sepoys and redcoats fell. Some crawled to safety, others were carried downstream, while the least fortunate were trampled by the boots of the men crossing the river. The leading troops of each column scrambled up the broken shoulders of the walls. The engineers shoved ladders against those shoulders, and still more men climbed their rungs to the ramparts.

And there the fight changed. Now, on the narrow firestep of the outer wall, the columns had to force their way forward, but the Tippoo's men were firing volley after volley into the attackers' ranks. The most damaging fire came from the inner wall, for there the Tippoo's men were protected by a parapet while the British and their Indian allies had no such protection on the inner side of the captured outer wall. Men fired at them from their front, and a torrent of fire came from their flank, yet still they pushed on, consumed by the blind rage of war. The only way to survive horror was to win through, and so they stepped over the dead to fire their muskets, then crouched to reload while the ranks behind pushed on. The wounded fell, some of them tumbling down to the inner ditch, while behind them, in the foaming river, the tails of the two columns hurried on toward the battle.

The breach had been taken, but the city had not fallen yet. The sepoys and the redcoats had taken a hundred yards of the outer wall on either side of the breach, but the Tippoo's soldiers were fighting back hard, and the Tippoo himself led the defenders north of the breach. The Tippoo had cursed Gudin for blowing the mine too early and thus wasting its terrible destructive power, but now he tried to revive the defense by his personal example. He stood in the front rank of his soldiers while behind him a succession of aides loaded jewel-encrusted hunting rifles. One by one the rifles were given to the Tippoo who aimed and fired, aimed and fired, and redcoat after redcoat was struck down. Whenever an enemy tried to rush along the ramparts, the Tippoo would drop that man, then pass the gun back, take another, step forward through the powder smoke, and fire again. Musket balls hissed about him. Two of his aides were wounded and a score of soldiers fighting at the Tippoo's side were killed or maimed, but the Tippoo's life seemed charmed. He stepped in blood, but none of it was his and it seemed as though he could not die, but only kill, and so he did, cold-bloodedly, deliberately, exultantly defending his city and his dream against the barbarians who had come to snatch his tiger throne.

The fight on the walls intensified as more men came to the threatened ramparts. The men in red came from the river and the men in tiger stripes came from other parts of the city wall, and both came to kill on top of the wall: a narrow place, scarce five paces wide, lifted in the sky.

Where the vultures flew, scenting death.

Sharpe scooped up three fallen muskets from the end of the alley where they had been blown by the explosion. He checked that his new guns were undamaged, loaded the two which were empty, then went back to Lawford. "You stay with the Colonel, sir," he suggested, "and put your coat right side out. Lads will be here soon. And when they're here, sir, you might like to find Lali."

Lawford colored. "Lali?"

"Look after her, sir. I promised the lass she'd come to no harm."

"You did?" Lawford asked with a trace of indignation. He was wondering just how well Sharpe knew the girl, then he decided it was better not to ask. "Of course I'll look after her," Lawford said, still blushing, then he noted that Sharpe, despite his own advice, had still not donned his red coat. "Where are you going?" the Lieutenant asked.

"Got a job to do, sir," Sharpe answered vaguely. "And, sir? Can I thank you, sir? I couldn't have done any of this without you." Sharpe was not used to offering such heartfelt compliments and he spoke awkwardly. "You're a brave bugger, sir, you really are."

Lawford felt absurdly pleased. He knew he should have stopped Sharpe from leaving, for this was no time for a man to be roaming Seringapatam's streets, but Sharpe was already gone. Lawford turned his coat the right side out and pushed his arms through the sleeves. Gudin, beside him, waved away a fly and wondered why the dust and smoke did not keep the pests away. "What will they do with me, Lieutenant?" he asked Lawford.

"They'll treat you well, sir, I'm sure. They'll probably send you back to France."

"I'd like that," Gudin said and suddenly realized that was all he really did want. "Your Private Sharpe . . ." he said.

"Sergeant Sharpe now, sir."

"Your Sergeant Sharpe, then. He's a good man, Lieutenant."

"Yes, sir," Lawford said, "he is."

"If he lives, he'll go far."

"If he lives, sir, yes." And if the army lets him live, Lawford thought.

"Look after him, Lieutenant," Gudin said. "An army isn't made of its officers, you know, though we officers like to think it is. An army is no better than its men, and when you find good men, you must look after them. That's an officer's job."

"Yes, sir," Lawford said dutifully. The first fugitives from the walls were visible at the end of the alley now, men in dust-smeared tiger tunics who staggered or limped away from the fighting. The noise of that fight was the continuous staccato of musket fire, shouts, and screams, and it could not be long before the first murderous attackers broke into the streets. Lawford wondered if he should have demanded Gudin's sword, then worried about having allowed Sharpe to go off on his own.

Sharpe lived so far. He had thought about putting on his red coat, then decided there was no point in making himself conspicuous, even though the coat was now so filthy that it hardly looked like a uniform any more, and so he left the turned jacket knotted about his neck and, with two muskets slung on each shoulder, ran northward through the city. The crackle of muskets was constant, but above that crisp sound he could also hear the roar of maddened men going into a brutal fight. In a few minutes that fight would spread into the city and Sharpe planned to use those minutes well. He ran through the small square where the rocket carts were still parked and then hurried past the Inner Palace where a tiger-striped guard, thinking that Sharpe was a deserter from the Tippoo's European troops, shouted a challenge at him, but by the time the guard had cocked his musket Sharpe had already disappeared into the labyrinth of alleys and yards that lay to the north of the palace.

He pushed through a crowd of fearful women, passed the cheetah cages, and so went back to the dungeons. The bodies of the three *jettis* were crawling with flies and beyond them the outer gate of the dungeons still swung open. Sharpe ran through the gate and jumped down the stairs to where his tiger lay dead.

"Sharpie!" Hakeswill came to the bars. "You came back, lad! I knew you would. So what's happening, lad? No! Don't do that!" Hakeswill had seen Sharpe take a musket from his shoulder. "I like you, boy, always have! I might have seemed a bit hard on you at times, but only for your own good, Sharpie. You're a good boy, you are. You're a proper soldier. No!" Sharpe had aimed the musket.

Sharpe turned the muzzle away from Hakeswill and aimed it at the padlock. He did not want to waste time with the picklock so he simply held the musket against the ancient loop of the padlock and pulled the trigger. The iron loop sheared and the lock fell from the hasp. Sharpe dragged the cell door open. "I've come to get you, Obadiah," he said.

"Knew you would, Sharpie, knew you would." Hakeswill's face twitched. "Knew you wouldn't leave your sergeant to rot."

"So come on out," Sharpe said.

Hakeswill hung back. "No hard feelings, lad?"

"I'm not a lad, Obadiah. I'm a sergeant like you are. I've got Colonel Wellesley's promise, I have. I'm a sergeant now, just like you."

"So you are, so you are, and so you should be." Hakeswill's face twitched again. "I said as much to Mister Morris, didn't I? That Sharpie, I said, he's a sergeant in the making if ever I did see one. A good lad, I told him. Got my eye on him, sir. That's what I told Mister Morris."

Sharpe smiled. "So come on out here, Obadiah."

Hakeswill backed all the way to the cell's rear wall. "Better to stay here, Sharpie," he said. "You know what the lads are like when their blood's boiling. Might get hurt out there. Best to stay put a while, let the lads settle it first, eh?"

Sharpe crossed the cell in two strides and gripped Hakeswill's collar. "You come with me, you bastard," he said, tugging the whimpering Sergeant forward. "I should kill you here, you scum, but you don't deserve a soldier's death, Obadiah. You're too rotten for a bullet."

"No, Sharpie, no!" Hakeswill screamed as Sharpe dragged him out of the cell, across the tiger's carcass, and up the stone steps. "I ain't done nothing to you!"

"Nothing!" Sharpe turned furiously on Hakeswill. "You had me flogged, you bastard, and then you betrayed us!"

"I never did! Cross my heart and hope to die, Sharpie!"

Sharpe spun Hakeswill up against the bars of the dungeon's outer cage, slamming him against the iron rods, then punched the Sergeant in the chest. "You're going to die, Obadiah, I promise. Because you did betray us."

"I didn't do nothing," Hakeswill said through his labored breathing. "On my mother's dying breath, Sharpie, I didn't. The flogging, yes. I did do that to you, and I was wrong!" He tried to fall to his knees, but Sharpe dragged him upright. "I didn't betray you, Sharpie. I wouldn't do that to another Englishman."

"You'll still be telling lies when you go through the gates of hell, Obadiah," Sharpe said as he grabbed the Sergeant's collar again. "Now come on, you bastard." He pulled Hakeswill through the dungeon's outer gate, across the courtyard, and into the alley which led south toward the palace. A squad of tiger-striped soldiers ran past the mouth of the alley, going to the western walls, but none took any notice of Sharpe. The guard on the northern palace gate did notice him and leveled his musket, but Sharpe snarled the magic words at the man, "Gudin! Colonel Gudin," and such was the confidence in Sharpe's voice that the guard lowered the musket and stepped aside.

"Where are you taking me, Sharpie?" Hakeswill panted.

"You'll find out."

Two more guards were stationed at the inner courtyard gate and they too pointed their muskets, but Sharpe shouted at them and once again Gudin's name was a talisman sufficient to allay their suspicions. Besides, Sharpe had a redcoated prisoner, and the two nervous guards mistook him for one of Gudin's men and so let him pass.

Sharpe lifted the gate's latch and dragged it open. The six tigers, already disturbed by the terrible noises that had been battering about the city, leapt toward the opening gate and their six chains cracked taut. Hakeswill saw the animals and screamed. "No, Sharpie! No! Mother!"

Sharpe dragged the struggling Hakeswill into the courtyard. "You reckon you can't die, Obadiah? I reckon different. So when you get to hell, you bastard, tell them it was Sergeant Sharpe who sent you."

"No, Sharpie! No!" This last word was a yelp of despair as Sharpe pulled Hakeswill into the center of the courtyard and there spun him around at arm's length. "No!" the Sergeant wailed as Sharpe spun him faster, then Sharpe suddenly let go of Hakeswill's collar. The Sergeant was unbalanced and out of control. He staggered and flailed his arms, but nothing could stop his momentum. "No!" he screamed a last time as he fell and slid across the sand to where three tigers waited.

"Goodbye, Obadiah," Sharpe said, "you bastard."

"I cannot die!" Hakeswill screamed, then his cry was cut off as a great yellow-eyed beast growled above him.

"They've got an early supper," Sharpe told the bemused guards on the gate. "Hope they've got an appetite."

The guards, not understanding a word, grinned back. Sharpe took one look behind, spat, and walked away. A debt, he reckoned, was properly paid. Now all he needed to do was hide till the redcoats came. And then he saw the pearl-hung palanquin, and another debt came to mind.

For a time it seemed as if the Tippoo could hold his city. He fought like a tiger himself, knowing that this blaze of violence beneath a smoke-shrouded sun would decide his fate. It would be the tiger throne or the grave.

He did not know what was happening on the southern stretch of the walls, except that the distant fury of constant musket fire told him that fighting continued there; he only knew that he and his men were taking a terrible toll on the attackers on the northern wall. The Tippoo had been forced slowly back by the sheer weight of numbers that poured onto the ramparts, and that bloody retreat had driven him off the western ramparts, back around the corner by the remnants of the northwestern bastion, and so onto the long stretch of northern wall which faced toward the River Cauvery, but there his retreat had stopped. A *cushoon* of infantry had been stationed in the Sultan Battery, the largest bastion in the north wall, and that garrison hurried along the walls to reinforce the Tippoo who now possessed enough men to overwhelm the musketry of the attackers on the narrow northern firestep. The Tippoo still led the fight. He was dressed in a white linen tunic and loose chintz drawers with a red silk sash about his waist. He had jeweled armlets, the great ruby glittered on the feathered plume of his helmet, there were pearls and an emerald necklace at his throat, and the gold-hilted tiger sword at his side. Those gaudy stones made him a target for every redcoat and sepoy, yet he insisted on staying in the very front rank where he could pour his rifle fire at the stalled attackers, and his charms worked, for though the bullets flicked close none hit him. He was the tiger of Mysore, he could not die, only kill.

The attackers suffered even worse damage from the men on the inner wall. That wall had not been breached, it had not even been attacked, and more and more tiger-striped infantry hurried up its ramps to reinforce the defenders. They fired across the inner ditch and their musket balls flayed at the crowded attackers and their cannon fire cleared whole stretches of the outer wall. Only the blinding powder smoke that hung between the walls protected the attackers, who either endured the terrible flank fire or else crouched behind dismounted cannon and prayed that their ordeal would soon end. They had captured the northwestern corner of the outer wall, but it seemed to have gained them nothing but death, for now it was the turn of the Tippoo's men to be the slaughterers.

Baird, heading south from the breach, encountered similar resistance, but Baird was in no mood to be delayed. He caught up and passed the survivors of the Forlorn Hope and, shouting like a demon, led a crazed charge past the ruined gatehouse where the remnants of the Tippoo's mine smoked like the pit of hell. Baird was a major general, but he would gladly have given all the gold lace on his uniform for this one chance to fight like a common soldier. This was revenge, and the great claymore hacked into the Tippoo's men as Baird bellowed his challenge that mingled fury with the agonized memories of his humiliation in this city. He fought like a creature possessed, stepping over the dead and slipping on their blood as he carried the battle down the walls. His men howled with him. They were caught up in Baird's madness. At this hour, under the fire of the sun and emboldened by the arrack and rum they had drunk in their long wait in the trenches, the redcoats and sepoys had become gods of war. They gave death with impunity as they followed a war-maddened Scotsman down an enemy wall that was sticky with blood. Baird would have his city or else he would die in its dust.

Appah Rao's *cushoons* defended the south-western corner of the city and Appah Rao watched appalled as the hugely tall Scotsman hacked his way toward him. He watched the torrent of redcoats swarming behind the giant, and he heard their shouts and he watched their victims fall off the ramparts. The brigade that defended that stretch of wall was being killed man by man, and those that lived were giving way and some were running rather than face the horror, and Appah Rao's men were next for the slaughter.

But to die for what? he wondered. The city was gone and the Tippoo's dynasty was doomed. Appah Rao knew his men were watching him, waiting for the order that would hurl them into battle, but instead the General turned to his second-in-command. "When were the men last paid?" he asked.

The officer frowned, puzzled by the question, but at last managed an answer. "Three months at least, sahib. Four, I think."

"Tell them there will be a pay parade this afternoon."

"Sahib?" The second-in-command gaped up at Appah Rao.

The General raised his voice so that as many of his men as possible could hear him. "The pay is overdue, so this afternoon we shall have a pay parade in the encampment. Men shouldn't fight without pay." He ostentatiously sheathed his sword and walked calmly down from the ramparts. Here, at the Mysore Gate, there was no ditch between the inner and outer walls, and Rao airily strode through the inner gate. For a second his men watched him, then first in ones and twos, and afterward in a rush, they followed. One instant the wall was crammed with men, the next it was emptying so that Baird, cutting his furious way through the last of the west wall's guards, suddenly saw that the city was his. He howled again, this time in victory. His butcher's sword was red with blood, his right sleeve soaked with it. A redcoat, perhaps forgetting that the Scotsman was a general, slapped his back and Baird hugged the man for pure joy.

The Tippoo still fought and still thought he could win, but on the northern wall, just twenty yards beyond the northwest bastion, a single cross-wall joined the inner and outer ramparts. The cross-wall served as a buttress for the old outer wall, and at one time it had been intended to thicken the buttressing cross-wall, then make the space it contained into an even larger bastion, but the work had never been done and now the wall, its coping just eight inches across, offered itself as a perilously narrow bridge to the redcoats and sepoys who were trapped by the Tippoo's fire. If they could cross that bridge they could assault the inner wall and scour its defenders from the deadly parapet. One man tried to cross and was shot down. He wailed as he fell into the ditch. A moment later another man dashed across and reached half-way before a musket ball shattered his lower leg. He dropped his own musket and fell onto the wall's coping, cursing as he tried to keep his balance, then a second shot tipped him over the side. For a second or two he managed to cling to the top of the wall, shuddering as pain shook his body, then he too dropped.

The Tippoo's men on the outer wall cheered and edged forward to drive the enemy away from the buttressing cross-wall, but a rush of sepoys checked their progress. A new musket duel broke out, Indian against Indian, a torrent of fire in which the Tippoo somehow survived like a charmed being. The sepoys fired volley after volley, came forward, died, and more men came to take their places.

The Light Company of the King's 12th regiment followed the sepoys. Captain Goodall, their commander, eyed the narrow buttress. It led directly to the inner wall which was heavy with defenders, but it was also a bridge to victory. "Death or glory!" Goodall shouted the cliché, but it was a truism too at that moment, and then he stepped out onto the narrow coping and fired his pistol into the lingering powder smoke that obscured the far end of the wall. "Come on!" he called, then ran along the top of the wall, miraculously keeping his footing. He jumped onto the inner wall's parapet and slashed down with his sword. A man fired up at him, but Goodall's Sergeant, coming hard behind, had unceremoniously shoved his Captain out of the way and Goodall fell down onto the inner wall's firestep and the bullet missed him. The Sergeant was next across the parapet, then a line of screaming men followed as Goodall fought his way eastward. The fire from the inner wall, which had been gutting the attackers, began to falter, and suddenly a rush of redcoats, who had been crouching for shelter from the inner wall's musketry, ran eastward along the outer wall toward the Tippoo. Others crossed the makeshift bridge to reinforce the 12th's Light Company.

The Tippoo saw the enemy revive. They were like a beast that had been wounded, but not killed, and the beast had life in it yet. Too much life, and the Tippoo understood that his night's troublesome dreams had been right after all. The turbid oil pot had told the truth. This day the city would fall, and with it his throne and his palace and his seraglio with its six hundred women, but the disaster did not mean the dynasty was dead. There were great forts in Mysore's northern hills and if he could reach one of those fastnesses then he could still fight on against these devils in red who were stealing his capital.

The Tippoo retreated fast and his bodyguard went with him. They left other men to defend the outer wall while they ran past the Sultan Battery to the ramp which led down to the Water Gate and there, at the foot of the ramp, the palace chamberlains had thought to have His Majesty's palanquin ready with its bearers. One of the chamberlains, oblivious of the bullets hissing through the sky, bowed low to the Tippoo and invited His Majesty to take his proper place on the plump silk cushions beneath the palanquin's tiger-striped canopy. The Tippoo turned and glanced up at the walls to see what progress the attackers were making. There was fighting on both walls now, and the city was plainly doomed, but the defenders were still resisting stubbornly. The Tippoo felt a pang at deserting them, but swore he would avenge them yet. He rejected the palanquin. It was a slow vehicle in which to make a retreat, while inside the city, just on the other side of the inner wall, he had stables filled with fine horses. He would choose his swiftest horse, snatch up some gold to pay those men who stayed loyal, then flee through the city's unthreatened Bangalore Gate and from there turn north toward his great hill fortresses.

Above the Tippoo the city's last defenders retreated slowly. The city was falling to the redcoats under a pallor of smoke, and God had willed it, but God might yet permit the Tippoo to fight another day and so, rifle in hand, he headed for the inner Water Gate.

The palanquin was carried by eight men, two to each of its four long gilded handles. When Sharpe first saw it, the clumsy vehicle was being hurried away from the palace by two robed chamberlains who lashed at the bearers with their tiger-headed staves. For a second Sharpe thought the Tippoo must be inside the palanquin, but then he saw that the side curtains were looped back and that the cushions inside were empty. He followed.

He could sense a panic inside the city now. It had been quiet until a few moments ago, crouching like a beast not wanting to be noticed, but now the city somehow sensed that its doom had come. Beggars huddled together for protection, a woman cried in a shuttered house, and the stray dogs yelped piteously. Small groups of the Tippoo's soldiers were fleeing in the streets, their bare feet pattering on the dried mud as they ran toward the Bangalore Gate where no enemy threatened. The sound of battle was still intense, but the defense was fraying fast.

The chamberlains led the palanquin toward the Water Gate of the inner wall. The gate lay close to the malodorous lake of sewage that so soured the air and some of the sewage, denied proper drains by the hastily constructed inner wall, had leaked into the Water Gate which was a brick-lined tunnel, fifty feet long, piercing the inner wall. An officer stood guard at its inner doors, but, as the palanquin approached, he unbarred the big teak gates and dragged them open. He shouted something as Sharpe followed the clumsy vehicle into the low tunnel, but Sharpe just shouted Colonel Gudin's name back and the officer was too confused to challenge him again. Instead, once the palanquin and the European soldier had gone through the tunnel, he closed the doors then glanced nervously up to where a mist of smoke betrayed the attackers' progress on the wall above him.

Sharpe paused inside the tunnel while the palanquin went on ahead. The tunnel's floor had sunk in places and the leaking sewage had gathered in those deep spots. The place stank like an uncleaned barracks latrine. The palanquin's bearers stumbled as they splashed through the pools, then the vehicle went into the sunlight beyond. Sharpe could see soldiers out there in the space between the walls. The soldiers wore tiger stripes and were watching anxiously westward. He had followed the palanquin instinctively, but now found himself in a bad place. The tunnel's thick teak doors were shut behind him, the air was foul and choking, and there was an enemy in front of him. He crouched beside the damp wall, trying to decide what he should do. He had four muskets, all but one loaded, but his spare cartridges were in the pocket of his red coat which, because it was still knotted around his neck, was hard to reach. He stood, propped the muskets against the curved wall, pulled the jacket right side out, and then shoved his arms into the tiger-torn sleeves. He was a redcoat again. He loaded the one empty musket, then crept toward the mouth of the tunnel.

And saw the Tippoo.

He saw the small gaudy man come running down the ramp from the outer walls. The Tippoo, surrounded by his bodyguard and aides, stopped beside the palanquin. Sharpe saw the Tippoo look back toward the fight, then shake his head, and immediately an aide broke away from the group and ran toward the tunnel where Sharpe waited. The Tippoo gave one last glance westward, then followed.

"Bloody hell," Sharpe cursed. The whole damned lot were coming for him, and he backed down the tunnel, cocked one of his muskets, and dropped to one knee.

The aide ran into the tunnel, shouting for the gate to be opened. Then he saw Sharpe in the gloom and his shout died away. He dragged a pistol from a green sash at his waist, but too late. Sharpe fired. The spark of the powder in the pan was unnaturally bright in the tunnel, and the noise of the musket was magnified to a deafening crash, but through the sudden smoke Sharpe saw the aide flung backward. Sharpe seized a second loaded musket and just at that instant the door opened behind him. He turned, snarling, and the officer guarding the gate saw the red coat and, without thinking, just slammed the heavy, nail-studded teak doors shut again. Sharpe heard the locking bar being dropped into place.

The Tippoo's bodyguard ran toward the tunnel. Sharpe fired his second musket. He knew he could not fight them all, so now his best chance of surviving was to deter them from coming into the tunnel itself. Then, blessedly, a roar of musketry announced that he had help and, with the third musket in his hand, he edged forward through the dense smoke to see that the Tippoo's bodyguard had been distracted by a new enemy. Some British troops had found steps down to the space between the walls, and those troops were now attacking toward the Water Gate. The bodyguard retreated from the new attackers, unmasking the tunnel's entrance, and Sharpe ran toward the daylight. He crouched just inside the tunnel and saw that the Tippoo had been caught in the open. On one side was the palanquin, with its dubious chance of a lumbering escape, and on the other was the threatened Water Gate which led through the inner wall to his horses. His bodyguard was firing and reloading, firing and reloading, while the Tippoo seemed frozen with indecision.

A cheer sounded to Sharpe's left. More muskets fired, then suddenly there were two redcoats taking cover in the inner tunnel. One saw Sharpe and whirled round with a leveled musket. "Whoa!" Sharpe shouted. "I'm on your bloody side!"

The man, wild-eyed and with his right cheek pitted by powder burns from the lock of his musket, turned back toward the enemy. "What regiment?" he called to Sharpe.

"Havercakes. You?"

"The Old Dozen." The man fired, and immediately sidled back to begin reloading the musket. "It stinks in here," he said, ramming a fresh bullet down his barrel. More redcoats were occupying the Sultan Battery in the outer wall. They had no British flag to show their conquest of the huge bastion and so they ran a red jacket up the flagpole. The jacket had pale yellow facings, showing that it came from the King's 12th, a Kentish regiment. "That's ours!" the man beside Sharpe exulted, then seemed to gurgle. His eyes opened wide with astonishment, he gave Sharpe a puzzled, almost reproachful look, then slowly toppled backward into one of the fetid puddles. Blood seeped onto his pale yellow facings. Up on the outer wall a mass of tiger-striped men charged to recapture the Sultan Battery and their courage gave new heart to the defenders between the walls who gave a cheer and fired a ragged volley at the redcoats edging toward the Water Gate.

The dying redcoat shuddered. His companion fired, then swore. "Bastards!" He hesitated for a half-second, then broke out of the tunnel's shadow and sprinted back to the west, back toward the rest of his comrades who had been advancing toward the tunnel. The Tippoo had made up his mind. He would ignore the palanquin and try to reach his horse, and so he had ordered his bodyguard to clear the tunnel's entrance. That bodyguard now charged, screaming, and Sharpe, knowing that he was trapped, splashed back into the inner Water Gate's lingering smoke. He stopped halfway, turned, and blasted the musket toward the mouth of the tunnel where he could see the leading men of the Tippoo's bodyguard silhouetted against the daylight. A man screamed. Sharpe had one loaded musket left.

Musket balls thumped into the teak doors beside him. He fired his last musket, then reloaded with a practiced, but desperate, haste. He was waiting for men to appear in the dense smoke of the tunnel, but none came. Sharpe knew he was going to die here, but he was bloodily determined that he would die in company. Let the bastards come. He was frightened, and in his fear he was crooning a mad tuneless song without words, but his fear did not stop him from loading a second musket. Still no one came to kill him and so he snatched up a third musket and bit the top off another cartridge.

The bodyguard had still not come into the tunnel. Sharpe, in his fear, had not heard the sound of battle growing at the end of the tunnel, but now, crouching and listening, he became aware of the shouts and volleys. The men of the 12th were pouring musket fire into the Tippoo's bodyguard and those men were staying close to their monarch and returning the fire. Redcoats attacked from the west and more fired from the Sultan Battery. The attempt to recapture the battery had failed, and a mix of sepoys and redcoats were now forcing their way along the outer northern wall. The ferocity of their fire had forced the Tippoo's bodyguard to crouch close about their monarch, and Sharpe had been given precious seconds in which to load his muskets. He had three charged guns now. Three bullets, and he wanted one of them for the heathen bastard who had poured salt on his back, the bastard who wore a great ruby in his hat. He again crept forward through the smoke, willing the Tippoo to come into the tunnel.

But the Tippoo was once again fighting off the encroaching infidels. Allah had given him this last chance to kill redcoats, and so he was taking the jeweled hunting rifles from his aides and calmly shooting at the men who had so nearly captured the inner Water Gate. His aides were shouting at him to flee through the tunnel and find a horse, but the Tippoo had been granted this final moment of battle and it seemed to him that he could not miss with any of his shots, and with each redcoat thrown back he felt a fierce joy. Then a new rush of sepoys and redcoats burst along the outer wall and those men came swarming down the ramp by the outer Water Gate to add their muskets to those threatening the Tippoo's shrinking bodyguard.

And as those new enemies appeared, the Tippoo's charmed luck turned. One bullet struck his thigh and another punched his left arm to leave a splash of blood bright on the white linen sleeve. He staggered, but kept his balance. It seemed that not a man of his bodyguard was left unwounded, but a score of them still lived and could walk. In a moment, though, the enemy must triumph and the Tippoo knew it was time to bid his city farewell. "We go," he told his relieved aides, and limped toward the tunnel. His left arm was numb, as though it had been hit by a giant hammer, but there was a horrid pain in his left leg.

A shot crashed out of the Water Gate's smoky gloom and the man leading the Tippoo's escape was snatched backward from the tunnel entrance with blood misting up from his shattered skull. Against the bright sunlight that glowed at the end of the tunnel the fine droplets of blood looked like powdered rubies. The man fell, screamed, and thrashed. The

Tippoo, stunned by the suddenness of the bodyguard's unexpected death, paused, and behind him a terrible roar
sounded as the assaulting redcoats closed in on the mouth of
the tunnel. The bodyguard turned back to face their attackers with fixed bayonets.

"Go, Your Majesty!" A wounded aide thrust a rifle into
the Tippoo's hands, then dared to push his monarch into the
tunnel. The Tippoo allowed himself to be pushed into the
shadows, but stopped close to the mouth of the tunnel and
from there he stared into the vaporous darkness. Was an
enemy there? He could not see because of the smoke.
Behind him were the harsh sounds of volleys and curses as
his bodyguard died, and as they died their bodies were making a terrible barricade that protected the Tippoo, but what
waited in front of him? He peered, reluctant to go forward
into the shit-stinking gloom, but then the aide snatched at
the Tippoo's elbow and dragged him deeper into the darkness. The few surviving bodyguards were defending the tunnel with bayonets, stabbing at the crazed redcoats who tried
to scramble across the bloody pile of corpses.

"Open the gate!" the aide shouted, then he saw the
shadow within the shadow at the end of the tunnel and he
dropped to one knee and took aim with his jeweled rifle. He
fired, and the golden tiger-mask doghead snapped forward
onto the frizzen. Sharpe threw himself to one side just as the
gun fired, heard the bullet snick the wall and ricochet into
the teak door, then he saw the aide pull a long pistol from
his sash. Sharpe fired first, the boom of his musket echoing
in the tunnel like doom's thunder. The ball hurled the aide
back into a deep pool, and suddenly there was only the Tippoo and Sharpe left.

Sharpe stood and grinned at the Tippoo. "Bastard," he
said, seeing the glint of light reflected from the ruby in his
enemy's helmet. "Bastard," he said again. He had one loaded

370 · BERNARD CORNWELL

musket left. The Tippoo was holding a rifle. Sharpe stepped
forward.

The Tippoo recognized the hard, bloody face in the gloom. He smiled. Fate was most strange, he thought. Why had he not killed this man when he had the chance? Behind him his bodyguard was dying and the victorious redcoats were plundering their bodies, while in front of him was freedom and life, except for one man to whom the Tippoo had shown mercy. Just one man.

"Bastard," Sharpe said again. He wanted to be close when he killed the Tippoo, close enough to make certain of the man's death.

Behind the Tippoo the bright daylight was dulled by the swirling gunsmoke where dying men gasped and victorious men looted. "Mercy is God's prerogative, not man's," the Tippoo said in Persian, "and I should never have been merciful to you." He aimed the rifle at Sharpe and pulled the trigger, but the gun did not fire. In the panic of the last seconds the aide had handed the Tippoo an unloaded rifle and the flint had sparked on an empty pan. The Tippoo smiled, tossed the gun aside, and unsheathed his tiger-hilted sword. There was blood on his arm, and more on his chintz trousers, but he showed no fear, he even seemed to relish the moment. "How I do hate your cursed race," he said calmly, giving the sword a cut through the smoky air.

Sharpe did not understand the Tippoo any more than the Tippoo understood Sharpe. "You're a fat little bastard," Sharpe said, "and you took away my medal. I wanted that. It's the only medal I've ever got."

The Tippoo just smiled. His helmet had been dipped in the fountain of life, but it had not worked. The magic had failed and only Allah was left. He waited for the snarling redcoat to shoot, then a shout sounded in the mouth of the tunnel and the Tippoo turned, hoping that one last body-guard would come to save him.

But no bodyguard appeared and the Tippoo turned back to face Sharpe. "I dreamed of death last night," he said in Persian as he limped forward and raised the curved blade to strike at the redcoat. "I dreamed of monkeys, and monkeys mean death. I should have killed you."

Sharpe fired. The bullet went higher than he intended. He had thought to put it through the Tippoo's heart, but instead it struck the Sultan in the temple. For a second the Tippoo wavered. His head had been whipped back by the bullet's force and blood was soaking into his cloth-padded helmet, but he forced his head forward and stared into Sharpe's eyes. The sword fell from his nerveless hand, he seemed to smile a last time, then he just slumped down.

The booming echo of the musket shot still battered Sharpe's ears so he was not aware that he was talking as he crouched beside the Tippoo. "It's your ruby I want," Sharpe said, "that bloody great ruby. I wanted it from the very first moment I saw you. Colonel McCandless told me, he did, that it's wealth that makes the world turn and I want my share." The Tippoo still lived, but he could not move. His expressionless eyes stared up at Sharpe, who thought the Tippoo was dead, but then the dying man blinked. "Still here, are you?" Sharpe said. He patted the Tippoo's bloodied cheek. "You're a brave fat bastard, I will say that for you." He wrenched the huge ruby off the blood-spattered feather plume, then stripped the dying man of every jewel he could find. He took the pearls from the Tippoo's neck, twisted off an armlet bright with gems, tugged off the diamond rings, and unlatched the silver-hung necklace of emeralds. He pulled on the Tippoo's sash to see if the dagger with the great diamond called the Moonstone in its hilt was there, but the sash held nothing except the sword scabbard. Sharpe took that, but left the tiger-hilted sword. He lifted the blade from a puddle of sewage and placed it in the Tippoo's hand. "You can keep your sword," he told the dying man, "for you fought proper. Like a proper soldier." He stood up and then, awkwardly, because of his burden of jewels and because he was suddenly conscious of the dying Sultan's gaze, he saluted the Tippoo. "Take your blade to paradise," he said, "and tell them you were killed by another proper soldier."

The Tippoo's eyes closed and he thought of the prayer that he had copied into his notebook that very morning. "I am full of sin," the Tippoo had written in his beautiful Arabic script, "and Thou, Allah, art a sea of mercy. Where Thy mercy is, where is my sin?" That was a comfort. There was no pain now, not even in his leg, and that was a comfort too, but still he could not move. It was like one of the dreams he copied each morning into his dream-book and he wondered at how peaceful everything suddenly seemed, as peaceful as though he was floating on a gilded barge down a warm river beneath a blessed sun. This must be the way to paradise, he thought, and he welcomed it. Paradise.

Sharpe felt a pang of sorrow for the dying man. He might have been a murderous enemy, but he was a brave one. The Tippoo had fallen with his right arm trapped beneath his body, and though Sharpe suspected there was another jeweled armlet on that hidden sleeve, he did not try to retrieve it. The Tippoo deserved to die in peace and, besides, Sharpe was rich enough already, for his pockets now held a king's ransom while a leather scabbard sewn with sapphires was hidden under his shabby coat, and so he picked up one of his empty muskets and splashed through the tunnel's bloody puddles toward the pile of dead that lay in the smoky sunlight. A sergeant of the 12th, startled by Sharpe's sudden appearance from the tunnel, snatched up his bayonet, then saw Sharpe's filthy red jacket and let the weapon fall. "Anyone alive in there?" the Sergeant asked.

"Just a fat little fellow dying," Sharpe said as he climbed over the barrier of the dead.

"Did he have any loot?"

"Nothing," Sharpe said, "nothing worth the trouble. Place is full of shit, too."

The Sergeant frowned at Sharpe's unkempt dress and unpowdered hair. "What regiment are you?"

"Not yours," Sharpe said curtly, and walked away through the crowds of celebrating redcoats and sepoys. Not all were celebrating. Some were massacring trapped enemies. The fight had been brief but nasty, and now the winners took a bloody revenge. On the far side of the inner wall Colonel Wellesley had brought his men into the streets and they now surrounded the palace to preserve it from plunder. The smaller streets were not so fortunate, and the first screams sounded as the sepoys and redcoats found their hungry way into the unprotected alleys. The Tippoo's men, those that still lived and had escaped their pursuers, fled eastward while the Tippoo, left alone in the tunnel, lay dying.

Sergeant Richard Sharpe slung the musket and walked around the base of the inner wall, seeking a passage into the city. He had only a few moments of freedom left before the army took him back into its iron grip, but he had won his victory and he had pockets full of stones to prove it. He went to find a drink.

Next day it rained. It was not the monsoon, though it could have been, for the rain fell with a ferocity that matched the fury of the previous day's assault. The pelting warm rain washed the blood off the city's walls and scoured the hot season's filth out of its streets. The Cauvery swelled to fill its banks, rising so high that no man could have crossed the river in front of the breach. If the Tippoo's prayers had been answered and the British had waited one more day, then the floods would have defeated them.

But there was no Tippoo in Seringapatam, only the Rajah, who had been restored to his palace where he was surrounded by red-coated guards. The palace, which had been protected from the ravages of the assaulting troops, was now being stripped bare by the victorious officers. Rain drummed on the green-tiled roof and ran into the gutters and puddled in the courtyards as the red-coated officers sawed up the great tiger throne on which the Tippoo had never sat. They turned the handles of the tiger organ and laughed as the mechanical claw savaged the redcoat's face. They tugged down silk hangings, they pried gems out of furniture and marveled at the simple, bare, white-painted room which had been the Tippoo's bedchamber. The six tigers, roaring because they had not been fed and because the rain fell so hard, were shot.

The Tippoo's father, the great Hyder Ali, lay in a mausoleum east of the city and, when the rainstorm had stopped, and while the garden around the mausoleum was still steaming in the sudden sultry sunlight, the Tippoo was carried to rest beside his father. British troops lined the route and reversed their arms as the cortege passed. Muffled drums beat a slow tattoo as the Tippoo was borne on his sad last journey by his own defeated soldiers.

Sharpe, with three bright white stripes newly sewn onto his faded red sleeve, waited close beside the domed mausoleum. "I do wonder who killed him." Colonel McCandless, restored to a clean uniform and with his hair neatly cut, had come to stand beside Sharpe.

"Some lucky bastard, sir."

"A rich one by now, no doubt," the Colonel said.

"Good for him, sir," Sharpe said, "whoever he is."

"He'll only waste the plunder," McCandless said severely. "He'll fritter it on women and drink."

"Don't sound like a waste to me, sir."

McCandless grimaced at the Sergeant's levity. "That ruby alone was worth ten years of a general's salary. Ten years!"

"A shame it's vanished, sir," Sharpe said guilelessly.

"Isn't it, Sharpe?" McCandless agreed. "But I hear you were at the Water Gate?"

"Me, sir? No, sir. Not me, sir. I stayed with Mister Lawford, sir."

The Colonel gave Sharpe a fierce glance. "A sergeant of the Old Dozen reports he saw a wild-looking fellow come out of the Water Gate." McCandless's voice was accusing. "He says the man had a coat with scarlet facings and no buttons." The Colonel looked disapprovingly at Sharpe's red coat on which Sharpe had somehow found time to stitch the sergeant's stripes, but not a single button. "The man seems very certain of what he saw."

"He was probably confused by the battle, sir. Lost his wits, I wouldn't doubt."

"So who put Sergeant Hakeswill in with the tigers?" McCandless demanded.

"Only the good Lord knows, sir, and He ain't saying."

The Colonel, scenting blasphemy, frowned. "Hakeswill says it was you," he accused Sharpe.

"Hakeswill's mad, sir, and you can't trust a thing he says," Sharpe said. And Hakeswill was more than mad, he was alive. Somehow he had escaped the tigers. Not one of the beasts had attacked the Sergeant who been discovered babbling in the courtyard, crying for his mother and declaring his fondness for tigers. He liked all pussycats, he had said to his rescuers. "I can't be killed!" he had shouted when the redcoats led him gently away. "Touched by God, I am," he had claimed, and then he had demanded that Sharpe be arrested for attempted murder, but Lieutenant Lawford had blushed and sworn that Sergeant Sharpe had never left his side after the mine was blown. Colonel Gudin, a prisoner now, had confirmed the claim. The two men had been discovered in one of the city's brothels where they had been protecting the women from the drunken, rampaging victors.

"Hakeswill's a lucky man," McCandless said drily, abandoning any further attempt to drag the truth from Sharpe. "Those tigers were man-eaters."

"But not devil-eaters, sir. One whiff of Hakeswill and they must have gone right off their feed."

"He still swears it was you who threw him to the tigers," McCandless said. "I've no doubt he'll try to take his revenge."

"I've no doubt either, sir, but I'll be ready for him." And next time, Sharpe thought, he would make certain the bastard died.

McCandless turned as the slow funeral procession appeared at the end of the long road that led to the mausoleum. Opposite him, behind an honor guard of the King's 73rd, Appah Rao, now in the Rajah's service, also watched the cortege approach. Appah Rao's family and household all lived. McCandless had sat in Appah Rao's courtyard, a musket on his lap, and turned back every redcoat or sepoy who had come to the house. Mary had thus survived unscathed and Sharpe had heard that she would now marry her Kunwar Singh, and he was glad for her. He remembered the ruby he had once promised to give her and he smiled at the thought. Some other lass, maybe. The Tippoo's ruby was deep in his pouch, hidden like all the other looted jewels.

The muffled drumbeat came nearer and the red-coated honor guard stiffened to attention. Mourners followed the coffin, most of them the Tippoo's officers. Gudin was among them. McCandless took off his cocked hat. "There'll be more fighting to come, Sharpe," the Colonel said softly. "We have other enemies in India."

"I'm sure we have, sir."

The Colonel glanced at Sharpe. He saw a young man, hard as flint, and the restless anger in Sharpe's heart made him dangerous as flint and steel, but there was also a kindness in Sharpe. McCandless had seen that kindness in the dungeons, and McCandless believed it betrayed a soul that was well worth saving. "I may have uses for you if you're willing," the Colonel said.

Sharpe seemed surprised. "I thought you were going home, sir. To Scotland."

McCandless shrugged. "There's work undone here, Sharpe, work undone. And what will I ever do in Scotland but dream of India? I think I shall stay for a while."

"And I'd be privileged to help you, sir, so I would," Sharpe said, then he snatched off his shako as the coffin drew close. His hair, which he had still not clubbed or powdered, fell loose across his scarlet collar as he stood to attention. Far away, beyond the river, rain fell on a green land, but above Sharpe the sun shone, glistening its watery light on the mausoleum's bulging white dome beneath which, in a dark crypt under their silk-draped tombs, the Tippoo's parents lay. Now the Tippoo would join them.

The coffin was carried slowly past Sharpe. The men bearing the Tippoo were dressed in his tiger-striped tunic, while the coffin itself was draped with a great striped tiger pelt. It was a mangy skin, uncured and still bloody, but the best that could be discovered in the chaos following the city's fall, and down one flank there was a long ancient scar and Sharpe, seeing it, smiled. He had seen that scar before. He had seen it every night that he was in the Tippoo's dungeons. And now he saw it again, scored into a tiger skin that covered a brave dead king.

It was Sharpe's tiger.

The siege and fall of Seringapatam (now Sriringapatna) in May 1799 ended decades of warfare between the remarkable Muslim dynasty that ruled the state of Mysore and the invading British. The British, under Lord Cornwallis, had captured the city before, in 1792, and at that time they decided to leave the Tippoo on his throne, but mutual antagonisms, and the Tippoo's preference for a French alliance, led to the final Mysore war. The aim of the war was simple: to do what had not been done in 1792, unthrone the Tippoo, to which end the British concocted some very thin reasons to justify an invasion of Mysore, ignored the Tippoo's overtures for peace, and so marched on Seringapatam. It was a brutally naked piece of aggression, but successful, for with the Tippoo's death the most formidable obstacle to British rule in southern India was removed, and with it the increasingly slim chance that Napoleon, then at the head of a French army stranded in Egypt, would intervene in the subcontinent.

The novel's description of the city's fall is mostly accurate. Two Forlorn Hopes, one headed by the unfortunate Sergeant Graham, led two columns of attacking troops across the wide South Cauvery and up the breach, and there the columns separated, one going north about the city's outer ramparts and the other south. Major General David Baird commanded the assault, and he, judging in the heat of battle that the resistance to the south was more formidable, turned that way. In fact the northern column encountered the stiffest opposition, most probably caused by the Tippoo's own leadership. Many eyewitnesses, from both sides, testified to the Tippoo's personal bravery. He was gaudily dressed and bright with gems, but he insisted on fighting in the front rank of his men. Further difficulties were caused by the defenders firing from the inner wall's sheltered firestep, and it was not until Captain Goodall, the commander of the 12th Regiment's Light Company, had led his men across the buttressing cross-wall and so began the capture of the inner ramparts that the defense collapsed. The fight was short, but exceptionally bloody, causing 1,400 casualties among the attackers and over 6,000 from the Tippoo's troops.

I did take one great liberty with the historical facts of the assault. There was no disused western gateway, nor any mine either, but the idea for the mine came from an enormous and spectacular explosion which occurred in the city two days before the assault. It is believed that a British shell somehow ignited one of the Tippoo's magazines, which then blew up. I changed the nature of that explosion, and delayed it by two days, because fictional heroes must be given suitable employment.

There were a few French troops in Seringapatam, but Nelson's victory at the Nile had effectively ended any real chance of French intervention in India. Colonel Gudin is a fictional character, though someone very like him did lead a small French battalion in the battle. Others of the novel's characters, like Colonel Gent, did exist. Major Shee, a somewhat intemperate and unfortunate Irishman, commanded the 33rd during the time Wellesley served as one of Harris's deputies and Lieutenant Fitzgerald, brother of the Knight of Kerry, was killed in the confused night attack on the Sultanpetah *tope*, probably by a bayonet thrust. That setback was

Wellesley's only military defeat and it gave him a lifelong aversion to night actions. Major General Baird did dislike Wellesley and fiercely resented the fact that General Harris appointed the younger man to be the Governor of Seringapatam after the siege, although, given Baird's hatred of the Indians, the appointment was undoubtedly wise. Baird's jealousy lasted many years, though in his later life the Scotsman generously admitted that Wellesley was his military superior. By then, of course, Arthur Wellesley had become the first Duke of Wellington. In 1815 only Napoleon still regarded Wellington with contempt, dubbing him the "Sepoy General," but the Sepoy General still whipped Napoleon.

The Tippoo Sultan, of course, existed. His defeat was celebrated in Britain where the Tippoo was regarded as a peculiarly brutal and ferocious despot and for years afterward, despite many other momentous victories over much more formidable enemies, the British still harked back to the Tippoo's defeat and death. The event was celebrated in numerous prints, it was turned into at least six stage plays, and it occupied many books, all tributes to the curious fascination the Tippoo exercised over his erstwhile enemies. Yet his death, despite being pictured and re-enacted so many times, was never fully explained because no one ever discovered who exactly killed him (it was most probably a soldier of the 12th's Grenadier Company). The Tippoo's body was found, but his killer never came forward and it is presumed that this reticence was caused by the man's unwillingness to admit to ownership of the Tippoo's jewels. Where many of those jewels are today, no one knows.

But much of the Tippoo's grandeur can still be seen. The Inner Palace of Seringapatam, alas, was demolished in the nineteenth century (local guides insist it was destroyed by the British bombardment, but in fact the building survived the siege intact) and all that remains of its splendor are a few ruined walls and some pillars which now support the canopy of Sriringapatna's railway station, but the Summer Palace, the Daria Dowlat, still exists. The mural of the British defeat at Pollilur was restored by Wellesley, who lived in this exquisite little palace while he governed Mysore. It is now a museum. The Tippoo's mosque still stands, there is another small palace in the city of Bangalore, and, perhaps most moving of all, the Gumbaz, the elegant mausoleum where the Tippoo lies with his parents. To this day his tomb is covered with a cloth patterned with tiger stripes.

The Tippoo revered the tiger, and used tiger motifs wherever he could. His fabulous tiger throne existed, but it was broken up at his death, though large parts of it can still be seen, notably in Windsor Castle. His dreadful toy, the tiger organ, is now in London's Victoria and Albert Museum. The organ was sadly damaged during the Blitz, but it has been superbly restored, though, alas, its voice is not what it was. The Tippoo did keep six tigers in his palace courtyard (Wellesley ordered them shot).

Sriringapatna's outer wall still stands. The town, which has fewer inhabitants now than it did in 1799, is an attractive place and the site of the assault, overlooking the South Cauvery, is marked by an obelisk that stands immediately to the north of the repaired breach. Just behind the breach, and filling the whole northwestern corner of the defenses, is an enormous earthen bastion—all that remains of the inner wall. The rest of the inner wall has disappeared completely, probably demolished by Wellesley shortly after the siege. Later, during the high noon of the Raj, various sites were identified in Sriringapatna as historically significant locations, but I believe the absence of the inner wall caused some confusion. Modern visitors to Sriringapatna will discover plaques or memorials displayed at the Tippoo's dungeons, at the Water Gate where he was supposedly killed and, much farther east, at the place where his body was found, but of the three I suspect only the last is accurate.

The so-called dungeons are beneath the Sultan Battery, and while it is quite possible they were used as cells in the 1780s (and thus the place where Baird spent his uncomfortable forty-four months) they were not so employed in 1799. By then the inner wall had been built (it was hastily constructed after Cornwallis's 1792 siege), and it is much more likely that the "dungeons" were thereafter employed as a magazine (a use for which they were obviously intended). The Tippoo's surviving prisoners all attested that they were held inside the inner wall during the siege, so that is where I placed Sharpe, Lawford, McCandless, and Hakeswill.

A plaque marks the Water Gate through the outer wall as the site of the Tippoo's death, but again this seems wrong. The evidence of Mysorean survivors, some of whom were close to the Tippoo at the end, clearly states that the Tippoo was trying to get inside the city when he was killed. We know he had been fighting on the outer wall and that when he broke off that fight he came down to the space between the walls, and there the story becomes muddled. British sources claim he tried to escape the city through the outer wall's Water Gate, but the Indian testimonies all agree that he tried to go through the inner wall's Water Gate into the city itself. That second Water Gate has since vanished, but I suspect it was there that he died and not at the existing gate. It might seem logical that he should have attempted to flee the city, but the remaining Water Gate led, and still leads, to the flooded ditch inside the glacis, and even if he had negotiated those obstacles (under fire from the attackers on the wall above him), he would only have reached the southern bank of the Cauvery which was under the guns of the British forces north of the river. By cutting through the city he could have reached the Bangalore Gate which offered a much greater chance of successful escape. Indeed, after the Tippoo's death, or perhaps while he was still dying, some of his loyal retainers found him, placed him in the palanquin, and carried him eastward, presumably in an attempt to reach the Bangalore Gate. They were intercepted, the palanquin was overturned, and the Tippoo's body lay undiscovered for several hours. It seems a pity to abandon the present Water Gate as the place where the Tippoo was shot, for its gloomy dank tunnel has a certain eerie drama, but doubtless the matching gate in the inner wall was equally atmospheric.

The Tippoo's body was treated with honor, and next day, as the novel describes, he was buried beside his parents in the Gumbaz mausoleum. Wellesley, meanwhile, stamped out the looting in the city (he hung four looters, a remedy he would employ in the wake of future sieges), but what the common soldier could not take, the senior officers happily plundered for themselves. The East India Company's Prize Agents tallied the Tippoo's treasures at a value of two million pounds (1,799 pounds), and half of that fabulous fortune was declared to be prize money, so that many senior officers became rich men through that single day's work. Most of the treasures returned to Britain, where they remain, some on public view, but many still in private hands.

Today the Tippoo is a hero to many Indians who regard him as a proto-independence fighter. This seems a perverse judgement. Most of the Tippoo's enemies were other Indian states, though admittedly his fiercest fights were against the British (and their Indian allies), but he could never entirely rely on his Hindu subjects. No one is certain that he was betrayed on the day of his death, but it seems more than likely that several Hindu officers, like the fictional Appah Rao, were deliberately lukewarm in their support. The Tippoo's Muslim religion and his preference for the Persian language mark him as being outside the mainstream of modern

Indian tradition, which is perhaps why I was assured by one educated Indian that the Tippoo had, in truth, been a Hindu. He was not, and no amount of wishful thinking can make him into a more acceptably "Indian" hero. Nor does his story need embellishment, for he was a hero anyway, even if he never did fight for Indian independence. He fought for Mysorean domination over India, which was a quite different thing.

I would like to thank Elizabeth Cartmale-Freedman who ransacked the files of London's India House and did much other research for *Sharpe's Tiger*, and for all the useful things she discovered and which I left out, I apologize. I must also thank my agent, Toby Eady, who went above and beyond the call of duty by accompanying me to Sriringapatna. Research has rarely been more enjoyable. As usual, when writing Sharpe, I owe gratitude to Lady Elizabeth Longford for her superb book *Wellington, the Years of the Sword*, and to the late Jac Weller for his indispensable *Wellington in India*.

Sriringapatna is still dominated by the Tippoo's memory. He was an efficient ruler whom Indians revere and the British consider a callous tyrant. That tyrannical reputation was caused, above all, by his execution of thirteen British prisoners before the assault (only eight of them had been captured in the night skirmish, the others were already prisoners). It is unlikely that the executions took place at the Summer Palace, but they were carried out by the Tippoo's *jettis* who did kill in the manner described in the novel. Those murders are reprehensible, yet they should not blind us to the Tippoo's virtues. He was a very brave man, a considerable soldier, a talented administrator, and an enlightened ruler and he makes a worthy foe for young Richard Sharpe, who still has a long road to march under his cold, but very clever, Sepoy General.

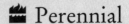 Perennial

Books by Bernard Cornwell:

STONEHENGE
2000 B.C.: A Novel
ISBN 0-06-019700-5 (hardcover)

An epic tale about one of the most mysterious and compelling creations ever conceived—Stonehenge—and the three men, brothers and rivals, who will be marked by its long shadow.

THE SHARPE SERIES:

"The world may have a new literary hero. His name is Richard Sharpe."

—*Philadelphia Inquirer*

SHARPE'S FORTRESS
Richard Sharpe and the Siege of Gawilghur, December 1803
ISBN 0-06-019424-3 (paperback)

In this explosive final installment of Richard Sharpe's India trilogy, Sharpe and Sir Arthur Wellesley's army try to bring down an impregnable fort in a battle with high stakes—both personal and professional.

SHARPE'S TRIUMPH
Richard Sharpe and the Battle of Assaye, September 1803
ISBN 0-06-095197-4 (paperback)

A riveting story of betrayal and revenge that marks the second volume of the India trilogy. Richard Sharpe must defeat the plans of a British traitor and a native Indian mercenary army.

SHARPE'S TIGER
Richard Sharpe and the Siege of Seringapatam, 1799
ISBN 0-06-093230-9 (paperback)

The first of Richard Sharpe's India trilogy, in which young private Sharpe must battle both man and beast behind enemy lines as the British army fights its way through India toward a diabolical trap.

SHARPE'S BATTLE
Richard Sharpe and the Battle of Fuentes de Onoro, May 1811
ISBN 0-06-093228-7 (paperback)

As Napoleon threatens to crush Britain on the battlefield, Lt. Col. Richard Sharpe leads a ragtag army to exact personal revenge.

SHARPE'S DEVIL
Richard Sharpe and the Emperor, 1820-21
ISBN 0-06-093229-5 (paperback)

An honored veteran of the Napolenic Wars, Lt. Col. Richard Sharpe is drawn into a deadly battle, both on land and on the high seas.

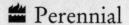 **Perennial**

Books by Bernard Cornwell:

REDCOAT
ISBN 0-06-101264-5 (paperback)

The young Redcoat, Sam Gilpin, has seen his brother die. Now he must choose between duty to a distant King and the call of his own conscience.

"A rousing adventure yarn ... [The] battle scenes are excellent."
—*Washington Post Book World*

THE STARBUCK CHRONICLES:

REBEL
ISBN 0-06-109187-1 (paperback)

When a Richmond landowner snatches young Nate Starbuck from the grip of a Yankee-hating mob, Nate is moved to turn his back forever on his life in Boston and agrees to fight against his native North in this powerful and evocative story of the Civil War's first battle and the men who fought it. (Volume One)

"Starbuck is a worthy hero ... and the battle scenes are presented with real mastery."
—*Kirkus Reviews*

COPPERHEAD
ISBN 0-06-109196-0 (paperback)

Nate Starbuck is accused of being a Yankee spy. In order to prove his innocence and prevent the fall of Richmond, he must test his courage and endurance, and seek out the real spy. (Volume Two)

"Always based on fact, always interesting, often exciting, always entertaining."
— *Kirkus Reviews*

BATTLE FLAG
ISBN 0-06-109197-9 (paperback)

This acclaimed Civil War series continues as Confederate Captain Nate Starbuck takes part in the war's most extraordinary scenes. (Volume Three)

"The best thing to hit Civil War fiction... one of the finest authors of military historical fiction today." —*The Washington Times*

THE BLOODY GROUND
ISBN 0-06-109198-7 (paperback)

The story of Nate Starbuck as he serves under General Robert E. Lee himself, culminating in the famous, bloody battle of Antietam. (Volume Four)

"Cornwell is more than a great storyteller. [He] has woven an excellent history of the Civil War..." —*Flint Journal*

Available wherever books are sold, or call 1-800-331-3761 to order.